Books by Dorothy James Roberts

A MAN OF MALICE LANDING

A DURABLE FIRE

THE MOUNTAIN JOURNEY

MARSHWOOD

THE ENCHANTED CUP

LAUNCELOT, MY BROTHER

MISSY

RETURN OF THE STRANGER

MORE THAN YOU PROMISE
with Kathleen Ann Smallzried

WITH NIGHT WE BANISH SORROW

FIRE IN THE ICE

KINSMEN OF THE GRAIL

KINSMEN OF THE GRAIL

KINSMEN OF

Dorothy James Roberts

THE GRAIL

Little, Brown and Company • Boston • Toronto

Published simultaneously in Canada
by Little, Brown & Company (Canada) Limited

PRINTED IN THE UNITED STATES OF AMERICA

To Genevieve and Anne McGuinness,
with my warmest thanks.

Foreword

MALORY GAVE US KING ARTHUR and the court of Camelot and the men whose names have stood like milestones in our literature: Lancelot, Galahad, Tristan, Perceval, Bors, and the others. After Malory, Wagner re-invented a vast, philosophical Perceval, and after Wagner Tennyson animated a gallery of pure-hearted, simple-minded Arthurian heroes. And nobody save these three ever wrote a word about the brotherhood of the Round Table.

This is a literary canon warmly accepted by moderns. It is convenient, but it has the disadvantage of falling wide of the truth. Yet partisans who hear it questioned feel as though a beloved landmark has been declared a fake. They do not wish to believe that Malory labored three hundred years after the "real" period of Arthurian Romance had flourished in the twelfth century and died away of its own overstylization.

The legend of Perceval le Galois, upon which *Kinsmen of the Grail* is built, is perhaps chief among the tales which owe nothing to fifteenth-century Malory's art of breathing new life into old, moribund materials. He made little of its complexities, and was satisfied with only cutting it, like a good editor, and improving the style of the remaining parts. In its written form the history of Perceval and Christ's cup was a product of the late twelfth century. It is probably a good deal older.

I do not mean that the twelfth-century poets of Arthur were more "real" than Malory. They were only the movers and shapers necessary to the evolution of his masterpiece. In some instances their king was a sort of Roman Emperor with a "floating" court of great splendor. In others he was a hunter or fighter or a lonely background presence, in others he did not appear at all. Camelot had not become the capital of a mystic realm, Guenivere's spell on Lancelot was not yet tragic and destructive, and the king and queen enjoyed a family, at least one son. In tales told in the far west of the British Isles the royal seat was Caerleon-on-Usk, a city which in the twelfth century still bore traces of its richness as an administrative center of the Roman occupation. More important for our purposes, Gawin (Gawaine, Gauvin, Gavin, Govan) stood shoulder to shoulder with Lancelot as the greatest hero of them all. Three hundred years were needed to reduce him to the noble wreckage Malory describes.

In the twelfth-century heyday of these tales of memorable men, storytelling devices were employed which were to become the work-horses of mediaeval narrative. The wicked dwarf, the damsel in distress, the giant's (or enchanter's) castle, the talisman, the magic weapon, these occurred with a regularity that could only mean they were recognized and loved by hearers and readers. Such a figure, for instance, as the drawing of a sword from a stone or tree trunk or door post or hall pillar is so common one feels a story without it can hardly be called mediaeval. The Arthur of Malory who drew his sword from the stone forty-nine days after Easter, on Whitsunday, had been preceded by dozens of earnest heroes who "enchieved" a talismanic blade, and so made their adventures worthy of becoming literature.

I am not ridiculing a supposed simplicity in the literary mind of the Middle Ages. If ever artists understood the ceaseless, tragic plight of man in nature, if ever they sought the soul's cure in the faith that men can prevail against their burden of suffering and evil, if ever they felt a warmth for living things and a pleasure in earthly joys, the artists of the twelfth century did. True, they failed to invent the modern novel, though they invented cathedrals. But as if to make up this narrative deficiency they left us rousing stories that have influenced every tale told since their time whose protagonist can truly be called a hero.

KINSMEN OF THE GRAIL

1

So, GAWIN THOUGHT, even the Romans got a bellyful of
this uncomfortable ledge when they were building road.
He looked back at the monumental headlands he had
crossed, then on to easier, descending ground down which
the track swung inland and a little south. The ancient highway, wooded on the landward side, was not in good repair.
Yet it stretched away before him with the forthright promise
of destination that spoke in every mile the legionaries had
hammered into the soil of their conquered worlds.

The dazzle of afternoon sun and the rumble of breakers
on naked cliffs had battered his senses, and Gawin pushed
against his stirrups and said aloud, "Eeee, I'm tired." He
lived too much on the back of a horse, he was not young
enough to wallop his bones day after day through bogs and
mountain passes. "I am too old," he spoke again, and
reached over the casque hanging at his saddle bow to give
his horse a companionable smack. "What do you think of
that, friend?"

The horse walked on, soberly footing its way down the
worn road. Gawin smiled at its ears as a man smiles who

has belittled himself for the sake of hearing his judgement denied. But in a moment he muttered, "Old. Tired." Am I old and tired? Am I Gawin, the knight ordained by Arthur's hands in his patched palace in the City of Legions? Then Gawin was a curly-headed squire dressed in yellow silk, kneeling at Arthur's feet and thinking complacently of the figure he cut before the ladies of the queen.

Yesterday. Where have I been since that young squire's yesterday of girls and yellow silks? He thought of King Arthur's Norgals, the rough west country of mountains and white-boiling streams, of glens and waterfalls and forests, of round, hazy valleys spread like checkered mantles between hills. He lifted his right hand and stared at it. The back was tufted with bleached hair, even between the leathery knuckles. And the chain-mail sleeve of his hauberk bagged at his wrist and was rusted and torn, some rents mended with bright new links. He raised the shield hanging on a thong about his neck and squinted at the blazon. But there was no blazon. Time and the blows of spears had worn its colors to flecks.

The horse, reaching a level stretch where the mossy Roman paving lay protected under a bank on the seaward side, slowed and stopped. A beech tree half uprooted by wind leaned into the road and offered a blot of shade.

"What's the matter?" Gawin said.

The horse moved toward the hollow from which the tree had been torn. A pool of ground water was caught there.

"With twenty rivers to choose from today," Gawin said,

4

"you settle on this hatful of mud." But he got down and allowed his horse to drink and nibble grass along the green edge. He knelt by the pool, slapped water over his head, then watched the small waves he had started smooth out.

His reflection, the face all seamed and scarred, eyebrows faded and coarse, looked up at him. The curls that had once made him strut before the queen's women had been flattened away (how long ago?) by the headgear of his trade, a steel helmet. Now his hair was a shag of sun-streaked light and dark.

He got to his feet, flung a stone into the water to destroy the image. Old. I have said it boastfully a hundred times when I made complaints that were no complaints. How can I be old at forty? Arthur is older than I, Yvain is older than I, Kei is older than I, Lancelot is older than I. But not Kei. Yet Kei looks older . . .

I need a night under the roof of an inn, he thought, a hot supper and good ale, fish and porridge for breakfast, and a walk in a garden where parsley and pinks are in bloom. I need a smith to clean my armor, and a clerk to cut my hair, and at bedtime a woman to lie beside me in the dark. I need to get the harness off my back.

He overtook the horse and led it to the fallen tree, whose trunk he used as a mounting stage. Heaving himself into the saddle he felt his schooled strength. "Move, now," he said. "If we find a town lying at the foot of these hills we will ride into it with style."

He spurred into an easy trot, sitting light and straight. He tried to keep his mind on the pleasure he meant to take, on the inkeeper's drudge who would help him out of his armor and prepare him a bath, on the steaming country supper. He made an effort to think about the girl, young but knowing, the warmth of her between the covers, and the sleep after love.

Were not these pleasures the best of life for a knight and fighting man in the very years of his prime?

2

HE SAW THE TOWN from above. It lay on spurs of its backing hills, now dipping into shallow ground, now huddling on the slope. Beyond it on the right was a rough sea margin which, in the summer dusk, showed nothing save foggy blue and purple. Small, but at least more than a monk's cell and mill, Gawin thought. "Pray God," he said to his horse, "that my bed and your stall will be clean and dry."

The Roman road wound north again, entering the town from the top. Gawin trotted along the single street of low, boxlike thatched houses, which were not yet lit by a candle or a fish oil lamp, though through some open doors hearths glowed with peat fires. Children ran out to peep at him, and dogs barked at his horse. He wondered what the cottagers lived on. Sheep, I suppose, they are weavers, and ship from the port, if there is a port. Unless they knead their bread out of the whin and heather growing on these stony coombs.

He reined in to ask a child where the inn might be, but

the child ran away. Coming around a curve the view of whose far side was blocked by an overhang of rock, he almost rode down a shepherd walking behind a herd. The animals clung to one another shoulder to shoulder, and their bobbing rumps stopped the road tight.

Gawin slid down and led his horse, falling into step with the shepherd. The stench of damp, befouled wool seemed thick enough to swim in. The sheep crowded together foolishly and cried in high, strangled voices at the two dogs that were driving them.

"A warm night after a warm day," Gawin said.

"Warm enough."

"Are you going home?"

"I'm following these sheep."

Crusty brute, Gawin thought, but a subject of the king. And therefore I shall not cut my way through this flock and leave its guardian in the ditch to meditate the duty of courtesy.

He said, "Is there an inn in this place, friend?"

"Might be an inn."

He grabbed a handful of the man's dirty homespun tunic and pulled him so close he could have counted his eyelashes. "In the king's name," he asked him, carefully gentle, "tell me the *where* of this inn."

"There. Right in front of you. In the king's name."

"Do you find fault with the king's name?"

"Not me, I am a herdsman, I am not of the rank of men who find fault."

"What ails you that you can't greet a stranger civilly?"

"I do not know what stranger you are. And in this corner of the west country we are not often bidden in the king's name."

"Tell me what you are called," Gawin said.

"Ewan."

"Whose herdsman are you, Ewan?"

"Do not question me, messire. I am a herdsman, and in the king's name, I am unarmed."

Gawin let him go. "Leave your dogs to watch the sheep a while, and come into the inn with me. Tell the pot boy in the kitchen you are to drink your ale on my reckoning. If he asks whose reckoning, tell him Gawin's, nephew of the king and knight of the City of Legions."

"Messire," the shepherd said in a quaver, "I did not know, I did not mean —"

"Why do you fear strangers?"

"Strangers are always to be feared, at least — that is —"

"I am an officer of the king's peace," Gawin said. "What is the uproar in this place?"

"It is a long story to tell standing here in the dark. Listen, messire, I must stay at the inn tonight too, only my bed will be in the fold with my sheep. I have not eaten since morning, and I believe you haven't either. Let me fold my sheep and eat."

"I'll make a bargain with you, Ewan. If you will not run away the minute you've swallowed your ale I'll come out to you, and you can tell me your tale where no one will hear it but me."

"You are surely Gawin, messire?"

8

"I am Gawin, believe me."

"And no one will hear my story?"

"I promise you."

"Then I will tell you. Only —"

"What now?"

"You will protect me?"

Gawin grinned with angry annoyance. "I'll protect you, I swear it, I'll be your mother."

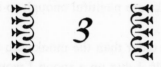

3

THE INN WAS an old, ruined stone house now mended with timbers and thatch. Its common room still possessed a huge fireplace and wall-oven above it. Its kitchen, washhouse, and storehouse were lean-tos added by the present landlord.

Gawin bargained for a bed on the ledgelike gallery running around two sides of the common room. He was the only guest.

"I shall need someone to squire me and prepare me a bath," he said.

"My daughter will serve you," the landlord said. He was a small man, thin too, dark and watchful. "While you eat your supper my daughter will play the harp and sing to you."

"I'm in need of songs and harp playing." Gawin wondered whether this girl was to be the one he hoped for. Some landlords hired compliant "daughters," but some were suspicious and raised an outcry if a guest took a daughter for granted. "What place was this before it became your inn?" Gawin asked him.

"I have heard it was the cooking house of a monastery, but pirates came down on it from Ireland or the North or somewhere and battered every wall into the earth except these. I have heard the monks made a fine thing of their living, and owned silver cups and jeweled mass vessels, and wrote books on sheepskin."

"By luck monks are plentiful enough so that we shall not miss a few."

"Objects even older than the monks are found in the soil hereabout. Myself, I dug up a spoon I would sell to a man who cares for such curiosities."

Gawin laughed and shook his head.

The landlord stepped close. "They say it is a tear spoon, very odd."

"What's a tear spoon?"

As the bargain approached, the innkeeper's eyes grew greedy. "In the time of our forefathers mourners weeping at graveside caught their tears in these spoons. The water of grief was held to be sacred." He shrugged apologetically. "Our forefathers did not know God, they were heathen, I mean some of them were heathen. They preserved their tears, for piety's sake, in little phials. My spoon is truly remarkable. Will you look at it?"

"I will look at it to please you, but I do not plan to catch tears and cork them up for piety's sake."

The landlord stepped into the kitchen and returned with

his treasure. The tear spoon was ivory, its shank slender and its bowl no larger than his fingertip. It was cleaned and polished, but its color had deepened to amber.

Gawin was touched by its antique strangeness. "What is the price?"

"What will you give me, messire?"

"Double my reckoning for food and bed."

"That is little for so rare a thing."

"Then keep it for a traveler who needs a tear spoon."

"I am a poor man, messire. Double the reckoning, and two shillings more."

"Robbery is robbery, whether a poor man commits it or a rich. Double the reckoning."

"Let it be one shilling, then."

"I will buy your spoon because I believe if I don't you will not pour my ale. Is the ale good? In this house it should have a decent religious flavor."

"The ale is good, messire."

The ale was not good. It had been helped with wormwood to conceal the fact that too few hops had gone into its brewing. But poor ale was better than none, and Gawin took the mug and sat down before the hearth and stretched out his legs. At once he fell into a doze, and only wakened when the fire heated his chain hauberk.

A girl stood before him. She wore a long gray homespun shift belted with rope, and over it a brown jacket, short and without sleeves. Her feet were bare. She had wrapped her head in a coarse veil so that her cheeks stood out like beacons, hard and round, each with a dimple. Her figure was young, firm, heavy, and she had brought with her a little rush of cool air.

"I have made you a bath," she said, "and I am to help you take off your armor."

"Here?"

"Yes, here is where the water has been fetched."

A round tub of coopered beech staves stood by the fire. The girl peeled him expertly out of his chain shirt, his tight leather riding jacket, his under-vestment, his kneepieces and mailed shoes, his leather riding breeches. Without words she indicated the tub, without words scrubbed him and kneaded his arms. When she was done she said, "Will you dry yourself or shall I?"

"Give me the towel."

"My father has sent you soft shoes and a shirt and tunic and long hose," she said. "On the bench. I am to sing to you while you dress."

"Do you sing to every guest?"

"If they wish to be sung to, I sing to them."

"I do not wish to be sung to," he said shortly.

"Then I will serve your supper. Do you wish to be sung to while you eat?"

"I'll decide later."

"Shall I go, messire?"

"Yes," he said.

She passed through the rude arch leading toward the lean-to kitchen. She believes me a churl, Gawin thought, and I spoke like a churl. But this female, as hard as an apple from head to foot, scrubbing me as though I were a scalded pig, she is enough to turn any man into a churl. He considered her coming into his bed with the same air of indefatigable competence, her eyes as round as plums and with the expression of plums. Would she say, "Shall I sing to you while you make love to me, messire?"

Gawin raked his back with the rough homespun towel. A girl, a girl, all soft and dainty, young, a little shy, was every maiden like that within her spirit, even such great, bustling, dull ones as the landlord's daughter? Once in a man's life a girl was like that. Or did memory only invest her with the sweet of flowers? I will not have a woman this night, he thought, unless . . .

The landlord's daughter sang to him while he ate his dish of boiled mutton and onions and the slab of white bread produced in honor of his rank. Her voice was low and pure, tender, hauntingly sad. When she finished her eyes filled with tears.

"That was a beautiful song," Gawin said.

"Was it, messire?"

"Do you like me a little, lass?"

"Yes, messire."

"I like you. Will you come to me tonight after your father is asleep?"

"Yes, messire, but —"

"But what?"

"My father will not go to sleep —"

"Then —"

"— unless you pay him," she said.

4

AFTER HIS SUPPER was cleared the innkeeper and his daughter left Gawin alone in the common room. To give me time, he thought restlessly, to whet my desire and to agree to the price, whatever the price is to be. Why not? I have seen such bargains done this way a hundred times. Why should it anger me tonight?

To rid his imagination of the fresh, broad-bodied girl who had unarmed him, he rose and left the inn. A long green summer afterglow lay on the horizon of the sea in the west. It gave the illusion of light, but not light itself. Gawin could see nothing that might be a stable or sheepfold, and under his feet the dark ground was uncertain. One stops at this house of dead monks as one stops at a place in a dream, he thought, without landmarks.

But he could smell Ewan's sheep and even hear a kind of rustle, like animals breathing or moving quietly. Stooping to bring the near horizon against the afterglow he saw low sheds. He moved toward them, reached a stone fence, stopped to listen, said, "I am here, Ewan."

Silence.

Curse him, Gawin thought, he's hiding his head under a louse-ridden fleece, afraid to answer me. He put his hands flat against the stone fence and vaulted it, coming down into soft earth, apparently a barnyard. As he stumbled through dung cakes and the irregular pits of animal tracks, Ewan, rising at his elbow, said, "I should have run away, Messire Gawin, but I didn't, and I ask you to remember your promise to protect me."

"Remembering such promises is my trade. Where shall we talk?"

"They gave me a hut beside the stable to sleep in. We can go to it."

Ewan led the way. The hut was so low Gawin had to stoop in order to enter, and within, it was smothering dark and evil smelling. "There is only one place to sit," Ewan told him, "the woolsacks I am to sleep on." And he tugged Gawin gently by the sleeve.

"Now," Gawin said when they were settled, "tell me who makes trouble here."

"Do you know my lady Iglais?"

"You mean a woman has frightened this countryside?"

"No, no, my lady is the widow of Allan the Fat. You must have known Allan the Fat, messire."

"I remember him, but it was long ago. I knew him when I was a young knight. He used to come to the City of Legions for the Whitsuntide assembly. He had brothers, hadn't he, a big family of brothers?"

"This is our trouble," Ewan said. "His brothers are dead, every one, and Messire Allan too. Some died in King Arthur's wars and some died across the sea. I mean they were killed bearing arms."

"Men who live bearing arms, die bearing them," Gawin muttered.

"All these deaths in war, they changed the nature of the lady Iglais. Some men think they turned her brain, but I am her chief herdsman, I have belonged to her household all my life, and I do not believe her brain is turned. I believe she only grieves. Being a woman, she does the foolish things women do in their grief."

"What foolish things does she do?"

Ewan sighed. "Well, this. After her husband lost his life she ran away to the most remote of the castles he held. He was a wealthy lord, messire, he had many houses. She garrisoned his other castles, but she did not leave enough men to protect them, and she did not send help afterwards. And I needn't tell you what happened."

"She lost her husband's holdings, then?"

"Yes, indeed, messire, she lost them one after another. A vassal of her husband has besieged and siezed all but one, the last, the house she lives in."

"What castle is that?" Gawin asked. "Where is it?"

Ewan's fear was so palpable that Gawin could hardly hold in his own moody impatience. The shepherd said, "I will tell you where it is in a while, messire. Now I am not done telling you the folly of my lady Iglais."

"Folly enough already. Yet a woman alone invites enemies."

"She has a son," Ewan said. "His name is Perceval."

"Why doesn't her son give her counsel?"

"He is not old enough to help her. He was born five months after his father fell with an arrow through his eye. He is a child, he is barely sixteen years old."

16

"Sixteen! What do you call a child in the west? At sixteen Perceval should be ready for knighthood."

"He is not to become a knight."

"Why not? Is he an innocent without sense?"

"I am telling you, this is the doing of my lady Iglais. Perceval is the real reason she fled to a castle beyond traveled roads. We live at the end of the world, messire, we see no knights. Besides she has ordered us never to speak the word *knight* to her son. We are not even to let him know that men of his birth bear arms."

"To raise a young man like a girl, that is a scandal," Gawin said.

"She has not raised him like a girl. He is wonderfully manly, he can sprint and leap better than any boy I ever saw, he can throw a peeled wand as straight as birds fly. He would make a worthy knight if he knew the arts of knighthood. But not knowing them, he spends his time playing games and running on the cliffs. They say he can swim after fish and catch them in his hands, though I have never seen him do it. I think it is only the way women speak when they praise their children."

"Does Perceval know how his mother has been robbed?"

"He does not. But now her enemy is threatening to seize our own castle. And my lady's real terror is not that she will lose her home but that her son will see men fighting at last. Therefore she means to yield without even trying to defend herself. She and all her household will be turned out onto the roads."

"The lady Iglais is touched," Gawin said. "She should

17

be put into a nunnery under the care of pious women."

"We no longer have farms enough to feed us," Ewan went on, "and soon we shall be hungry. This is why I was sent to the mainland to buy sheep. It was why I did not wish to tell my name — for fear you were a soldier of our enemy. But I have had time to think, messire. If you are an officer of the king's peace, isn't it your duty to defend my lady Iglais?"

"Yes, yes," Gawin said wearily, "it is my duty to defend her. Who is your enemy? Will he agree to fight a champion of the lady Iglais?"

"His castle is called The Moors, and so he is called The Moors, or Knight of The Moors. I am no soldier, I do not know whether he will agree to fight a champion."

Gawin rose incautiously and knocked his head against the stinking thatch. He sat down again. "Tell me where her castle is."

"Do you know the west country, messire?"

"Not as a native, but I have ridden it over and across many times on king's business."

"Do you know the strait of salt water that runs between this coast and the shore opposite, to the west?"

"I know it. I have never crossed it, but I have seen it again and again."

"Then you know it is long and narrow and that tides entering it twist into dangerous currents. Yet many men in this village live by ferrying passengers across. Once you reach the western side you see good land, not rugged, but rolling and rich. You see fine cattle too, and excellent grain. All the same, these fields mislead the stranger, for as you keep on going westward the soil becomes rocky and less fruitful. And finally when you have gone as far as you can go, and reach the sea again, the land is nothing but stone and birds. Just before the rocks turn into bald cliffs, there my lady has hidden herself and Perceval."

"How many days after the ferry will you need to come home?"

"Two days driving the sheep. If I could walk alone it would be one day. It is twenty-four miles as miles are reckoned in Norgals."

"What day did the Knight of The Moors set for his siege?"

"A fortnight from today."

Gawin rose again, more watchfully. "I shall go with you and your sheep in the morning."

"Will you send a runner to the king first, messire?"

"No. I am here to prevent runners trotting all over Norgals with begging messages to King Arthur."

Ewan, who had been blowing sighs throughout his narrative, fetched another, the deepest of all. "I am afraid for my lady. How can one knight prevail against so much trouble?"

"One knight, any knight, he can only abide the event," said Gawin.

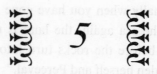

5

THE INNKEEPER was waiting for him in the common room, whose only light now came from the hearth. "Have you had a walk, Messire Gawin? Without your sword?"

"Yes," Gawin said.

"That was a risk. But we are too poor here to attract desperate men, and so we live with a measure of peace. Will you drink ale before you sleep?"

"No. Fetch the ladder and I'll go up to my bed."

The landlord did not move. "The west winds blow cold gales at night on this coast. I shall be glad to arrange whatever you wish for your comfort."

"Nothing, but thank you for your willingness." From his traveling pouch, which he wore inside his borrowed shirt, he extracted a few coins and dropped them onto the table.

The man was too tactful to seize them. "I understand, Messire Gawin. You wish nothing." His hand crept toward the money pieces and covered them.

"Except the ladder."

"The ladder is already in place."

"Share my thanks with your daughter," Gawin said with scorn.

The ladder, hardly visible in the flicker of the fire, led him to the gallery, where shadows were dense and the air hot and dry. The floor was uncaulked planks laid over beams, and cracks of light from below showed him a dark patch which he took to be his bed. It was only a pallet of blankets made up on sheepskins, but a little comfort was promised by a sheet spread between the hides and covers.

He removed the garments lent him by the innkeeper and stretched himself naked on the pallet. The blankets seemed as heavy as iron, and, besides, smelt stale. If he threw them off he was cold, if he pulled them up his body steamed. I've had better beds in a hayloft, he muttered aloud. Why can't I sleep? Kei says I can sleep hanging from a peg, he likes to pretend I am all beef and fat in the brains. I shall have to deal with Kei one of these days.

The wind blew steadily, crying about the corners of the monks' cooking house. Much glory had decayed on the soil of Britain and left its signature in pathetic remnants like the tear spoon. To catch tears, what an idea that was! Weep all men for lost delight.

Was it a yellow surcoat he had worn over his mail the day his uncle, King Arthur, knighted him? Yes, his mother had made it for that very office. She looked feminine, charming, sitting before her embroidery frame working with threads of gold and silver and colored silks from Byzantium. On the morning of his knighthood Arthur had said, "Do all things knightly." But his mother gave him no advice, only told him, "No knight who kneels to be invested with the arms of the Round Table will be as handsome this Whitsuntide as you."

Handsome? Perhaps the yellow surcoat made me shine among the squires, but Lancelot in his plain, blue woolen tunic was the handsomest knight in Britain that day. Yet handsome or not, I have tried to do all things knightly. Only it is no longer a trying. Doing all things knightly is a habit we are dyed with when we are being schooled as pages and squires. It is our trade, we do not think of it any more than a baker thinks of kneading bread. At least we do not think of it after the first year or two. Our bones have learned to recognize the unlawful and the unjust, and our hands to administer the correction. And between whiles we are wet or dry, we catch sword cuts or give them, we eat flabby mutton and onions in some fallen cooking house of monks, and we think of the daughters of innkeepers to whom shillings look larger than gold crowns. What if a man found a labor that was not habit, a labor he could think of with surprise and joy, even love?

When I was a page I thought about knighthood with joy and love, when I was a squire too. When I became a knight I thought about it with surprise. I, Gawin, in yellow silk, armed by my uncle's hands on Whitsun twenty years ago and more. I have had them, the surprise, the joy, the love. Where are they? Gone, so much needless baggage dropped in the bogs of Norgals. I lost a horse once in quicksand at a river estuary near the City of Legions. Does one's knightly joy sink into bottomless sand, like a poor brute that can't escape?

Perhaps surprise and joy and love do not live in the spirit, but, like treasure, are bred by the sweat of the body, and, like treasure, must be paid as the fee for life. Perhaps they are the price we yield for lasting out years enough to make us forty. I envy Prince Tristram, Gawin thought, and sat up on the pallet and pushed his hands into his hair. Tristram died young, he was barely twenty, he never knew how soon surprise and joy molder into gray, he never loved with any love but his first love for the Irish wife of King Mark of Cornwall. And at the end he claimed his death gladly, as though it were a royal kingdom.

But one must be young to believe death a royal kingdom. Tristram lacked years enough to teach him that death is the eyeless end of life, that it sweeps our manhood away. If our souls escape, they are no longer ourselves, they are wrenched from all that made us men, and venture heaven with no arms save ignorance and terror, like half-schooled squires.

Shall I pray God to mend my knighthood? Gawin began to pray, woodenly and without attention. How could one trouble God with a demand for joy? How could one beg fretfully for the morning light of surprise? One was no longer a child coaxing for a wooden sword.

"Messire," said the landlord's daughter.

Against the firelight glancing below, Gawin could see the girl's head at the top of the ladder.

"My father is asleep," she said. "Are you awake, messire?"

"Yes, I am awake."

She climbed the remaining rungs and moved toward his pallet.

"Wait," Gawin said. He pulled a blanket loose and threw it onto the floor beside him. "Sit here, lass."

"Why, messire?"

"Let us talk."

"Talk?"

"Tell me your name."

"Luned, messire."

"Don't go on calling me messire, Luned. Is the innkeeper your true father?"

"Yes, mes — yes, gentleman, he is my father."

"Ah!" said Gawin, and gently put an arm around her. "Poor Luned!"

"Do you pity me, gentleman?"

"Gawin is my name, you must call me Gawin. I pity you if you need pity for having such a father."

The girl was silent.

"What do you wish of this world, Luned?" he asked her.

"Nothing," she said. "At least whatever you wish. At least —"

"At least what, lass?"

"Perhaps you could give me a shilling for myself."

"Oh," he said. "But I have paid your father."

"I only mentioned it because you asked me what I wish."

"Do you wish to sleep with me tonight? Do you wish for love, Luned?"

"I have come for that," she said, "messire."

6

GAWIN HAD AGREED that Ewan was to make the first start. The morning was cold. Inland a vast bruise of sulphurous clouds dragged the sky low, and brown mist hid the mountains to the east. The innkeeper came into the yard, offered his hand at the mounting stage, and watched Gawin ride off. But Luned did not. She had failed to show herself at breakfast too, and she had not helped him arm, leaving that duty to her father.

As Gawin struck out across the heathery waste he felt galled by the indifference of the girl who was to have given him again the lost flavor of joy. Had their warm closeness in the night meant so little that she had no memory to cherish worth a smile of farewell? But she has her shilling, he thought, and the shilling outweighs Gawin. And so my vice of vanity is rebuked by her vice of greed. For a shilling spent I have bought a shilling's value, and it wasn't Luned's fault, but mine, that I expected more.

He had been riding up a low roll of ground, and now, reaching its crest, he stopped. Below him stretched a brushy flat, and then the sand, dull brown under dull light, marked at low tide by frost-colored streaks of wet. Mist hung over the water, and the far shore was only a thickness in the mist. In the immeasurable distance lay a yellowing gleam, as though at the world's edge light was to be found.

Blur, silence, birds half heard and half seen, this is the coast of Norgals, this is where I follow my trade of knighthood. He was moved, seeing his land new. If my wife had lived, he thought, but turned from the memory of the girl who had been his such a little while. It was long ago. A man on king's business could not gnaw away his strength with the grief of loss. If she had lived, my sweet maid! He could not recall her face, not the pretty brow under russet hair, the amber-clear eyes, the full mouth. She was gone with his yellow squire's silks. In the mist, after Luned, she was long dead. It was only that he could not forget her, neither today nor yesterday. He had loved her, and he had loved no other woman. Except for a price.

On the foggy beach he found Ewan awaiting him with new complaints. Had Messire Gawin overslept, or been delayed by the blind weather? The tide would soon turn. They must get aboard. He had been lucky enough to find a boat of eight oars which would ferry the sheep in one passage, but its owner took advantage of honest men in need by charging an outrageous fee.

The sheep had to be driven aboard over a gangway of roped planks. They refused to step onto it and broke apart and ran about the sand. When the dogs collected them and drove them onto the planks one fell and was almost lost in the sea before the cursing oarsmen could head it toward shore. Ewan scolded like an old woman, shrilling that if a single animal were drowned he must be paid, by the king's law that protected poor men. The crew were wet and short-tempered before the boat lunged into the sawing currents of the strait. As they crossed, the sheep cried, cried, in the voices of lost souls.

The uproar raised Gawin's spirits. "Ewan, I will lay you a groat that I am a better shepherd than you."

Ewan's face was red and streaked with nervous sweat. "It pleases you to believe transporting twelve sheep across the strait is a simple matter, does it?"

"At least it pleases me to be on the sea this fine, weeping morning."

"You may have all of that pleasure for yourself, Messire Gawin."

"What is your plan when we come ashore?"

"To go home with my flock safe."

"As for me," Gawin said, "I shall ride ahead. Tell me the roads and crosses I am to follow."

"Very well, messire, if you wish to leave me alone with the animals. When we make our landing I'll draw you a map in the sand."

"Between me and God!" said the steersman. "The sun is going to shine!"

Gawin looked back at the low coast. Its broad, green-brown lap was wiped clear of fog, which was now boiling up the mountain flanks beyond the village. Blue-walled heights were sometimes revealed, sometimes veiled, heavy and featureless against the eastward-running clouds. Under these immensities Luned lived her life, each day bounded by the double prison of stone and sea. What would she buy with her shilling? A silver ribbon? A few mouthfuls of Frankish wine? A red-coated puppy from Ireland? Or would she hide it with others her arts earned until she had accumulated enough to break out of her suffocating world? Luned, he thought, it is for you and your kind as well as for the lords of this realm that I wear the arms of the king.

"I suppose the sun will shine," Ewan said, "if it doesn't rain."

EWAN WARNED HIM that if he rode a straight line inland he would pass through forests held by the Knight of The Moors. The route along the north shore would be a few miles longer, but safer. "You will find a fishing village," Ewan said, "and ten minutes' ride beyond it a church. Turn left at the church."

Gawin said, "I will see you tomorrow."

"God go with you, messire."

"And with you."

Gawin had never passed the strait until this day. But he knew much old lore about the countryside lying beyond it. His father had been a Scot with the Scot's fondness for the tradition clinging about the ancient Britons. Long ago he related to Gawin how the Romans crossed the strait; how they found drawn up on the shore to oppose them a black-robed host chanting heathen spells; how the magic of the Britons did not prevail that day; and how the blood they shed ran into the sea and turned it red.

Hence he expected to find the remains of a Roman road. But the trail by the strait was no more than a narrow path, now of earth, now of the stone of its bed. Perhaps, he thought, the druids scared the Romans away before they could begin to level and dig. Or perhaps nothing is here worth a road — more likely, since it was not easy to scare Romans away from any land they meant to keep.

Gawin made his turn toward the north coast. The countryside was shallow, its marine meadows green with grain. But as he approached the slanted shore the road rose a little, then wound about the flanks of a high-domed hill. On the far side of this hill the sea washed into a peaceful crescent bay whose northern arm was also a high headland.

The sun strengthened in a clearing sky. Near the shore the sea was thin over brown sand, above deep water it was glowing blue-green. The sands were broad and empty, quiet too save for the plaintive mewing of birds and the rustle of their wings. I must grant Luned one thing, he thought, she has given me a day when I feel whole.

He turned his horse to look back at the girl's home. Down the coast the mountains marched, and right across they reared high, darkling peaks, slopes bare hoary-gray, or deeply velveted with grass, or trimmed with torn white streams and waterfalls. Their ponderous heads were mottled by running shadows. On their skirts purple heather and the bold gilt of blooming gorse laid rich stains. My little kingdom is always drowned in color, he thought, but never such color as now. Looking north again he wondered whether the smoky step on the sea's horizon was Ireland, and believed it was.

For three hours he rode, often in sight of the sea, often with limitless prospects of dyed mountains opening in the east. As he lengthened the distance between him and the mainland he saw the ranges behind him rising more massive, more deeply glowing. And presently he had come far enough to discover among them local rain squalls, all purple and black. Nothing is better, he thought in high good humor, than to have a sunny dooryard when your neighbor's is wet.

He did not stop at the fishing village, which lay under a coastal bluff. At the church he entered and knelt before the altar to pray for his mission. The old edifice, half hidden by wild brush, was dusty with decay, yet the more solemn for being ruined. Beyond it lay a disorder of great stones of the kind the ancient Britons used for temples, and still beyond, a circular mound, some forgotten earthwork, perhaps Roman, perhaps already timeworn when the Romans came. A grove of walnuts had once flourished in the church demesne, but now the trees were wind-split and fruitless.

At this point he found Ewan's left fork, and turned inland. The road dipped through a straggling forest, skirted a few unfertile fields, then led once more into trees. Gawin had not met a soul since he left the strait, and so he was startled when he saw a man running across an oat field. He was leaping along swiftly, his hair blowing out from his head and his tunic flattened across his breast. He sprang into the first thin margin of trees, stopped, and turned to watch.

Gawin reached for his casque, which he carried on his saddle bow. But he did not put it on, for the man was unarmed. Indeed he was not a man at all, he was only a lad, a country hobbledehoy, staring with open mouth and round eyes.

"Good day to you," Gawin said.

"Good day to you. Who are you? Are you an angel?"

Gawin laughed. "Not yet, at least. I am a knight from the City of Legions, and I am here on king's business."

"Is 'knight' another way of saying 'man'?"

This must be the foolish son reared by a foolish mother, Gawin thought. "Are you Perceval? Was your father Allan the Fat?"

"I'm sure you are an angel," Perceval said, "if you know my name without being told. What is your name — if angels have names?"

"Why do you think I'm an angel?"

"Because I saw a creature like you once, wearing iron clothes, and my mother told me he was an angel."

"Your mother was wrong, Perceval. These iron clothes are armor, and I am a man who wears them to protect himself against swords and spears."

"I am better protected than that," Perceval said. And he felt about the neck of his shirt and drew out a chain on which hung a gold cross. "Our priest says this will defend me against every evil. And look here, knight." From his

31

pouch he pulled a flat fragment of stone. "See those lines? They are magic. They will protect me too."

Gawin took the fragment. The engraved lines were feathered with barbs and cross strokes, the mysterious symbols old Britons used on pillar stones and roadside posts. In these days nobody knew what they meant.

"I must not argue with the Druids and your priest," Gawin said, smiling. "I'll get down and walk with you, if it suits you to have company."

"Then let me ride your horse."

"Why?"

"Because I have never ridden a horse. Ours work in the fields, and they are small and have woolly coats."

"This fellow isn't an easy horse to ride unless you know him," Gawin said. "But one of these days I'll teach you."

"It must be now," Perceval said. "My mother will not let you teach me if we wait until she knows."

"You're a man. You must decide such things for yourself."

The youth began to caper about him. "Then let me wear your iron clothes, let me ride your horse."

"Sit here beside me on this stone, Perceval. We have much to talk about."

"I can't sit, I hate sitting, I shall say rude things or fall asleep if I sit."

"I promise you I shall keep you awake."

Perceval flung himself onto the stone. He was an attractive boy, fair and high colored, with manly features and the grace of a strong body. But he wriggled like a child of seven, scuffed his feet, picked up pebbles to throw, blew great sighs.

"Tell me," Gawin said, "how far is it to the castle of your mother, the lady Iglais?"

"I don't know, three miles I suppose."

"Are these woods hers?"

"Yes, and the farms too. The day I saw the knight I had gone farther than I'm allowed to go — that way." Perceval pointed east. "He had a pot on his head just like the pot on your saddle. What is your name? You haven't told me your name."

"Gawin of Rhos. I used to live in Rhos, but when I was knighted I went to the City of Legions to live with the king. Do you know the king, Perceval?"

"No. I have heard there is a king, though. I think he does not like my mother."

"He loves all his subjects. His name is Arthur, and I am here to do something for him, for you too."

Perceval leaped up. "What, Gawin? What will you do for me? Let me ride your horse?"

How am I to make him listen? I must get him on my side. If I put him on the horse and lead it, no harm will come worse than a roughing up if he falls off.

He said, "A horse thinks, just as you do. A horse wants this and doesn't want that. If you are to ride him you must not believe for a moment that he will be charitable and full of love."

"Then tell me what I am to do."

"You're to sit still, you're not to jabber and shout, you're

33

not to kick the horse or strike him. Do you understand?"

"How am I to make him go?"

"I'll attend to that. You must promise you'll do what I tell you, nothing more."

"I promise, I promise."

"Listen to me! If he throws you you'll have only a second to remember to land on your shoulders and roll. Roll away from him. This will keep you from being stepped on, and if you fall correctly you won't break an arm — or your neck."

Perceval listened like a monk saying prayers. "I am to turn in the air and fall on my shoulders. I am to roll away from his feet."

"Are you afraid?"

"No."

"Good. Come meet him, now. Gently, gently! He doesn't like to be run at. So, here, pat his nose." Gawin held the charger on a tight rein close to its cheek.

"Does he like me?" Perceval whispered.

"We'll soon know. I'll lead him back to the stone. Stand on the stone, step your left foot into the stirrup, balance your left hand on his neck, spring up lightly and straddle him with your right leg. Be dainty, now! Don't hurl yourself. Pretend you're dancing."

Perceval planted himself on the stone, thought over all Gawin had told him, again oddly like a man at prayer. Then with a gesture so precise and swift that Gawin felt it in his heart he stepped into the stirrup and settled himself on the saddle. The big war horse shivered, laid back its ears, pranced against the taut rein Gawin still held. Gawin tensed himself for a struggle, but needlessly. The horse steadied and moved forward.

Oye, Gawin thought, feeling the sweat of excitement between his shoulders, what a mount that was! I have seen new knights after years of training do worse. This lad is one of the rare ones who seem born with their schooling already laid into their nerves and sinews, he is made for excellence.

"I feel wrong," Perceval said. "I feel as though I should have the reins in my hands."

"In time."

"But I *know* such things," Perceval insisted. "Whenever a matter is intended, I do not have to be told, I know it, I am sure."

"All the same," Gawin grinned at him, "I will lead this horse."

AFTER A SILENCE in which Perceval thought so intently he seemed almost rapt, he said, "What would happen if I held the reins?"

"The horse would bolt and throw you."

"I don't think so, Gawin. He feels as though he is willing to obey me."

"Remember, you were only to do what I allowed."

Perceval sighed. "I remember. But it seems a pity, the only time I'll ever ride a horse, not to —"

"You'll ride a horse every day, at least as long as I am a guest of my lady your mother."

"Is your business with my mother?"

"Yes."

"I wish to hold the reins," Perceval said.

Gawin made no answer, and they walked awhile in silence.

"Gawin."

No reply.

"I am sorry, Gawin."

"If you are to become a knight you must not forget your promises."

"I made the promise before I realized it was intended that I should know what to do. Tell me why you say I am to become a knight."

"All boys of good blood become knights and serve the king."

"When? Today?"

"No, no, it needs more than a day."

"Why? I am ready to become a knight now."

"Here is what you must learn first." And Gawin told him how, when he was a lad of seven, he had become a page in his father's house, and practiced every day at games meant to toughen him and harden his sinews. "I was taught to sing, too," he went on, "and to sit with ladies and converse politely, and to feed and fly the hawks in the mews, and to skin and part the carcasses of deer and boar and all game. I was taught the proper form of address to men of every rank, and to know precedence, and to give alms, and to tell the truth. These were my lessons until I was fourteen. Then I was made a squire, and my training was the use of arms."

"I am already older than squires," Perceval said.

"And so you have much to learn in less time than I had."

"I do not *feel* as though I have much to learn. I feel as though I already know these things."

"Keep your mind on the horse," Gawin said. "When we reach the ruined woodsman's hut he will try to surprise you."

The horse did not shy at the hut, but, testing Perceval's control, ten steps beyond it. The youth flew off its back, remembering, Gawin noted with a thrill of unbelief, to turn himself by means of an airy somersault and fall on his shoulders. He rolled away from the hooves as though he had done it a hundred times before.

He sprang up, his face scarlet. "What did I do wrong?"

"You let the beast outthink you. This is a good lesson to learn the first day."

"I did not need the lesson, I only forgot what I was doing because I was planning my knighthood."

Gawin mounted him again, and they passed on through the trees, which grew small and wind-gnarled. At last they left the stunted forest and emerged onto a long, rising slope of meager grass. At its upper edge a little castle seemed to have been born through slow time from the stone upon which it stood. It presented a front wall blind except for a low port at the end of the drawbridge, two slip windows halfway between top and bottom, and a row of exceedingly short and narrow archer's slits just below the flat roof. The house was about half as deep as it was long, one end almost closed by a rude round tower scaly with age. A round bartizan pierced by two archers' slits in the shape of a cross overhung the forward angle of the other end. The effect was primitive, solitary, yet somehow fantastic because of its toylike size.

A dry moat encircled it. The gate was, in fact, a barbican, and stood across the moat from the castle. It was a small, blocklike structure of two battlements, lacking windows. Its port was too narrow to admit more than a single horseman. The rear door onto the portcullis was not visible as they approached.

"I shall get down here," Perceval said.

"Why?"

"Because if I don't my mother will say that I have disobeyed her."

"You must ride all the way to the barbican, Perceval. You must not care who sees you. This is the way men live their lives."

"Oh. Then will you help me tell her this?"

"If you wish, I'll tell her myself."

Perceval considered it with his strange, unyouthful absorption. "I was wrong to ask you to help me. I must tell her."

"Knightly said."

They ascended over a pebbly road choked with weeds. Heavy shoulders of rock bared themselves, and grass gave way to thistles. At the castle no flags were flying, no guard was to be seen. Nothing seemed alive but the swooping, white-winged birds.

They reached the barbican. It too was unmanned. The portcullis was a narrow span of three rotting beams, and was drawn up at the portal on the castle side. It was unguarded. Gawin thought, how does one enter this desolate house?

"We can't take the horse across the bridge, and my mother hasn't seen us," Perceval said, disappointed.

"Is there a chief ostler? Where are the barns?"

"Nobody comes here, Gawin. If you need a chief ostler I'll be the chief ostler."

"Lead the way."

They followed the dry moat to a huddle of buildings outside the castle oval: a sheep house, a dairy, a hut for tools and storage, a small defensive fort in ruins, a dovecote. The barn was stone, and in good repair. A servant ran from the sheep house to meet them.

"Messire, messire," he said, "what have you done to Perceval?"

"I have come with a message for my lady," Gawin said, "and I need care for my horse."

"I shall be turned away!"

"Stop roaring that you'll be turned away, Thomas," Perceval said. "See to this knight's wants. Do not treat his horse like one of our farm animals."

"Who told you he was a knight?" Thomas called after them, but Perceval was marching back to the barbican.

At the gate he shouted, "Let me in, Iorworth, lower the

bridge." Anger turned him pale, and he shuffled back and forth, drawing deep breaths.

Presently the portcullis began to descend, its crazy machinery groaning. A servant in a coarse brown tunic and soft house boots appeared at the castle port. He stopped them at the inner side of the moat. "Messire, you must tell me your name."

"I am Gawin, knight of the City of Legions."

"No knights come to this house, messire. Here you are a gentleman but not a knight."

"I will not hear any more of this foolishness," Perceval raged. "Run to my mother at once, Iorworth, and tell her I have brought a guest."

"You do not know what you are doing, master, you must not alarm my lady, you must —"

Perceval, white with fury, raised his fist.

Gawin caught it. "Not that way. Iorworth is your servant."

"He shames me."

"The better reason not to shame yourself. Let us go in."

They entered the tower. No garrison occupied the single guardroom, and the little armory behind it was as bare as a cell. An inner door opened onto the great hall. Gawin expected it would be dank, gloomy too, but the room was pleasant. Logs burned in the fireplace, bright hangings covered the stone walls, lamps hung on chains from the beams. Couches heaped with cushions and chairs draped in silk covers gave it comfort. All its furnishings were worn, yet their old richness gleamed in the warm lamplight.

The lady Iglais sat at her frames near the fire.

"Mother," Perceval said.

"Are you home, Squirrel?"

"I have brought a guest, and you must not call me Squirrel."

Iglais rose.

Her son said, "This is Messire Gawin, from the City of Legions."

Iglais was a pretty little woman, younger than Gawin anticipated. Her clothing was old-fashioned, but it had been costly once, and the close bodice and flowing skirt were becoming to the gentle fullness of her figure. She wore no veil, allowing her corn-colored hair to fall in a soft roll about her shoulders. I have seen such women, Gawin thought, they have the gift of sounding reasonable when they talk nonsense.

She said, "Give me leave, messire," and turned to Perceval. "Did you go past the farms again, Squirrel? Each time you do, you spoil a little of our peace."

"No," he answered shortly. "Pay attention to our guest, mother."

She pushed her frames aside and faced Gawin, looking at his worn arms, looking with a kind of desperate eagerness into his eyes. "Did you tell him, messire?"

"Tell him what?"

"What man you are?"

"Yes indeed. I am King Arthur's knight and officer of his peace."

Her soft little face seemed to congeal. "Now you have

41

ruined me, messire, you have scattered all the quiet life I have guarded with such care these sixteen years. I wish God had stopped you before you broke into my home."

"What peace do you mean?" Gawin said. "You are under threat of seizure. I have come in the king's name as your champion."

"I do not ask a featherweight of help from the king and his meddling champions. You have taken my son away from me, and I do not care what happens to my castle and my life if you drag my son into the abomination of knighthood."

"I am intended for knighthood, mother," Perceval said.

"Believe me," Gawin said, making an effort to speak to her as a man speaks to a sweet, desirable woman (she was sweet, desirable), "my service is yours. Accept me as your champion, and I will do my best to cure the wrongs The Moors has made you suffer."

"If anyone has made my mother suffer," Perceval said, "I should correct the wrong. What wrong do you mean, Gawin?"

Iglais sat down again. "Be quiet, Squirrel. As for you, messire, you see how eager he is to help you destroy me. I have protected him for sixteen years, but every day of those sixteen years I woke in dread of this very thing. Go away. Leave us alone. I would rather face the Knight of The Moors than you."

Gawin took her hand. It was warm and small, and she let it lie in his as though it had died there. He said, "We must trust the king, we must trust God."

"God does not love me," she said.

9

THE NEXT MORNING Gawin discovered that Iglais did not maintain an armorer. But the smith in charge of farm tools agreed to beat the dents out of his helmet and shield, and to do what he could to mend his chain shirt. From him Gawin borrowed a little rancid fish oil, rags, and pumice, then went to the guardroom in the tower to furbish his steel himself. While he was scouring rusty patches on his knee pieces Perceval's mother entered through the door of the great hall.

Gawin got up from the puncheon stool. "Good day, my lady. You find me smutted and unfit for company, I'm afraid."

"I have brought you some polishing leather," she said. "I have not seen much armor in sixteen years, but I remember that my husband, Messire Allan, supplied his squire with soft rawhide."

"Sit here, my lady." Gawin offered her the puncheon, wondering whether the change in her appearance and bearing served some end he couldn't foresee. She looked peaceable and well rested, color in her little face, and her hair carefully dressed. She hardly resembled the perturbed, unforgiving woman who had greeted him yesterday.

"I hope you slept well," she said. "We aren't used to

guests here, and I've almost forgotten how to make them feel at home."

Gawin had spent the night in the guardroom on pallets and cushions laid over two benches pushed together. He had not slept well, yet better than he expected. He said, "Sleeping is a habit of mine. And to see you happier this morning is all I need for comfort."

She sat down on the stool, and Gawin moved to the bed-benches. He rested his armor across his knees and worked on it with the rawhide as they talked.

"Well, well," Iglais began, "when a situation can't be mended one is best served by not thinking of it, though I have been thinking about you, Messire Gawin. I suppose you realized that I was angry with you yesterday, for I have tried to bring up my Squirrel kindly, without the horrible knowledge of war that knights must have. But I decided last night after I had gone to bed that the time was bound to come when a knight, you or another, reached us and changed things so that I could no longer keep my home in the way that seems best to me. Besides, I *am* beleaguered by a cruel man just as you said, though how you knew it is rather a mystery unless the king sends out spies, and if he does, it would have helped had he sent spies here sixteen years ago when my husband was being attacked. But I don't mean to criticize the king, I only mean that if I do not have a champion I suppose it won't matter whether I have brought up my Squirrel to live in peace or to gallop about armed with murderous weapons."

Gawin listened to her low, pleasant voice as a man

listens to water, accepting it as a sound of nature. "You have had a difficult time, my lady."

"I did not think it too difficult."

"Can you tell me anything useful about your enemy?"

"Useful? I don't know. He is a tyrant, and I have no doubt he started to be a tyrant when he was a little boy, and I am sure you know that tyrants look for undefended victims, people they can frighten and unnerve. He probably enjoys thinking he makes me tremble, and don't you agree that manners of this kind are particularly stupid and discourteous?"

"Is he the same baron who seized your husband's other lands?"

"Yes indeed, the same man, and the thing that makes him a trial is that he was Messire Allan's vassal once. And I remember well my husband telling me that he was an overbearing, ambitious man, and that someday he would give him trouble. It seems so long ago," she finished with a sigh.

"But even old wrongs can be righted."

"Last night when I decided I would have to have a champion whether or not I desire one —" she broke off, embarrassed. "I do not mean to be rude, Messire Gawin, I only mean it occurred to me that we should send a man to The Moors to say you have come and wish to fight for me." She gave him a sad little smile. "So many years have gone since this trouble began. Women feel time passing more than men feel it."

"Not you, my lady. Time seems to have stood still for you."

"Do you truly think so? I was unhappy in the night, I thought, 'Messire Gawin will see only an old and foolish woman.' It is hard to make a person one does not know understand that living contentedly, living in peace, robs time of the sorest blows it strikes. Until last night I had forgotten I was old and foolish."

Gawin was touched, amused at himself too, for being vulnerable, in the same moment, to her courage and her daft charm. She was, he thought, an entrancing little woman, and he wondered why the Knight of The Moors had not forcibly taken her along with her lands.

"You see?" she said, "you are too honest to deny that I am old and foolish."

"I was only devising a courteous way to contradict you, my lady."

"Let us not 'my-lady' and 'messire' one another, Gawin. I remember your name. I remember hearing my husband speak of you. Aren't you a cousin of the king's?"

"His nephew. My mother was Arthur's sister."

"How is your mother?"

"She is dead, my father too."

"Oh, I'm so sorry, I'm so sorry. One never grows old enough not to miss one's parents, does one?"

In spite of himself Gawin felt his face arrange itself in a pious grimace of agreement.

"But let us not speak of sad things. Did you tell me what I should do about sending a message to Messire of The Moors?"

"Do you have a steward?"

46

"I'm afraid not. I had one, but after he died I let things slip. We seem to get along comfortably without a steward."

"What kind of man is Ewan? Could he act as steward?"

"Do you know Ewan?"

"I met him on the mainland. He told me your trouble. We can hardly send our message by a herdsman, and it would help if Ewan could serve as your steward. Can he ride?"

"Yes indeed."

"Then we'll ride together. I'll back him."

"Poor Ewan," Iglais said. "He's a very nervous man."

"All he need do is inform the baron that, in the king's name, I offer him combat, body for body, on the day he set to attack you, and state that the outcome will decide the ownership of these lands."

Iglais hugged herself in a shiver. "Body for body, how dreadful that is!"

"This is the way officers of the king must settle matters that can't be taken to the City of Legions."

"And what if you lose, Gawin?"

"I suppose the day will come when I can't defend the king's law, but we must hope the day has not come yet."

She leaned forward, chin in hands, and studied him. Her eyes were exceedingly blue and clear. As blue as Lancelot's, Gawin thought.

"I can understand why you have bewitched my poor Squirrel," she said. "You are so sure you can do what you promise."

"May I offer a suggestion about Perceval?"

47

"You wish to make him a knight."

"I was only going to tell you that when I was a page my father called me Heatherhead. But one day it made me feel belittled, and I told him he must never call me that name again. I believe Perceval has reached the time when Squirrel offends his pride."

"Heatherhead," she said, charmed. "What a sweet, funny name. Your father must have been a loving man, Gawin."

Gawin found himself without an answer.

"Poor Perceval, he does object, you're right, and I mean to stop it. Yet it seems harmless to give him a fond name."

"As for his becoming a knight," Gawin said, footing his way with care, "what lies ahead for a strong, wellborn young man if he can't have the brotherhood of his fellows? He should be schooled enough here so that you can send him to the City of Legions feeling assured he is ready for knighthood."

Her eyes filled with tears. "Yes, yes, yes, yes, I know, I suppose I have always known. Only time passes so swiftly. Just yesterday he was a little boy." She wiped her eyes on the sleeve of her gown. "I have been chattering like a sea gull, haven't I? For so many years I've had no one to talk to except my servants and Squirrel. And I am glad you have come, not because I need a champion, but because," she said, "because this is a lonely life."

"You must return to the world, Iglais. You must see the City of Legions again."

"No, I have no wish — except to turn time back. What

were we speaking of? You asked me questions, and I am afraid I didn't answer."

"About what happened between you and the Knight of the Moors."

"Oh. Yes. But it doesn't seem important any longer. Well. My husband once held all the land west of the strait. He garrisoned it with castles, and he made The Moors the captain of all the garrisons. When Messire Allan was killed, the baron simply said the castles were his, and the farms, and everything. We had loyal soldiers, we had good officers too, and they fought for me with all their hearts, but my husband was gone." She spread her hands. "What could we do? And that is all, I suppose. He was my enemy, he wanted my lands and took them, and my husband's old soldiers have been killed or accepted his service. It's a simple story, isn't it? A strong side and a weak side."

"Has he ever offered you conditions?"

"No."

"Have you allies?"

"No. I mean I have three brothers, but one is old and sick, and one has become a hermit, and the third is a man like The Moors, ambitious and greedy. Besides, my brothers are so far away, I haven't seen them for years, and I only hear news of them when a priest who learns what is happening in the world comes to give my priest comfort and assistance."

"So," Gawin said lightly, "you and I, we must hold this castle."

She nodded. "Do you think it is truly worth holding?"

"That is not always the issue," he said, "when we have a duty to do."

10

"Now," GAWIN SAID to Ewan, "Do you understand what you are to do?"

"I understand but I cannot do it, messire. I am a shepherd, I am a peaceful man, I have never held a weapon in my hand except an ax, and then not as a weapon. No," he said, "war is for men of birth."

"If Iglais orders you to perform this errand, do you mean to refuse?"

"She will not order it. Here no one gives hopeless orders, not even my lady. We live in peace, though I suppose I cannot make a knight of the king understand what peace is."

Ewan was manly in a way Gawin had not expected. They stood looking into one another's faces, and it was Gawin who turned away. The dreamlike air of this place of rocks and birds has addled my brain, he thought. Who would believe that in Norgals, in all Britain, a household could melt and shift until every man was the equal of every other man, until my lady is less concerned with her enemy than with her shepherd's nerves, until the shepherd dare reject a king's commission? I must take these children under my wing, like a priest.

The priest, there must be a priest. I will ask him to ride with me.

"Where is your holy man's cell?" he said.

"In the grove beyond the oat farm."

"Do you have an altar within the castle where you hear mass?"

"Yes, but —"

"But what?"

Ewan shifted his feet. "Well, the fact is, we do not hear mass regularly. I suppose you will charge us with a lack of religion, but — this matter is hard to explain to a soldier."

"All the same, try."

The shepherd sighed. "We seem to live with God all the time, messire. Our land is very old. Many gods have made their homes in our woods and on our cliffs. And," Ewan said, turning red, "our Lord Christ and His Father are friendly to — to —"

"To what, man?"

"You must speak to the priest. Don't question me, a shepherd, let me go to my work." And without a by-your-leave Ewan hurried away.

Gawin went to the barn, asked Thomas to saddle his horse, mounted, and set out for the oat farm where he had first seen Perceval. What do they mean by peace, these poeple who have been robbed of land, soldiers, castles, farms, almost of bread itself? Here is peace which is only their failure to defend themselves against evil, an unjust peace that encourages tyranny, an unknightly peace, an unlawful peace, no peace at all, but weakness. Yet it is hard to lay hold of this weakness which behaves so strangely like strength.

Beyond the oat field stood a grove of gaunt trees. Grass grew under them, and in the grass lay patches of harebells, freshly blue. As he entered the cool shade he saw that the flowers grew thickly, like a lovely mantle borrowed from the color of heaven. He followed a dim footpath, stooping now and then to pass under branches. The priest's house was backed against a stone slab. It was a neat little cottage, its walls dry stone and its roof thatch. It lacked windows, and its open door was topped by a square stone lintel.

Gawin dismounted and wound his reins around a branch. He peered through the door, saw a plain table and chair, a narrow couch, a puncheon stool, a hearth over which hung cups and a pan, and at the room's end, a crude stone cross. The priest sat before the empty hearth, his hands folded on his knees.

"Good day to you, father," Gawin said.

The man rose. He was tall and spare and his gray hair had not been cut for so long it had overgrown his tonsure. His robe was a brown homespun shift, ankle-length, tied at the waist with a cord. His feet were bare.

"Good day to you," he said. "I heard you riding through the trees. I heard you stop to look at my parishioners, didn't I?"

"Your parishioners?"

"The harebells, the harebells," he said with a soft laugh. "Aren't they beautiful this morning?"

52

"Harebells," Gawin said.

"Will you honor me by eating bread with me?"

Gawin stepped into the cottage and sat down in the chair which the priest pushed forward. "I have come from my lady Iglais," he said. "I am Gawin, an officer of the king."

"Thomas told me of your arrival." He opened a coarse sack and withdrew a loaf and cut a slice. From an earthenware jug standing on the floor by the cross he poured a mixture of milk and water. "Thomas brings me these meats each morning, cheese too. Will you taste my cheese, Messire Gawin?"

"No, father, just a mouthful of bread."

"You have a mission with me?"

Gawin found himself unable to state his mission. A barefoot priest with a parish of harebells, how could this man represent the household of Iglais when the challenge was carried to the Knight of The Moors?

"You find things a little strange?" the priest said.

"Yes, between me and God, I find things more than a little strange! Did Thomas tell you my business with my lady?"

"He spoke of your teaching Perceval to ride your horse."

"Did he mention that I wish to be her champion against the baron who threatens her?"

"Oh, yes, that too."

"And do you find it larger that I put Perceval on my horse than that I hope to deliver Iglais and restore her land?"

"It is hard to know what matters are large and what

53

small, isn't it?" The priest gave him a childlike smile. "The fact that you have reached us at all may be larger than anything you do."

"Why?"

"Because we live with truths that are not forced to take many shapes in many circumstances. Our truths may seem puzzling to you because their shape is always the same."

"Do you mean the shape of your truth, as you say, will alter my duty?"

"You will learn that yourself, Messire Gawin."

"I only wish to know — I am only asking — it is only that —"

"Yes?"

"— why you do not sing regular masses," Gawin finished, defeated.

"Oh. Does this displease the king?"

"It is uncustomary."

"I suppose it is. I sing a mass when someone wishes it, or when I feel that a mass is waiting to be sung."

"Ewan told me — Ewan said — he spoke of many gods who have lived in your countryside."

Soberly the priest nodded. "That is true. God wears the weather — seasons and tides. Men have known this since the beginning of the world, and have spoken to Him through the garments He puts on. Do you find it a fault that we remember God's ancient robes of Summer and Winter?"

"Summer and Winter, these were feasts of the pagans," Gawin said. "They do not concern Christian men."

"Look here, Messire Gawin." The old man rose and

moved to the cross. It was a tapered column. Its squared edges still showed worn engravings of barbs and hatches, the kind Gawin had seen on Perceval's ancient charm. Into the upright had been mortised arms formed of the same stone.

The priest rested his hand on an arm. "I made this cross. I found its two pieces in the rubble of a fallen temple built by our forefathers in my grove I do not know how long before God died on His cross."

"It was a heathen temple, then."

"They say my cross was a pillar so shrewdly placed that its shadow fell on the temple altar only once during the year, at sunrise on midsummer morning."

"Have you put it in your cell to cleanse it of its old evil?"

"Why do you say evil, messire? Men's lives were in God's care then as ours are now. Our forefathers needed His help, without Him they could not feed themselves, without God's summer sun they would have starved. And so when they saw God, they saw Him wearing His fertilizing sun." The priest spread his hands. "The sun is not all of God, but to the men who built the temple in my grove it was the greater part."

Gawin was struck silent.

"We ask God to feed us too," he went on. "But we remember that He died for us on the cross, and that His death gives us the bread of life. His vessel of divine bread in which He lives again nourishes us as the ram sacrificed on midsummer morning nourished our forefathers of the temple. And this is why I believe my cross shows forth two of God's shapes, one Who died there, and one more ancient than the cross."

For a moment Gawin felt himself persuaded, not by the outlandish words of the priest but by a quiet wonder, a moment of joy in which many things appeared to be one thing.

"Who sees all of God?" the priest murmured. "Our fore-fathers? Ourselves? No man can see His total, Messire Gawin. But each man sees a part. Some behold Him most clearly in the relics He has left us. You are an officer of the king, your hands are occupied each day with objects you can touch, your sword, your shield, the armor given you by the king. These things are the clothes of your duty. And I believe, when you begin to look for God, you will see Him most clearly in a shape you can hold between your hands. I believe you are a man who needs a talisman, you are a man who needs God's Grail."

Gawin stammered, "I need — I need only to seek justice on the body of The Moors."

The priest did not appear to have heard. "Perceval too," he said. "He will also need to touch God."

11

AS HE AWAITED his combat Gawin slept unevenly at night and was restive by day. His fixed sense of purpose seemed to lie thinly over a danger unrelated to his duty. Wasn't he, in confronting Iglais's enemy, becoming her more deadly enemy? In Arthur's name he was shattering a peace he had not even recognized as peace.

I must not weaken myself, he thought again and again, I dare not. And to keep himself at the pitch of intention he occupied all his time. Most of it he spent with Perceval, fulfilling his promise to explain the skills of knighthood.

Perceval was not only unnaturally quick to comprehend what he saw and was told, he was magical in performance. He made no errors of awkwardness, his strength did not blunder, his balance never failed. He learned, moreover, not to coax for privileges once ruled out. For his mother's sake Gawin did not wear armor or allow Perceval to strut about in borrowed chain. The boy accepted the rule with nothing worse than a sigh.

One morning they were exercising in the grassy field below the castle. As a shield Perceval used a barrel head to which an armstrap had been nailed. Gawin struck at it with a weighted shaft. But no matter how swift or crafty Gawin was, the makeshift shield always caught his thrust.

"It is time you admit who trained you," Gawin said. "Your skill is more than accident."

"Nobody trained me. But —"

"But what?"

"You will tell my mother. She thinks I play games to amuse myself."

"Power and grace like yours are not acquired in play. I have been using strokes no beginner I ever saw could parry, yet you turn every one."

"It is intended," Perceval said.

"Intended?"

"Yes. I mean that I parry your thrusts. I always know if a thing is intended, Gawin. If it isn't, I am stupid, I forget, I can't think what to do."

Here is the pride of youth, Gawin thought, the belief that one is infallible. "The feeling that victory is intended is a fine way to stumble into defeat," he said. "Besides, there is more than feeling in your action with that shield. There is schooling too."

Perceval dropped the edge of the barrel head onto the grass and leaned his two hands on it. "I have watched falcons and porpoises and hares. Our farm horses are fastened into straps and led, they walk slowly without rhythm, they hang their heads. If they come to a stone they have to go round it. But a hare leaps over a stone, even if it is ten times as tall as himself. I would rather leap than walk like a farm horse, so I watched hares until I learned how. I can't fly like falcons, but I can swing to right and left, I can turn as fast, I can go straight to a mark each time, as they do. I know how to swim, but not to live in the sea with the porpoises. All the same I can curl myself around whatever is in my way as sleek and close and swift as they, I can keep my balance by remembering how the water helps. If this is what you mean by schooling, I am schooled."

"And no knight helped you?"

"No. Will you tell my mother?"

"Not if you don't wish."

Perceval said, "I would like to fight The Moors in your place, Gawin."

"Now that is *too* much."

"Then let me go with you."

"Not that either."

"But I know you need a man to carry your challenge. Let me do that. I am the son of the family he has injured."

"Wait awhile," Gawin said, pleased with him. "A time will come when you fight for justice in the king's name."

Gawin's own day was nearing, and he himself conveyed his challenge. He stood at the drawbridge of The Moors and called out the set phrases: he had come on the part of Iglais, he impeached the knight of treason against King Arthur, he would meet him to prove the impeachment, body for body, on the appointed day. He heard the baron's response: I accept my lady's champion, I shall be here to defend the charge and prove it false.

He returned to Iglais, found her working at her embroidery frame by the hearth, and told her the combat was set.

She drew a sigh. "I should be thinking of things to help you, Gawin, since you insist on fighting this fight for me, but I have already made up my mind it is men's business, and I don't know what to do for you except keep you amused while we are obliged to wait until it is over. If you like, we can carry our lunches to the cliff, but the weather is so changeable, and nobody enjoys coming home soaking wet. Or I could sing to you, except I haven't sung for a long time, and I'm not sure my voice is pleasing, though I can still play the harp. What would make you happy?"

"I would feel happier if I believed you are satisfied with what I must do."

"Yes indeed, Gawin, it is good of you to care about my difficulties. It will be useful to have the farms again, though we have made out without often feeling hungry. You have only to look at Squirrel to see how strong he is, and the servants, they seem to keep up too."

"Yours is a matter of the king's justice, Iglais. This is why I can't ignore it."

"The king must be a busy man, a whole kingdom needing justice to worry about."

"The king is only the vessel of justice, the fountainhead. He obeys the laws as we must."

She nodded wisely. "I should think he might find it wearing sometimes; I should think he would like to stay at home now and then and have cozy suppers and talk. I'm afraid he doesn't have much time just to live, as though tomorrow were another part of today."

"It is his calling to protect the law of the realm."

"I was just saying so. He has a son, hasn't he? Is the son a nice young man?"

"Lohot? Yes. He was knighted at Whitsuntide three years ago. When he was a squire I trained him. He was fourteen when he came to me, and I had him until he became eighteen."

"And I suppose you taught him all the things you wish my poor Squirrel to learn?"

60

"Iglais, Iglais —"

"Have I been upsetting? I'm so sorry, I do realize you have made Squirrel happier than he has ever been. And this is what I want for him — to be happy, even if his happiness is rather uncomfortable for me."

If I were to love any woman again, Gawin thought, it would be this maddening, small Iglais. I am already half in love with her, and if I am not watchful I shall end squatting here on these bare rocks like a sea gull mewing little songs. He said, "I spoke with the priest a few days ago. He thinks Perceval may wish to take orders."

"My priest, you mean? By the oats?"

"Yes."

"I don't like to be rude and say you didn't understand him, Gawin, but Squirrel isn't in the least religious. What an odd notion," she finished with a smile, "Squirrel in orders!"

"The priest said — I don't remember precisely — he spoke of the vessel of the mass. He said Perceval would need a Grail."

"Oh. The Grail. Yes, we're all fond of speaking of it, it's a relic in my family, you know."

"What is? What relic?"

"The Grail. It belongs to my brother, the sick one."

"Tell me what this Grail is, Iglais. Have you seen it?"

"No, I haven't seen it, my brother lives a long distance away. He's been sick for years, though perhaps I've mentioned that?"

"Yes."

"I'm afraid the story is immensely long. It tells how the relic came to Britain because Joseph of Arimathea, who was a friend of Our Lord, had to run away from the Romans, or perhaps it was the Jews, after Our Lord was crucified. And he had a cup with him when he boarded ship to sail to the west. They say it was the cup the Disciples drank from at the last supper they ate with Our Lord, and some men say it was the very same cup that caught His blood when He hung on the cross. Anyway, Joseph reached Britain and hid the cup, nobody knows where, or how long it lay concealed. But when it was recovered it passed to Joseph's descendants, our family, I mean, my brothers' and mine. And we have had it ever since."

"What is your brother's name?"

"Peleur — King Peleur. My brothers are all kings."

"Could a man see this cup?"

"You might go to Peleur and ask. The priests who visit my priest speak of it sometimes. They say no woman can see it, no man either until he has made certain preparations. But priests are gossips, they like to invent little mysteries, it makes their work exciting. I wish I could tell you more about it, but I can't."

"Where is Messire Peleur?"

"He built a grand house for the relic, in the north somewhere. But since I never see him I am not sure where. Perhaps you could find out from the priest."

She turned back to her frame tranquilly and began to work with a long, scarlet thread. Gawin made little sense of what she had told him, he was confused about the words of the priest, each moment he understood less of the substance of his errand with The Moors. Yet he felt superbly clear. He would search out Peleur, and he would see the cup in which Christ's blood once glowed. He would hold it between his hands. And in that moment the scarred deceits of life, the meanness, the insane follies of life would be cleansed away, in that moment he would know the perfect name of joy.

12

NO MAN OF GENTLE BIRTH was maintained in the household of Iglais. Though Thomas was capable of discharging the duties of squire his base blood barred him from appearing with Gawin on the field of combat. But he could watch from a distance, care for Gawin's horse if it were wounded, and see that no treachery of The Moors was left unreported. The importance this gave him inspired him to hear the battle mass which Gawin had asked to have celebrated at the castle on the morning he was to fulfill his challenge.

When Gawin arrived Thomas was already present. The small room used as a chapel was not much more than a stone cell furnished with an altar and cross. The priest wore the same brown robe, but now he had put on cordwain sandals and hung his beads from his rope girdle. Gawin had not expected Iglais, but she appeared a moment after him, a light blue veil folded over her blond hair. She seemed weary and she had been weeping.

Poor, sweet lady, he thought, I must not look at her or she will unnerve me. And he knelt and fixed his eyes on the cross. The priest went slowly through the sacred Latin, gave Gawin sanctified bread, absolved him, and blessed his arms. Iglais rose and went out swiftly. Leaving Thomas to collect his armor Gawin followed and waylaid her in the narrow passage before her private chamber. "Bless me too, Iglais."

"I wish you well, Gawin, and I shall be praying for you. I would be unhappy if any bad thing happens to you when you are doing this for me."

"Give me a kiss of farewell?"

"Don't say farewell! I suppose you must be right since you feel so strongly about it, and if you are right we must believe you will prevail." She stood tiptoe to kiss his cheek.

"If I fall, you must send a runner to the City of Legions to report the manner of my death to King Arthur."

"Yes, yes, I understand." Her lips trembled, but she had shed her tears. "Goodbye for a little while, Gawin, and now you must let me go."

"Where is Perceval?"

"He has said he means to ride with you today, but I told the servants not to awaken him. Please don't send for him unless you must."

"No need to send for him, though if he is awake and wishes to follow me you must not try to stop him, Iglais." His heart knotted itself into a lump of cold misery. "I know this is hard for you, but men, they must live men's lives."

She drew the veil across her face and turned away.

It was a morning of heavy air, clouds rolling in sodden

haste on a west wind. A poor day to fight, he thought, damp will choke the lungs, and I'll sweat like a porter, and if I bleed my armor will stick to my flesh, and, bleeding or not, the salt will chafe me. But fighting is not meant to be done in ease.

He went to the guardroom where Thomas had transported his mail. "It is time to prepare me," he said. "Do you know what to do?"

"Between me and God, messire, I have never armed a man before in my life."

"Then arm your first one with care. Eeee! You're buckling the straps too tight. Easy man, the chausses are meant to protect my legs, not cut them off at the knee."

"Why don't you wait until you get there to put on all this iron, Messire Gawin?"

"Because we may be ambushed along the way."

"A fighting man must think of everything," said Thomas admiringly.

Without flags or trumpets to hearten their departure, with no one except Iorworth and the undergroom to bid them Godspeed, they trotted down the slope of grass. Gawin was beginning to feel the readiness that made a man conscious of his strength and sharpened his will to fight warily and well. The baron is short and heavy, he thought, he will come on like the wind and try to unseat me with sheer weight. But he will tire. I must get at him on the ground, we must finish it on foot. Against a thick man of low stature my advantage will tell after ten strokes. I am ready, he thought, and unless a man is ready in his mind, his body can't fight, not even if it is as strong as Samson's.

He had forgotten Iglais and all the perplexities of her household. This is what it was to be ready.

After a ride of two hours through forest they reached the hold of The Moors. Scarlet pennons were flying on the two towers. Outside the moat on the grassy battle green stood a pavilion of blue and yellow striped silk. Near it was a portable mounting stage and a horse caparisoned with a bright, brocaded housse, as yet riderless. The baron's shield, emblazoned with a ram's head, hung on a stake by the open fold of the pavilion.

"Stop here, Thomas," Gawin said. "Keep your position under this tree. You know what you are to do if my horse is cut, or if there is treachery, or if I fall."

"I know, I know, messire. I wish I had been born of gentle blood, but I will try to do as well as if I were your true squire."

"Goodbye, Thomas."

"God go with you."

Gawin closed his ventail, seated his spear in the saddle feuter, threw his shield onto his left arm, and rode forward. At the pavilion he struck the baron's shield a light, ringing blow. "Messire of The Moors, prepare to answer the king's charge of treason."

The baron emerged. Over his mail he wore a loose surcoat, sleeveless, belted with a baldric bossed with silver. Below the head of his spear, which his squire still held, a swallowtail pennon of scarlet silk was fastened with two gold rings. His squire mounted him and handed up his shield and spear.

"Go to your lines, messires," the squire said.

A page in scarlet silk, who stood on the curtain wall before the keep, blew a long note on a polished horn.

"Take the south line," the squire told Gawin.

Gawin rode to his quarter of the grassy field, The Moors to his. They turned their horses and faced one another, a shabby knight in an old surcoat of faded colors, a splendid one polished at all points and gleaming in the sun. The page blew the charge. Gawin touched his horse with the spur, leaned forward easily, watched his enemy's shield, which seemed to fly toward him. As he expected, the baron charged at a furious gallop. His spear hit Gawin's shield like a falling house. Gawin felt himself rise out of his saddle and sail weightless over his horse's crupper. With a thud that rattled his helmet he came down on his feet, staggered for balance, and discovered that he was still holding the butt of his shattered spear. In the same gesture he flung it away and drew his sword.

The baron was also unseated. Gawin grinned, and felt his lips stick to his teeth. This teaches you to respect a man with longer arms than yours, he thought. I hit you half a second before you hit me.

They approached cautiously, circling for advantage. He's too short to try for my head, he will hunt an opening under my shield or cut at my knees. I'll offer him a target and overreach him. Gawin dropped his shield invitingly, but the baron was not fooled. He probed at Gawin's legs. Not too much of that, friend, Gawin thought, I've no mind to limp the rest of my life. He gave ground, gripped his sword with both hands, leaped forward, struck, and on the recoil leaped back. He had felt the baron's mail open and saw an ooze of blood below his ear. His sword had taken off a wedge of his steel casque and cut through the rings of his camail. The muscles of his neck were grazed and bleeding.

There's something for you to think about, Gawin muttered aloud. Now you must defend your bare flesh. And while you worry I'll break your elbow and after that —

The baron rushed all at once upon Gawin, raised his sword above his head, and brought it down with a deafening crash of metal on Gawin's helmet. Gawin had not expected the maneuver and was not ready with a parry. He only deflected the blade a little, so that the blow fell flat. But it was of such terrible force that it knocked him backward. He rolled onto his hands and knees, hampered by his shield. He saw the baron's feet running across the grass, and, still on his knees, covered himself with his shield. While his enemy was wasting a blow on the shield, he would slash him across the ankles, between his chausses and champons.

He balanced forward, but the baron did not come on. It had happened so swiftly that Gawin lacked even a second to peer through the slits of his ventail toward the baron's head. And therefore, when his enemy's feet paused and seemed to dance insane steps, he was overbalanced by his expectation of the charge and would have toppled forward had he not leaned on his shield. He looked up at the moment when the baron fell like a crashing tree and lay spread-eagled on his back.

Gawin pulled himself to his feet. A great burst of blood spurted from the baron's neck. In the wound, bathed red, stuck a short arrow with a weighted shaft.

Gawin stood still, stupidly looking down at the dying man.

"I saved your life, I did it, I saved your life!" A voice like Perceval's rang about the green.

"Thomas!" Gawin shouted.

"It wasn't Thomas, it was I, Perceval. I saved you."

"Where are you?"

"In the tree right over Thomas's head."

"Get down. Come here."

The baron's squire spurred forward, knelt beside the fallen man, raised his master's ventail, called him by name. Then he sat back on his heels and spoke to Gawin. "He is dead, messire, his face is turning blue. Your unlawful weapon has all but beheaded him."

Perceval capered across the grass. "I walked all night, I have waited since daybreak, and I saved you."

Gawin grabbed him by the shirt. "Did you shoot this arrow?"

"Don't try to conceal your crime by blaming it on a boy, messire," the squire said.

"It is not an arrow, it is a dart," Perceval said. "Iorworth told me it was a dart."

"Where did you get it?"

The baron's squire rose. "This is treachery. I must report

69

it to my lord's brother. If you run away while I am gone, you will be accused as recreant in the City of Legions before King Arthur." He mounted and galloped toward the castle.

"What does he mean?" Perceval said.

"Never mind what he means. Where did you get the dart?"

"In the armory. It was sticking in a crack, I found it and cleaned and polished it, and Iorworth showed me how to sharpen it. I have practiced throwing it at birds. I can bring down a flying gull with it. It is truly mine, you need not fear I stole it."

Groaning, Gawin let him go. "You've killed the Knight of The Moors, Perceval."

"He knocked you down. I killed him for you."

"Listen, I was fighting on a challenge of the king. It was lawful combat. But your act was murder."

"What is murder? If he hadn't hit you with his sword you would have killed him anyway. Why does it matter if I did?"

"We were two against one. If you can't understand the law, can you understand that?"

Perceval's wild blush ebbed from his face and left him pale. "You said your cause was the king's cause, Gawin, you said it was just, you said you would win this fight because it was just. I meant to help you, I meant to help the king too."

Behind them they heard the sudden thud of horses. Gawin turned. The squire was returning from the barbican of the castle, and with him a man who was unarmed save for a

70

shield and sword. They galloped past the pavilion and onto the battle green. The unarmed man flung himself from his horse and ran forward, his sword gripped in his right fist and his shield thrown before his breast.

"I appeal you for treason, Gawin of Rhos," he said. "You murdered my brother from ambush, the squire saw it all."

"It was no murder. It was —" Gawin gulped at the explanation as though at salt — "an accident. A misunderstanding."

"You lie," the brother said. "The squire heard you call it murder."

"Whatever I called it, I do not abide your charge of lying. Arm yourself."

The brother was a slight man, younger than Gawin by fifteen years. He had the unskillful look of a clerk or a student. His rage seemed to make him ill, turning his mouth purple and his swarthy skin chalk-yellow. "I will prove the charge on you body for body," he said, and flourished the sword.

"Go and arm, then."

"Do not order me to arm, messire!" His teeth chattered. "I'll decide when you answer the charge, not you."

"Set the time, then, and make an end of talk."

The brother let his shield slide forward on his arm and his sword hang slack. He turned his back on Gawin and moved away from the group about the dead man. Perceval had not said a word, he had only stood looking first at Gawin, then at the dark-skinned kinsman of The Moors.

Now he asked, "Is this how justice is?"

Gawin was watching the brother, who stood alone a moment, then faced them. His mud-colored cheeks were streaked with tears. "Gawin, my brother possessed himself of the lands of the widow of Allan the Fat because he had made agreements with Allan that he held to be sufficient. He accepted your challenge believing in his rights, and he would have adhered to the outcome. I mean, had he not been treacherously murdered."

Gawin said, "He was not murdered, he —"

"Be silent, messire. I wish to be bound by my brother's given word for his sake. Therefore, let the widow of Allan the Fat hold her lands for the space of one year. At the end of the year, return here and answer my charge of treachery and untruth."

"I will answer your charge then or now or whenever you wish. But I will not hazard the lands of the lady a second time on such an unworthy pretext."

"You have no choice," said the kinsman of The Moors. "I will defeat you if I can, and then it will be I who says what happens to the lands. Either pledge me your presence on the day, or be appealed before Arthur at the City of Legions as recreant."

"I shall be here," Gawin said. "Now let us make an end of delay and lift this man onto our shields and carry him to the chapel." He spoke to Perceval. "You must come with us."

Perceval stared into Gawin's face, then stooped and drew the dart from the baron's wound. Without waiting even to wipe it with grass he ran away at the top of his speed. In a moment he was out of sight in the trees beyond the green.

"He is a wild animal," Gawin said. "He is a youth who has grown up without training. But I promise you he will do his penance."

"You will do his penance for him, messire, one year from today."

13

GAWIN'S HELP in carrying the dead knight to the chapel was refused, and he and Thomas began their homeward journey.

"I wish you had followed Perceval when he ran off," Gawin said. "Did he speak to you?"

"Not a word. As for following him, you ordered me to keep my post under the tree. Besides, I do not understand why his action is so very wicked. And besides that, did you ever see a dart thrown as he threw his?"

They will all feel as Thomas does, Gawin thought, they will all ask me reasonably why, if I were trying to kill the baron, it was wrong for Perceval to try. They will ask me again what justice is, as though it were a foreign language beyond their comprehension.

"It is born in you," Thomas said with an envious sigh. "No man can learn to use his arm as Perceval uses his."

"Do you mean he threw that dart by hand?"

"Yes. How else could it be thrown?"

"But this passes belief," Gawin said. "Surely he had a hurling device, at least a bow."

"Believe me, he did not."

In spite of himself Gawin felt a thrill of admiration. To aim at a running man whose only vulnerable spot was no larger than a bird's wing, and to hit him with force enough to kill, this was marvelous.

He said, "You know Perceval, Thomas. What will he do?"

"I can't answer you, Messire Gawin. Nothing like this has happened before."

"Will he go home?"

"I suppose he will, since he has no other place to go."

"Then we may overtake him. Keep watch in the woods."

They kept watch but they did not see Perceval. When they were nearing the oat fields Gawin said, "Go on without me and be careful not to show yourself. I shall turn north and search the shore road. It may be four or five hours before I return."

"What about my lady? This will be a long day for her if she hears nothing from us."

"I do not want her to learn what occurred until I have talked with Perceval."

"If you will listen to me, I believe it is better to tell her first and hunt for the boy afterwards."

I know, I know, Gawin thought, Perceval is young and full of the passions that keep a man warm, but Iglais is sitting before her frames in the still suffering that has no nourishing heat of life in it. He was ashamed, realizing he had desired her praise, and that now he dreaded facing her.

"I'll agree to your suggestion, Thomas. Let us go on."

They rode up the tipped field to the moat. The drawbridge was down, and Iorworth was waiting in the barbican. When he saw them he ran out.

"God be thanked, Messire Gawin, you have prevailed. Will you tell me how the combat went?"

"Thomas will tell you." He dismounted and passed over the crazy planks, dragged himself through the guardroom and armory, where he laid aside his weapons, and entered the great hall. Iglais, still wearing the blue veil, sat before the hearth with her hands in her lap. The embroidery frame stood ready, as though it waited in the silence with her.

If I could have gone in to her and taken her in my arms and said, I have done my utmost for you — this was what I hoped, Gawin thought. She had not looked up, and he stood for a moment too moved to speak. What have I to hope for now? Her hate?

He stepped toward her. "I am here, Iglais."

"Where is Perceval?"

It was more than vanity, he went on thinking, I wished to be her fortress, I wished to protect her.

She said, "He was not in his bed when I went to rouse him an hour after you left. Did he follow you?"

"He went before me," Gawin said. "He left at some hour in the night and reached the combat rendezvous at daybreak."

"Is he dead?" she said, quiet.

"No, no, no, he is whole."

"And he watched you shed the blood of the Knight of The Moors?"

"Let me sit down, Iglais."

"Oh," she said, "I am a selfish woman, I thought of Squirrel and not of you. Do you need medicines or a healing bath?"

"I am not battle-worn, I hardly struck a blow. And I've come back with news for you. Your lands will be restored. I mean they will be returned to your use for the length of a year." He forced himself not to watch for a gleam of surprise and joy in her eyes.

"It will be pleasant to see the forests and fields my husband was so fond of," she said, "and I suppose we shall have a greater household now, or shall we? What happens to the baron's men?" Her face was still wan, but a little color was rising, and she seemed to be making an effort to fix her attention on his words.

"Free people living in a demesne which must be handed over to a new master can choose to go or stay. Usually they stay and become part of the new household. The slaves must remain."

"I hope all these strange men understand how to live in peace."

"When a year has passed," Gawin said, hearing his heart march through his head in heavy knocks, "I must prove your case again."

"Oh, is this the king's law you have been explaining so well to Squirrel?"

76

"It is not the king's law. I have been challenged by the brother of your enemy."

"But how unfair," she said, "though I suppose one might have expected it, since that family is full of violent ideas and can't abide seeing things go on without uproar. Thank you, Gawin, but one battle is enough, and if the baron's brother will only agree to leave me in peace he may keep the farms. I would rather give them up than have all this painful stir again." She offered him a timid smile. "You realize I'm grateful, don't you?"

Gawin dropped his head into his hands.

"Now I've troubled you, I'm afraid I have said stupid things, and you must forgive me if I have. I suppose it would be foolish to deny that I've been a little disturbed, thinking about the — the — about Squirrel watching what happened this morning and enjoying it as though it were a game. I had hoped he would never see —"

"Stop, Iglais. Please let me speak."

"Something *has* happened to him, then."

"In a way, something has happened to him. He hid himself in a tree at the edge of the battle green. I did not know he was there. The baron and I were unseated in the first rush and were fighting on foot. I wounded him in the neck, it was slight, but I sheared off a handbreadth of his mail. A wounded man defends himself by striking heavy blows, and the baron knocked me off my legs with the flat of his sword. He was coming at me while I was rising, and Perceval saw this and believed I was near my death. He threw a — a weighted dart, he hoped to help me, his aim was

77

perfect, and the dart flew straight into the neck of the baron, precisely where I had cut off the mail." Gawin could not keep hidden his wonder at Perceval's skill.

Iglais did not say a word. After a long pause Gawin went on, "The brother of your enemy considered this a treasonable blow, and while I was questioning Perceval he rode out from the keep and charged me with treachery. This is why I must fight again in a year."

"Squirrel," she said. "He does not understand all this talk of justice. Has he become a traitor too?"

"No. It is my right to defend the charge."

Again she let a long silence stretch between them. "Did you give him the dart, Gawin? Did you teach him to throw it?"

"I did not. He found it. He says he found it long ago. He has perfected himself secretly by hurling it at flying birds."

She nodded, despairing. "It was in his nature. I tried, but—"

"It was an accident of ignorance," Gawin babbled, "no one is to blame, not you, not Perceval. Men are men, Iglais, and something profound in them tells them to become men when their childhood is done."

"Does he understand that he has done wrong?"

"Yes."

"Then he will not come home," she said.

"He will come home, Iglais. But when I leave I must take him with me to the City of Legions. To keep the king's honor clear, he must do his manly penance. It will not harm him, it will help him, and after it he will become a squire in the king's household and be taught the conduct of proper knighthood."

Tears filled her eyes and spilled slowly down her cheeks. "It is intended. He will not come home," she said, "ever."

14

GAWIN SEARCHED FOR Perceval along the coast road, while Thomas and Iorworth rode back and forth in the woods beyond the oat farm. The next day they hunted again. That evening the drawbridge was lowered in the hope that he would come home in the night. All this while Iglais moved from duty to duty in a silence that affected Gawin like fever in a wound.

On the third morning, before the hour of prime, he was awakened in the guardroom by a hand on his shoulder.

"Messire." The voice was that of the priest. "Let me speak with you."

"Have you news of the boy?"

"Yes."

Gawin jumped out of bed an began to pull on his clothes. "Is he safe?"

"He was safe when I saw him last, but how long he will remain safe I can't guess."

"In God's name, tell me what you know."

"Is there a candle in this black room, Messire Gawin?"

"By the door."

"I have left my tinder box in my cell. Do you have tinder and flint?"

"No, no, but can't you speak in the dark?"

"I am used to the dark. I thought you would wish a little light."

"I wish to hear your story," said Gawin through his teeth.

"Yes, my story. Well. I had got up to say the office of lauds. I suppose I'm not faithful in observing the canonical hours, on many mornings I sleep until the sun wakes me, but this morning I had started awake, and I felt an impulse to kneel at my cross and say the prayers of dawn."

"Perceval —" Gawin said.

"I am coming to him. I lit a candle and I was kneeling when I heard a man walking down my path. I was still at prayer, and so I did not rise. Perceval entered my house and stood inside the door and waited for me to finish."

"Did he say where he has been? Did he send his mother a message? Had he anything to tell you of —"

"Patience, patience," the priest said, "I must relate all as it happened. When I rose I hardly knew him, he was dressed so outlandishly. He wore a kind of wild armor, Messire Gawin, not true armor. He had woven himself a shield of green twigs, and a helmet too, and made a baldric of braided rope. In his baldric he carried a little arrow, the same, I suppose, that he used against The Moors."

"We must bring him home at once, father."

"He has gone," the priest said.

"Gone! How could you let him go!"

"I did not let him go, he went off so swiftly that I could

not stop him. He is young, Messire Gawin, and I am an old man."

"Didn't he say a word?"

"Yes indeed. He knelt and asked me to bless his knighthood. I blessed him, hoping prayer would calm him. When I had done, I asked him whose knight he meant to be, and he answered, 'King Arthur's. I am going to the City of Legions to ask King Arthur what justice is.' "

"Was he ill?"

"He seemed sound, his mood was gentle." The priest made a rustling sound, as though he ran the cord of his robe through his fingers. "He has the gift of seeming sensible in his unsensible moments. He almost persuaded me, at that hour, after my prayers, that his going off to King Arthur wearing a kind of basket on his head and demanding to be told the nature of justice was a reasonable act."

"Did you appeal to him in the name of my lady?"

"I spoke of her suffering, I asked him to remember her love. But he only gave me a message for her. He said, 'Tell my mother I shall come back when I know what justice is.' "

Gawin knocked his knuckles against his forehead. "Father, what is justice? I wish I had Perceval's hope of finding the answer."

"Do you blame yourself for this unhappiness?"

"Yes. I don't know. Blame — who is to blame? I am an officer of the king's peace, I have a duty, I do my work. How did Perceval leave you?"

"He seemed to melt through the door while I was talking

to him. I followed him outside and heard him running through the trees."

"Does he know how to reach the City of Legions?"

"I can't tell you that," the priest said. "Perhaps you described the roads when you were teaching him to become a knight?"

"No."

"And so the lad is loose on the highways of Britain, with no money in his pouch, nothing to protect him but a harness of green withes, no knowledge of his journey. This is a sorry thing, Messire Gawin."

"How long since he left you?"

"Not more than half an hour."

"Return to your house, father. I'll tell my lady what occurred, and then I'll overtake him."

"I hope so. Now God go with you."

A little gray light eased the darkness of the guardroom, but in the great hall the smothering blackness was only broken by the hearth embers. Gawin felt his way to Iorworth's bed in the porter's cubicle, roused him, and asked him to summon Iglais. "Then go to the stable and tell Thomas to saddle my horse," he said.

He returned to the guardroom and put on his chain shirt and girded himself with his baldric and sword. Perceval is a better animal than I, and he can escape me in the woods if he wishes. I'd best be prepared to follow him all the way to the City of Legions in his game of hide and seek. I must say goodbye to Iglais this night, and —

The thought of her turns my blood to milk.

He waited at the hearth of the great hall. Presently she entered, slipping like a ghost over the floor rushes, her white robe painted in wavering colors by the flicker of the embers.

"I am sorry to disturb you," he said.

"I was not asleep."

"The priest has seen Perceval."

Iglais sat down. "Tell me what Squirrel has done."

Gawin repeated the story of his coming to the holy man's cell in fantastic armor, and of his mission with King Arthur. "I must follow him, Iglais. And I must leave without knowing whether I shall return — when I shall return, I mean."

"I do not believe Squirrel will let you find him," she said.

"If I don't find him before, I shall find him at the City of Legions."

"He is gone," she said faintly. "I gave him up the morning I heard what happened at the combat."

"Perhaps he has gone for a little while, but you must take heart. He sent you a message, remember."

" 'When I know what justice is,' " she murmured.

"Iglais — Iglais — I have not loved a woman in twenty years until now."

"Do you love me, Gawin?"

"Yes. I am your knight from this morning."

"How pleasant our lives might have been," she said, her voice a whisper, "if we had cared for nothing except life."

He longed to do something meaningful, to set things right, to give her a gift worthy of her. Set things right? He must hope they could be set right. Give her a gift? He had only the clothes he stood in. And the ivory tear spoon.

"I have nothing to offer you in parting," he said, "but my service. And perhaps you believe you have had too much of that."

She rose with a little leap of angry impatience, turned away from him, then with a sigh turned back. She laid her two hands on his shoulders. "Take care of Squirrel," she said. "If he is anyone's now, he is yours." And she stretched to kiss his mouth.

15

THE BARN WAS DARK save for a candle stuck to the bottom of a tin basin which was standing on a puncheon stool. The ceiling's heavy beams were hardly visible, and the rough-cast walls above the horse boxes were only a veiled glimmer. On either side of the candle the faces of Thomas and Iorworth, usually so bland, were distorted in the shadowy gloom to fiend-like malice. They were abusing one another in loud voices. Gawin's horse was still unsaddled.

"What do you find to fight about at daybreak?" Gawin asked them.

"Iorworth is a filthy coward," Thomas said.

Iorworth defended himself. "It does not make me a filthy coward only to be reasonable."

"We have small time to be reasonable," Gawin said. "Lead out my horse."

"You see, messire agrees with me," Iorworth said. "I told Thomas to saddle first and look for his own nag later."

"Nag?" Gawin said.

"His carelessness has let a horse get loose."

"What horse is loose?"

"My best plow horse," Thomas told him. "And if Iorworth weren't so stinking frightened of a thief he would help me hunt it before it is taken too far to find."

"Thief!" Iorworth spat into the straw. "It ran away while you snored."

"Let me see the stall," Gawin said.

Thomas was eager to show him. "Messire, you can clearly tell that the rope has been cut. This means a thief, it does not mean the beast hacked its own rope — whether or not I was snoring."

Gawin carried the rope to the candle. It was fresh-cut, every strand sheared. "Perceval has taken your horse," he said.

"Perceval!" Thomas said. "Why would Perceval creep home in the middle of the night and lead off my best plow horse?"

"God be thanked if Perceval has been here," Iorworth said. "How do you know, Messire Gawin?"

"He visited the priest and said he meant to ride to the City of Legions. And he would need a horse — this horse, I think. I must ride after him."

"God guide you to him," Thomas said.

"God will guide me only if you decide to saddle my horse."

The big charger was brought from its stall. Unable to stand idle, Gawin gave the groom a hand with the cinches, then mounted and walked the horse along the moat. The early light was feeble, and the ground stony — no chance to discover and follow tracks. At the farms he drew up to orient himself and choose direction. Perceval would know this much: that to reach the City of Legions he must ride to the strait and cross it. And since he was a person who did things in the most direct way, he would probably head due east and follow his nose to salt water.

I needn't hurry, Gawin thought, I'll follow him east, but I'll ride back and forth, quartering an edge of the forest on each side. Even if he beats me to the strait he must stop to find a boat of some sort. Unless yesterday he stole a boat and hid it on the beach? I must hope he hasn't been as long-headed as that.

Gawin had ridden down many an escaping man, and as he put his experience to work his mind kneaded thoughts of more than Perceval. Iglais, she had kissed him. "How pleasant our lives might have been if we had cared for nothing except life." What did these words mean? They were women's words, the desire of a gentle lady for a quiet existance. Women were like cats who curl themselves into a ball of sleep in which the dreams are better then the awakening. In her dreams, hadn't Iglais invented a world (an impossible world) where men could be good? And now, because she was wise as well as foolish, she knew she could never creep back into her dream, and she held him, Gawin, accountable for its ruin.

If I had not met Ewan on the road before the monk's cooking house, would Iglais's world have remained? Never, it could not. Before I came Perceval had found the dart, he had taught himself to kill gulls on the wing, he had run beyond his mother's boundaries. I only hurried her discovery that no world exists where men can be good, I had the ill luck to become the messenger who must tell her hers was an impossible dream.

I have never in all my life met such a woman as Iglais, such a place as her land of stones and birds. Here things are not what they seem. Why is it an impossible dream that men can be good? Because men are evil. Or if not evil, because they are restless, because they are cursed with the desire for joy, because in love they are always tainted with the taint of necessity. Because men are men. She has lived with servants and a child so long she forgets men are men.

I, Gawin, forty years old, I have fallen in love, he mumbled aloud. She does not love me. And because I am Gawin and forty years old, I will not be a fool and cherish this love. I will forget Iglais.

He dragged his thoughts back to Perceval. The strengthening light disclosed a cloud-burdened morning. As he rode into the forest beyond the farms (Iglais's forest now) he studied the dew hanging like honey to every leaf for signs of a rider's passage, watched for hoof marks, trampled vines, fresh horse droppings. Perceval may have gone by the cliff road after all. Or to the south. Is there a route to the south? I could ride back and ask Iglais to tell me the paths that run to the strait. Will she have returned to her bed to

lie there, alone, thinking of the ruin of her dream? Of me?
Has she dressed, is she wearing her blue veil, has she walked
through the harebells to the priest's cell? Will she tell the
holy man she cannot forgive me, and will he urge her in the
name of Christ's charity to forgive all blind and blunder-
ing men? And will she kneel before the cross of druid stones
and weep?

Iglais, he said aloud, my love Iglais.

16

RAIN BEGAN TO FALL, not as a thickening of the mist, but
as a sudden drench so heavy it seemed a wall of water into
which he must ride. He slung his shield over his horse's
head, but presently the beast began to breathe moisture
into its nostrils and blow and cough. Gawin took such
shelter as a pair of trees grown together allowed. And now
the rain soaked him less like a torrent than a bath. The
wet inside his chain shirt made his skin crawl, and he could
see driblets running out the toes of his champons. Sighing,
his horse hung its head straight down, crooked one foreleg,
and stood still.

"Patience, friend," Gawin said. "We are uncomfortable
this moment, but when the sun comes out and we begin to
steam, we'll look back to our discomfort as to pleasure."

Now and again the downpour eased but only as though
it drew breath for a fresh attack. It filled the woods with a

pulseless roar and turned the road into a stream. "We are cursed on this search," Gawin said, "and if I am not to drown you I must get you under a roof. But where am I to find a roof?" He crowded the horse close to the twisted tree trunks, covering its head as best he could with the shield.

And then the wind rose, a west wind which shook the water-heavy branches and added a wild tone to the bawling rain. It was cold, and turned Gawin's chain shirt into a chilling shroud. Moreover the horse began to shiver. "Come on, then," Gawin said. "At least the wind will blow at our backs and the rain won't whip into your nose and ears."

Once more he took the road, trusting the animal to find its own footing on the flooded trail. After they had covered a slow half mile the rain dazzled into silver, thinned, stopped. Above, masses of smoking clouds scudded east, leaving long tatters of gray on a clearing sky. Now he could hear water gurgling in the road, and a loud patter-patter among the foliage as wet fell from branch to branch. The storm had washed from the air its familiar smells of salt and rock, and the sodden earth gave up drifts of freshness, scents of mosses and roots, even a false scent of flowers.

But if the road had held the tracks of Perceval's plow horse it held them no more. Every sign of animal or man had been leveled as though from the world's beginning. Gawin could only plod ahead toward the strait, calculating for comfort how much delay the storm had cost him, and before the storm, the priest's deliberation, and the quarrel of Thomas and Ioworth. "Perceval is ahead of us by two hours," he told his horse.

The forest frayed out, and he entered a countryside of meadows whose drowned grain could not lift itself to bend to the wind. No farm hands, no herdsmen were in sight, and Gawin began to feel that he was riding through a land sunk under the sea.

He was hungry, worried too lest his chilled and panting horse, which had been given no fodder since yesterday's sundown, develop a fever in the chest. Often he muttered aloud. "Old campaigners, you and I, we must endure a little fasting, we must live through some storms . . . If Perceval were my son I would offer him a lesson in knighthood to remember for this prank . . . If he should reach the City of Legions before me . . . I hope he has the luck to run onto Lancelot or Yvain first, not Kei . . . Lancelot has a sympathy for wild boys . . . Lohot, now, Lohot would be a friend to Perceval . . . Ah, ah, I am wet to my soul's shinbones . . . Ale," said Gawin, "ale, it would . . . As God sees me, there goes a man."

The man walked rapidly toward the east, head bent. He was protected by unshaped sheepskins sewed together save for a neck-hole. His hat was a thick hank of straw tied under his chin with a rag. Its ends stuck out a foot both ways, front and back.

Gawin rode up behind him. "Good day to you, friend."

"Good day," the man mumbled.

"You and I, we are the only creatures of God brave enough to face this weather," Gawin said.

90

"That may be."

"Can you tell me whether I can get meat for my horse nearby? And a fire for myself?"

"No."

"Why not?"

"Because I don't know."

Gawin felt a moment's dull anger, but he said, "We're in the same plight, brother, we should be better friends."

At last the man raised his head. "I have nothing to be friends with, messire. What do you want of me?"

"I am looking for a young lad on horseback, not a good horse. Have you seen him?"

"A strange one, that one? Wearing a sort of — I don't know — a — a —"

Gawin nodded. "Yes, a basket shield and helm."

"I saw him."

"When was this?"

"I suppose it was before the storm."

"Are we near the strait of salt water?"

The man pointed ahead. "Just over the long rise, and across two farms, and there is the sand."

"You must belong to the household of the Knight of The Moors."

"The Knight of The Moors is dead, messire."

"All the same," Gawin said, "I think you are a homeless man who would be glad of a new master."

The farm hand was silent.

"Go back the way I have come," Gawin told him, "until

you reach the castle of the widow of Allan the Fat. You know the place?"

"Yes, I know it."

"Tell her Gawin is your friend, and that Gawin asks her to put you to work in the barn under Thomas. What is your name?"

"Bruns. Is this true, Messire Gawin? Will the widow give me shelter and work to do? The Moors was her enemy."

"I promise you."

"Then I will tell you something more, since you call yourself my friend. The lad you are hunting, he is gone. I mean he has crossed the salt strait."

"But you are walking toward the strait, not away from it. How can you know he crossed it?"

Bruns moved on a few rapid steps, then turned back. "It is true, I have already been to the shore, and I saw him cross. I suppose I have told you a lie, but a homeless man without friends, it is not good for him to speak the truth."

"Tell me when you saw him cross, Bruns."

The man twisted his hands, one inside the other, though rather from the habit of unease than from fear. "I met him a while after daybreak, I don't know how long." He pointed westward toward Iglais's land. "That way. He asked me if I knew the strait, and I said I knew it, and he wanted to know if I would guide him to it, and I agreed. We rode two on the horse, and an uncomfortable brute it was. I went all the way to salt water with him. And I was coming back again when I heard your horse, messire. And I pretended that I was walking to the strait instead of away, because I hoped if we were going in the same direction you would not stop me."

"You mean you have just left him?"

"Oh, no, I stayed to watch him cross."

"And I suppose you found him a boat?"

"He did not ask me to find a boat. He swam."

"Swam!"

"I knew you would not believe me, but as God sees me standing here in sheep hides, he tied his basket work to his back and put his javelin inside his shirt and went right into the water and struck out for the mainland."

"With his horse?"

Bruns did not speak.

"Tell me," Gawin said, "did he lead his horse into the water too?"

The field hand fell onto his knees. "I did not steal the horse, I swear it by God's body. I guided him until we reached the strait, and he gave me the horse as a fee of gratitude. And I have hidden it. I knew my kind of man could never explain a horse."

Gawin was tempted to dismount and kick Bruns into the ditch for helping Perceval escape, but he was used to holding in his impatience. He said, "The horse belongs to the widow of Allan the Fat. And since you have been willing to spill a little truth for me, tell her Gawin asks her to give you the worth of the beast for the sake of your courtesy to her son."

Bruns was still crouching on the road. He looked up. "Was it her son, messire? The innocent they call Perceval?"

"You knew it was Perceval. Don't tell me you didn't know it, and that he was running away."

"He seemed to me a good man. And in this hard world, why should a good man be driven to earth like a hare before dogs?"

17

THE EFFECTS OF THE STORM or the difference in light seemed to alter the margin of the beach, and Gawin searched for some landmark that would tell him whether or not he had come to the place where he and Ewan landed the sheep. The grain fields were no longer the same, being a fortnight older, and the emptiness and silence of the strand were strange. Everything is shifted, he thought, for lack of a frightened shepherd, a boat, and a dozen bleating sheep.

He stopped at the crest of a low, sandy cliff to look across the ruffled strait at the mountains of Norgals. About their heads the storm still hung in packs of thick cloud, and he could see purple squalls that hid everything but themselves. Yet the sky was clean in places, and against its glassy clarity lay flanks of the range. The mountains appeared enormously high and heavy, and he let himself marvel that such locked walls could open into roads and passes, even into little hanging valleys down which summer streams sparkled through pastures colored with wild flowers. But at this moment

94

summer peace had deserted the mass, and no scented calm gleamed through the weight and gloom.

He rode south, following the shore. The strait widened somewhat, its hues showing the shallowing of the water. The cold west wind wrinkled its surface and blew up leaden patches of whitecaps. Sea birds were flying again, at first in twos and threes, but as the sky cleared, in larger flocks, and finally in whole populations.

He became aware that a boat was in mid-channel, sailing from the mainland. It was small, single-sailed, wallowing awkwardly across the currents. Sometimes he lost it in a sun dazzle, sometimes he was sure two men worked it, again, only one. He hunted for a trail down the cliff, found it, and rode along the brown sand, timing his passage to meet the arrival of the boat. A fisherman, he thought, and I hope he does not share the terror of this countryside that a man on horseback has come from the devil.

A hundred yards offshore the boatman threw in his anchor, a flat stone looped with line.

"Hoy!" Gawin called. "Will you land?"

"I am fishing."

"I'll buy your catch."

The man sat awhile, considering it, then pulled up his anchorline hand over hand, and, using oars, rowed within a dozen yards of the strand.

"Good day to you," Gawin said. "If you'll ferry me across I'll buy your catch and pay for the fishing time you lose."

"I can't do it," the fisherman said. "Your horse will swamp me."

"I know that, man. My horse has had its troubles today, but it still owns the courage to swim behind us."

"It's a long swim for a horse that has had troubles."

Gawin abandoned argument. "Two shillings."

"What if you knock me in the head and steal my boat?"

"If I steal your boat I shall have to turn my horse loose. And this fellow outweighs you and your boat and all the fish you'll catch in the next year. Be clever, friend. I'm an officer of the king, and my business is not to steal boats."

"Three shillings, messire."

"Two. One, if we must discuss the price."

"What choice have I got, if you're a king's officer?"

Gawin grinned. "I leave you to decide."

Using his oar as a pole, the fisherman brought his clumsy little craft into shallow water. He tossed out a line, which Gawin looped through the reins of the horse.

"Your valuable beast can walk a fair distance before he needs to swim," the fisherman said. "On this side the strait is like water in a pan."

"How are the middle currents?"

"Not so bad here where it is broad — not the rip and saw they are to the north."

"Can the horse make head?"

"We must find that out."

Gawin entered the boat, which the fisherman had brought around. They began to move from the beach. The horse neighed and resisted, but Gawin talked to it, tugged its line, coaxed it to take the water. Their progress was erratic and exceedingly slow, yet they inched safely into the deep reaches. The horse floundered after them, ears laid back and whites of the eyes glaring with panic.

The current carried them far below their starting point. But on the mainland side a curve to westward and a sand bar shortened the distance somewhat. "With God's help we'll come ashore," the fisherman said. "Look, the horse has found its feet."

"What is this place?"

"If you ride south about a mile you'll reach the camp city the Romans built to guard the coast, messire. Do you know the coast?"

Gawin studied the ground, which rolled upward from the apron of shingle. The scrub gave way to a forest of big trees. "Do you mean the point where the old Roman road turns southeast?"

"South and a little east," the fisherman said. "That's the point I mean."

God's help indeed, Gawin thought. I'll find a royal fort there, and provision for my horse, and, with luck, news of Perceval.

The boat nosed into the shallows and gently grounded. The beach was empty and all grown over with thick-leaved salt weeds. The horse stumbled onto the wet sand. Trembling so that it swayed on its feet, it stood with its hind heels in the water, hung down its head and coughed in great, heaving moans.

"Your animal that is worth a year of my life is done for,

messire," the fisherman said. "This swim needed more than courage."

Gawin began to hate the man. "Build us a fire, and fetch a sheet from the boat that I can cover it with."

"I haven't time to build fires, but if you pay me I might be able to find an old sail."

Gawin's rage ran along his nerves like a hot knife. This horse had taken him through eight years of Arthur's business in Norgals and Britain. They had ridden in war games together, in feast-day parades and royal assemblages. They had fought armed men, they had pursued fugitives, they had outrun or overleaped peril. They had lived through sleet storms, through nights without shelter, through thirst and hunger. Like himself, the horse was schooled to its work, and, like himself, performed it with conscience.

With an oath he drew out the two shillings and flung them onto the sand. "As a favor to me, tell your priest Gawin cursed you."

"Messire, messire —"

"Stand back. Take yourself off."

"The sail —"

"Your stinking sail would poison my horse. Be gone before I knock you into the sea."

The fisherman slowly moved away, staring over his shoulder. He climbed into his boat and sat there, round-eyed.

Gawin's cloak had dried a little in the wind and sun of the strait. He removed it, laid it over the horse, and led the animal south along the beach. It staggered like a drunken man, gasping hoarsely for breath, now and again vomiting foam and water.

"Come on, brother," Gawin said, "take heart. Don't show your pains to a slavish fisherman who weighs our lives at a shilling." He stroked the horse's withers. "We have endured more than this."

They reached a marshy inlet where there was no footing. The only possibility of passing it was by way of a steep path opening onto higher ground. The horse refused the ascent.

"A little more," Gawin said, "only twenty steps. Then we'll be in the forest, then on the Roman road, then in camp, then warmth and a good stall and fresh fodder."

The horse struggled upward, stretching its neck and scrabbling among the stones for footing. At the top it stopped. Its head drooped to its knees, which folded under it with awful deliberation. It fell, tongue protruded and eyes walled in their sockets.

Gawin knelt beside it. His horse was dead.

For men who had fought beside him and lost their lives he had dug graves with his sword and buried them. But this protection against wolves and vultures was more than he could afford his horse. All he could do, when he could bring himself to do it, was to walk away and leave the faithful beast lying in a copse of beach trees.

I'll send men to bury him, he promised himself, from the king's fort. This is my old sin of wrathful pride. I should have built the fire, I should have bought the sail, I should have led the horse back and forth on the sand until he was rested and warm. I should never have made him swim the strait when he was already half-drowned by the storm and shaking with wet and cold. I should have made better plans to follow Perceval, I should have used the time to get men and a boat fit to cross with horses aboard. I should not have been Gawin, I should have been a wiser and more patient man.

He felt tired and ill. He plodded along, seeing himself, feeling himself awake from the dream of infallibility. For what? For a boy who runs off to ask what justice is, for the boy's mother, for the Gawin who dares not fail. Why could I not believe that Perceval will get safely to the City of Legions? He will, he is born for it, no doubt it is "intended." Arthur and Lancelot will take him under their care. Was it Iglais? Yes, some of it was Iglais. Some of it — he shook his shoulders wearily. I must overtake Perceval, he muttered aloud. I am not Gawin if I fail to find him.

He trudged through the beech woods, up rising ground. Perceval is a man with a secret, and the secret torments me. He is a boy and not a boy, something different from a man. A sprite, a being not all flesh, he has a destiny, and even before he knows what it is, he wears his destiny in his face. The face started before Gawin's imagination, longer than it was broad, well-boned, ruled by the brown eyes and the smooth, square brow. Strong yet delicate, masculine, it was not a child's face, it would never be the face of an old man. I must find him, Gawin said.

He climbed a low knob and saw the camp city of the Romans lying under a shoulder of land and facing the strait where it widened into the sea. It had been walled once, but its walls were breached in many places. The old governor's palace was unroofed, and the masonry of the fort had been plundered to make a stout keep, yet its foundations were still visible. Grass grew in certain of its streets, in others thatched cottages straggled along the ancient, sunken paving. This combination of ruin and revival lay in the afternoon sun, peaceful, smoke rising from its fires, and children running about its ways.

Gawin stood still to look at it. Love, joy, victory, were they not patches among ruins?

18

THE ROYAL FORT occupied a narrow promontory protected on two sides by the sea and on the third by a swampy stream running into salt water. Its landward side had no moat, being defended by a curtain wall. The battlemented bartizan at the upper corner was manned by a single sentry, who challenged Gawin.

"I am the king's nephew, a knight of the City of Legions, Gawin by name."

"I know you, Messire Gawin," the sentry said, "and I thought I recognized you, though I was in doubt because you come on foot."

Gawin only nodded. "What knights are within?"

"Messire Kei arrived this morning. Our regular garrison

is here, but the knights usually with us are on their way south."

"Let me enter," Gawin said. "I need rest and a meal, and then I shall need a horse. Can you spare me a strong, well-schooled animal?"

"Certainly, messire. You will not stay the night?"

"I must go on."

The sentry shouted an order, and the heavy door was unbolted and unchained. Gawin moved into the outer enclosure. The keep was a solid chunk of masonry, pale yellow, with towers at each corner. Its lawn was beautifully green and mowed to velvet — a sign of peace, Gawin thought. He was passed through the inner barbican, across a narrow isle of grass, and into the heart of the fort. Around the central hall, armories, storage rooms, quarters, a chapel, and an emergency kitchen were built against the walls. The battle flags which usually draped the central hall were missing, and the stone seemed cold in spite of a fire burning on the broad hearth.

The hall was empty save for a squire assigned by the sentry to unarm him.

"What news?" Gawin asked him.

"Little news," the squire answered. He was so young that he could hardly have laid off his page's silks, a bright-eyed lad who watched Gawin alertly. "The times are dull here, and our garrison doesn't have much exercise except to recover stolen cattle or put down spite raids. Now the knights have left for the Whitsuntide assembly at the City of Legions." He gestured toward the bare walls. "Without banners the place seems strange. I wish I could see the knights riding into the City of Legions with their flags on parade."

Gawin smiled. "It is a sight when you see it first."

"I have heard of you, Messire Gawin. My fellows will envy me when I tell them I squired you."

Me, I envy this lad, Gawin thought, whose largest wish is to see a parade of flags. "What mission brings Kei to the fort?"

"He is on his way to the City of Legions too. He has been riding through Norgals to proclaim the King's Justice at Whitsun. Perhaps you and he will return together."

Gawin said, "I am on a mission, and I may or may not be in time for the King's Justice."

"The sentry told me you have lost your horse."

"Yes, two miles northeast, in the beech copse, and I would be glad if a detail goes there and buries him and brings his gear to me."

The squire did not find this request remarkable, knowing well that a good horse was part of the knight who rode him. "I am sorry. It is bad to lose a friend. May I know how he was killed?"

"I killed him," Gawin said shortly. "I over-rode him."

"Your mission must be urgent."

"Tell me, have you had a visitor today?"

"No, no knights except yourself and Messire Kei."

"I mean a boy, a lad of sixteen, tall and fair, with brown eyes, and wearing a — well — a basket on his head."

"Oh." The squire laughed. "Yes, indeed, I did not think of him as a visitor."

103

"When did he arrive?"

"A few moments before noon. Very wet, very pale, saying nothing except that he must have a horse — for the king's sake, if you please."

"Did he tell you anything else? Why he was wet, why he wore the basket?"

"Nothing at all. He only demanded the horse."

"Was he given a horse?"

The squire was young enough to blush with embarrassment. "Well, you see, our Captain was already on the way to the City of Legions, and the youth only spoke to the soldiers, and they — we squires too, if I am to be honest — we all thought him a figure of fun, and we — I hope you will not be offended, Messire Gawin."

"You played him a trick, then?"

"We put him on the stable mule — the old mule that quiets the colts when they are being schooled. I am sorry. No one imagined he was the object of a mission. And the mule seemed to suit his armor of twigs."

"And then you let him and the mule go on alone?"

The young squire was almost ready to weep. "It seemed funny — I cannot understand why it seemed funny, messire."

"The boy was Perceval, the son of Allan the Fat. His father was a loyal servant of King Arthur. Perceval's mind is disordered by an accident in which he killed a man. And here is a lesson for you, Messire Squire. Trouble wears many shapes, and it is not knightly to make sport of any shape of trouble, even a foolish one."

The lad hung down his head. "Give me a penance, messire."

"You will know how to choose a penance for yourself. Now," Gawin said, pitying him and laying a hand on his shoulder, "send me a servant with food, and see to the burying of my horse. Where is Kei?"

"I do not know, but I'll find him and ask him to come to you in the hall."

"Did Kei have a part in this mischief against Perceval?"

"I — I — you must ask him, I — I —" and the squire backed away hastily and left the hall.

So, Gawin thought, it was Kei's doing, he behaves like a malicious child, it is easy for him to forget his knighthood. Why does Arthur protect him, why does he find excuses for his folly and rashness? I suppose because he is a strong, crafty soldier. If I could get through his thick hide I would read him advice to remember, but the only way to read Kei advice is to knock him over the crupper of his horse.

Two servants entered the hall, one carrying a basin of warm water and a white towel, the other a platter on which lay a half loaf of dark bread, a meat pudding, and a great wedge of cheese. As a small table was being set before him Gawin washed his face and hands. While he was eating his meal Kei appeared.

"Gawin himself," Arthur's seneschal said. "I hear you have been going afoot."

"True," Gawin said.

"A pity you rode your horse to death. Did you misjudge its endurance?"

"I rode my horse to death, but me, I survived, Kei."

"Lucky you judged your own strength more cannily than the strength of your horse. I must find a horse that will do my fighting for me."

"I advise it," Gawin said. "It leaves one all the more vigorous for planning foolish pranks, and carrying them out."

Kei laughed and sat down. "In an evil humor? Not you, Gawin, you're the envy of every unbearded squire longing to be known among ladies for smooth temper and courteous manners."

"I am glad someone finds qualities in me to envy — to emulate too, let us hope."

"What brings you so far from easy living?" Kei asked him.

"I am looking for the son of Allan the Fat. Do you remember Allan the Fat?"

"Very well. He was as gross as an autumn hog."

"He was trusted by Arthur. His son is Perceval. I am told Perceval stopped with you at noon today."

"Nobody stopped at noon. I reached the fort an hour before midday, and I assure you, nobody stopped."

Gawin smiled. "Then I needn't fear that Perceval was sent on his way without the horse he requested."

"God's body!" Kei said. "Was *that* lump the son of Allan the Fat? You're joking, Gawin."

"I hope to live long enough to let you know I am not joking. As for now, I shall only render you whatever thanks you deserve for the service you offered a brave young man."

106

Kei stood up, wrathful color mantling his dark, narrow face. He was tall and graceful, but never quite still. He was a man who hooked his hands into his baldric, or pulled at his sleeves, or felt about the neck of his shirt with a finger. He was a man, too, who did not look directly into another's face save when he was watching the result of a scornful remark or a painful jest. Now he yawned, stretched, pressed his hands against his ribs. He said, "I'll remember your thanks, Gawin."

19

GAWIN WAS TOO RESTIVE to let his fatigue delay him. He requested a dry shirt and breeches, dressed himself, was rearmed by the squire, and went to the mounting stage to learn what horse had been allotted him. The animal, saddled with Gawin's gear, was a tall gray, seven years old, broad in the chest and thick-muscled.

"He is no beauty, messire," the groom told him, "but he is strong, and his disposition is steady."

"Well, my friend," Gawin addressed it, "you and I must get along peaceably together." And he stepped up the mounting stage and settled himself in the saddle. The horse bent its hind legs and pranced, as though to establish the fact that it had a mind of its own, but when Gawin put it in a walk it moved willingly.

"God go with you, messire," the groom said.

"And with you."

Only a few hours of summer daylight remained, and as he passed through the fortified door and turned southeast on the Roman road he wondered whether he might not have saved time by staying the night in the fort. "Now," he explained to the horse, "we have about twenty miles to go before nightfall if my reckoning is right, and so let us not waste time feeling out one another's weaknesses."

Below the castle, the road was in bad repair, its pavement broken or weedy or missing altogether. The track went straight into the forest, ascending a stream valley to a ridge and watershed. The woods were dense and old, slopes cut by steep ravines into whose clefts the sun never shone. Little noisy brooks skimmed down rocky beds, hurrying into waterfalls or idling in pools about which leaned moist bracken and small, colored flowers.

Perceval has never seen such forests as this, Gawin thought. He is used to wide spaces and the sky above him. Will he be afraid? Not Perceval. The longer I hunt him the bigger he grows. I misread him in that desolate corner where I found him, I took him for a half-mad child whose mind leaped from toy to toy without purpose. Now he goes before me like a man stronger than I. He bores through this Norgals of Arthur's without sleep or food, without direction, without friends, day and night equal for him, pursuing justice on muleback as one pursues a fox. And I who know justice cannot be dug out of a barrow, I believe he will find it.

The gloom of the woods oppressed him and he was eager

to reach the pass. But the pass let in no light save what glanced off a narrow tarn in which a stream rose to find its ways down the far side of the watershed. On the descent the ground opened out somewhat, to the right falling away in small valleys on whose moist grass sheep grazed. At the foot of the mountain the Roman road led him onto the sands of an estuary where salt and fresh water met. Here it had once passed over a causeway, but now the causeway was tumbled into ruin.

"I've no mind to lose you in quicksand," he said to the horse. "And if we ride around the head of this estuary we shall find ourselves belated, with no hope of a bed except in some deserted camp of outlaws or a woodcutter's hut, and I have no mind for that either."

He drew up and stood still to study the oily shine of the shingle, which spread itself broadly on both sides of the water. Risk it? I have never heard of quicksands here. But quicksands do not announce themselves, and I would be a fool to take the chance. It occurred to him that Perceval was unaware of this peril, and he felt the hair on his neck stir as he wondered whether boy and mule were dead beneath the dangerous gleam now beginning to be streaked with the reflected hues of sunset. He rode back and forth looking for tracks, but the ground was mossy and the light deceptive.

What had Perceval done? Been wise enough to turn away from the Roman road westward, toward the coast? I pray God he has, Gawin thought. And that is what I must do. Over the sea the sky had broken into red and saffron and pale green, and from these celestial dyes the oozy shingle took new colors. He followed the estuary along its north side, pushing his horse through scrub or over patches of spongy grass.

Less than a mile from the coast he came upon the mounds and scattered masonry of a Roman villa. About it, old lawns and gardens of vegetables were overgrown with a thick scrub of oak and beech. Among the straggling trees he saw what he was searching, a stout, one-roomed house of stones taken from the fallen villa. Gawin dismounted. The trees were taller by a dozen feet than when he had seen them last, and he felt a premonition. Did time fly so fast? He moved up to the tiny square of dooryard garden, but now the parsley and savory were choked with grass. With his sword hilt he knocked lightly on the closed door. No one answered the knock.

Dead, he thought, my friend the old hermit has died here alone, and no young hermit comes to take his place. Why wasn't the news of his death brought to the City of Legions? Gawin made the sign of the cross. Then with his mailed foot he kicked the door, but it was strong and locked and it did not give. He gripped his sword in both hands and raised it for a blow on the wood of the door.

He did not deliver the blow. Shouts were lifted below him toward the shore, shouts and the sounds of combat that were his familiar knowledge. The hermitage lacked a mounting stage, and armed as he was he could not heave himself onto his horse. He could only run in the direction of the stour.

Vines matted under the trees slowed him, and the sunset dazzled his sight. The battle was loud, but it was short.

110

When he leaped out onto the beach he saw an enormous man in the brown homespun of a hermit kneeling above a fallen man. Beside the hermit stood an armed youth holding a drawn sword.

"Hoy!" Gawin shouted.

The armed man turned.

"I'm a friend," Gawin said. "Put up your weapon."

The man did not put up his weapon, but came on, prepared to fight.

"Stop, Davith," the hermit said without looking up. He was binding the fallen man with rope, hands and feet. "If messire says he is a friend, he is a friend."

"What is happening here?" Gawin said. "I require you in the name of the king to answer me."

"We have caught a felon," the hermit said, tightening his knots expertly. "Or rather Davith has caught him and I have tied him up. We divide our labor this way."

"What hermit are you?"

"Joseus." The huge, brown-clad man rose. Against the vivid sky he seemed tall as a church. His head was tonsured Celtic fashion, and at the back dark curls tumbled in disorder. He was grinning, and even in the uncertain light his teeth gleamed marble-white.

"Hfff!" he said. "That was soon over."

"You, a man of peace," Gawin said, "why do you brawl with felons?"

"Someone must brawl with felons if God's law is to be served. Besides, I have been a man of peace only a little while. This brave fellow —" he clapped the armed man on the shoulder — "was my squire when I was in the world. He draws the sword, not I. I content myself with wrapping evildoers in rope and delivering them to the king's fort."

Gawin could not forbear a laugh. "It's an odd way to catch felons, I must say. What has this one done?"

"He waylays travelers. At the causeway. You know the causeway?"

"I've just passed it."

"My fine rogue hides in the scrub above the sands, and when a rider stops to wonder how he is to cross, he jumps out with a club and knocks him off his horse, and then steals the horse. It is my Christian duty to see that wayfarers are not molested near my hermitage, and so I have given him a lesson. Or," he added wistfully, "Davith has given him a lesson."

"Will you send him to the king's fort tonight?"

"No, I'll pray with him at my chapel, and take him myself in the morning."

"You'll pray with him while he lies bound?"

The hermit laughed an easy laugh. "I wish him to listen to the prayers, messire."

Gawin sheathed his sword, and so did Davith. "I am glad the king has such a stout advocate in these marshes, Joseus. Do you hold the hermitage above the beach?"

"Yes. I have lived there since the old hermit died."

"I knocked at your door. I need a bed tonight. I am Gawin, king's officer and knight of the City of Legions."

"Ah, Gawin!" To Joseus's smile was added the gleam of

112

his strong, white teeth. "I have heard many a time of you. Welcome to my house."

They walked back together, Davith following with his evildoer slung over his shoulder like a grain sack. At the Roman villa the hermit and squire carried the captive to a little chapel of timbers built against a ruined wall. And as Gawin waited, walking in the blasted garden, he heard Joseus's voice loud in prayer. If I were a felon with that bass voice roaring in my ears, he thought, I would make haste to repent my crimes. What a soldier Arthur has lost! Will those terrible shoulders serve God as they might have served the king?

The hermit returned presently and, stooping, brought a key from under his doorstep. "I must keep my house locked," he explained, "because I am a hospital too, and wounded knights have enemies." He opened the cell door and invited Gawin to step within. As he warmed their supper he tumbled out questions. What knights had his guest seen recently? How were affairs at the City of Legions? Was he riding to the Whitsuntide assembly to attend the King's Justice? Often he interrupted himself with good-natured admissions that he talked too much.

"You must feed, Gawin. Pay no attention to me. While you wash I'll carry a basin of stew to Davith and our thief, and then we'll eat, and as we sit by the fire perhaps you'll humor a man of peace with a little talk of war."

Like two old campaigners, Gawin thought, reminiscing with their heels on the fender.

20

TO THE USUAL spare bread and cheese of holy men Joseus added dried puffin boiled with carrots and onions. "On Sabbath days I make a week's mess of this stew to avoid needless concern with the body's wants," he said. "In time, I believe God will strengthen my will so that I can live on herbs and bread, but now my soul cries for the taste of flesh."

"I know this house well," Gawin said. "Often when I have been in the north I have stayed a night here."

"With the old hermit? Then you know he has been dead these four years."

"Is it four years? I lose count."

"I hope I may attain his holiness," Joseus said.

"It is strange that a man like yourself should have chosen this life. I would like to hear your story."

Joseus leaned forward to stare into the fire beginning to blaze on the hearth. "I am a sinner, Gawin. That is why I chose it."

"Our priests tell us we are all sinners."

"My sin was murder."

Gawin was silent. Joseus sank forward, clasping his hands as he considered his sin. Tears welled into his eyes and ran down his cheeks to lose themselves in his beard.

"God's forgiveness is large," Gawin murmured.

114

"We must hope it is large." The hermit wiped his eyes with the backs of his hands. "I killed my own mother."

"Do not speak of it, Joseus."

"I can speak of it. I am a little better used to it, now that I live with God."

"Then you wish to tell me how it happened?"

Joseus nodded his big head. "It is a penance I have laid on myself to tell every one who asks. Let me go back a little. My father was a rich lord, a man who would have been called a king in the days before Arthur made this a land of one king. My younger brother and I were his only children. My father was a saintly man, Gawin, and he began to hate the uproars of power, he began to think wars were a work of the devil. In the end he determined to give up the world and become a holy man."

"He was a hermit like yourself?"

"Not like myself, but he is a hermit. He is still living God's life in his old age."

"You might have been a rich lord, Joseus."

"Yes, yes," he answered, glancing restlessly about the narrow room. "I believed the lordship was my right. When my father retired from his titles I informed my mother that I meant to be a king. But my mother said I was too impatient to govern others, that I overbore any will but my own. She said she would not support my claim of inheritance. It was her intention to see it fall to my younger brother."

"Many a man would have resented that."

Joseus leaped up, his body seeming to cram the cell. He paced back and forth as far as the room's limits permitted, fresh tears bursting from his eyes. "If I had done nothing more than resent it! But I was so enraged I was blind and crazy, and when I came to my senses my mother was lying before me dead."

"You drew your sword?"

"No, no, no, I thank God I did not commit that deliberate wickedness. I struck her without intention or plan, as an evil child strikes. The blow felled her, and whether the blow killed her, or the fall, she was dead."

"Joseus, you can fairly accuse yourself of unchristian wrath, of impatience that is less than human, of greed, of violence, but not of murder."

"I do not need any man's comfort, Gawin, though I thank you for the kindness. I have dealt with this sin between God and me, and I know what I must accuse myself of."

"Have you asked peace from your father?"

"Yes, in time I confessed myself to him and begged his forgiveness, and he forgave me as far as one man can forgive another. I have not seen him since that day, but I hear of him, and he of me."

"Tell me where your father holds his hermitage. If I travel near it I'll carry him a message from you."

Joseus sat down again and turned up the skirt of his long robe and wiped his eyes and beard. "I couldn't weep at first, and I take it as a sign of God's loving correction that I can weep now."

What a bitter tale, Gawin thought, as the memory of his own mother, so charming and elegant, rose before him. And what a strange man. It is hard to believe he wouldn't have been a worthy lord. Men need such nobles as this to make them lawful and brotherly.

"You think I should have been a soldier," Joseus said. And his mood, which shifted so erratically, shifted again, and he smiled his white-toothed smile. "I enjoyed being a soldier when I was in the world, and I was a good one — a big one, at least. But now I only watch Davith fight. The time must come when I send Davith from me, but God is good to me, He gives me my teaching in little steps. He will decide when I can do without the joy of seeing Davith wield his arms, and then I shall be a little farther along the way God has set for me to travel."

Gawin stretched his legs to the warmth of the fire. "I'll tell you something, Joseus. I meet people on this journey of a kind I've not known before. I have never known a man like you."

"What has your journey been?"

"I was riding in the usual way on the king's peace. That is my work, to visit Arthur's people in Norgals, and to settle such matters as seizures, the stealing of women, unjust imprisonments — you know the work I mean. At the strait I heard of a widow whose lands had been taken from her, and I went to her castle to fight her oppressor on the king's challenge."

Joseus listened eagerly. "Did you fight him?"

"But it was not a case of simple justice. The widow prized a quiet life even at the expense of losing her holdings. And I began to feel that my coming was a worse injustice than the rape of her houses and farms. Besides," Gawin added slowly, "she had a son."

"You did not fight her enemy, then?"

"I do not know how to tell this story," Gawin said. "The bare events do not speak truly of it."

"Try to tell me, I am hungry to hear of such deeds."

"Well. I went out to fight. The son — he was a — I mean he had not been trained. His mother would not permit him to hear a word about knighthood. But he was on fire to become a man, and in my contest with her enemy he intervened and killed the man — by throwing a dart into his neck. He said he had done this for the king. And now he has run away to find the king and ask him the nature of justice. It is my mission to find him."

"This does not seem a strange story to me," the hermit said. "What was the widow's name?"

"She was the lady Iglais. Her husband was Allan the Fat."

Joseus fell silent, not as a man who ceases to speak, but as a man to whom silence has suddenly become a deep, physical change.

"Do you know her?" Gawin asked.

"She is my aunt, my father's sister."

"In God's name, is Peleur your father?"

"Peleur is my uncle. Do you know Peleur, Gawin?"

"Not yet, but —"

"Are you seeking him?"

"I am seeking Perceval. Your cousin."

"What do you mean when you say you do not know Peleur *yet?*"

The soldier and the hermit eyed one another in a silence so tightly drawn that even the small noises of the fire seemed loud. Then Gawin sighed. "The lady Iglais, she spoke to me of a relic in your family, a Grail. I wish to see this Grail. She said Peleur keeps it."

"What do you know of it?"

"Nothing. I did not understand what Iglais told me."

"Listen, Gawin, the Grail is a mystery. It is a secret handed down in my family from the old times, from the times of Joseph of Arimathea, they say, and they say too that Joseph was the founder of our blood in Britain. I do not know what the Grail is, but I know this much, that it deceives many men who wish to hold it in their hands."

"Is there no relic, then? Only a secret?"

"I don't know, I don't know, I do not meddle with the Grail," Joseus said. "Sometimes I believe it is a madness that does not come from God, but sometimes I believe it is a piece of God's truth that is shown to men who must see before they have faith. I do not know what the Grail is," he concluded with great force.

"Your father, does he know the secret of the Grail?"

"I don't know that either. I do not wish to know."

"Who is your father, Joseus?"

"His name was Pelles, but he no longer uses his name. He calls himself only The Hermit. Yet the life he lives is so holy that men who remember him and the goodness of his lordship still call him king, they call him King Hermit. And

119

many people know him only by that name, King Hermit."

"And your other uncle, the third of my lady's brothers?"

"Mortelle. His name is Mortelle."

I have crossed Arthur's Britain ten times, Gawin thought, but I have never heard of this family. And he wondered uneasily whether Joseus was mad. Did madness run in the blood? And was Perceval tainted with it? Or had his own journey been a dream from which he would awaken? No, he told himself, Iglais was not a dream.

"You think all this is madness," Joseus said.

"You read me, friend. Twice you have told me what I was thinking."

The hermit smiled his ready smile, boyish and keen. "God looks through every man's eyes," he said, "and sometimes He is playful and tells us what He sees."

21

JOSEUS INVITED GAWIN to use his pallet in the cell, insisting that he himself would be serving both God and the king were he allowed to sleep on the chapel floor before his cross. Nor would he permit Gawin to attend to his horse, assuring him that Davith would feel honored to rub it down and lead it under shelter.

"Besides being an inn and a hospital," the hermit said, with his particular kind of gayety, "I'm a posting station, and if some guest of mine has overcome an enemy and brings me the horse he has gained in battle, I keep it until a luckless man reaches me on foot. For such beasts Davith and I have hidden a little stable in the woods."

"I could be no better cared for at the City of Legions," Gawin said. "God soften your bed in the chapel, Joseus."

"God give you sound sleep."

Somewhere in the country of Iglais, Gawin had lost the gift of sound sleep, and it was late when he drifted into a dream. The dream was of Perceval and Peleur and the huge figure of Joseus in brown homespun, wearing a helmet and sword. Through the ventail of the helmet he kept crying, "Ask, ask, ask."

In the morning when he awoke Gawin felt himself alone. He got to his feet, noticed that a fire of kindling was prepared on the hearth, the pot of last night's stew hung on the spit, and the table laid with a wooden plate and spoon. He opened the door and discovered his horse already saddled and tied to a tree in the ruined garden. The light is late, he thought, probably after prime. Why didn't they rouse me? Turning back he saw the door key, and with it a message, lying on the puncheon stool by the fire. The message was a flat board upon which was drawn in charcoal a lively picture of a large, robed man leading a smaller one by a rope attached to his bound hands. Bringing up the rear was a figure of a squire. Under his picture Joseus had drawn a cross.

Gawin was amused, disappointed too, since he had hoped to see Joseus at breakfast. But the picture was plain. The hermit and squire had already set out with their felon for the king's fort. For them day began after the prayers of lauds.

Without stopping to light the hearthfire Gawin washed, dressed, ate a little cold stew, then struggled into his armor. He locked the door and stowed the key under the squared log outside the cell. This step was not high enough to act as a mounting stage, and nothing in the garden would serve. He untied his horse. "We'll have to walk awhile," he told it, "until I find a stone tall enough to mount me. Though perhaps Joseus has a block near his stable. Come on, friend, we'll hunt for it."

He led the animal back and forth through the ragged second growth. The stable was well hidden under the overhang of a rocky bank, brush piled before its front wall. Gawin looked at the stout shed curiously, pushed the brush aside, and tried the heavy door. It gave slowly, and he stepped inside. Two stalls, now untenanted, and a feed bin were constructed against the backing-wall of stone, and on one side lay a pallet stuffed with straw.

But Gawin hardly saw these things. With an oath he knelt and put his fingers inside animal tracks showing moist and fresh on the dirt floor. They were mule tracks.

Why did Joseus lie to me when I asked if he had seen Perceval? Did I ask? But he knew my mission and it was the same as a lie, to withhold the fact that Perceval was sleeping within a quarter mile of me. And now I suppose Perceval has gone with him and Davith. Or more likely, Joseus has already started him on his way to the City of Legions, roused him after lauds and led him through the estuary sands by some secret route he did not describe for me. Even given him a horse? Gawin smote the stable wall. *I am dogged by every unlucky delay a man can suffer.*

He left the stable without replacing the brush, wishing to make it plain that he understood the hermit's deception. He followed the small mule prints until he lost them in ankle-deep vines tangled through and through last year's dead weeds. *With God's help I'll pick them up again at the estuary — if Perceval still rides the mule.* But the tide was low when I reached the estuary yesterday, which means it was low this morning three wasted hours ago. *Even if I find hoof marks I won't be able to cross where Perceval crossed. Iglais told me Perceval would not let me find him.* And all the way to the City of Legions I shall lag behind a boy who never bestrode a horse until a few days ago, and discover him sitting at the king's table in squire's leathers, looking as bland as a girl!

He laughs at me, Joseus too, these cousins who lay their heads together to befool a king's officer. Let him go, let him reach the City of Legions riding a mule, let him explain himself to the king. But Gawin went on looking for tracks, for a stone or bank from which he could mount his horse. He must find Perceval. He would find him. It was no longer a matter of protecting a helpless boy on the perilous ways, it was no longer a desire to interpret the murder of the Knight of The Moors in terms that would appeal to Arthur's mercy, it was no longer even an eagerness to console Iglais. It had become a conviction of destiny, it had grown into the will to succeed in a mission laid on him not by the accident of circumstance but by his need to find joy again, to revive his own lost innocence with the secrets of joy and innocence Iglais and Perceval shared.

22

WHERE THE FOREST FELL away above the broad valley of the estuary he found a pile of logs hewed all the same length and stacked to await the cart of the woodcutter. Gawin used them to help himself mount. Below him the strand seemed alive with birds and fishermen casting their nets into the flow tide. He rode down and inquired whether he could safely cross. A man carrying a seine pointed out water still shallow over firm bottom, promising him his horse would not have to swim. He could learn nothing of Perceval.

Gawin passed without harm. On the far side the claws of hundreds of feeding sea fowl had printed the beach in hatchings so closely set that no sand remained smooth. If I crawled back and forth among these claw-marks, he thought, I might discover traces of Perceval's mule. Better to take on faith the fact that he reached this shore.

Above the east bank of the estuary the Roman road turned inland, ascended a low ridge, and came down to a valley village still called Mound-and-Wall by the Norgalois who had helped themselves to the stones of a military station to build the walls of their cottages. Gawin had a friend in this village, an ancient herb-seller, who eked out her living by giving a bed to a traveler if she knew him and, besides, cooking him a breakfast of duck eggs and oat porridge. He found her bent above her garden rows, loosening the earth around rue and rosemary with a pointed stick.

"Good morning, mother," he called to her.

She straightened and peered at him under her hand.

"I am Gawin."

"Ah, Messire Gawin." Leaning on her stick she tottered to the road.

"I hoped to spend last night with you, but I was belated and had to stop with the hermit west of the estuary."

Her chin trembled ceaselessly, its long, gray hairs catching the light. "I am sorry for that, Messire Gawin. I am sorry you did not come as far as Mound-and-Wall."

"Here's a shilling for the welcome you would have given me."

"Keep the shilling, keep the shilling. It is the pleasure of hearing your news I missed, not the shilling." But she took it in her brown claw and slipped it into her mouth.

"Have you seen a stranger this morning, mother? A youth riding an old mule? Or perhaps a horse?"

She pushed the shilling into her cheek. "What hour this morning?"

"Between lauds and prime."

"I don't get up with the first light as I used to. My bones are old and I let them lie snug as long as they will."

"Then," he asked explicitly, thinking of Joseus's equivocation, "you did not see him?"

"Not a hair of him. Will you come inside and drink a cup of herb broth? Or milk and water?"

"Thank you, but I must go on. God defend you, mother."

"God go with you, messire."

At the lower end of the village the Roman road divided, one fork running east, the other bending back south to follow the coast, though by a few miles inland. The coastal road avoided the endless ridges and peaks of central Norgals, but it was the longest way home to the City of Legions. What advice had Joseus given Perceval, to go the long, easy way, or the short, rough one? It must have been the long way, Gawin thought, since it is plain, and Perceval knows nothing of the difficulties of Norgals.

At the milestone he turned his horse south. As was their habit, the Roman builders had laid the road straight, pushing it up ridges and down them, and carrying it across streams by causeways or fords. Sometimes from high points where woodcutters had thinned the forest Gawin had glimpses of the vast bay forming the west coast of Norgals. But more often he saw no horizon, only armies of trees marching into shade, through whose trunks a round valley might be visible, its floor checkered with pastures and grain fields. The west wind blew steadily hour after hour, fetching squalls of cold-fingered rain from the sea. Between squalls the sun dragged at the mists or burst free to paint patches on the slopes with the bright, changing hues of heather.

He stopped at every village to ask whether Perceval had ridden through on mule or horse. He put the same question to solitary farmers and herdsmen he could hail from the road.

Nobody gave him news of the boy's passing. Once more he has fooled me, Gawin thought. No matter what advice Joseus might have offered him, Perceval took the shortest road to the City of Legions. And I suppose at this very hour he is riding miles to the east of me, hauling himself up to the high passes and pouring himself down the defiles, his body still as fresh as morning and his mind on fire with his quest of justice. I hope Joseus remembered to warn him about the baron Logrins.

The memory of Logrins added a new depression to the depressions Gawin already dealt with. This man, once king of a powerful clan, had resisted Arthur longer and more cleverly than any chieftain in Norgals. Indeed, Arthur had never wholly subdued him, and Logrins still conducted murderous raids against farms and churches, even against royal forts. Recently he had begun to waylay travelers, hold them for ransom, then hide in a mountain stronghold whose site Arthur's soldiers could not succeed in uncovering.

It was too late to ride back to the milestone and take the other fork. Now all Gawin could hope was that with a better mount and a faster route than Perceval's he would reach the City of Legions first and so turn north above it to meet the boy as he came down from Logrins's country. He must hope, too, that a youth on an old mule, wearing basket armor, would not seem to the baron a subject worthy of capture.

Gawin no longer paused to inquire whether Perceval had been seen but made only such stops as his horse required for food and rest. Meanwhile his spirit drifted among the sights and sounds which had pressed themselves upon him since the evening he met Ewan at the strait. Iglais was always with him, though less as a present memory than as the sill under the structure of his thoughts. From her as from a window he looked out at the stony cliffs, the priest's house on the lawn of harebells, the empty guardroom, the useless armory, most of all at the quiet evenings before the hall fire. From her he looked at her unknown brothers, at Pelles who in his holiness was still called king, at Mortelle, the greedy oppressor, at the chief of them all, Peleur, who guarded Christ's cup in its splendid house. Where were they, these brothers united by the mysterious relic of their blood? Iglais had suggested the north, but Gawin was a northerner born in Rhos, and in no north he remembered were they spoken of. Would Arthur know them, or Lancelot? Or were they no real men, only the proud creations of a lady who had lost much? Joseus, at least, was not the creature of a lonely mind. And Joseus had said he was the son of Pelles and the nephew of Peleur. Perhaps these were not their true names, perhaps they were designations assumed to set them apart from men who had not inherited Christ's cup. Perhaps like masons and pilgrims the family of the cup chose to wrap their lives within a mystery known only to themselves.

Gawin was uneasy, and stirred in his saddle. In the sequestered valleys of Norgals, on farms folded between the peaks, he had heard of the old religion followed by the Britons before they had been taught God's gift of His Son. He had heard whispers that the old religion was a Mystery whose disciples could wring secrets from the pagan Spirits

Who were Lords of Summer and Winter, and Who watched over sowed fields, and animals about to bear young, and women with child. This was blasphemy, he knew, and he shivered as he wondered whether the family into whose hands Christ's cup had fallen dealt in such unlawful secrets.

"Oye!" he said aloud. "It is late, I must begin to think of day's end." He leaned forward and stroked the neck of his horse. "For a stranger you have used me well, friend."

An hour before dusk he reached a village where the road divided again. As the north fork occurred at the head of the great, western bay, this fork occurred at its base. One branch ran on south, then hooked westward to stretch toward the cliff-walled promontory which was an enclosing arm of the bay. The other bent eastward, pushed right across the broad, southern lap of Norgals, and entered the City of Legions like a spoke in the wheel of roads turning on the hub of Arthur's royal seat.

He was well acquainted with the village of the road fork. Once it had been a receiving station for the tin that Roman overseers and British slaves mined from works a mile or two south. Now, with the Romans so long gone that not even their word for *tin* was remembered, many of the village families still lived by making pans and cups which their masters collected to sell all the way to the east, even as far as Byzantium.

Gawin rode into the innyard. Watching the groom who lugged a portable mounting stage across the cobbles, he thought, will the innkeeper have a daughter? And he was filled with revulsion.

129

23

By MID-MORNING the next day Gawin had reached the headwaters of the river down whose course he meant to ride all the way to the City of Legions. The wind had fallen at last, and blue sky planted with white-flowering clouds seemed only an extension of the bright air. Mountains lay on every side, forming lovely curved lines above vast green and purple slopes; and high passes opened clear, distant views that sometimes stretched as far as salt water in the south. To Gawin, the northerner, these mountains seemed peaceful. Through pleasant valleys on either hand many small streams joined the river, and all day the sound of water was in his ears, water and birdsong.

He never passed this mountain trail without thinking of the Romans. The dead conquerors of Britain had laid a line of fortresses down the river, not mere frontier stations, but leveled acres as large as towns, enclosed by walls. And before the Romans his forefathers, the Britons, reared earthworks and triangular strong places of stone, and before the Britons, nameless men dug defensive ditches deep in bare rock. It was a good land, Gawin thought, whoever had lived on it considered life not too much to spend in its protection; an old land, an experienced land, Arthur's and his. And now God's houses followed the ancient tracks of its past, churches, monasteries, cells of holy men. Gawin was moved as he thought of the antique voices sighing in the mountain breeze.

The next afternoon at yet another ruin he reached the junction of his road and Perceval's, where the river turned south to the sea. And an hour later he rode under the north gate of Arthur's royal city.

And so I have come home, he thought, without Perceval. He wondered restlessly whether the boy had arrived, what he made of the proudest of all Roman cities in Norgals, home of the legions, of governors, of rich provincial princes. Did he even know that Romans once walked the busy streets along which their houses, patched by British masons, still stood? Would he stop to stare, open-mouthed, at the great buildings preserving a faded air of palaces, gilded lead roofs peeling, and gardens a little wild and weedy, and baths whose conduits would have leaked away the hot water had any furnaces remained to heat it? Who would tell him the market was the ruin of a theater? Or that the ring-shaped earthwork outside the walls was the most prized of Roman pleasure spots, an amphitheater?

Making his way among the merchant booths, and hurrying women, and foreigners from Africa and the Rhine, and children running after dogs, and priests, sailors, craftsmen, servants of the rich, Gawin planned what he would do — go to the church and say his prayers, wash, report himself to Arthur, find a fresh horse, and ride north, beyond the junction, into the mountain country through which Perceval must still be toiling. I have not found him but I will find him, he promised himself.

Arthur had built two churches, one for his knights, one for the queen and her attending ladies. Gawin entered the knights' church, knelt before the altar, and muttered the prayers of thanksgiving for a safe return. His mind was not on the words, and he left the church without the satisfied feeling of journey's end. He rode past the mended palace of the Roman governors which was Arthur's residence, and entered the lawns of the hall raised by the king's masons for the brotherhood of the Round Table. This structure was less magnificent than the carved and pillared imperial buildings, being low and long and without grace, only plain walls encircling a vast chamber along whose inner sides were ranged armories and quarters and all the necessary rooms for a company of soldiers.

At the row of mounting stages he surrendered his horse and asked that a fresh animal be held ready for him. He passed through the guards and porters in the fortified porch and entered the great hall. He meant to go on to the common room where he hoped to find friends playing chess or hashing over old battles. If he had the luck to meet Lancelot or Yvain they would tell him quickly such news as he should hear.

But at the Round Table chamber he stopped. The king, Arthur himself, sat in his high seat. Pressed close about him as though in emergency were knights, perhaps as many as twenty. And of all people Gawin did not expect to see, Kei was there, his shirt still showing the marks of lately removed armor. He had put himself by the king, displacing young Lohot, Arthur's son, who stood between Kei and Yvain.

Lancelot was not among them. Through this tense group ran the sound of conversation, not loud, not the talk of men discussing a mission, but low and slow and strange.

"Messire Arthur," Gawin said.

Arthur raised his head. Though he had reached the age of grizzled men he was still all one color, eyes, hair, beard, skin, brows, a faded reddish brown. He was an immense man, yet not as Joseus was, not great cords and bony joints. His years had altered his grace somewhat without despoiling it. His russet eyes moved slowly to Gawin. "Is it you, nephew?"

"Yes, uncle. I've just ridden in from the west on the Roman road."

The king rose. He stood half a head above all his men except Lohot. "Welcome, Gawin. We have had a wonder here that I wish you had seen."

"Let us not call it a wonder too soon," Kei said.

"What was it," Lohot said, "if not a wonder?"

"An outlandish accident satisfies me," Kei answered.

"It is wonder enough that you are here, Kei," Gawin said. "You must have flown over the mountains like a kite."

"I made an easy ride — without flogging my horse to death, either. But then, covering ground is a skill one is born with or not born with."

"Enough, Kei," Arthur said. He moved from the group and laid a hand on Gawin's arm and push him forward. "Come here, nephew. Look at this." He stopped before a square oak pillar as thick as a man which stood in the

133

center of the hall, its head supporting the midpoint of the low, curved ceiling. "Do you see?"

"The sword," Gawin said.

"The sword." With his forefinger Arthur traced a stained slit in the pillar. This scar was five inches in length and breast-high from the floor. As long as Gawin could remember, even when he was a page of seven visiting the City of Legions with his father, a sword had stood in the slit to its hilts. Above it were carved letters:

Draw me, best knight.
Mine be your might.

Gawin felt as though he had been struck in the lungs. *Who put the sword there?* he asked his father before his voice deepened. I don't know, son. *Who is the best knight?* He will be the knight who can draw the sword from the pillar. *Shall I be the knight who draws it?* I hope so, but you must grow big and do your work knightly first. And then at home he had asked his mother, *Who drove the sword into the pillar at the City of Legions?* I have heard that warrior kings who wish to make their knights valiant have such swords, Gawin. *Why, mother?* Oh, each knight hopes to draw it. They say a cunning workman of the king's fastens the sword so that it can never be drawn. And as the young knights are made all try and all fail, yet all hope to improve in strength and courage in the faith that they will draw it next time. And so the king is served. *Mother! That would be a wicked lie!* Perhaps it is not a lie, my son, I am only telling you old tales I have heard told.

Gawin had put his hand to the hilts not once but twice. He had seen Yvain throw against it the whole might of his heavy shoulders, he had seen Lancelot attempt it with the swift power that no knight owned but Lancelot, he had seen Bedwyn and Bleheris and Erec and Gareth and Blamor and Lionel and Sagramor and Balan and Lohot try it one after another as the years passed. And he had forgotten the sword finally as one forgets objects one sees every day, though the words carved above it ran through his head sometimes in the way a child's rhyme is remembered.

"Was it Perceval who drew the sword?" he said.

"He did not tell us his name." Arthur passed his hand across his eyes. "I ask myself if it happened. He was a lad, a — a —"

"Wearing mimic armor woven of withies?"

"It was the same fool you killed your horse for, Gawin," Kei said, "and I will never believe he was helped by anything but fool's luck. He had no idea at all how to handle a sword. Luck," Kei said, "the luck of an oaf, the luck of a thick-headed, walloping peasant-heathen."

"Where is he?" Gawin said. "Where has he gone?"

Lohot would have answered, but Kei interrupted. "As God sees me, this oaf has gone to fight a rogue-knight who challenged the king."

"I said hold your tongue, Kei," Arthur reminded his seneschal. And in a dry, flat voice he told Gawin the story. This was his manner when he was moved.

"I and these knights had eaten together, and we still sat at table discussing the war games to follow the assemblage

135

at Whitsuntide. A porter entered and informed me of the arrival of an armed man who asked for me. I received him. He announced that he was a knight from Little Britain, that he had heard of the annual Whitsuntide games, and that he wished to try his skill against the best knights of the Round Table.

"I answered that he must give his name to the herald of the games, and issue his challenges in the lawful way," Arthur went on, looking neither at Gawin nor any knight, looking at nothing. "He made a show of anger, accused my knights of hiding behind the laws of tourney fighting, demanded a bout at once with anyone who dared accept his challenge. I ordered him to conduct himself peaceably and reminded him we were unarmed. He took a goblet from my table and shouted that whoever restored it must win it from him. And he ran through the postern —" Arthur turned a hand toward the door opposite the porch — "and so avoided the guard in front, who would have halted him."

The king sat motionless in the remoteness that was his habit. "The youth you call Perceval must have entered while the stranger was making his uproar. I had risen to take down my weapon, and when I saw him first he was standing by the pillar. He reached out and plucked the sword as one would pluck an ear of grain." Arthur raised his hand and closed his fist as though about the pommel of a sword.

"Did he speak?" Gawin asked.

"Not a word. Oh. Yes. He said, 'I'll return your cup, Messire King.'"

"'Messire King!'" Kei mocked. "'Messire King!'"

"Before we had taken in the fact that a boy armed with reeds could draw the sword he followed the stranger knight through the postern. All this had just occurred when you arrived."

"And no one tried to stop him?"

Arthur smote the pillar. "We must stop him. I did not think of stopping him. See that he is stopped."

"I'll follow him," Gawin said.

"No. I wish to speak with you. Yvain will go."

"Uncle, permit me —"

"Go on, Yvain," said the king.

24

THE KING WALKED HEAVILY to his high seat. "Give us leave," he said to the knights.

"As for me," Kei said, "I shall go after Yvain."

"Not you, Kei," Arthur said. "You will frighten our Knight of the Basket away. Yvain will deal best with him."

Gawin stood still, his head bent so that he would not have to see the pillar. What had happened? A miracle? An ignorant youth deceived by a trick of sovereignty? If I had been here, if I could have defended him against matters he didn't know, if I could have presented him to the king!

"I am glad you have returned, cousin." Lohot's hand fell upon his shoulder. "Welcome home."

Gawin looked up. The king's son stood some inches

taller than he, a leaner, more vivid Arthur, yet not altogether a mold of his father. He had the blue eyes of his mother Guenivere, and, too, a kindliness of bearing, a confiding warmth that Arthur lacked. "Thanks for the welcome, Lohot. I wish I had seen what you just saw."

"Yes, it was a moment. Since I was a little lad in page's silks I have dreamed so many times of the drawing of the sword that when I saw it I felt —" the young man spread his hands. "I don't know what I felt, an emptiness, perhaps."

"Gawin," Arthur said.

Gawin began to move toward the king. "Tomorrow we must talk of the war games."

Lohot's fair face warmed. "It is good you will be here for the games, cousin. But do I need to prove again that I have learned the lessons you taught me when I was your squire?"

"I have forgotten you were ever a squire."

"Not Kei," Lohot said. "I believe Kei is still of the opinion that I am not ready for knighthood."

"Kei bites at every man's heels. You must show him your metal by prevailing at the tournament."

"Listen, Gawin." Lohot detained him by holding the cuff of his chain shirt. "I would rather have a mission of my own than prevail in the games. My father has never given me a mission. Perhaps you will speak to him in my behalf?"

"Messire Gawin," Arthur said.

The knights who had been present at the drawing of the sword were moving toward the common room. "Let us meet later," Gawin said.

138

"Sit here, nephew." The king flicked a finger toward an audience chair placed below him.

Now I must tell him, Gawin thought. How am I to tell him?

But Arthur began at once to speak of Norgals. "You have been absent three months, and I hope these three months do not mean you found affairs in the north in turmoil."

Gawin took his place in the audience chair at which the king still pointed. "I rode right around the borders of Norgals, I visited your barons, I called on your hermits and priests, and inspected your churches and forts. Except for one, the upheavals I met could be settled on the spot."

"You didn't ride through the interior, then?"

"I intended to quarter back and forth from the coast to the eastern border, through the country of the baron Logrins. But," said Gawin, gathering his will, "the matter I spoke of made me wish to get back to the City of Legions as soon as possible."

"Logrins," said Arthur. "Logrins has been a thorn too long."

"Has he given fresh trouble?"

The king watched Gawin from under his tawny brows, yet without appearing to see him. This blind stare was a tool of his, and men not accustomed to him were diminished by it. He was not dressed for armor, but wore a long, belted tunic of scarlet silk furred at the hem with ermine, and over it a sleeveless surcoat, white silk embroidered with gold. His shield and the baldric on which hung his sword were sus-

139

pended from carved pegs above his chair. "The fact that Logrins is alive at all gives trouble, Gawin."

"Is it your wish that I hunt the mountains once more for his stronghold?"

Arthur considered it. "We have done that too often. I believe he moves from cave to cave, or wherever he keeps himself. I get reports of remote places where ashes or dead animals show he has camped. Now we must make an attack of a different kind. I am thinking of asking knights to go out alone, each man against him body for body. It is time to give up our little useless sallies and try to take him in single combat."

"I have thought this myself, uncle. But only such knights should go as choose the mission."

"Yes. Men are keener when they elect hard labors of their own will. The best things are always done this way."

The king's words made them think of Lancelot, and they spoke his name together.

"Lancelot," Arthur repeated. "Logrins is a mission made for Lancelot's hand. But he is absent, out of the country."

"Where is he?"

"I sent him to settle a problem as knotty as the problem Logrins gives me. He and forty knights he chose have gone to pacify Bryant of The Isles. I am sure you remember Bryant."

"I remember him," Gawin said. "He was a man I never trusted."

The king allowed himself a moment of chilly amusement. "Yes, yes, you told me to my face that I misread Bryant, and now you are congratulating yourself that you were right. But let me tell you this, Gawin. A sovereign who rules a land must use men to help him. And men are not perfect, each man has a thin spot, like old cloth. Time wears men as it wears cloth. I knew Bryant was proud and envious, but I knew too that rewards were always large in his thoughts, and I had to hope that giving him rank as a royal governor would knit him to me. You believe I was wrong. But this is the way a king rules — through prizes and advantages ambitious men desire. More often than not it works."

Gawin was silent.

"You do not agree," Arthur said.

"I have seen you rule since I was a page," Gawin answered. "From the first days of my knighthood you have done me the honor of speaking frankly with me. I have been trained in your methods. And —" he broke off.

"And you do not agree with me."

"Messire," Gawin said, "I can't explain myself. On this trip — one day — there came a day — when I felt old. One day I was sitting under a tree while my horse fed. And I looked back on my knighthood and saw it all one color, the color of regret."

"What has this to do with Bryant? He may be a poor tool, but I can build with him."

"Before that day I would have said good things are spoiled if we build them with poor tools. But time has made it clear that poor tools are all we have, and turn our labors to less than we hope. This is what I regretted while I waited for my horse to feed."

"Ah, Gawin, you have only arrived at the secret of every wise man. As for Bryant, he has not been the tool I needed in The Isles. He oppressed his people. They asked me for help. And I sent them Lancelot."

"When?"

"Soon after you left the City of Legions. He has been gone almost as long as you."

"And what has he done in The Isles?"

Arthur showed his teeth in a grimace of satisfaction. "He decoyed Bryant to the beach by a false landing. While Bryant watched one ship Lancelot came ashore in another and attacked his rear. First he cut Bryant's troop into thirds, next he drove each third methodically into the water, next he took Bryant, next he imposed his terms, next he —"

Gawin laughed. "I recognize the style. Why doesn't he come home?"

"The people of The Isles love him. They wish me to make him the new governor."

"No, no," Gawin said. "You will not make him governor, and if you do, Lancelot will refuse."

"But meanwhile I leave him there."

"And Bryant?"

"Lancelot sent Bryant to me. He is here. In prison."

"Waiting a day to be hanged?"

"Waiting, at least," Arthur said. "I still need Bryant. I am teaching him a lesson."

"Do you believe he is tractable enough to learn lessons?"

"I believe what I believe, Gawin. One thing I believe is that the time has come to send for Lancelot."

142

"I shall be glad to see him. When I return at the end of a mission I look for Lancelot first — after yourself, I mean."

"We have let Lancelot lead us away from Logrins. We will talk of him again, but at the moment I wish to hear your report region by region. Tell me the event that was unlike the others, the one you say hurried you home."

Now that he must speak of Iglais and Perceval and their land of clouds and harebells Gawin felt his heart turn. All he had prepared himself to say left him. "It was in the northwest, as far as one can go. After the death of Allan the Fat, the lady Iglais, his wife, went to this desert place with her son."

"I remember her," Arthur said. " She was a pretty woman but rather foolish."

"She is a lady in whom wisdom and folly are mixed."

"Indeed."

"The baron of The Moors had seized certain of her holdings."

"I do not remember any baron of The Moors."

"He was her husband's vassal. I summoned him to combat on the king's challenge and," said Gawin, unable to do what he had hastened home to do, "he was defeated."

"Killed?"

"He is dead, messire."

"Are the holdings restored to the lady?"

"For the term of a year. The baron's brother has challenged me to defend them again at the end of a year."

"I can't have it," Arthur said. "I will not have my officers challenged and challenged again by men who think themselves larger than common justice. I will send two knights to take the brother. Where is he and what is his name?"

"I have engaged to return, uncle, and I wish to return."

"Oh," said the king, "some circumstance makes this affair more than mere seizure."

"Yes."

"What circumstance?"

"The lady Iglais — it is her son who came into the hall today and drew the sword from the pillar."

"What! That basket-wearer is Allan the Fat's son?"

"Perceval. I do not know how to describe him. He is — is — a — he is not what every man is. He has a — a —"

"Come, Gawin, what about Perceval?"

"He is the best knight. He will become the best knight. Hear him when Yvain brings him before you. He must show forth his own story."

"I do not understand a word of what you are saying."

Gawin rose. "May I ask you a question, uncle? It is a question I can't ask without your indulgence."

Arthur stared, his red-brown eyes cold. "If it is an outrageous question you must abide the result."

"The sword," Gawin said. "Was it fastened into the pillar by artifice?"

"Do you believe it was?"

"I do not know what I believe."

"You are forty years old, nephew. You are beyond lamenting the taste of life, like any disappointed squire. Your question is too late. As for its answer," he said, "let the son of your wise and foolish lady render it."

144

25

GAWIN FOUND IT HARDER and harder to keep his mind on his replies. Under Arthur's dry, deliberate questioning his own thoughts swarmed. No one here has heard of Perceval but me, he told himself, no one could have expected him to come to the City of Legions, therefore no one could have given secret orders to loosen the sword so that he could draw it. What can I believe but that he was helped by a miracle? How can I accuse him of murder if he is to be the best knight?

"— and how did you find them garrisoned?" Arthur said.

"Forgive me, I am over-ridden, and my ears buzz, and I did not hear your question."

Arthur studied him briefly, then said, "Go and unarm, Gawin. Bathe and eat. We will meet again in the morning."

"With your permission I would like to be present when you question Perceval."

"I will speak with him in the morning too. The hour is already after vespers. Goodnight, nephew. Rest well."

Gawin hastened to the common room. This chamber opened from the postern end of the Round Table hall. It was low, floored with stone, and lit by two narrow, deeply embrasured windows. On its walls hung the flags of the brotherhood, among them Gawin's banner of scarlet silk

145

embroidered with a gold hawk. Shields of dead knights were also displayed around the walls. Prince Tristram's hung between that of The Morholt, the Irish champion upon whose body Tristram first proved his knighthood, and that of King Mark of Cornwall, for love of whose young wife the prince took his death.

Knights stood together discussing the drawing of the sword. Gawin saw that Perceval was not with his friend Yvain.

"Where is he?" Gawin said.

"Your bird has flown," Kei told him. "He is not a man who understands the command of a king."

"Yvain," Gawin said, "you were sent to bring him."

"I was sent to bring him. But hear me out, Gawin. Sit down, drink ale. You look worn enough to need a little mending."

"If we are friends, Yvain, tell me what you know of Perceval."

Yvain answered him with a brotherly, familiar smile. "I went out to the mounting stages. I asked a groom whether our guest with the reed shield had taken a horse. The groom said he had mounted his own horse, a tall bay."

"Joseus after all," Gawin mumbled.

"I asked the groom whether the stranger knight who had stolen the king's goblet had taken *his* horse. The groom had not seen him. This seemed to point to the stable at the sally port where the domestic horses are kept, and I walked there and questioned the ostlers. They had seen the stranger, as it proved. He had left his horse with them and come on foot

146

to the porch. Later, when he ran out at the postern with the king's goblet, his horse was exactly where he needed it, and he galloped away westward, not following the river road."

"Yes, yes," Gawin said.

"Patience, brother. Perceval followed him. Me, I told the ostler to saddle a horse, and I went after the pair of them. You see, Gawin, that time was lost with all my trotting back and forth from the entrance porch to the sally port."

"And so you missed them," Gawin said.

"I found them, but too late. Perceval overtook the stranger and challenged him. You have heard, I suppose, that this fellow was boiling to fight someone, anyone, from among Arthur's men. All the same he answered Perceval that he would not engage an unarmed man."

"Make an end of all these words, Yvain."

"I am telling it as speedily as I can, believe me. The end was that Perceval admitted he lacked a spear, but demanded that the stranger dismount and fight on foot. And he showed the sword he had drawn from our pillar. The stranger ridiculed his shield of twigs, and so Perceval pulled him by the foot and unbalanced him and tipped him onto the grass. This changed the stranger's mind, and they fell to it, sword against sword."

"Who taught Perceval to handle a sword?" Gawin said.

"How can I tell you that?" Yvain said. "I know nothing about him, I never saw him until this afternoon. But someone must have taught him, because by the time I arrived he had not only cut the stranger through the helmet but

147

through the brains too, as deep as to the shoulders. And I found him trying to pull the dead man out of his armor."

"What did he say? Tell me what he said."

Yvain wagged his head. "He said, 'Messire, show me how to squeeze this man out of his iron clothes'!"

Kei said, "This simpleton of yours deals in treachery, Gawin. He is plainly not what he pretends."

"Pretending or not," Yvain said, "he did not know how to unfasten armor. I showed him the straps and buckles, and as we worked I questioned him, and he told me about his fight with the thief of the goblet, and all else as I have told you. He gave me the goblet too, I supposed for safekeeping. I have fetched it back."

"He's a murderer," Kei said.

"He is not a murderer, Kei," Yvain answered. "The stranger had issued a challenge, remember. He said before us all that if the king's goblet were restored, a knight must win it from him. It was a lawful invitation to combat."

"Murder, however you defend it. The stranger said nothing about combat to the uttermost."

"Oh, come, Kei," Yvain said reasonably. "The stolen goblet was a challenge in itself, he wished to insult the king, he walked up to the royal table and snatched a feeding vessel. He dared the *king,* he did not dare Perceval. And a dare to the king *must* be answered to the uttermost."

Angrily Kei turned his back. "You are as infatuated with this stable-clown from the north as Gawin. I am glad Arthur has one friend among his knights."

148

Gawin said, "Go on Yvain. What occurred after you helped Perceval unarm the dead knight?"

"He asked me whether he was entitled to the dead man's 'iron clothes.' I told him he was. He asked if the horse was his too, and I said yes. Then he asked me to help him put the armor on. Next he asked me to mount him." Yvain crumpled his homely, dark face into a grin of regret. "You needn't say what you are thinking, Gawin. I should not have let him mount. But wouldn't you take it for granted that a young knight who had just avenged an insult to the king would want nothing so much as to return and hand the king his goblet? And so I was left standing with my mouth open when Perceval wheeled the horse and said, 'Farewell, Messire Yvain, I will remember your help. Tell the king I will come back and ask him what justice is' — these were his words, 'what justice is' — 'when I have proved that I am the best knight.' And he rode off like a demon. I hadn't an ounce of armor on my body. I had come out on a domestic horse. What could I do but watch him go?"

Gawin sat down and dug his hands into his hair.

"I believe he will return, brother," Yvain said. "He would be foolish not to come back and receive the king's thanks. Do you hold me at fault in this?"

"No, no. I should have followed Perceval myself."

"Since I've played squire once today, let me unarm you, Gawin. Then —"

"No, I must ride after Perceval."

"Now? Late as it is?"

"Some daylight is left, an hour or more."

"Has the king given you leave to depart?"

"I am summoned to speak with him in the morning." Gawin rose. "And this means I must finish my errand with Perceval tonight."

"Let me come with you."

Gawin shook his head. "Thanks, Yvain, but in this matter I must go alone."

26

AT THE MOUNTING STAGE the groom who held his fresh horse said, "It is so nearly night, Messire Gawin, that I hope you need not ride far."

"It is not yet dark."

"Not black dark," the groom said. "But would you not be wise to take a squire with you?"

"I am not afraid of a few shadows. Now let me mount."

"God go with you," the groom said.

Gawin knew his errand was hopeless, but he was driven to turn west nevertheless. He told himself that landmarks were still plain. To the north he could see the great stone mountain that was as round as a wave arrested at its crest. Before him, like a deeper dusk in the thin dusk of evening, the phalanx of mountains marching down from the north stretched themselves onto the plain. And at their end stood the strange guardian tumulus which the forefathers of his forefathers had raised.

He lacked the easy passage of the Roman road, for it continued south from the City of Legions. Westward he had only a rude earth trail that began at once to ascend the slopes. Between woods on either side the darkness was heavy, though above him the sky offered a lane of pale gray light. What will Perceval do, he asked himself, push right on as though night could never fall? Perhaps he has already marked a hermitage where he means to stay. Yet Gawin knew of no hermitage among these forested ridges whose defiles were as familiar to him as the streets of Arthur's capital.

At the crest of the first hill his horse stopped.

"Come on, brother," Gawin said, and gave its neck a gentle slap.

The horse did not respond.

"Let us not quarrel with one another," Gawin said. "Move." And he touched the animal with his spur.

It crouched, circled, refused to go forward. Gawin was used to trusting the instinct of a horse for danger, but he was impatient, and struck the spur smartly into the animal's belly. It gathered its feet under it to buck, and he was surprised and wasted the second he needed to pull up its head and prevent it from arching its back. He only managed to kick free of the stirrups before he was thrown right over its ears.

He sat in the road, hearing his ears buzz. He bent his arms and legs and found himself whole. "So, brother," he said, "you have made yourself clear." Cumbered by his hauberk and chausses, he got awkwardly to his feet. The horse did not attempt to shy away from him, but let him take the rein and wind it about his hand.

The two stood together, listening. Gawin began to hear footfalls approaching from the west. The walker advanced without much noise, his steps slow and shuffling. The tread was not that of an armed man, but seemed rather to be made by an old woman.

"Hoy!" Gawin said. "What are you?"

"A friend, Messire Gawin."

"You know me and I don't know you."

The walker coughed or chuckled or made some sound of satisfaction. "And this means I listen to voices more carefully than you."

"Merlin! What are you doing on this hill?"

"I am walking home."

A slight, shapeless lump emerged from a patch of deep shadow. Gawin did not have to see the man's features to know he was the ancient who, so the story ran, tutored King Arthur in his boyhood and became his foster father. Since Gawin first knew him he had been a small, hoary gaffer of a man, raisin-wrinkled, faded black eyes peering from under grizzled brows. Foul luck, Gawin thought, to meet him here. He will talk and talk and talk.

Merlin said, "Walk with me, Gawin, since it appears you must walk."

"Yes, I must walk, thanks to you. This beast and I aren't well acquainted, and he threw me before I knew you had scared him. Have you met a rider on this slope?"

"Tk, tk. A pity. I'll wager a groat no horse has thrown you since Arthur knighted you."

"Sooner or later any horse throws any rider," Gawin said, as though it were a point he were obliged to make.

"This is the reason I prefer to go on foot. Will you walk with me?"

"I will walk until I find something I can use as a mounting stage." Why do I let him double me back, why don't I simply say goodnight and leave him? But this was Merlin's way, to hold men fast whether or not they wished to be held.

Merlin was toddling slowly eastward toward the city. "It is not late for a man who depends on his feet to be abroad, but it is late for a man who depends on his horse. Surely you will not mount again this evening, Gawin."

"I have a mission."

"What mission is this?"

No affair of yours, old crock, Gawin thought. But you must stick your snout into everything that happens at the City of Legions. Here is the fruit of Arthur's tolerance of you at court, of his letting you sit at whatever audience you choose and stroke your beard and play the wise counselor.

"What mission, Gawin?" Merlin repeated.

"If it concerns you," Gawin said, determined to assert himself, "I am looking for a youth who has just ridden away from the Round Table hall."

"Perceval? Is it Perceval who brings you out to listen to the owls?"

"How do you know Perceval!"

"I met him a while ago," Merlin said contentedly. "I have

153

talked with him. Indeed I have had the luck to send him to a friend of mine."

"Ah, Merlin, keep your hands off this mission. Tell me where he is."

"He is safe."

"Don't make a mystery of it. Where is Perceval?"

"The evening is going to be pleasant," the king's counselor said. "And I believe we shall see the stars when we come from under the trees."

Gawin stopped. "I'll say goodnight. I must go the other way."

Merlin did not interrupt his soft shuffle forward.

"Tell me what was spoken between you and Perceval."

"He said, 'Good day,' and I answered, 'Good day.'"

They walked a few steps in silence. "Listen, Merlin, I have never been a bad friend to you. Why do you wish me ill in the matter of Perceval?"

Merlin sighed. "You young men live by bargains. You hope to buy your news from me with the reminder that you have been my friend."

"I only suggest that friends should help one another."

"I suppose so, though it may be that you and I do not think in the same way. And since you will have an answer even when you understand I do not care to give it, I must tell you that I do not wish to have Perceval followed."

"How can it matter to you? You don't know him, you have only just met him."

"I know his mother, I know her kin. And I will not answer your question, Gawin. Return with me. Now I will speak as a friend and tell you that you will hardly find your right hand in this gloom."

I've lost him again even without Merlin, Gawin thought. If I stumble through the night hoping to uncover the cell in which the old toad has hidden him I shall miss my audience with the king, and my duty is to the king.

"Since there's no help for it, pluck up heart," Merlin said.

"Well! Since there is no help for it, I shall do what you are too crabbed to do for me — tell you a piece of news."

"About the sword?" Merlin's voice was tranquil. "Perceval told me he drew the sword from the pillar. Is this your news?"

Gawin stood still in the road.

"You must not be impatient with me," the friend of Arthur said. "I ask pardon. To amuse myself I have been playing a little game with you, and I am sorry I have added anger to your despair. Forgive an old man."

"Why?"

"Why what?"

"Why have you spoiled my hope of finding Perceval?"

"Let me ask a question. Why do you hang so much hope on finding him?"

"I must know —" Gawin began, helpless. He made a fresh start. "What was the sword, Merlin? Do you know its history?"

"I have heard that Arthur's father, Uther Pendragon, gave the pillar to Arthur with the sword already standing in place, I have heard he made this gift when Arthur was crowned. I have heard too that Uther Pendragon told Arthur it was brought to Britain by a holy man who saw Christ crucified. But these may be tales."

"Lies, you mean? Was it you who fixed the sword in the pillar by artifice?"

"No, not I, I had no part in any artifice."

"Yet you conceal Perceval from me because he drew the sword, I think."

"If I conceal him — and I do not admit it — I do so because he has business of his own."

Gawin said. "The king expects to see him in the morning. Is his business greater than the king's?"

"It may be."

"If you love God, Merlin, tell me what was said between you and Perceval."

Merlin paced along softly for several moments. Again he sighed. "Well, well, now that you mention God, I will tell you this. Perceval asked me who I was."

"And then?"

"And then he listened to my reply."

"What was your reply?"

"I answered, 'Merlin.' Perhaps I added a few simple words about myself too," he concluded modestly. "Then Perceval asked me what justice was."

"And I suppose you told him in a few simple words what justice is?"

"No," Merlin said. "I only told him where to look for it."

27

THROUGH THE DAYS before the King's Justice, Yvain stayed close, coaxing Gawin to visit the armorers who were preparing their mail for the war games, or ride a few courses on the practice tournament fields outside the city wall. Together they attended the fêtes that preceded the assemblage, and Gawin dutifully took his place among the queen's ladies performing round dances on the lawns, or opposed the young knights playing at bowls, or cheered on the squires, candidates for knighthood at Whitsun, showing their skills in foot racing, riding, and weapon handling. But nothing mended his wooden spirits.

"What ails you, brother?" Yvain asked him. "The king did not reproach me in the matter of Perceval, and I hope you aren't doing what Arthur didn't."

"If I am poor company," Gawin said, "it is my fault, not yours."

They were sitting on the grass near the squires' training green, which lay at the bottom of the long fields behind the sally port. Yvain wished to show Gawin a young cousin of his, the son of a chieftain from the west by a bondwoman. The youth's birth was against him, yet he displayed such promise that Arthur had received him and entrusted his education to Yvain. They watched him ride at a target shield hung from an arm hinged to a wooden post.

Yvain said, "Something weighs on you, that's plain. Can you speak of it?"

"I don't know how to speak of it. This journey — no journey I have made since I was a knight was like it."

"Look at my squire manage his spear!" Yvain said. "He has hit the target shield right in the center three times out of three."

"A target shield doesn't move, and a man on a horse does," Gawin reminded him. "All the same this fellow will make a good soldier."

"How was your journey different from the others?"

"I've ridden through Norgals I don't remember how often," Gawin said, "without meeting such strange people as I met last month."

"Strangers aren't enough to muffle you in gloom."

"I do not mean strangers, I mean strange people. Tell me, have you heard of a family of brothers whose names are Peleur and Mortelle and Pelles?"

"I may have. If I have it was so long ago that I remember nothing of them clearly. Are they your oddities?"

"I was told their lineage is the most ancient in Britain. Besides," Gawin went on slowly, "the oldest brother, Peleur, owns a relic so holy that no man can see it without performing certain acts, I don't know what acts."

"Relics," Yvain said comfortably. "Relics fly about our land as thick as bees."

"Your cousin has just hit the shield on the rim, and the recoil came within an inch of breaking his nose."

"I saw it, he forgot the reins in his left hand and pulled

158

his horse over when he leaned into the charge. We must allow him an error now and then." Yvain rose and called to the young man and explained what had happened. Then he dropped onto the grass again. "What is Peleur's relic?"

"A cup," Gawin murmured. "Our Lord's cup that He shared with His disciples at the last supper. So I was told."

"Ah! I have heard of this cup. Some men say Joseph of Arimathea or Nicodemus or another friend of Our Lord used it to catch the blood that dropped from His wounds as He hung on the cross."

"In Norgals they call it the Grail."

"They call it the Grail wherever it is spoken of, Gawin. Surely you know its legend? When I was a young knight — you were still a red-headed squire — we said among ourselves that good soldiers would see it."

"Has any knight seen it?"

"Come, now, a story of this kind is meant to ennoble us and give us a mark to achieve. We say we shall see the Grail, but we do not wallop about on horseback looking for it." Yvain gestured toward the laboring squires. "These fine fellows sharpen their courage on such high hopes."

"You believe it is a fable."

"I believe it is a — a — something a good soldier's mind has both right and reason to guide itself by."

"Peleur's Grail is not a fable," Gawin said. "I stayed a night with a hermit who told me he is nephew to Peleur. He told me there is a cup of Christ and that it can be seen if the seeker does not fear its perils."

"Hermits live lonely lives, and when they grow old their

minds often wander among fancies that seem real to them."

"Joseus was young — not much older than Lohot."

"Is this your trouble, Gawin? You wish to search for the Grail?"

"I don't know, I don't know. I am a plain man, I do not understand mysteries, I have appetites and evil tempers. Yet —"

"Yet you wish to see it."

"I wish to see Perceval, at least. Do you know what Merlin told me? He told me the sword in the pillar was put there by a holy man who saw Christ crucified, and we know — we have been urged to believe — that it has waited all these years for the best knight." Gawin looked at Yvain to discover whether some madness of his own was reflected in his friend's face. "And what if the best knight is the knight who requires the sword to help him in whatever must be done to achieve the Grail?"

Yvain said, "Now I realize why letting Perceval escape was a blow to you."

"Perceval is of the lineage of the brothers. His mother is Peleur's sister."

"You believe his drawing the sword was a miracle? Because of his lineage?"

"Yes," Gawin said, "I believe it was a miracle."

"I see," Yvain said. "Plain Gawin with his appetites and evil tempers has been touched on the head by an other-worldly finger that has given him a headache. Tell me, brother, was Perceval's mother one of the strange people you spoke of?"

160

"She is a widow, she is a gentle, innocent lady, she knows how to make life gentle and innocent too. I promised her I would bring Perceval back, and I don't wish to see my promise turn into a lie."

"Oh, oh, what problems you have!" Yvain's rough features seemed to stretch with sympathy. He was an ugly man, his face all lumps and creases and bright, deep-set eyes. Moreover, his complexion was swarthy, and his streaked black hair fell into coarse curls. Yet Gawin knew that the more one saw this unhandsome mask the better one liked it, until after years it assumed a manly sweetness, a brave goodness that did not belittle its strength. "A lady who attracts our ladyproof Gawin, and a son marked with a wild sign! I am sorry for you."

"Her name is Iglais," Gawin said, glad of a chance to speak it, "and you are right, Yvain. I think of her oftener than I have thought of any woman since — since I had reason to think of one special woman."

"And you can't explain her son to her or to yourself. And both mother and son are wrapped in a mist with the Grail. And you don't know whether the Grail is a truth or a lie. Aye, aye, you have a mind full of stones, Gawin."

"But the heaviest stone," Gawin said, and became silent.

"Still another?"

"In the buried corners of Norgals you can find people who have twisted our faith," Gawin said. "They mix it with the old beliefs of our forefathers, they put ancient Demons beside our God, the pagan Demons of Winter and Spring."

"Now here is one matter you don't need to carry on your

161

back," Yvain said stoutly. "All country folk believe in elves and sprites and unhuman maidens who can turn themselves into white hinds or swans. Why should these silly notions be a stone for you?"

"Listen, Yvain, the priest of Iglais was the first man to speak to me of the Grail. And he dealt" — Gawin dragged his hand across his eyes — "or seemed to deal with pagan gods. What if the Grail is evil? What if it is a temptation?"

Yvain's good-natured face sobered. "I know only one medicine for ills like yours, Gawin. A moment ago you called my squire a good soldier. We are good soldiers, you and I. But we live in a wicked world. Evil creeps into us with the drawing of each breath. We can't keep ourselves free of evil, we can only confess ourselves, hear our soldiers' masses, fulfill our missions, be faithful to Arthur, and forget matters that are deep beyond our power to comprehend. If this Grail is evil, don't think of it again."

"And if it isn't evil?"

"If it isn't, then you will miss something you would have been better for having. But you will still be a good soldier."

"A good soldier — is that enough for you, Yvain?"

"Yes."

"And it never seems too little, too poor, too fruitless? You never feel you have grown old missing the true prize?"

Yvain said, "Certainly I do. But this is what piling up years means. And even in face of it, I believe still that being a good soldier is enough. Ask yourself what is better, Gawin, ask yourself whose lot you would exchange for yours."

Whose lot? Gawin wondered. Perceval's?

162

28

AFTER THIS conversation Gawin took care to avoid the look of a disappointed man. Unless Arthur gave him leave he had the duty of remaining at the City of Legions; and as Whitsunday neared and old friends began to arrive for the Round Table assembly he did not need to force the pleasure he felt in seeing them again. These were men with whom he had fought the king's battles and ridden on the king's missions.

On Whitsunday morning at the hour of prime he went with Yvain and all the knights to hear mass in the king's church. It was Arthur's custom to fast for three days before he met the hundred and forty knights of his fellowship, then, bearing the cross, to walk barefooted from the hall to the minster. Robed in a plain white shift tied about him with rope, he entered before the bishop, carried the cross to the altar, knelt, and remained on his knees throughout the service. Gawin thought the bowed figure stripped of all signs of kingship still showed forth the sovereign courage that supported him through the rigors of his condition. And he rose from the bishop's benediction feeling that men endured their common burdens best by not showing the galled marks the burdens imposed.

Outside, Guenivere and her attendants were emerging from their mass in the church maintained for the queen's use. All the ladies, all the knights, all the royal household moved onto the lawns about the Round Table hall. Here each year the parade formed that accompanied the king to his field of justice. Kei, the seneschal, and Lucan, the chief steward, acted as marshals, helped by Elifri, the chief groom, and Rhyferys, the chief huntsman, and their corps. Gawin saw that horses, as many as two hundred, were already caparisoned and being led in a double line to the mounting stages.

He and Yvain chose their animals, mounted, and waited together.

"We shall not be rained on," Yvain said. "The law that requires rain to fall on Whitsun has been suspended today, I guess."

"Do you see Lancelot?" Gawin said. "I hoped he would reach us by parade time."

"Even on Whitsun Lancelot hates mobs. But that doesn't mean he hasn't come home."

"If he were here he would ride. He does his honor to the king the same as the rest of the Hundred and Forty."

"True," Yvain said with a grin. "But think. Hasn't it often happened that his missions were so urgent he could only arrive when it was too late to appear in the parade? Yet for a man who dislikes hearing his name screamed out by pot boys and carls, he manages to be a greater lure to the curious than any knight."

"He attracts the people because he is the best of Arthur's men."

"I agree, I agree," Yvain said in high good humor. "I am

not abusing your hero. I love him as you love him. That's another of his qualities — to earn the admiration of every man of the Hundred and Forty without earning the edge of their jealousy."

Gawin said, watching Kei expertly maneuvering the columns of horsemen "Wrong, Yvain. I can name you men who are jealous of Lancelot. But they don't display it, because biting at him means they also bite at the king."

A huntsman in the king's livery rode up to them. "Will you take your ranks, messires?"

"Are we on the move?" Yvain said.

"Yes, messire, the procession is about to start."

Gawin's spirits rose. No matter what gnaws the mind of a soldier of the Round Table, he thought, the Whitsunday parade is a cure. The ladies wore every color of fine stuffs, and the knights dressed themselves in surcoats and long, stiffly embroidered capes cherished from year to year for this very occasion. The furs and brocades, the silks and soft leathers, the great clasps of gold or silver or bright Irish enamel, the polished dress shields and light arms, above all the noble host of battle flags were such a sight as one could never forget, and Gawin thought of the Norgals squire who had wished to be in Arthur's city today.

Bedwin, Arthur's bishop, and the chapter priests rode first, then the king himself, alone, then Lohot and his mother, Queen Guenivere, then the Queen's squires and ladies, then Merlin on a white hackney. Gawin, sharing the royal blood, might have accompanied Lohot, but years ago he had chosen to ride with the men most trusted by Arthur:

165

Yvain and his kinsman Bedwyr, old Ector, still as lean and straight as men thirty years younger than himself, Bors, the kinsman of Lancelot, Bleheris, who could make poetry as well as wield a sword, and little Dinadan of Cornwall, Prince Tristram's friend. Behind the Round Table knights followed princes of the provinces, Anguissh of Ireland outshining them all by his size and the blaze of his red beard. Last came the young men in squires' silks who hoped to kneel before the king at the Round Table assembly after the Justice and hear themselves named to their seats.

The parade began slowly to move. It passed through the gate of the Round Table enclosure and turned toward the Roman road over which provincial lords of the Empire had once ridden to the amphitheater. Every condition of man who could reach the City of Legions had ridden or walked or hobbled or been carried there. And throngs of beggars, tumblers, masons and smiths seeking work, pickpockets, friars, sick men trusting a sight of the king for cure, minstrels, musicians, hawkers of food and drink and magic potions and charms against ills of the flesh pushed one another to see what could be seen. Foreign knights had come from Spain and Africa and the islands of the Northmen to behold Arthur's fellowship, and London merchants and Irish sea captains had schemed to arrive in time to watch the king pass by. Hordes of children and stray goats and dogs and barnyard fowl boiled in and out of the press.

This crowd of men and animals was noisy, bawling with the joy of holiday and shouting for favorites as the knights rode on. Gawin heard his own name roared again and again.

166

He dreamed of Iglais, of Perceval. I am alone in this throng, he thought, but if those two had come with me I would be less alone.

At the amphitheater the king and the Round Table brotherhood dismounted and entered on foot through a passage walled with masonry. Arthur, Bishop Bedwin, Lohot, and Merlin walked the length of the grassy oval and took their places at its far end. A broad length of silk brocade tied at each corner to spears whose shafts were thrust into the ground made a royal pavilion on the earthwork where once Roman benches had stood. The queen and her party sat under a similar cover at the king's right. And the knights disposed themselves on either side of the amphitheater right around the continuous earthwork. The bishop invoked God's guidance, a trumpeter blew a few clear notes, and the King's Justice began.

On Whitsunday Arthur heard only extraordinary causes which needed special wisdom or mercy, remedies roomier than law. Suppliants came before him, sometimes frightened to find themselves face to face with their sovereign, sometimes sullen or desperate because hope for the evil afflicting them was worn out. They stammered, or wept, or stared, or cried out loudly like children for the relieving care of a father. And they brought gifts, fruit tied up in a cloth, a jug of fresh milk, a new-baked loaf, a wreath braided of flowers and sprays of grain. These were Arthur's people for whom his knights took their vows.

Gawin thought of the years he had spent in the king's service. Yvain called us good soldiers, yet we never make an

167

end to the misery that crawls to the City of Legions each Whitsunday. They appear summer after summer, these destroyed souls, looking through the same eyes as their kinsmen of last year and speaking in the same voices. What hope is there for men, for a poor tanner whose daughter has been debased, or for a knight who longs for a joy he can't name? But the king gives his justice as though the sores of human creatures could be healed. Perhaps this is what it is to be a good soldier.

The morning wore on, the sufferers were heard and departed. Gawin stood in a solitude as real as a walled cell. He did not know that a man had stepped between him and Yvain until a hand took him by the elbow.

"Greetings, brother," Lancelot said.

"Ah, Lancelot! Yvain told me you would miss the parade and come to the King's Justice."

"Yvain will be a wise man by the time he is as old as Merlin. I am glad to see you, Gawin."

Gawin said nothing. He only looked at Lancelot, the tall, blue-eyed knight who moved and spoke more softly than most men, but in whose movement and voice was such strength.

29

ARTHUR'S WHITSUNTIDE fast continued through the giving of justice, and on that day no knight took food until the king sat to meat. After three hours of standing inactive in a cool wind Gawin was hungry, fighting the depression, too, that had renewed itself, once the excitement of the parade was past. And in the same moment that he felt himself fortified by Lancelot's presence he was critical of him. Lancelot is a willful man, he thought, he puts his own comfort before his respect for Arthur.

Bishop Bedwin rose to recite the final prayer, the trumpeter blew the close of the King's Justice, and the Round Table brotherhood began to descend the low earthwork and move toward the walled aisle and the field beyond the amphitheater where the horses waited.

"If I had wagered on you today, Lancelot," Yvain said, "I could have won a gold besant from Gawin."

"What wager?" Lancelot said.

"That you were already in the City of Legions when we left the hall, but would tell us you weren't. I would have taken 'aye,' Gawin 'nay.' "

"A fool's wager, Yvain. If I swear I was not here, how will you know the truth?"

"We would have trusted your word as an honorable knight."

"Then as an honorable knight I'll say nothing at all. You didn't wager, and so you can't object that a gold besant hangs on my silence."

Their frivolity fretted Gawin. He said, "I hear that Bryant's people have asked the king to make you the new governor of The Isles."

"Yes," Lancelot said, "but —"

"You refused?"

"I hope I shall never refuse any mission Arthur gives me, but if he asks me what I wish I shall say I am not cut to the pattern of governors of men."

"Why not, Lancelot?" Yvain said. "You have everything needed in a ruler, strength, wit, military skill, and —"

"And the sense to read flattery for what it is, Yvain. Tell me your news."

"While Gawin was in the west last month I was in the north," Yvain said. "If you can believe it, they lacked rain, something I never heard of in the north. They expect famine."

"Do you know the king is holding Bryant in prison?" Gawin said.

"Is he?" Lancelot smiled at Gawin's impatience.

"He says he is teaching him a lesson. He means to release him. This Bryant who talks so smoothly and is every man's friend, I never trusted him. A knight who has once defied the king is no fit knight."

"If Arthur believes Bryant can learn a lesson we can believe it too," Lancelot said.

"I hope you are right," Gawin said. "We have restless men in the kingdom who only need a traitor to unite them."

"Tell Lancelot about the family you heard of in Norgals," Yvain said.

They had passed the exit of the amphitheater. Gawin covered the fact that he did not intend to reply by walking toward the mounting stages. He found his horse, stepped up the stage and into the saddle, and sat watching Yvain and

Lancelot, who had laid their heads together and were speaking like men exchanging a confidence. He thought, Yvain is repeating what I told him of Peleur and Perceval, he is saying I have turned foolish and wish to fly off on a young man's errand. I am weary of all men, I must get away from the City of Legions, I must ask for a mission. If I had not allowed Merlin to turn me back, Gawin thought, if I had plucked up the fortitude to leave him, if I had kept my confidence that I would reach Perceval . . . Merlin, he thought. Merlin. Merlin said, "I know Perceval's mother, I know her kin." He said it and I let his words drift over me without taking in their sense. Why didn't I wring the story from the old man then and there? I shall get to Merlin today and squeeze what he knows out of his skinny gullet.

The parade moved slowly into the Roman road. The crowd of spectators had grown, and grooms and huntsmen rode up and down the route pushing men back who were bent on seeing the king and touching him too, if they could. They discovered Lancelot, shouted his name, swept toward him in convulsive waves. Lancelot looked straight ahead, his face pale. It is not the mob he hates, Gawin reflected, but something within that makes him vulnerable. Gawin would not permit himself to give words to what all men knew of Lancelot, his love of Queen Guenivere. For all men knew, besides, that Lancelot avoided the king's wife, denied himself even the nearness to her that his nearness to the king would have made lawful.

The sense of festival rose among the brotherhood as the knights dismounted and entered the Round Table hall. The chamber was draped not in parade flags but in banners once carried into battle. Some were torn, some were stained with dust, some with blood. Around each clung the memory of an act of courage or the death of a soldier who had yielded his life in Arthur's service. Under the flags hung the battered shields, the split helms of brothers who would come no more to the City of Legions.

The company broke their fast with new ale and first fruits. Then Arthur received the young knights who had taken their vows at mass and seen their pristine armor blessed, walking with each to the seat assigned him at the great table that had given the fellowship its name. Now all ceremonial duties were finished. Lucan, the chief steward, carried in the symbol of Whitsun, a whole roast ewe lamb garlanded with flowers and sprays of herbs and grain. He set the gilded platter before the king, who cut the first slice. Chief cooks brought the roast joints, the baked fowl, the fish puddings, the stews; apprentices, the honey, eggs, white bread, cheese, fruits, ale.

The feast continued until dusk. By then the talk was loud, the musicians seemed to be playing in dumb show among voices bawling songs of their own, the storytellers had abandoned their tales of old wars. At last Arthur rose.

"Before I bid you goodnight, messires," he said, "I wish to tell you that the baron, Bryant of The Isles, has been defeated, and sent to me, and held in prison. I have had him fetched to the common room. In presence of my fellowship, and Lancelot, who conquered him, I am ready to receive his surrender and his oath of loyalty to Britain's king. Let Bryant be led in."

Old Ector, Arthur's chief captain and still the best military strategist of the brotherhood, rose and left the hall and returned with Bryant. The baron of The Isles was a big man, handsome in a gleaming, overfed way, with great mustaches and thick, curling hair. In spite of the fact that he was stripped of all marks of rank, dressed in a coarse homespun shift and walking barefoot, in spite of the fact that his hands were tied before him, he managed to move with a kind of noble ease, as though he chose his lot.

He knelt submissively before Arthur and bowed his head. His gestures were calculated, like those of a minstrel.

Arthur presented him with the hilts of his sword. "Lay your hands on this cross, Bryant, and acknowledge that you betrayed your duty as my governor, and were defeated in a fair fight, and are my prisoner."

Bryant raised his bound hands to the cross formed by the blade and hilts of the sword. "Arthur of Britain, I acknowledge that I betrayed my duty as your governor, and was defeated in a fair fight, and am your prisoner."

"Let his hands be loosed," Arthur said.

Ector unfastened the tie.

"Repeat the words the bishop speaks to you," Arthur said.

The bishop wrapped his beads around Bryant's hands and placed the crucifix between his palms. "On Christ's body I swear my faith to Arthur of Britain and to the realm of Britain. On Christ's body I swear to be the loyal man of

173

Arthur, to obey and defend him, and to avoid all treachery to him and to Britain."

Holding the crucifix, Bryant repeated the solemn oath, then put his hands between the king's and repeated it again. His voice was strong and pleasant, and all the while he exuded a certain cheerful willingness, even a relish, as though he were accepting an honor.

"Now," Arthur said, "let him be taken away and clothed and given arms."

"Bryant is a man who swears by Christ's body as you and I would say 'by my head,' " Gawin muttered to Lancelot.

"Swallow your rage, brother," Lancelot said. "The king is not done."

"My second word," Arthur told them, "deals with the outlaw Logrins. We have tried to hunt him down and failed. Bands of troops can't avoid announcing themselves, and this gives him time to escape. Therefore I wish to make his capture a matter of single combat, body for body. I shall not ask any knight of mine to try this mission. But if any knight elects it willingly, let him declare himself." Arthur did not look in Lancelot's direction.

"I elect it, messire." Before the king had finished speaking Lohot sprang from his chair immediately below the royal seat. "Give me this mission."

Lancelot got to his feet. But Kei, who had sat with Lohot, bounded forward and put a quick hand on Lohot's shoulder. "Let this mission be shared between the prince and me, messire," he said. "We are friends. He is a young knight, I am an experienced one. Give me leave to go with Lohot."

Lancelot, who had been shouted down, said again, "I elect the mission, messire."

Gawin too had risen. "And I, messire."

Lohot watched his father keenly. "It is your custom to accept men in the order in which they offer themselves, messire. My offer was first."

"Ah, Lohot!" Arthur said. "Give me time."

"Lohot has justice on his side, messire," Kei said. "It has always been your custom to accept the first knight to request a mission. As for me, two men will alert Logrins no more than one. Let me go. Ask Lohot if he will receive me."

"I would willingly go alone, but if you wish I will go with Kei." The young man approached Arthur and knelt before him. "Messire, I am five years older than you were when you became king of Britain. I am shamed if you refuse me missions worthy of my blood. Give me your blessing," he said, "father."

Arthur stretched his hand over his son's blond head and made the sign of the cross. His hand shook.

Knight, I am an experienced one. Give me the leave to go with Lohot.

Lancelot, who had been looking at us, said again, "I elect the mission, my love."

Gawin too had said, "And I, liege.

zon than one. Let me go. Ask Lohot.

30

Lohot and Kei did not remain in the City of Legions for the war games, but departed on their mission against Logrins at dawn of the first day. Their absence overhung the festival. The king paid his usual sober attention to the feats of his young men, and awarded prizes with words of praise and encouragement. Yet Gawin missed in his uncle the disciplined sense of pleasure with which he observed the growth of his best men.

Gawin took no part in the games of the opening day. This was a time for new-made knights and for squires nearing the end of their training. They competed in pairs, man against man. The squires carried blunted spears and were allowed to ride only one course. They were aware that they had no second chance to show off their skills before the king, and they galloped together furiously, each hoping to win the spurs with which Arthur awarded the judgement. The new knights were permitted to use true battle spears, and to ride two courses. To earn the notice of their sovereign they crashed at one another's shields as hotly as the squires.

On the second day the Round Table knights fought individual challenges. Gawin rode three courses against Lancelot's kinsman, Bors, who had been trying year after year to defeat him with the sword. In the final rush on horseback both men were unseated, and finished on foot. Feeling the pleasure of meeting an old opponent again, and being over-confident, Gawin pressed Bors too early, saw his sword fly out of his fist, and took a flat blow across the breast that felled him.

Bors stood over him, grinning. "This year, brother," he said, "I have learned from the defeats you've given me in the past."

"I was careless," Gawin said. "I ran into your parries too fast."

"You taught me last year, and the year before that, and the year before that, that you would run into my parries too fast." Bors picked up Gawin's sword.

Gawin gathered his legs under him and rose from the grass. "Do I show my weaknesses so clearly?"

"Ah, Gawin!" Bors handed him his sword, grasping it below the hilts. "No man can say you have weaknesses. You fight like a north wind full of hailstones." They moved together toward the king's pavilion at the edge of the jousting field, where Bors would receive his prize, a silver-studded bridle, from Arthur's hand. "Being impatient is your strength," he said.

"And my weakness." Gawin laid a hand on his friend's shoulder. "And in this I think you have interpreted my mind as well as my right arm."

The third day was given over to a grand tournament in which the Round Table brotherhood and its guests competed. The day began with a parade past the pavilions of the king and queen. The whole household marched: eight head porters who shared out the gate among them during twelve months; heralds and trumpeters; corps of foresters, huntsmen, fishermen, falconers, grooms, each led by its own chief officer; squires who were chamberlains of the bedchamber and hall; stewards and purveyors, smiths, saddlers, woodcarvers, masons, each corps carrying its own banner, even the physicians, even the priests and scriveners. Non-military officers wore buskins of soft leather buckled over the instep, embroidered frontlets, silk tunics, and brocaded mantles. Carls and freemen were dressed in trousers tied at the ankle, soft boots, broad leather girdles, linen surcoats, and short woolen mantles. Knights wore long capes over burnished battle armor, and rode on caparisoned horses.

Bedwyr, the captain of the tournament, took command of four bands of knights, Bleheris another four. Arthur put himself at the head of the ninth band, whose duties were to relieve men trapped by odds, to keep the battle within lawful boundaries, and to answer challenges offered them to engage in single combat. Squads of grooms and foresters were detailed to lead away riderless or wounded horses and to provide fresh ones.

At mid-morning the fighting men left the City of Legions and rode together to high, level ground outside the walls. Here the prize was displayed. Two forked stakes of polished wood were driven into the sunny sward, supporting a crosspiece of chased silver. A sparrow hawk was chained to this perch, its jesses jeweled and its hood ornamented with gems and gold embroidery and trimmed quills. If through three annual tournaments a knight carried off the prize Arthur awarded him a hawk each year thereafter for the length of his life. Lancelot had won his hawks, and so had Gawin, and so had Kei. Gawin said in the common room that Lancelot hadn't entered the games in order to give other men a chance at victory. But Kei denied he had gained his hawks through Lancelot's forbearance.

The trumpeter blew the order of ranks, and then the first charge. I will learn from the lesson Bors gave me and be a canny man today, Gawin promised himself. But at the shock of encounter he forgot his plan. Fighting with Bedwyr's men he grouped friends about him and led attack after attack, broke spears on shields whose blazons were as familiar to him as his own, wielded his sword in close quarters when plunging horses made calculated blows impossible, threw his weight into the defense of comrades who were giving ground. The crash of metal on metal, and sparks streaking from helms and hauberks entered his senses not as sound and sight but as clues to action. He heard his own shouts and the shouts of his fellows without knowing whose voice raised them. His mouth swelled with thirst, but he did not realize his need for water. His skin was scraped raw with sweat and dust, but he was not aware of his pain. He knew only one thing, that his body was the body of a crafty, embattled animal who must win or fall helpless. This is what it was to be schooled, this was twenty years of knighthood under proof. And at vespers when the end was blown he felt that time had stood still.

In the stunned silence of exhaustion the tournament companies returned to the City of Legions. Baths and medicines were prepared. It was late when they went in to meat, later when the king declared Bedwyr the winner of the hawk. Ale and the pleasure of retelling the events of the day revived the talk, and when Arthur rose to bid them goodnight the room was loud with argument.

By twos and threes they stumped into the common room. Gawin sat a distance from the hearth so as to avoid the sting of heat on his mauled legs. "I shall sleep like a pillar of stone tonight," he said to Yvain.

"I too, brother. You and I, we aren't as young as those gaudy young cocks who flapped out in their first armor this morning."

"A strange thing happened to me today," Gawin said.

Yvain cracked his knuckles slowly, one after the other.

"Stranger still," Gawin said, "I forgot it until we were sitting to ale in the hall. I remembered it like a dream just as Arthur was presenting the hawk to Bedwyr."

Yvain yawned so enormously that his jaws clacked like dice. "If you wish me to listen you must show a little haste. My eyes will shut themselves in another moment no matter what spirit revealed itself to you on the field."

"Oh, you would cackle out a joke with your head on a pike! I am only saying that once when I was unhorsed and being pressed by two men, a knight rode between me and them and drove them off. The strange part was this, that he was wearing a blazon I never saw before. What man who is not a friend would offer me his help?"

"A marvelous tale!" Yvain said. "A miracle!"

"I know the blazons of our Britons' shields, and I had

180

memorized the blazons of the guests and foreigners. I swear this knight was not of our company. He must have come up long after the combat began."

"What was the blazon?" Yvain said.

"No blazon, in fact. He carried a plain shield, but it was painted scarlet from top to bottom."

"Oh," Yvain said, "a red shield." And he hunched his shoulders and peered at Gawin out of eyes puffed almost shut with fatigue. "A plain red shield?"

"Do you know it?"

"I know it. It is Perceval's. The shield he took off the knight who stole Arthur's cup, it was plain red. And I am afraid your innocent from Norgals has challenged more man than he could deal with."

"No," Gawin said. "If it was Perceval's armor it was Perceval himself."

"You told me he has had no training in the skills of war. He would have to be madder than a loon to enter the Round Table games. Perceval has met a knight who hit him down and took his armor as a lawful prize, and then wore it to our games."

Never, Gawin thought, it was Perceval or it was a betraying demon. Perceval. I have missed him again.

31

WHEN GAWIN went in search of Merlin the next day the king's counselor was not in his quarters in the hall, or on the artificial island he had built in the river for his own use, or with the scriveners, or in any place where he was sometimes found. A boatman told Gawin, "I have not seen him since the King's Justice, messire, and I do not believe he returned to the City of Legions from the amphitheater." His failure to find Merlin was a disappointment that haunted him.

Through the following weeks knights who had met for the Whitsuntide assemblage departed, some to take up new duties, some to return to districts whose peace and safety were their concern. The crowds of sight-seers and petitioners thinned away too, with the minstrels and acrobats, the sick and the poor, who had profited by the royal distribution of alms. Gawin felt that Arthur's capital was an abandoned place. Yvain remained, and Lancelot, but Lancelot spent much time with the king.

"I am no man to get fat by the fire," Gawin complained to Yvain. "And if the king does not think of giving me leave himself I shall ask for a mission."

"Take some sport," Yvain advised him. "Me, I like nothing better than to dawdle beside the hearth, but I'll be energetic for your sake and go with you to join the hunters or fly hawks."

"No," Gawin said, "I am not in need of a time-waster."

Yvain studied him, then said, "Talk to the king, brother. Tell him the matter that weighs you down. You can trust him."

"I have trusted him since I was seven years old," Gawin said with a sigh. "But trusting him is not the same thing as begging him for favors."

"I think you doubt his willingness to show you comprehension less than you doubt yourself."

"I do not doubt myself," Gawin said shortly.

"Not your courage. But this Grail of yours, it makes you afraid you are seeing shadows. Go to the king. You will never be a contented man until you prove the cup, aye or nay."

"Would you join me, Yvain?"

Yvain shook his dark head. "It is not for me. I am older than you, enough older at least to live more comfortably if I do not have to worry out the final word on our lives. I am a shallow man, I like best to eat and sleep and handle a spear and watch a wild boar turn at bay. Grails, they embarrass me."

"I do not believe you," Gawin said. "You have not thought about this quest."

"I don't wish to think about it. Listen, Gawin, God makes rules for men. He deals with most of us at arm's length, knowing His secrets would crush us. But if a man is fit to hear His secrets, He calls that man. And this is why," Yvain finished, his face blooming with childlike faith, "I tell you to go to the king. Arthur will know, if anyone knows, whether God has started you on His Own mission."

Gawin was touched by the simplicity of the man with whom he had lived shoulder to shoulder so long. Yet I am a simple man too, he thought, Yvain and I were as alike as two hares until I rode into the country of Iglais. But now . . . Now I am mad. God does not call men of forty to show them His secrets. I will never carry this matter to the king.

A fortnight later Arthur sent for him.

Gawin asked the messenger, "Where is the king?"

"In his cell off the Round Table hall. You are to go there, messire."

"Are any knights with him?"

"One. The new knight, Bryant of The Isles."

The messenger, a page of thirteen, preceded him from the common room, across the empty, dark Round Table hall which had grown dead-cold, as far as the door of Arthur's private cell, which was let into the wall beside an armory for short swords and bolts and crossbows.

This little chamber was unlit by any window. In an iron sconce standing by the door burned a candle as thick as a man's wrist. The room was bare of all furniture save an oak prayer-desk, a clerk's stool, and the king's chair, which was barrel-shaped and carved around the base with intertwined beasts. Rushes covered the floor.

Bryant stood near the door with Arthur, who was saying, "Thank you for your care in this matter, Bryant, and we will consider it again tomorrow."

"At your convenience, messire." The big, gleaming knight could not resist giving Gawin an equivocal smile.

What an oily traitor he is, Gawin thought. He has crawled his way into the king's confidence in the time most recreant men would have needed to lick the wounds of their shame. What charms Arthur in men like him? Has he summoned me only to show me how much he trusts this tub of lies?

The king actually went to the door with his deposed governor. "Are you comfortable in your quarters?"

"Perfectly," Bryant said. "I am comfortable in my quarters and in my service too, messire, and," he said glancing over the king's shoulder at Gawin, who stood waiting to be greeted, "I count myself fortunate to have a sovereign whose mercy keeps pace with his judgement."

"God go with you." Arthur turned back to his chair. "Sit here, nephew." He gestured with his finger toward the stool. He was unarmed; indeed, he wore a plain brown robe without surcoat, and rawhide buskins. But on the wall above his chair hung a helmet, a shield, and his battle sword. "You are still displeased with me in the matter of Bryant of The Isles, I see."

"Lancelot says you have the gift of turning disloyal men into loyal men, messire." Gawin took his place on the stool.

"That is not quite an answer," the king said.

"If you demand an answer, messire, I think Bryant has shed his treachery more easily than a snake sloughs off its old skin. It is barely two months since he was led before you at Whitsuntide in chains."

"Besides, you dislike his bearing and language," Arthur said. "You speak one word where many men would speak twenty, Gawin, you can't feel confident of Bryant, who speaks twenty words where many men would speak one. Yet in all that speech he wraps some nourishing grains of truth."

"I am glad you find him wise, messire."

"Three 'messires,' nephew? We are at home here." His easy manner, his familiar dress, stirred in Gawin the memory of Iglais asking, Does the king ever have time to enjoy himself?

"What long thought are you thinking?" Arthur said.

"I ask pardon. Much has occurred. I mean much always occurs at the Whitsuntide assemblage."

"I am not satisfied with you," Arthur said.

A wave of humiliated blood rushed into Gawin's face. "If I have failed any duty —"

"No, no, I am not speaking of your duty. I am your kinsman, you are mine. Except Lohot, no one is as close to me as yourself. Why have you not told me what troubles you?"

The blood that had risen at his uncle's charge banged in his ears. He knew he was sitting as mute and awkward as a squire, but he could not choose among his tumbling thoughts.

"Merlin seemed to think you distressed yourself about the youth who drew the pillar sword. Perceval the Norgalois. I have sent for you in order to hear from you the story of this young man."

"I have told you the story, uncle."

"Yes, but not all of it. What occurred in that barren region of Norgals?"

To give himself time Gawin began, "The Knight of The Moors —"

"You have reported the Knight of The Moors. I do not wish to wring your confidence from you, Gawin. If this matter of Perceval is private beyond what an uncle can assume —"

"I do not know where to make a start," Gawin said. "We do not think of happiness, we knights who do your work. We think of peace and safety and obedience. But the lady Iglais, she thought of happiness. I do not know how to describe a happy human soul."

"Was it for the sake of the mother's happiness that you did not inform me of the murder of The Moors?"

"You know that?"

"The news was brought to me a day before you reached the City of Legions."

"Then why did you let Perceval escape?"

"You forget what happened," Arthur said. "He came into the hall when a stranger was raising an outcry. He drew the sword, he remained only a moment, he left. I did not know his name. I heard it only after you returned and told me."

"If I had followed him —"

"Yes," Arthur said, "perhaps you would have made him

your captive. You were armed and Yvain wasn't. But I did not expect Perceval to prevail against the stranger."

"You expected his death?"

"His death," Arthur said without a show of concern, "or that the stranger would ride away in contempt of the shouts of a wild boy. Do you wish me to admit my judgement was faulty?"

"The sword," Gawin said. "If you had told me the real nature of the sword —"

"Never mind that. Relate the whole affair of Perceval."

"I could not accuse him of murder after he drew the sword reserved for the best knight." Gawin rose and walked restlessly back and forth over the creaking rushes. "Even if the pillar was a device, too much had gone before." And, words bursting from him like blood from a wound, he told Arthur about the priest whose cross was engraved with demonic signs, and Peleur, the sick old man who guarded Christ's cup, and his kinsman Joseus, who warned Gawin of the cup's perils and concealed Perceval because he was of the lineage of Peleur.

"Why would Joseus, a holy man, deceive me if not to protect a mystery? And why was Perceval helped at every point, but at every point I was delayed? When I learned he had drawn the sword —" Gawin heard himself speak as though from a distance, "I believed I had been in the hand of a miracle."

Arthur creased the skirt of his robe into a short fold, ran his finger along the fold, smoothed it out. "I see, I see. And now you wish my leave to —" he raised his head and smiled the warm, rare smile that sometimes touched him, "you wish my leave to look between the fingers of this miraculous hand."

"Yvain ridicules me too."

"Yvain doesn't ridicule you, and I don't. I give you leave, Gawin. Go and find Perceval or Peleur or only —" he smiled again — "the lady Iglais. But I lay certain conditions on this mission. Men in search of miracles carry a contagion with them, an — a fever of purpose that infects others in ways it has not infected themselves. And in unprepared men it becomes an illness of the mind. Do you understand?"

"No."

"I mean," Arthur said with force, "that you must go alone. You must not din this Grail into the ears and hearts of your fellows. Particularly," he said, "you must not dangle it like a golden apple before Lancelot."

"I will not speak of it to any man."

Arthur opened his hands over either arm of his chair, leaned back, looked beyond Gawin at the nothing which was his private view. "And you must wait a while, nephew. Before you leave Britain's affairs behind I must send you into Logrins's country to —" he broke off.

"You wish me to protect Lohot?"

Arthur turned the stare on him. "Protect him? Do you question Lohot's prowess? I only wish you to go into Logrins's stronghold and — hm —"

"See that order is restored?"

"Yes," the king said. "See that order is restored."

32

IN THE CITY OF LEGIONS Gawin slept in the hall of Arthur's royal residence. This house had been the Roman governor's palace, a villa with a wide pillared porch, airy chambers, hot baths. Many of the pillars had been pulled down by war or fallen with age, the subterranean spaces were long decayed, and the gardens, though they were cared for, no longer showed the Roman splendor of walks and fountains. Arthur used the central block of the palace, which was still intact, but allowed the ruined wings and porticos to stand. These yellowed skeletons, Gawin thought, against which clean turf washed like sea against cliffs, were more beautiful in their desolation than they might have been in their glory.

On the morning after his interview with his uncle he emerged and saw the familiar masonry lying under the shine of a clear sky, with the bright grass spread about it. A man only beholds his home earth when he is happy, he thought. He moved toward the Round Table hall, thinking, on such a day as this any man but Yvain would be outdoors. But I'll find him hunched against the fender dreaming of ale and cheese. If I were as lazy as Yvain I wouldn't be able to lift my sword within a week, but he can drowse and eat and sprawl and gossip and then rise up like a freezing wave and sweep away everything before him.

He passed through the guards and porters. The chamber

190

of the Round Table had been allowed to grow cold after the assemblage, and for several weeks had been unlit. But as Gawin entered he saw old Ector sitting between two tall candles in the audience chair below Arthur's high seat. This was the place of the chief captain when he acted as Arthur's surrogate. A knight and a squire and two guards in the king's livery stood below him.

Gawin walked down the long room. He did not recognize the knight, who wore his mail, but whose helmet, shield and sword lay on the floor before Ector.

The king's venerable captain was speaking. "I accept your surrender in the name of Arthur. On your good faith, remain in the City of Legions and present yourself to the king in the morning."

The stranger said, "I will do that willingly."

"The guards will give you quarters. Now take your leave."

Gawin watched while the stranger was led away. He had seen such surrenders often. This was the way captives taken at a distance from the capital were made to submit themselves to Arthur. He said, "Good day to you, Ector. What knight of ours has sent his prisoner to the king?"

Ector smoothed his neat, small beard. It was snowy white, as was his hair, which he wore short, in the fashion of young men. "The stranger says he doesn't know. He says he was defeated by 'a good knight,' who spared his life on condition that he yield himself to Arthur. The 'good knight' wore a shield without blazon."

"What was the offense that brought the unknown knight down on him?"

"An uproar at a ford." Ector rose and moved the captured man's relinquished weapons together with the toe of his boot. "He says a knight 'appeared from nowhere' as he was waylaying a train of monks, though he maintains the monks had trespassed by cutting harvest on his field. He says the knight challenged him, then knocked him flat in the first charge. They fought on foot and he lost his sword after only two passes. He means it," Ector said with a dry grimace of amusement, "when he says he was beaten by a good knight."

"Why doesn't he know the good knight's name?"

"His captor refused to give it. He only said, 'Yield to the king or lose your life.'"

Gawin, in whose mind Perceval was always a presence, thought of the youth in red armor who had ridden away to prove his right to question the king concerning the nature of justice. This affair had the mark of his fearful directness. But Ector said, "It may have been Lohot. Lohot has felt shamed by being passed over when missions were awarded, and I believe he will try every feat he can find to try before he returns to the City of Legions. What are you doing here, Gawin?"

"I am looking for Yvain."

They walked together to the common room. Yvain was not huddled before the fire as Gawin expected. He bade Ector farewell and left the hall through the postern.

Two royal stables were maintained at the City of Legions.

192

One stood at the sally port of the Round Table hall, and housed horses suitable for use within the City, and mounts prepared for state excursions. The other was much larger, and occupied several acres in the fields beyond the postern. It housed heavy chargers and animals used in goods trains.

Gawin stopped at the domestic stables. "Have you seen Messire Yvain?" he asked a groom.

"He passed half an hour ago, and walked down the fields. I think he has gone to the armorer's."

"Saddle two horses," Gawin said.

"Will you and Messire Yvain ride together?"

"I want his help in picking a new charger. We will go only as far as the combat stables."

He moved on toward the smithy and forges of the royal armorers at the bottom of the fields near the city wall.

Yvain was sitting under an oak tree watching a smith work steel for a spearhead.

"At least," Gawin said, "I was right in thinking I would find you sitting down. Get up. Come with me to select a new war horse."

"Ah, the king has given you a mission at last." Yvain rose.

"I am to ride to Logrins's country to see order restored."

"Good, good! Now you will rub the rust off your spirits. Tell me, brother, did you speak to the king of your other matter?"

"One thing at a time," Gawin said smiling. "Logrins is enough for one man's hands."

"You look less disgruntled," Yvain said.

"I deny that I have looked disgruntled. Where is Lancelot?"

"I don't know. I haven't seen him today."

"Well, then, we must choose the horse without him." They moved up the long field toward the postern. "Though," Gawin went on, "in these days I think you and Lancelot and I and all Arthur's old friends would do well to stay together."

"Now what do you mean by that!" Yvain stopped and took Gawin by the sleeve and held him.

"I mean I do not like the way Bryant of the Isles has pushed himself into the counsels of the king. Just two months after Lancelot delivered him recreant, Bryant is cuddling up to Arthur as to a new-found father."

"Oh, come now, Gawin, you can never keep a cool head about Bryant. Arthur saved him for the sake of his shrewd counsel, remember."

"If Bryant continues to be received with more love than the king shows his tried friends, we shall have a misery here we've never had in the life of our fellowship."

"Spleen, spleen!" Yvain said.

"We shall have two parties, you and I and Lancelot and Ector and Bedwyr and the others on one side, Bryant and —"

"Stop, Gawin. Don't name our knights in any party against the king. If we trust Arthur, we trust his friends."

"All the same, before I leave the City of Legions I shall warn Lancelot. Bryant hates him. Lancelot must not forget that."

Yvain gave him an angry grin. "I never knew a man like you, Gawin. You have got to have a bone to gnaw no matter how fortunate you are."

33

THE MORNING of Gawin's departure was cloudy and unseasonably warm. In the vale of the river the air seemed clear, softly lighting the reaped fields above the north gate of the City of Legions, and deepening the colors of amber and rusted green on the gentle slopes. But beyond, where the mountains lay, the distance was blue and thick and without modeling.

Yvain, who was riding with him to the point where the road turned westward, said, "Today will be sticky, the weather will worsen."

"I believe you," Gawin said. "But the weather usually worsens in this dripping land."

"Autumn is a poor time to stick your nose into the hills, and I wish Lohot had seen fit to come home." Yvain nodded toward the flat wall beyond. "While your bones shake in the gales up there, think of me warming my shins in the common room."

They rode in silence to the milestone where Yvain was

to turn back. Moved by the emotion of parting, Gawin was ashamed of his doubts of Arthur and his sullen resentment of Bryant's preferment. He regretted too that he could not tell Yvain of the mission awaiting him after the matter of Logrins was settled, and he felt divided from the dark, homely man who had been his closest friend. Arthur's caution that seekers of miracles were possessed by contagion recurred to him, and with it a premonition that, if he lived to return to the fellowship of the Round Table, he would come home a stranger.

Yvain drew up his horse. "Rest easy about the king, Gawin. He knows what he is doing."

"It is not the king, it is — I mean, much has happened. And our lives run on in new directions."

Yvain grinned. "I know. This is the way a man's heart turns over when he buckles on a hard mission with his mail. God go with you, brother."

"I shall be back in a month," Gawin said, unable to find words. "God go with you, Yvain." And he wheeled his horse out of the Roman road onto the narrow trail that was to lead him into the vast, desolate uplands, where only outlaws and holy men found a living. He knew Yvain was watching him, but he could not bring himself to look back.

He rode west six or seven miles through tamed land rolling into pastures between low swells of forest. At length he struck a wider road running north almost parallel to the one at whose milestone he had left Yvain. And three hours after his departure from the capital he reached the junction of two rivers where a village hung on the slope under a tall, loaf-shaped hill. This village lay in the southern angle of a rough square of mountains. The main spine of the mass stood almost north and south, to the east great fingers of highland spreading like a hand. The range did not break into ragged peaks, but folded long curve on curve, blue, lofty, separated by round valleys or narrow glens. Trees marched up the slopes, crests peering above them. The domelike summits, made bald by winter wind and sleet, afforded summer grass for herdsmen hardy enough to drive their cattle to the dangerous solitudes.

Roads stretched like a necklace around the four sides of the mountain square, Roman to the south and west. But Gawin knew he had ridden all the highway he was to see until he found Lohot, or Lohot's grave. His business now was in the rising forests, in the swampy dales where head-high bracken and thickets of sycamore echoed no sound save water and storm and the voices of birds and wolves.

Under fee to Arthur the village was required to maintain a post for a royal forester. The quarters were a stout, thatched hut and a stable for two horses. Gawin found the place, dismounted in the dooryard, and cried, "Hoy!"

The forester in king's green appeared at the stable door. A dog walked out and stretched his head forward and winded Gawin.

"Good day to you," Gawin said. "I am here on king's business."

"Good day to you. Aren't you Messire Gawin?"

"I am Gawin. Can you find feed for my horse and time to talk with me awhile?"

"Yes indeed, messire. Come in." The forester's hut was warm and clean, furnished with a chair, a table, a sleeping pallet, and the puncheon stool that was always part of the gear of humble homes. A peat fire burned on the hearth. "Wash and rest yourself while I care for your horse." He set an earthenware bowl on the table and poured water into it from a wooden pail. "Will you eat bread with me?"

"Willingly," Gawin said.

The forester went out, and returned presently with the dog, which lay down and put its head on its paws. From an oak chest on the hearth he produced a dark loaf and a wedge of cheese. "If I had expected you, Messire Gawin, I would have made you a stew of venison. Me, I do not hunt for myself. When I am hungry for flesh I get a little fish from the monks, who have a pond at the end of the village above their house."

"You foresters who spend most of your lives in the woods believe deer are your brothers," Gawin said, breaking off a piece of the loaf.

"That is true, messire." The forester ducked his head in embarrassment. "We are used to thinking of them as creatures of the king. Besides —"

"Besides, you love them. Well. Bread and cheese are nourishing food."

"What mission brings you to my post?"

"I am going up there —" Gawin pointed to the mountains, "to discover what I can about the outlaw Logrins. Have you heard of him?"

"Anyone in this village has heard of him. He used to ride

down on us, and I have seen his men roaring into the village with lit torches, looking for treasure in the church. But many months have passed without his raiding in the near regions, and it is my opinion he has moved west to the mountains close onto the coast."

"Why west?" Gawin said.

"I have heard of a raider who troubles that land, though I am bound to say some men think he hides on an island in the sea. It could be Logrins, could it not?"

"Yes, if Logrins were the only outlaw in the world. Do you know that at Whitsuntide the king sent two knights to take him?"

"I know that. Messire Kei rode into the village and questioned me, just as you have."

"Messire Kei alone?"

"Yes, he was alone. He told me he and the other knight had agreed to ride one east, one west."

"When was this?" Gawin asked him.

"Soon after Whitsun, I am not sure of the day."

"And since then you have had no news at all?"

"None, messire."

Gawin considered it. "Soon after Whitsun" must mean that Kei and Lohot separated almost at the gate of the City of Legions — bad faith on Kei's part, since he had promised to ride with Arthur's son. He said, "It would help me if you can remember how close to Whitsun Messire Kei called on you. A week later? A fortnight?"

The forester leaned his elbows on the table and gave the

matter glazed thought. "I am trying to recall whether the cloudberries were ripe."

"Well?"

"The cloudberries *were* ripe, messire, I mean they were just beginning to be ripe in a few favorable spots. I remember, because while Messire Kei spoke with me two children of the miller came through my dooryard with a basket partly filled. If the cloudberries had been ripe everywhere their basket would have been filled to the brim."

"And when do the cloudberries ripen?"

"About a fortnight after Whitsun when Whitsun is as late as it was this year," the forester said in triumph. "There, Messire Gawin, I have remembered. At the earliest it was a fortnight after Whitsun."

A fortnight, too long, Gawin thought. Why, when he was still only three hours distant from the City of Legions, should Kei have needed a fortnight to appear at the village? "Since you have done well for me once, tell me which way Messire Kei rode when he left you."

"He said he was going to the west. The road runs northwest, and I suppose he meant he would follow the road."

But Logrins's country tended toward the east. Kei must surely have abandoned Lohot. And I must find out why, he thought. He rose. "Thank you for your help, friend, and now describe the best way to quarter these mountains."

"If I had to do it I would follow the valleys up to the passes."

Gawin questioned him about the passes, about caves and hidden glens, about fords across streams. The forester's knowledge was precise, for in these matters he was on his own ground. He named landmarks, calling off outcrops and blasted trees and waterfalls as though they were features of his dooryard. At last he said, "But remember, Messire Gawin, it is already autumn in the valleys, and in the high slopes it is almost winter. If you are looking for any man, even an outlaw, you will do better to hunt him where the weather helps and does not hinder."

"Thank you for your good counsel, your bread too, and your care of my horse. Now God go with you."

"God go with you. And I hope He will lay His hand between you and the cold and starvation up there." As though in benediction the forester leveled a finger at the slopes and slowly made the sign of the cross.

AT THE MILITARY STATION in the village Gawin provisioned himself with a roomy sack of the black bread that time hardened without spoiling, and the pale cheese made by every farmer in the neighborhood who grazed cows or goats and could reach a cave in which cheese would ripen. Slung from his back this was his baggage, this and his traveling pouch in which he carried coins and, like a secret plucked from the land of Iglais, the tear spoon he had bought from Luned's father.

He rode to the milestone where the road divided. The

old Roman road ran northeast, the other, an earthen trail, northwest. At the milestone he stopped to consider his course. Strike into the trackless hills, or act on the forester's hint that Logrins had gone to the sea?

My affair is here, he thought. Logrins has always been a cave-and-glen fighter, never a man for boats. I must quarter these uplands just as I expected to when I left the City of Legions. And if I do not find Logrins — or Lohot — that will be the time to go to the coast.

"We're for it, friend," he said to his horse, "and now I shall learn whether Yvain and I were wise to pass over the handsome animals with wide nostrils and big, moist eyes and small feet on slender legs." The beast was broad-chested, short-necked, and heavy in the flanks and withers. Gawin listened with satisfaction to the solid thun-thun of its hooves, remembering poems his father was fond of reciting in which horses flew with the speed of lightning and flung clods to the stars as their feet struck earth, manes and tails streaming like comet hair. He grinned, thinking, comet hair is less than useful when a horse has got to scramble down the perpendicular side of a ravine and dig his way up the wall of moss and rock chips on the other side.

He left the road and pushed into rising fields where the stubble of harvest had turned rusty pink. They quickly gave way to bracken, then to brush, then to small trees escaping the deep shade of the woods, then to old forest. Generations of fallen leaves choked the vines and blossoming wild plants that knit younger growths together. Lack of these weeds shortened the common food of birds, so that among the great trunks he missed singing voices. Or perhaps the year is too late for birds, Gawin thought, too late for any creature except a man on king's business.

The forest was dark, close and silent too, inhabited by a spirit of malign antiquity. Above him wind complained huskily among drying leaves. He had no path to follow, he could only pick his way, winding from slit to slit among the black boles, ascending always, orienting himself when he could by a shadow falling on a bare haunch of rock or athwart a trickle of water. He tried to hold a zigzag course whose direction would still be north, watching all the while for signs that riders, one rider, had gone before him. In the vast region ahead, crest upon crest, long eastward-thrusting outliers and valleys hiding between the masses, would he find vales where a lonely cottage squatted under the protection of a shouldering slope, a square of dooryard before it, a child, a dog, a few hens, and smoke rising softly from the hearth fire? "I doubt we shall see a thatched roof anywhere," he mumbled to his horse.

At times he heard rain above him, at times a few drops slid through the forest roof to sting his cheeks. He believed he had been riding for hours, that dusk had fallen. And when he saw warm gray light ahead between the trunks, when he rode out of woods whose edge seemed almost drawn by a knife and found open slopes brown and thick, when a cold wind charged him like an enemy from ambush, he was surprised to recognize that the hour was still afternoon.

"Well done, friend," he said to the horse. "You and I

are fair climbers. And I was right to choose muscles before grace. We'll go on until we can see where we are."

Below, the forest still closed his view, above, rugged slopes of frost-cured heather and whin, and still above, grass covering the crest like a brown-gilt fleece. Behind the mountaintop the sky rushed in a seethe of gray and purple, as though it were pouring into the next valley. And all around, the ground rolled into miniature ranges of ridges and shallow vales, strong-scented of water and stone and wet heather and the thin, clean air of height. In the bottom of one of these lofty vales he surprised wild deer grazing, and for a moment schemed to stalk them, but resisted. No need to kill for food until his sack of bread and cheese was empty.

The freezing air chilled his chain shirt, and he wrapped his cloak close. He thought, I'll stow my mail and trust myself to my leathers. Any man who keeps alive in these altitudes can't survive in Perceval's "iron clothes," and therefore I shall not be at a disadvantage if I ride without mine.

He stopped his horse, dismounted, laid aside his cloak and surcoat, and struggled out of the calf-length hauberk of linked steel rings which he wore over a tight leather jerkin and breeches. Shall I leave my mail on the heather like a fallen battle flag to say that a knight has been defeated by the weather? No, I'll live to need it one day. And he pushed it into the bag with his bread and cheese.

He did not remount, but led his horse, resting it and relieving his own weariness. He grew warmer at once in spite of the gnawing wind. The rain had passed on east and hung at his right in a dense, sightless wall. To the west he could see long yellowish glints behind the clouds, and at last small vents of blue.

The mountaintop seemed to move as he approached it, grassy reaches unfolding endlessly. Then without expecting it he gained a knob from which miles opened before him, stretched, empurpled curves whose crowns gleamed russet and gold and dark lavender. Eastward, vales formed what might have been bottomless chasms, so black they were with shadow.

He shaded his eyes with both hands and studied the view in all directions. There was no house, no man, no thread of smoke, no cattle, nothing but creased domes drowsing above forests, tending always north. Where in all this tumbled sea of earth was Lohot, the brave son of Arthur, on whose blond head no winter sleet had fallen until now? With a sense of doom Gawin thought of the Lohot who had been his squire, so hardy, so young, so at home in the comfortable life of his father's palace. If he had lived to cast accounts with Logrins, had he lived to escape this freezing silence?

"We shall not ride on north today," Gawin said to the horse. "We must quarter the west side of this mountain, down by nightfall, up again in the morning. Then the east side the day after. Does that please you?"

At sundown he was in a deep vale by a stream, black walls of trees above him. He chose a spot for camp that was out of the wind, a little bare earth under an overhang. He watered the horse, led it up and down the narrow banks while it fed, tied it to a branch. Himself, he slept in his cloak. In the morning he built a fire, warmed the aching stiffness out of his limbs, ate bread and cheese, drank from the stream. Unhindered by the weight of armor, he mounted from the ground.

They rode to the top again, choosing an ascent north of their descent of yesterday. The next day they performed the same maneuver on the eastern side. The day after, they dropped into the valley lying between them and the summit beyond. Again and again they ascended, descended, while days passed in a numbing pattern, one day, three days, a week, a fortnight, day and night finally running into a long ordeal, timeless — of motion, of cold and hunger and un-healing sleep, above all of deathlike solitude.

All horses have died but mine, Gawin thought, all men have laid down their lives but me.

And because he could not bear the void stillness through another heartbeat he shouted aloud. Over and over he shouted the word Joseus had cried in his dream, "Ask, ask, ask . . ."

35

ON A CERTAIN MORNING Gawin was leading his horse up a long, steep hillside, seeing below him the vale of a river. The low countryside seemed familiar, and it occurred to him that during a season of stormy weather he had lost his way and come south again. But if I am lost, he thought, the only cure is to keep moving. He decided not to ride down any declivity but to hold to the ridges. He was worn out with the laboring climbs and the wracking descents; moreover he had all but lost hope of accomplishing his mission. He had searched caves and glens, he had turned over the rotted ash of campfires, seeing evidence in decayed bones sinking into the earth that whoever had paused there to roast a hare had gone on a year ago. Now he longed to escape from the rugged trap of mountains and head westward.

I will give myself one day more, he thought, and if I find no trace of Lohot I'll go to the river road and follow it toward the coast. Seeing the watercourse from above, he could not be sure it was the stream that flowed finally into the City of Legions. Yet he believed it was, and the realization that he had circled and missed a destination oppressed him. These hills that looked so soft and bland from below seized the man who dared them with a kind of evil magic, stunning him with the muffling close of forests first, then, when he reached the crests, blinding his senses with rain and wind and the smothering hands of clouds.

I should have requested that the king give me the forester at the village, he thought, or I should have brought a squire, or asked Yvain to share this mission. But I am Gawin who never waits long enough to prepare, I am the knight who must prevail alone. And now I have failed with Lohot as I failed with Perceval.

Under the trees the light was aqueous and strange. This slope — whatever slope it was — was rough and difficult and very long. At a time he judged to be near noon he stopped to water his horse and let it feed beside a small lake lying in a cup of clustering knolls. His own provisions were gone. His supper of yesterday had been the last meat of a hare caught in a springe made of thongs and green twigs. Now he was too numbed with loneliness to care that he was hungry. He stretched himself on the mat of fallen weeds by the water and slept.

A breeze woke him, gentler and warmer than the winds that had worried him in the morning. He sat up feeling fresh and comforted, feeling too a renewed hope. His horse had finished grazing and was standing nearby as though it protected his rest.

"Come on, brother," Gawin said. "Let us not give up so easily. If something lies ahead, we'll find it."

Though he hadn't known it, he was within a few yards of the top. At the heathy crest he looked down an immense depth to a mountain-locked valley, hidden, remote, yet peaceful. The airy distance, the steeps, the homely promise of the vale overwhelmed him. For one thing, the meadow wore, miraculously, the green of summer. For another, he saw on its secluded floor what he took to be a house and a church. Sight of the quiet settlement shielded on all sides by sheer mountain buttresses wrung him, and he wept.

On the vale side, the slope seemed to have been cleared once, and was now overgrown with young trees and breast-high bracken. Gawin helped himself go down by grasping the brown ferns and skidding from tuft to tuft. His horse was uneasy, but it was also experienced, and it found its own footing, slipping and recovering as it threshed through the brush. At the bottom, two meadows divided by a low stone wall lay between him and the house. Gawin considered feverishly whether to delay long enough to put on his mail, but he could not. He mounted and rode swiftly across the fields, in which grazed a cow, a mule, and a goat.

The house was a well-built and rather large stone cell, the church a humble square structure of wood surmounted by a cross. An old man dressed in the brown shift of a hermit emerged from the cell and raised his arm, then laid his hand over his mouth in a gesture asking for silence. Gawin flung himself from the saddle and ran to the holy man and knelt before him. "Father, father, God has led me to you."

The hermit hastily blessed him, then said in a low voice, "Speak softly, messire, I have a man in the church who is sick enough to die unless Our Lord saves him."

"What man, father?"

"Come into my house. Will you do me the honor of eating bread with me?"

Gawin could hardly hold in his impatience through the formal courtesies of his host. Words crammed him, he wished to relate his own story, to hear his voice and the hermit's, to laugh with excited joy. But the hermit walked rapidly before him through the cell door, pausing only to turn and beckon him in.

The house was part dwelling, part stable. A curtain of hides divided the living quarters from the stalls. A peat fire burned on the hearth, an iron spit supported a kettle

209

above the embers, and a plain table and two chairs stood near the chimney. A few cups and pans and jars of dried herbs occupied a shelf beside the hearth. The end of the room opposite the curtain was filled with a stone cross under which lay the hermit's pallet.

The ancient man poured water into a pan and gave Gawin a towel. He was exceedingly tall and straight. Great white ruffs of brows protected his eyes, which were so deep-set that their color was only a darkness in his weathered face. The face itself was too gaunt for wrinkles, its severity relieved by an expression of patience.

While Gawin washed, the hermit led the horse into the stable, unsaddled it, and reentered the room by lifting the curtain of hides. Without words he began to cut bread and cheese.

"I have wandered through these mountains since early autumn," Gawin burst out. "I have been on a mission of the king. This is said to be the country of Logrins the outlaw, and I have searched him up and down the mountainsides and in caves and along streams and —"

"Forgive me, messire, I was about to carry a little milk to the injured man. I must be absent awhile."

"Let me carry the milk, father."

The hermit did not respond, only picked up a bowl and went out. He moved swiftly, like a young man.

Gawin felt rebuked. How could I have offended him? He doesn't understand the need I have, he is used to living in isolation, he forgets the sufferings of cold and silence. Gawin passed his hands over his head, making an effort to control his wild eagerness. He could not eat. He rose and paced the cell, counting his footsteps so as to calm himself and estimate the passing of the moments.

The hermit was absent through what seemed an immeasurable time, and when he appeared his face did not show what he felt about the condition of the man he cared for. He gathered his skirts about him and sat down, an orderly man who had accomplished one duty and was proceeding to the next.

"Have I welcomed you, messire?" he said, speaking softly in his throat. "You mentioned that you have had a difficult mission."

"I am Gawin, father. The king sent me to seek the outlaw Logrins. His son Lohot has been absent too long on the same quest."

"Logrins has ceased to trouble these mountains," the hermit told him.

"I believe that. I have seen no man, no sign of man, since I visited the village by the river." He wished to ask what the hermit knew of Logrins, whether he had heard the fate of Lohot, but found himself unable to put the questions.

"You will remain with me awhile, Gawin." It was not a query, but a statement.

"I shall be glad to rest before I ride toward the sea."

"Do you know me? We have met before."

"No," Gawin said. "I do not think I would forget you. It must have been long ago."

Finally the hermit smiled. "I met you in the north at your father's house when you were a little lad four years old."

Gawin half rose. He remembered, or seemed to remember, or dreamed, or imagined a day when this very face, lean and fierce and deep-eyed, bent above him. In that day of dreams the head had been dark and the breast covered with mail.

"Ah!" Gawin said. "I believe — I think — you said —"

"I said, 'When you wish to know, my child, you must ask . . .'"

"Ask!"

"I am the man called King Hermit. But in the world my name was Pelles."

36

AFTER A PAUSE in which not even the lapping of the hearth fire made a sound Gawin repeated, "Pelles."

"I have heard you were in my country, and I believed you would find me," the old man answered.

"Your son, the hermit Joseus, I spoke with him before Whitsuntide."

"I do not often have word of my son," Pelles said, still smiling his remote smile. "Does he improve in holiness?"

"He thinks much of his need to improve, messire." Gawin broke off, embarrassed. "Forgive me that 'messire.' It came naturally because you were a king once, and because," he said, "you still bear yourself like a king."

"If I have not outgrown the habit of arrogance you must

lay the sin to my old body, Gawin, not, God lets me hope, to my spirit. Is Davith with Joseus?"

"Davith was with him when I saw him in the west. Joseus spoke of you. I promised I would bear you his message if I found you."

Pelles looked up, surprised. "Did Joseus tell you where I hold my hermitage?"

Gawin tried to remember. "I do not think so. I asked him, and now it seems to me he did not reply."

The holy man nodded as though to some consideration of his own. "In our family it has never been a custom to send travelers from kinsman to kinsman."

Gawin's mouth was dry. He said timidly, "I know your sister Iglais and your nephew Perceval. And I have heard of your brother, Messire Peleur."

Composed, his hands clasped in his lap, Pelles took time for some intense communication with himself that seemed to add silence to the silence already in the cell. At length he said, "Are you ready to begin your search for my brothers, Gawin?"

"I am not seeking both your brothers, only Messire Peleur. The king has given me leave to find him, though I do not understand how you know. It was a secret between Arthur and me."

"Both my brothers, the younger and the older. You must seek both Peleur and Mortelle."

"Why do you give me this counsel?"

"Tell me first why you wish to reach Peleur."

"Because of the relic of your family," Gawin said, "Christ's cup."

"Do you mean the vessel called the Grail?"

"Yes, if it truly exists. Have you seen it?"

"I have seen it," Pelles said. "I have seen one of its aspects. It resided here in my church. When I was its keeper it appeared as a vessel in which lay a lance, and the lance bled new blood from its point to signify God's fruitfulness."

"But your sister, your son too, told me the relic was the cup of Christ's last supper."

"Its purest aspect may be that." The hermit laid a hand on his breast as though he had felt a pang. "My brother Peleur is more fit than I to be the keeper of Christ's cup."

"Your brother Mortelle, has he been its keeper?"

"No."

"Then why must I seek him?"

"Because he will try to prevent you from seeing it. And so it is better if you seek him than if he seek you."

Gawin fell into an uneasy silence. The religion of the old Britons dealt in aspects of their sacred Demons, he knew, and in secret studies that were said to carry disciples from lower to higher knowledge through perilous stages. It occurred to him that Pelles, living long in solitude, might have been tempted to pry into heathen mysteries.

"Do you see how green my meadows are?" the hermit asked him.

"Yes."

"Since the Grail left me they have never ceased to wear the good grass of summer whatever the season."

Gawin got to his feet. "Farewell, Pelles. Lead out my horse."

"Sit down," the holy man said.

"Your Grail is evil."

"Do you think God despises the grass of summer, Gawin? Do you think God is not capable of keeping two small meadows green if He wishes to keep them green?"

"I think God has set His seasons to work according to His just plan. I think He cannot be summoned like a field hand to alter the rules of His Own year. I think when men believe they can fetch summer untimely with the help of a Grail or any pagan thing, they have given their souls to demons."

"And perhaps you think too that demons, as you name them, are not God's creatures?"

"I am sure they are not God's creatures if I am sure of anything. I am sure they war against God."

"You young men," Pelles said, "you are certain of God! Are you as wise as God, Gawin?"

"I will leave this place, I wish to go away, let me have my horse."

"You are free to leave, your horse too. Will you allow me to saddle it? Will you accept my blessing? Will you take a little of my bread and cheese against your hunger this evening?"

Gawin fell upon his knees and covered his face with his hands.

"When you rode across my meadow a while ago," Pelles said gently, "you cried out that God had sent you to me."

"I had been alone too long, I had been beaten by storms, I was lost."

"Oh," Pelles said. "You were lost?"

"I had failed my mission."

"That too," the hermit said. "You had failed?"

"And I saw your green meadow lying at peace in the sun. And I thought I saw a miracle."

"On top of all, loss and failure, you saw a miracle?"

"Will you receive me, Pelles?"

"I am here to receive you," the holy man said.

37

GAWIN DID NOT RECKON the time he spent with the regal old man who was of the blood of the Grail. Later when he thought of it he sometimes believed it was days, sometimes weeks, or, it might be, years. Even as he lingered at the hermitage in the green and hidden vale time was unreal. And now and again he remembered how he had fallen asleep by the high mountain lake and been awakened by a warm breeze. Then he would ask himself whether the breeze were an enchantment ferrying dreams from old, unknown islands, from strange countries buried under the heights through which he had toiled.

Yet his hours were crowded from morning until night. He shared the common labor of food-gathering and housekeeping, he milked the cow and the goat which grazed in the two meadows, churned butter, chopped curds for cheese. Moreover he cleaned the stable, groomed and fed his horse and the hermit's mule. And day after day he walked with Pelles up the slopes, where they dug healing roots from the frosty ground. He had never before performed such labors, had never seen them performed save by lowborn carls. Yet they seemed a natural part of life.

Pelles would not permit him to enter the church and tend the sick knight, nor would the holy man answer questions about his guest. He took care of their religious needs by celebrating simple masses before his cross in the cell.

In the evenings as they sat at dusk over the hearth fire the old man spoke to him of the wonders of life in all the wild creatures of the forest, of their mating, and the birth of their young, and their death. The quick flesh, he said, the warm blood, were not mere gifts of God, but members of God Himself, and in their responses to heat and cold and fear and hunger and love they showed forth the very Body of God. But above all, death was God's purest shape, and until he, Gawin, beheld God die in the death of His creatures, and restore Himself in every fresh life, he would not understand the quest he wished to undertake, or accomplish it either.

And there was more, always more, revealed in Pelles's low speech as they sat before the fire. There was more too as they walked through the winter-struck heights; there were ordeals of instruction and observation and labor that wrung Gawin's endurance to its uttermost and left him gray with fatigue, even terror. He learned to look at a leafless tree,

217

a burst and dried seed pod, a frozen root, with the eyes of Pelles who, so Gawin came to believe, at certain times looked through God's eyes. Gawin would feel himself grow faint as he contemplated a withered beard of oats or a wild apple split with cold, perceiving in the seed they bore the seed of his own life, and the seed of God's life glowing in theirs.

"All this multitude," Pelles said, "is One. Life and death," the holy man murmured, "are One." And he would scatter a thin layer of ashes upon the hearthstone and draw the symbols of the Many and the One. He would draw the Holy Vessels of bread and wine, saying, "God enters into the blood and flesh which have experienced death, and they live again, being God."

"Learn," he said to Gawin. "Ask," he said. "Remember."

One early morning when the cold was deep and they could hear in the forest above their valley the crack of freezing branches, Gawin said, "Sometimes your teaching mixes itself with my mission, and I am afraid I have betrayed the king."

"You have not put your mission aside?" Pelles asked.

"I am the king's man. How can I put my mission aside? Moreover, Lohot was my squire, he was a brave man and he was dear to me."

"Your mission has not succeeded," Pelles said.

"I know, I know. But I should report that it has not succeeded. I am sworn."

The old hermit sighed. "Yes, you are a man who has sworn the king's oath. Yet the king knows you are more than a sworn man, since he has given you leave to seek my brothers. In this search for them, are you not sworn?"

"No," Gawin said, "at least not to the king."

"Now I shall be alone," Pelles said, "for after you leave me no other knight will find me before my life is finished."

It was the old man's way to speak of his life and death as parts of one existence, and the thought of his end did not move Gawin to pain. He said, "You will not be alone, Pelles. Your sick knight will be with you."

"My sick knight is gone. Did I forget to tell you?"

Now Gawin did feel a pang. Though he had not seen the man in the church, he had experienced him as a strong presence. The long struggle to live had overhung the green vale day after winter day, and many times Gawin had paused to stare at the church and think of the brave young soldier in whose flesh health contended so narrowly with death. Was he young, brave, a soldier? Gawin knew nothing about him, not one fact beyond the fact that he lay ill. Yet he had given him size, age, complexion, valor. And now he missed him. "When did he leave you?"

"I do not quite remember," Pelles said. "Perhaps it was a fortnight ago."

"But you have entered the church each day as though you still watched his cure."

"I have entered the church to say my prayers."

"You have told me many things, Pelles," Gawin said, "yet not the name or condition of the wounded man. Am I never to know?"

The hermit tucked his hands into the sleeves of his robe.

"He was my kinsman. A friend of mine — his too — sent him to me. On his way to my hermitage he was struck under the arm by a spear and overthrown. My friend, who was following him, brought him to me."

"Perceval, then?"

Pelles nodded. "Yes, yes, it was Perceval."

"And the friend?"

The hermit made a denying gesture. "The friend is not your concern, Gawin."

The sense of time rushed back to Gawin, the feeling of winter and snow on the crests and the long darkness of the days of weakened sun. Stirring within him like the effort of enfeebled muscles was the fear of enchantment. The smile of Pelles seemed equivocal, sly. He said, "You have been my teacher, old man, you have received me with generosity, you have shared your food and your house. In the name of the good things you have given me, tell me whether the friend of Perceval was Logrins."

"Logrins!"

"That is my question."

Pelles shook his wintry head. "Logrins, Logrins, he is only a growth of these hills, like lichen. No indeed, my friend and Perceval's was not Logrins."

"Will you tell me his name?"

"And if I don't tell you, what will you do, Gawin? Will you leave doubting me, will you go away believing my valley is an evil place?"

Gawin began to sweat.

"I do not need your answer," Pelles went on. "You will

misread me if I tell you, and distrust me if I don't. Therefore you must know that the name of my friend is Merlin."

"Merlin is Perceval's friend, and brought him to you?"

"I have known Merlin longer than you have been alive. Because you are young and he is old he seems to you only a weary fumbler. And I think you will not believe me if I tell you his wisdom is wider than the wisdom of most men."

Gawin stood still, hands on hips and head bent. He could not raise a single word to reply.

"Now," Pelles said, "we have finished our term together. It is time for you to depart. I will saddle your horse and fill your food sack. Go down to the river road and ride west before you return to report your mission. In a little while you will reach the coast, and there you will hear news of my younger brother, Mortelle. When you have done what seems best to you, go home to the City of Legions."

Gawin still stood silent.

"Shall I bless you, my son?"

Without willing it Gawin knelt and bowed his head to receive the sign of Christ's cross made by the hands of Perceval's uncle and the friend of Merlin.

38

HE DESCENDED from the high valley of the hermitage through a series of winding passes which Pelles described. The way out was less laborious than the way in, and avoided the long ascent and descent that Gawin remembered. He did not find the lake on whose bank he had slept, or the crest from which the view had opened, or any landmark he recognized. Moreover he reached the Roman road in so short a time that he could not believe the hold of Iglais's brother, whose remoteness seemed absolute, could be near at hand. From the road he saw above him glittering fields of snow. Yet while he was among the lofty slopes the paths had not been icy, and the air had blown mild.

However deceiving the winter was in the passes, it was plain on the downs through which the road pushed westward. Trees were black and bare, fields brown. In shaded hollows snow hid the depths and chilled the winds that blew across them. Cattle and sheep had been brought down from the mountain pastures, and only in an occasional field beside a farmhouse did he see any animal.

At noon he stopped at a royal fort, and, by a careful guiding of the talk of its garrison, discovered the day and the month. Among the familiar soldiers of the king he felt foreign, ill almost, like a man who has lain near death and lost all knowledge of daily circumstances. He learned that the date was midwinter as he might have heard news of outlandish islands where, it was said, men had but a single eye.

This strangeness drugged him with a curious kind of peace. He did not think of Pelles, of the time that had slipped away from him, of the evenings before the hermitage fire when he had absorbed the secret lore of his teacher. He did not even brood over the misfortune of having lived by Perceval as close as a brother only to lose him again. He rode on westward as though the jog-jog of a man in a saddle were the whole of life. Yet this peace was not blindness. His senses were alert to sights and sounds, he slept with a refreshing sleep and awoke with a sense of purpose whose nature he did not need to comprehend. As he experienced the cold, the raw winds, the fatigue and stiffness of the winter journey, as he watched over the well-being of his horse, sparing it the freezing shocks of fords and drifts, he seemed to be observing another man and animal. Once, after turning aside to find an easy stream crossing, he heard himself murmur, "So. They have passed this difficulty safely."

On the third morning he left the village of tinsmiths where he had stayed on his return from the country of Iglais. Here the Roman road divided. He followed the arm that continued southwest into the great promontory which formed the base of the bay of Norgals. Beyond the village the track was much decayed, and after half a day of riding Gawin could no longer see it at all. It had brought him to an estuary bitten deep into the southern coast, and there it ended in the scattered rubble and wall fragments that meant the Romans had once built a fort or camp on the spot. Perhaps, Gawin thought, this was the last mile of Roman road in Britain. Perhaps this was the final outpost of the imperial legions who guarded their captured country against raiders from the sea.

He pulled up his horse. The land was level and stood above the sea in a low plateau. The shore had been gnawed away by white-ruffed waves that ran upon it so close one might almost have jumped from crest to crest. The river had dug itself down too within its own stunted cliffs. Now at ebb tide it had shrunk, and frost or salt rime or some effect of light silvered its margins and spangled the wet shingle. Gawin stood still, considering the most favorable ground to cross. He said to his horse, "We shall stop for a mouthful of food and a little rest."

Since he was wearing his mail he did not dismount, but munched bread while the horse fed on the weather-cured sea grass. Presently he heard a rider approaching over the Roman road. He pulled up his horse's head, turned, and with bread still in his hand, faced inland. The rider was hidden by the ruins among which weeds stood tall. When he emerged from cover he was close enough to be clearly seen.

"Messire Gawin," he called. "I never thought I would find you riding with your hand full of bread and your helmet on your saddle bow."

"As I stand here, you are Davith!"

"Davith I am, messire. I was eating my meal in the ruin when you passed, and so I saw you before you saw me."

"I was never so willing to see any man as I am you," Gawin said. "Where is Joseus? With you?"

"No indeed, Joseus is at home in his hermitage. Or so I suppose. He has let me go, he discharged me of my service to him seven days ago this day." The squire spread his hands. "And so we must believe God has made him holy enough to shut his eyes to the use of the spear and the sword."

224

"What brings you to this place, Davith?"

"Perhaps I am going home, or perhaps I am sent to meet you, who knows such things? In any case, we have met. And I will ask you the same question. What brings you to this place?"

"I am riding on a mission of the king."

"Will you tell me what mission?"

"It is a long story, but the end of it is that I am hunting an outlaw who seems to have left his glens and caves back there —" Gawin pointed to the country behind them, "and come west to harry the villages from an island in the sea."

Davith nodded. "I believed this was your mission."

"Do you know Logrins, then? Have you heard of his raids?"

"Logrins? No, I have not heard of Logrins. If Logrins is your mission we are not speaking of the same outlaw."

"Oh," Gawin said. "The man who troubles this coast is known, is he? And his name is not Logrins?"

"His name is Mortelle. And though I would be glad if I did not have to mention it, he is a kinsman of my master Joseus." Davith took no notice of Gawin's frozen stare. "Yet I am sure you understand that in most families of good birth one member outrages the customs of men. Mortelle is the bitter apple in the fruit of the family of Joseus. To be plain, messire, he is a robber and a murderer."

Gawin rode close to Davith and caught his rein. "Tell me the truth. Were you sent to meet me?"

"No, no, it was only a manner of speaking. I have lived with a man of God so long that I drop into his language without considering it. Joseus believed God shifted him about like a chess piece, and so I said, 'It is meant that Messire Gawin and I should meet,' just as Joseus said it of you when you visited him at the hermitage."

Gawin drew a long breath. The dreamlike peace in which he had been moving was at an end. He let Davith's horse go. "Where is the island of Mortelle?"

"I don't know, messire, I have heard men say 'the island' as though only one island ever stuck its rocks above salt water. Will you go to it?"

"I will go if I can find Mortelle."

"Then spare yourself," Davith said, grinning at him. "He is gone."

"First you say he is on an island, then you say he is not. Which do you mean, man?"

"I mean he was on an island once, but is on it no longer. Didn't you hear the wonder they relate of him when you came through the village of tinsmiths? Every man in the place is longing to tell a stranger how Mortelle was chased away."

Gawin thought bitterly, in this I am again too late as I was too late for Logrins. He turned back from the estuary and began slowly to ride toward the Roman road.

"Will you not let me tell you about the knight with the white shield blazoned with a green cross?" Davith said.

"Yes," Gawin said dully, "tell me."

"It was this white and green knight who did battle with Mortelle. They say he was young and brave beyond the bravery of men, they say he was stronger even than Mes-

226

sire Lancelot. They say he lay hidden on the shore watching for Mortelle's boat, and saw it, and rose up and shouted his challenge across the water. Mortelle took him into the boat, I suppose he considered this would be an easy way to rid himself of an enemy. And they fought for hours together on the deck. They fought away the daylight and into the dark. Men say they struck each other such frightful blows that sparks flew from their armor and could be seen like stars by watchers on the shore."

"What blazon is a white shield with a green cross?" Gawin said. But he knew. Now he recognized Perceval. Now he had learned that Perceval always ran before him, in red arms or white, or lying unarmed and ill, or riding a mule, or wielding the sword of the best knight. Now he knew that Perceval's triumphs were the other face of his own failure.

"I asked the same question," Davith said, "but no one could tell me. All I can report is that the green and white knight called Mortelle 'kinsman,' and cried that it was a shame against heaven that they were of the same blood."

"What was the outcome of the battle on the raider ship?"

"It was a draw, a kind of draw, at least. Mortelle was wounded, but not the green and white knight. Yet the knight was flung into the water and would have been dragged under by the weight of his mail except the sand formed a shallow spit, and he waded ashore. No one knows where Mortelle went. Some men say he sailed away to the north. Everything is said, even that he has a kinsman in the north against whom he wages a war. Yes," Davith told him

227

wisely, "everything is said, but nobody knows the truth. As for the green and white knight, he is gone too. They say he is galloping north to fight Mortelle again. But this is more tale than needs to be told. I say that he is gone and that I have related all God will allow me to call truth.

"It is a wonderful thing to live with a holy man," Davith finished in high good humor. "And if I have the luck to see my master Joseus again in this life I shall tell him God plays chess with squires too, and that today on the south coast of Norgals He moved me face to face with you, messire."

39

"WHERE WILL YOU GO when you leave the estuary?" Gawin asked Davith.

"Home to see my old father, if he is still living. I have not been at home these five years."

"What place is home?"

Davith pointed southwest toward the sea. "My family lives on the coast, messire. It is a good land, good for vines and grain. We have a fish pond and an orchard of fruit trees, and the grass is the best in Norgals. Will you ride with me and be my father's guest? You will be welcome."

"No," Gawin said, "but I am grateful. I was thinking of asking you to come with me."

"Where to?"

Gawin paused. His will ran this way and that, unable to decide.

"But I suppose," Davith said, "that you will return to the City of Legions, now you no longer need to hunt Mortelle off this coast."

"Yes," Gawin said, relieved that Davith had chosen for him, "I shall go back to the court."

"It is a long ride, messire, and I am near home. In half a day I shall see my father. And unless you require the service of a squire —"

"No, no, I only lack company. Go on to your home."

"Thank you, and God go with you."

"And with you, Davith."

Gawin watched the servant of Joseus ride inland around the shallows of the estuary and pass from sight under the cliffs. I must either believe that God is moving me like Davith's chess piece, or I must deny it, he thought. If I am to believe, Davith has been the instrument setting my destination. If I am to deny it I must ride back to Arthur in any case. "So, friend," he said to the horse, "we shall go eastward by the Roman road."

He returned to the village of tinsmiths, and the next morning began to retrace the journey he had made before Whitsuntide. He passed from fort to fort, from church to hermit's cell to house of monks. A cold wind blew at his back, snow fell on him in the passes, the frozen road made his horse's hooves ring. Yet he hardly noticed the weather, only pushed slowly forward as though the element of a soldier were hardships he could no more question than a fish could question the sea.

After the hour of vespers on the third day, when dark had already thickened, he reached the City of Legions. The north gate was closed, and Gawin could see the small light of a candle in the slit of the archer's window at the top of the gate tower. He struck the massive oak of the fortresslike City door with his spear.

The sentry emerged from the tower and stood on the wall. "Who are you, messire?"

"I am Gawin."

"Are you alone, messire?"

"Yes, I am alone, and if you doubt I am Gawin send a squire to fetch Messire Yvain." He considered this a rebuke.

"If you are Gawin I am sorry I must keep you waiting. I will send a horseman to Messire Yvain at once."

"Nonsense, man, someone on your post will know me."

But the sentry had left the wall, probably, Gawin thought, to descend the inner stair to the garrison at the base of the tower, where a mounted troop was always stationed. He rode restlessly back and forth, keeping his horse warm and easing his own angry impatience. The sky was black and gleaming with a frost of stars. He heard no sound outside the wall, none from within. The cold silence, the blind dark, seemed to have an effect on time, and Gawin believed an hour had passed before he heard himself hailed from the tower.

"Hoy!" Yvain's voice called him. "Are you Gawin?"

"I am Gawin, and never before in my life have I been kept standing like a suppliant before this wall."

Yvain laughed. "Gawin it is, captain, I know him by his wrath. He is safe, he will not burn the city over our ears. Admit him."

Presently Gawin heard the sound of chains, a turning winch, and the grate of iron-shod bars. The portal moved slowly, like some immense, cold-blooded animal, opening a slit wide enough to pass a horse and man.

Yvain was waiting, mounted. "I did not believe the guard when he said it was you. I am glad you have come home, brother." He leaned from his horse and took Gawin by the shoulder. "Are you whole?"

"I am whole except in my temper. What is this folly of refusing me passage?"

"I am sorry, messire," the captain said uneasily, "but I can only obey my orders."

"Come on, Gawin," Yvain said.

"First I will question this captain who locks out king's knights."

Yvain said, "Not now. Come with me." And he turned his horse and trotted beyond the military compound by the gate.

Gawin overtook him. "Why were you so tender of the captain's feelings, Yvain?"

"He was only doing his duty. Besides, I have much to tell you. And besides that, I was never so willing to see you in all the years we have been soldiers as I am this moment."

Gawin's anger began to clear. The familiar bulk of

Yvain in the dark rid him of silence and mystery and the prison of long solitude. As they rode together into the City he felt the homing sensation of never having been away.

"You were gone an age of months," Yvain said.

"It has seemed long to me," Gawin said, "until now."

"I suppose you have been thinking how you will shed your mail and wash away the miles and sit to ale," Yvain said. "But will you delay awhile?"

"Yes. Why?"

"We need to speak together before you tell your story in the common room."

"Is there trouble, Yvain?"

"I think we will go to The Frank's, if you are satisfied."

They walked their horses side by side. The Roman road ran through the City of Legions, but Yvain turned out of it into a lane so narrow it was no more than a byway for men on foot. It was crooked and dark and full of the smell of filth, even in the freezing cold. They rode single file, trusting their horses. Finally the alley turned sharply to the right and ended at a cobblestone yard before the doorstep of a thatched house.

This was the hold of a foreigner known as The Frank. He had been a sailor once, and now he lived by petty deals in hides and tallow, by dispensing bad ale to servants and squires looking for excitement, by a small trade in the goods of pickpockets, but particularly by offering privacy to men in need of it. Gawin had known him for twenty years. He was tolerated in the capital because he was useful.

They dismounted at the horse trough which did double

232

duty as a mounting stage. Yvain knocked at the door with the hilt of his short sword.

The Frank opened to them, holding a candle in a tin sconce. He was so nearsighted that his squint buried his little eyes in rolls of pasty flesh. He wore an unbelted shift of coarse brown stuff which sank at his chest and bulged over a soft paunch. A ruff of long, floating white hair around a bald dome gave him an odd, priestly look.

"Good evening to you, friend," Yvain said.

"Ah, Messire Yvain. Good evening to you. Will you honor my house by coming in?"

"Good evening, and I have not seen you for a while," Gawin said. "Do you know me?"

"Perfectly, Messire Gawin. Almost every holy day I watch you riding with the king on the street of the Roman road."

"Can you give us a quiet corner?" Yvain said. "And see that our horses aren't stolen?"

"Yes, indeed, messire, I am alone tonight, this being Christmas Eve."

"Christmas Eve," Gawin said. "I lost count of the days."

The Frank shuffled before them into a snug, small room where a fire burned on the hearth. From the ceiling beams hung cups, dried herbs, strings of onions, cured hides, horse bridles. An ale cask stood on a puncheon, and beside it a table was spread with a loaf of bread under a white cloth and a wedge of pale yellow cheese.

"If you require a meal," The Frank said, "I can give you a boiled fowl. I was cooking it for my Christmas dinner.

Or you might prefer a dish of cold mutton and onions."

"I have eaten," Yvain said.

"I shall try your Christmas fowl," Gawin said. "I have seen rather more cold mutton and onions than I care for."

The Frank served them, drew them a pitcher of ale. "Now, messires, shall I leave you?"

Yvain laid coins on the head of the ale cask. "God go with you, old man. I'll knock on the floor when we need our horses."

The Frank toddled away, his soft buskins slip-slopping across the floor rushes. His white hair swayed like a nimbus above the candle.

"It is good to see you scowling at me across a mug of ale," Yvain said.

"It is good to see your ugly face grinning because mine scowls," said Gawin.

40

WHEN GAWIN had picked the bones of The Frank's Christmas dinner he said, "I was too hungry to wait for your news. What mischief has fallen in the City of Legions, Yvain?"

"First, tell me what you learned of Lohot."

"I learned nothing. I rode up and down and across Logrins's country, I asked everywhere I met men, I searched for his grave. And nobody could tell me a word."

"What do you believe?" Yvain asked him.

234

"I believe he is dead. No man can disappear so wholly even in the mountains. All the while Logrins was troubling us we knew this or that about him, we saw the smoke of his fires on one ridge when we were riding on another, we found herdsmen who had watched him drive off their cattle. But Lohot, he is gone."

"I agree with you," Yvain said. "And I did not need your news to persuade me he is dead."

"My mission was a failure. I did not find Logrins, either, and only once, the very day I left the City of Legions, did I discover anything of Kei."

"Kei is here."

"Is he! When did he return?"

"In the late autumn, before Allhallows."

"How does he explain the absence of the prince?"

"He says after they had ridden together a week or more Lohot wished to continue alone," Yvain answered. "He says Lohot insisted they separate, one to ride east, one west."

"And I do not think this pleases Arthur. The king expected Kei to stand with Lohot throughout. It was Lohot's first mission."

"But Kei came home with the head of Logrins preserved in lead and presented it to Arthur."

Gawin smote the tabletop with the flat of his hand. "I heard everywhere that Logrins had left the mountains and gone west. Why didn't some herdsman or forester know Kei had killed him? Where does Kei say the killing took place?"

"In the wild mountains, he mentions a vale, a swamp,

beech and sycamore trees. But he says clouds wiped shadows away and he lost himself and cannot be sure just where he was. But the head, Gawin, the head was Logrins's head. Arthur recognized it."

Gawin brooded through a long silence.

"What are you thinking?" Yvain said.

Gawin beckoned him forward and put his mouth close to Yvain's ear. "Listen, Logrins had disappeared long before Allhallows, I heard it wherever I heard anything. What if Lohot met him almost on the day he and Kei separated? And what if Lohot killed him? And what if Kei discovered Lohot bearing home Logrins's body? Lohot trusted him, it would have been easy for Kei to —" Gawin looked over his shoulder at the arch through which The Frank had departed, then raised his finger and ran it across his throat. He went on in a rapid mutter, "What was Kei doing until Allhallows? If he had two bodies to hide he would need time alone."

Yvain shook his head vehemently. "No, no, too many ifs, Gawin. Besides, what had Kei to gain? Even if Lohot caught the outlaw it was no disgrace to Kei."

"Do you believe Kei's story?"

"No."

"Neither do I. If it isn't true, what is true? What fits the facts we know? Tell me what Arthur believes."

"He rewarded Kei, he gave him two castles and a village and a toll bridge."

"And you still think Kei had nothing to gain!"

"Ah, Gawin!" Yvain said.

"I do not understand why Arthur doesn't suspect him. His story is as full of holes as a fowler's net."

"No it isn't. You underestimate Kei, Gawin. Let me tell you something. Through the autumn and winter we have had a stream of defeated men trickling into the City of Legions to yield themselves to the king. All relate the same story. They were caught in some unlawful act large or small by a knight without blazon they call 'the good knight.' The good knight does not tell them his name, only pounces out and upends them in a furious charge, then flails them with his sword, then orders them to hand themselves over to Arthur or die. The king has faith that this boisterous conqueror is Lohot."

"He is not Lohot," Gawin said.

"But he is a mighty comfort to Kei, let me tell you. Kei praises him to Arthur, speaks of him always as the prince, blows on the king's pride with each new arrival. Kei receives the beaten men and says to them, 'Lohot, the king's son, overcame you, he is the best knight of our fellowship.'" Yvain tipped up his chin in a haughty gesture, staring above Gawin's head. His mimic of the seneschal bore the perfection of long observation.

"Why does he make such a point of the good knight being Lohot if he hasn't got something to hide?" Gawin said.

"At least it works."

"And why does Kei receive the captives? That is Ector's duty. Ector is the king's chief captain."

"No longer. Ector is displaced. Kei bought the post of chief captain with the head of Logrins. And this is why the closing of the gate is tightly enforced. Kei wishes to know where men are."

"By God's body!" Gawin said. "Tell me why, with you and Lancelot and Bedwyr in his service, the king should make a murdering animal like Kei his chief captain!"

"I have told you, I am telling you. He believes Kei rid him of the only man in Britain who has successfully defied him. Besides, Kei comforts him with the faith that his son overtops us all in knighthood. These are profound services, they are worth a fee."

"Not to Arthur," Gawin said. "His judgement can't be tricked by any malicious dog with a lust for preferment. He is a king, a sovereign. He knows men."

"He is also the father of Lohot, and in his heart he is afraid Lohot has lost his life." With a drop of spilled ale Yvain drew a bearded face on the tabletop. "I seem to remember you questioned his judgement in the matter of Bryant of The Isles."

"Bryant had proved himself a traitor."

"You were right about Bryant, Gawin. Bryant is Kei's man now. He and Kei are a party of two. They study the king as though there is no subject in the world to study but the king. They know almost before he does what advice he will seek and what answer he wishes to hear. And they are ready. We old soldiers," Yvain said, rubbing his ale picture away with the back of his hand, "we are babes in policy. We do our duty and we believe we have done enough. But this pair of rogues have devised something new. They have learned how to flatter a man who despises

238

flattery, how to weaken strong places in his soul and destroy weak ones." He looked up, his unhandsome face scarred into long wrinkles of grief.

"I will not believe it," Gawin said. "Arthur — I have sometimes thought he defended Bryant only because the distrust of his knights offended his pride. He is entitled to pay off a score now and then. As for Kei, he has always indulged him as men indulge willful sons. But he would not, he cannot set Kei ahead of you and Bedwyr and Lancelot."

"And yourself," Yvain finished. "But he has."

"What does Lancelot say?"

"He says nothing and he will never say anything. Lancelot will go to his death with his loyalty unlessened by so much as a raised eyebrow."

"Yes, but he must think thoughts when he looks at the work of Kei and Bryant of The Isles."

"What Lancelot thinks is of small account these days, Gawin. Kei and Bryant have considered him as carefully as they have considered the king. And they work without sleeping to remove him from Arthur's love."

Gawin spat into the floor rushes. "No man can remove him from the king's love. Arthur would no more turn his back on Lancelot than on Lohot."

"Our scoundrels have a convenient poison to sicken the king with." And without voice Yvain formed the word *Guenivere*.

"No, no, no, whatever Lancelot may feel, his conduct has been as clean as innocence."

"But a husband with a beautiful wife can be pulled this

way and that by suspicion, especially if the suspicion is nourished under the pretense of sorrowful necessity."

Gawin rose and prowled back and forth under the low ceiling beams. "Listen, Yvain, if what you say has gone far enough to become a truth, I mean to stand with Lancelot. I would rather exile myself than stare in other directions while traitors pull him down."

Yvain nodded. "We owe our loyalty to the king, but to a king who upholds his faithful men."

"I did not say I would put off my loyalty to Arthur. We have served him too long, we are his. I only said I would exile myself if —"

Like a man whose endurance has suddenly reached its end Yvain sprang from his chair and seized Gawin by the arms. "If what, brother? If Arthur imprisons Lancelot?"

"Imprisons, in God's name!"

"This is what is whispered at court. The jealous men, they run after Kei and Bryant, they clamor in words Kei puts into their mouths that the purity of our sovereign's house must be defended. They are the swine who squeal that Lancelot must be put in chains."

Gawin said, "The king would need to be wood-mad to put Lancelot in chains."

"Yes," Yvain said, "he would. Ask Kei what drives men wood-mad and he'll tell you, 'Their wives and sons.' "

 *41*

ON CHRISTMAS MORNING Gawin went to the knights' church to hear the bishop conduct the mass of the holy day. He entered early in order to say the prayers of thanksgiving for a safe homecoming, but more than this, to see Kei and Bryant and Lancelot and Arthur before they saw him. He did not know what other members of the Round Table fellowship would attend, since many were absent from the City of Legions. It was not the king's custom to call an assemblage at Christmastide.

The church was cold, and save for the candles on the altar it was dark. Gawin knelt on the freezing pavement and quickly ran through the prescribed phrases, then rose and stood with his back to a column. The dim interior, breathing old odors of wax and incense and stone, quieted the restlessness which had kept him awake the better part of the night, and moved him with the feeling that the teachings of Pelles were growths still so new in his spirit they could wither in the heat of wrath and surprise and the passion for action. He called the figure of Pelles before him, seeing the old man draw out his lessons in the ashes by the glow of the hermitage fire. God's purest shape is death, Pelles had said. This flesh dwelling in the food of the mass, this blood dwelling in the food of the mass, have experienced God's death, and are restored to life, being God. The mighty sentence fell upon Gawin with meaning as clear as light.

But at that moment a priest bearing the cross entered the church, followed by Bishop Bedwin and two deacons, who carried tall candles. Arthur and a small band of body knights walked behind them, then Kei, then Bryant of The Isles, then old Merlin scuffing along, his hands tucked into his sleeves.

In the candle flicker the rich colors of the bishop's robes gleamed like wine. He wore a long white shift embroidered above his feet in a heavy rectangle, over it a knee-length purple gown of watered silk edged with scarlet and pearls, and finally a draped blue cape of double silk lined with gray fur. A white linen cap broadly banded with gold covered his tonsure. Wrapped in all these fine things his heavy body waddled forward with immense dignity, his jewels and gilt fringes casting rainbow glimmers. Remembering Pelles in his worn brown shift and rope girdle, Gawin watched him, feeling he was in a foreign country.

From the shadow of the pillar he peered at the tall, graceful man who was his reason for life. Arthur's face was unreadable seen in the dimness from the side. Yet the long, firm stride, the inflexible back, the bare, sand-brown head inspired in Gawin a wave of awe and love, a sense that whatever seemed to be wrong in the kingdom of Britain, nothing could remain wrong.

Kei and Bryant revealed themselves no more than the king, and only Gawin's revulsion invested them with new and insulting arrogance. Kei, who usually affected plain, dark woolen tunics, was luxuriously dressed in a stiff silk surcoat worked in many colors. Bryant contented himself with a modest blue robe and dark green cape. Not ready yet to play the conqueror openly, Gawin thought. The group proceeded to the front of the church, knelt, rose, and stood waiting for Bishop Bedwin to begin.

Gawin clung to his pillar. Several knights entered and moved toward the party of the king. When Yvain appeared Gawin stepped out and gestured to attract his attention. "Where is Lancelot?" he muttered.

"Just coming in with Ector," Yvain told him.

"In nomine patris, et filii, et spiritus sancti," the bishop intoned.

If Lancelot entered the church he did not advance as far as Gawin and Yvain. Gawin tried to fix his mind on the service, but his thoughts would not settle. I will speak with him outside the porch, he said to himself, unless the king delays me, and if I am stopped by Arthur I will speak with him in the common room.

The familiar Latin rolling about the almost empty church fell upon him with an uncomfortable sense of strangeness. He was nudged by memory after memory — Joseus kneeling above the felon captured by Davith, the priest of Iglais saying, "Aren't my parishioners beautiful this morning?," the monks' cooking house whose earth had given up the pagan tear spoon, the lonely wayside crosses by Roman roads, their arms enclosed in stone circles engraved in the delicate spirals of the old Britons, and the older wayside stones made mysterious by the lost letters of the druids. He thought of Iglais slipping into the chapel cell at dawn on the day of his combat with The Moors, a blue veil over her head and her eyes swollen with weeping.

The bishop placed the palms of his hands together, spread them, said, *"Oremus, fratres."* Oh, Iglais, it seems a year of lifetimes since I saw you first sitting at peace before your embroidery frames! In those cold mountain months I forgot you again and again, yet I know I have never forgotten you. Iglais is a woman who lies within my spirit like my own name. I forget her this moment and that moment, and the very forgetting is a promise that she is always with me. Will she welcome me when I return at the beginning of summer to do battle with the brother of The Moors? And will she forgive me because Perceval is not with me?

Crowded with memory, his will not yet bound to any purpose, one moment longing to depart on his quest, the next vowing himself to stand with Lancelot against Kei, he heard the bishop's prayers as a sick man might hear through his weakness the phrases of absolution. And when the service was finished he felt relieved of an ordeal.

"Welcome, Gawin," Arthur said as they emerged from the church. "I learned last night that you had returned."

"It was late, messire, between vespers and compline, beyond the hour when you receive homecoming knights. But I was satisfied that the sentry at the gate would report me."

No visible sign had altered Arthur's appearance, yet it was altered. He said, "I will hear what you have to tell me one day soon, nephew. I will send for you."

"You know why I have nothing to report of the outlaw

244

Logrins," Gawin said, and glanced at Kei. The seneschal stood a little distance off, staring fixedly over the king's head.

"Yes, I know." Arthur brought his gaze back from his private landscape and offered Gawin a smile. "How are you? Winter missions thin men out."

"Not me, messire, a little wind only seems to tan me into leather."

The king stretched out a hand and dropped it heavily onto Gawin's shoulder. "I know, I know, you endure like a stone. God go with you, nephew. Hold yourself ready to speak with me." And he let him go.

"Greetings, Gawin," said Kei, making it clear he was doing a duty.

"Kei, greetings to you. Though I didn't hear it from your sentry, I have heard the wonders you performed on the mission you shared with the prince."

Kei's face pinched itself closed, like the face of a man who thinks more than he says. He made no reply.

The king's party passed on. All this while Bryant of The Isles had said nothing, only stood by meekly, appearing to be present by accident. They know, Gawin thought. I have put this pair of rogues on notice that they are at war with me.

"We may still find Lancelot in the common room," Yvain said. "I believe he took himself away while the bishop was droning his last *benedictus*. Lancelot does not push himself before Kei's eyes oftener than he needs to."

"I have been gone four months," Gawin said, "and in four months Arthur has changed."

"How changed?"

"It is hard to put words to it, Yvain. You said last night that in his heart he fears Lohot is dead. Just now when he took me by the shoulder I saw his fear."

Yvain's mouth was set. "Yes, I have seen it. The look of fear, even Arthur can't hold it off."

"I could not make myself believe last night that Lancelot is in danger," Gawin said. "I fought my blankets until after I heard the bell of lauds, and I could not accept it. Now, when the king looked at me, I understood what you were telling me."

"You know what a boar does when it turns, brother. It attacks whatever is nearest, a tree or a stone even. I have heard old hunters say," Yvain mumbled as they crossed the frosty church lawns and moved toward the hall of the Round Table, "that a boar at bay will gore its own flesh."

42

WITH YVAIN he waited in the common room, but Lancelot did not appear.

"I hoped he would speak with me," Gawin said.

"He stays by himself," Yvain answered, "and I suppose this is because he does not wish to turn his friends into a party against Kei."

"When I come home from a mission I begin to think of his greeting while I am still riding up to the gate."

"What do you plan to say to him?"

"Oh — warn him, tell him I will always stand with him."

"He knows, he knows." Yvain stared into the fire with a sad grin. "He knows his friends. As for warning him, it is useless. He is not a fool, he is aware of the situation with Kei, but I told you last night that he would let himself be locked into prison before he would defend himself against Arthur. For some men, loyalty and the consciousness of innocence are all the defense they wish."

After a long silence Gawin said, "What shall we do to celebrate the holy day, brother?"

"We have already repeated our prayers. This evening we will take our meat at the king's residence. Meanwhile I propose to keep warm by the hearth."

"What a sluggard you are! I can't squat over a burning log through all those hours before meat."

"Sit down, be still. You have surely walloped yourself through enough winter weather to earn an idle day."

But Gawin was too restless to follow Yvain's advice. As he stumped back and forth it occurred to him that Merlin would know whether treachery was plotted in the City of Legions — if he could be found, and if he would talk of what he knew. He said, "Should Lancelot look for me, tell him I have gone to the scriptorium."

He wrapped his cloak about him, stopped at the light arms dépôt beside the Round Table chamber, chose a short sword in a chased scabbard, and buckled it on. In the porch the wind raked him, and he raised the cowl of his cloak and drew it tight around his chin. He passed through the guards, who wore sheep-lined cloaks in the hopeless attempt to turn the cold before it chilled their mail, paused at the mounting stage, then decided to walk to the scriptorium, where brothers trained in the art of lettering copied manuscripts for the bishop's collection of sacred works.

The monks attached to the court maintained a series of stone buildings standing one against another: a church, an oratory, dormitories, a refectory and kitchen, a dispensary where the poor were fed and medicined, an armory, a library, and the scriptorium. The whole complex was built in the shape of a cross. One of its arms housed the library and manuscript room, which opened onto the lawns by their own oak door.

Gawin entered the library. Wan sunlight showed him a few precious parchment books chained for safekeeping to their lecterns, and rolls of vellum in cases on the walls. The room was deserted. He passed through a carved arch into the scriptorium. No one occupied the stools before the two high, sloping writing desks or sat at the table where sheets of prepared parchment and pots of ink and colors and gold leaves lay in orderly confusion with brushes and quill pens and scraping tools. Wintry daylight fell upon the stone walls and seemed rather to add to the barrenness of the interior than to warm it. There was no fireplace, only a perforated kettle in which a few lumps of charcoal were burning with ghostly blue tatters of flame.

The king's counselor was sitting on a puncheon stool beside the brazier. He said, "I have believed this past hour that someone was coming to visit me here. And as I live, it is Gawin."

"What do you find to do in this room, Merlin?" Gawin said. "Are you reading God's word on His birthday?"

"I am only trying to keep warm, occupation enough for a man of my years. But I am glad to share my coals, and I will be twice glad if you are willing to draw up a stool and sit with me."

Gawin looked at the small, huddled figure, remembering with a pang that this was the friend of Pelles, of Perceval too. To the dark robe he was accustomed to wear Merlin had added two or three brightly colored cloaks, the top one lined with fur. He had pulled up the cowls, so that his face was only a patch of pink skin between the white hair of his beard and eyebrows. He held his hands to the heat, moving the bony fingers slowly, like the winter-stiffened feet of a bird.

Gawin pulled up one of the tall desk stools and perched on it above the old man. "I have not seen you since we met in the pass outside the City of Legions," he said.

"Let us not dwell on a meeting that inspired some ill humor, Gawin. I believe we are better friends on this Christmas day than we were then."

"I suppose we are. Since that night I have been the guest of your kinsman Pelles."

"Pelles is no kinsman of mine, only a faithful, old friend. I have heard you received some teaching in the hermitage."

"Pelles sent you word?"

249

"I have heard it," Merlin said, setting his childlike mouth stubbornly.

Indulging his appetite for mystery, Gawin thought. The gesture awoke the anger Merlin could make him feel. He said, "Have you heard too that Kei and the traitor Bryant of The Isles conspire against Lancelot? Here is a matter nearer home and more fitting to be discussed between loyal men."

" 'Conspire' is a large word, Gawin. Yet it may be that these two do conspire."

"You are the king's trusted counselor. Why do you not help Arthur see the truth of this filthy affair?"

Merlin rubbed his hands slowly, then patted them together as though he hoped to restore the blood in them to living warmth. "You believe Arthur doesn't see its truth?"

"I believe fear of the prince's death disorders him. I believe Kei uses his disorder to enlarge his own powers. I believe Kei is afraid of Lancelot's strength and good faith, and labors to divide him from the king."

Merlin bobbed his head alike in agreement and disagreement. "It could be possible, or it could only seem possible. Whichever way it is, I am the king's counselor, I am not his panic and despair. With these he must make his own settlement."

Gawin too stretched his hands to the brazier, seeing their bleached hair and heavy cords of muscle in naked contrast to the transparent skin that covered Merlin's bones. "I do not hold with your 'it might be or it might not.' I wish to know what a knight who loves Arthur should do. I cannot

250

sit still and see this matter unroll like words on a parchment. I do not believe God writes our destinies on sheepskin as our monks write the story of Creation. We are men, we can alter the threat of evil."

Merlin sighed. "Your opinions are always large and round, Gawin. Let me tell you something about Arthur. Do you know how he was born?"

"No."

"He is the son of the lady Igerne. She was once the wife of the king's vassal, a baron who held Cornwall. The king I speak of was Uther Pendragon."

"I know Uther Pendragon was Arthur's father."

Merlin wagged his white beard in assent. "But Uther desired Igerne while she was still the wife of the baron of Cornwall, and by means which needn't be mentioned after all these years," the old man said blandly, "he made his way into her bedchamber and lay with her and got a son with her. This occurred before her husband died."

"But," Gawin objected, "Uther Pendragon was the lawful husband of Igerne. I have always heard it. My father told me when I was a lad."

"He was. The baron of Cornwall attacked him and was killed three days after Uther Pendragon had lain in the bed of Igerne. When she became a widow, Uther married her. But she was already with child. And the child was Arthur."

"I do not wish to hear such a story," Gawin said.

"Not many men understand it, but I remember," Merlin went on. "Arthur and I, we know. Arthur realizes his blood carries the stain of illegitimacy. This is the shame he lives

251

with, and a man who lives with shame is vulnerable throughout."

"What you say is treachery," Gawin told him. "If it is true you should keep it secret. If it is not true —"

"It is true, and I do keep it secret. I have told you for reasons which seem to me sufficient. Listen, Gawin, the time we call the future resembles a sphere hanging on a single chain. It turns, turns, and as it shows us new segments of itself we see events which have been laid up and finished before they become apparent. The future is the future only to ourselves, who must wait to see the turn of time. But to God, who beholds in one moment the near and the far face of time, and its upper and lower faces, the future and the present and the past are all the same."

"And what has this wonderful matter of time to do with Arthur's birth?"

"It is yourself I am speaking of. It has to do with you."

Gawin felt the hair on his neck rise. "Why?"

"Because you must be reminded that you have begun your mission. Time, the future if you like, has delivered you to the quest. Whatever inheritance of sin may shape the affairs of the king, your future is already prepared. You must go on with your search for the brothers Mortelle and Peleur."

Gawin was seized again with the terrible fear of enchantment. In the cold scriptorium, with winter sun the color of ice falling upon the pale stone, and the small, blue flame flickering above the charcoal in the brazier, he cast about for some familiar thing to fix like armor to his spirit. His eyes found the carved crosses hanging above the writing desks, each bearing a stiff, crucified Figure. He said, "This is all very fine, Merlin, but it does not help me know why you have told me the story of Igerne and Uther Pendragon."

"Doesn't it?" Merlin said. "I thought I had explained that each man's destiny has three parts, in the past, in the present, in the future; and that these three parts become one in the sight of God. If you wish me to speak to you as to a child, I must tell you plainly that you cannot alter whatever is reserved for Arthur, the son of a sinful father. And therefore you must take up the thread that draws your own life forward."

Gawin rose. "There is not enough heat in your pot of coals to warm us both, Merlin. Thank you for your counsel, and I will bid you good day."

Merlin made no reply, only pulled his hood closer about his face and closed his eyes. To Gawin he seemed to have gone instantly to sleep, like a babe.

43

THE SEASON OF CHRISTMAS advanced, and the king did not send for Gawin. They met almost every day, sometimes at meat, sometimes in the morning when Arthur emerged from his bedchamber to greet the knights who slept in the hall of the royal residence. His uncle would stand beside him a moment, speak a few friendly sentences, then pass on.

He has lost confidence in me, Gawin thought. Or perhaps he does not wish to hear me, perhaps he knows what I have to tell him will end his hope in the good knight. Yet to keep me hanging as he does has the feeling of a game of cat-and-mouse, and I am not hardy enough to endure much of that. I will ask his leave to depart on my quest.

But until he had spoken with Lancelot he could not make up his mind to quit the capital. Whatever Yvain said, Lancelot in simple self-preservation was bound to have an opinion of the situation between Arthur and Kei and himself — plans too. And though he may not have wished to discuss these matters with Yvain he would surely not refuse to discuss them with Gawin. I must know what Lancelot believes, Gawin thought restlessly. I must know whether he thinks this conspiracy of Kei is still small and weak or whether something deep and ruinous to the king's old friends is taking place. Gawin thought for the hundredth time how blind the whole affair seemed without Lancelot's counsel. Would he, as Yvain suggested, truly let himself be imprisoned rather than defend himself by means that could be called disloyal? No man will, Gawin thought, it is against courage and the will to live.

Lancelot was elusive. He showed himself at Church, and, if he were bidden, at the king's board. Between whiles he seemed to disappear right out of the City of Legions. As time passed Gawin grew more and more disturbed. Finally, on the morning of Epiphany, at the end of twelve days through which he had cursed Merlin, treated Yvain to morose moods, and quarreled constantly with himself, he swore he would either speak with Lancelot or leave the royal city.

Since it had proved impossible to waylay Lancelot at mass, Gawin did not attend the service of Epiphany. He waited until he was sure the prayers had begun, then went to the church and stood in the porch. When time enough had passed to allow the bishop to reach the Latin phrases of dismissal, Lancelot emerged. Gawin jumped forward and caught him by the cloak. "Greetings, brother."

"Greetings to you, Gawin, and I see you have taken me captive."

"I have taken you captive because you avoid me. I am afraid I have offended you."

Lancelot readjusted his cloak. "We have been friends too long for such words. If I avoid you, it is because of my old custom of spending holy seasons alone — or as nearly alone as our duty allows."

Lancelot kept no such custom. He was only evading an explanation of his isolation. Gawin fell into step beside him. "The holy season is over today, and if we are friends, spare me some time. We need to speak together."

"I am about to take my morning meal with the monks. Come with me to the refectory."

They left the church. The monastery lay a quarter of a mile beyond, across lawns traversed by a flagstone path. The day was warm and foggy, and Gawin felt the flags slip a little on the thawed earth.

Lancelot loosened his cowl. "The wind is milder today, isn't it? I hope better weather is a good omen for the new year."

255

"Much has happened to make us welcome good omens," Gawin said, hanging to his purpose. "I have heard from Yvain that the king puts more trust in Kei and the traitor Bryant of The Isles than seems wholesome."

"Come, brother, you must not say 'traitor' of men who have settled their troubles with the king. Bryant's outbreaks are in the past. Arthur will convert him into a useful servant of Britain."

"The king has old friends who have served him longer than a mere half year," Gawin said. "And I do not share your unconcern when I see doubtful men displacing them in our sovereign's confidence."

"Look," Lancelot said. "The clouds are breaking. We shall have fair weather after all."

The words were not delivered in a tone of rebuke, but Gawin felt rebuked. While he was digesting what Lancelot had said a voice hailed them from behind. He turned. Yvain was hastening along the flagstone path, his cloak blowing back from his heavy shoulders.

"Where are you off to in such a hurry?" he said. "Are you going to the monks? I should have thought one dose of piety would hold you for the day."

Gawin welcomed him lamely, but Lancelot broke into a grin. He laughs at me, Gawin thought.

"We are on a mission leading to hot broth and porridge," Lancelot said, as cheerful as a squire in a new surcoat. "Come break your fast at the monks' table with us, Yvain. I needn't ask you whether your appetite is sharp-set."

"Cold churches make me feel starved," Yvain said, "And

so do sleepless nights in poor beds, and winning a fight with swords, and falling into a rage."

"We were speaking of Kei and Bryant," Gawin said.

"And I was about to ask Gawin how long he will remain in the City of Legions," Lancelot said. "I suppose the king will not give him a new mission before Easter, since he has been riding in the weather."

"Gawin can't sit still until Easter," Yvain said. "He is wild to get astride a horse again."

"You two are wise," Gawin said.

"We know you, brother." Lancelot fell into step with him and laid a hand lightly on his shoulder. "Has Arthur told you the nature of your next mission?"

"No," Gawin mumbled.

"Gawin wishes to ride on a mission of his own," Yvain said.

"Listen, Yvain," Gawin said, "I am here beside you. You do not need to speak of me as though I were in another country."

"What mission do you hope for, Gawin?" Lancelot asked.

"I do not know what Yvain means by this mission."

"I mean," Yvain said explicitly, "the search for your relic."

Gawin said, furious, "I have never spoken to you of any such mission."

"You do not need to speak of it. A man who knows you can see it emblazoned on your chest."

"What is the relic, Gawin?" Lancelot said.

They have put me in the wrong, Gawin thought. Lancelot rebuffs me, and Yvain sees in Christ's cup only a feverish whim. I would tell them nothing even if I were not vowed to silence. And he stumped along the flagstones, his head down and his teeth clamped tight.

"Forgive us, brother," Yvain said. "When you turn grim you tempt us to make a little sport with you. Tell Lancelot about the Norgals family who guard the Grail cup."

"Ah! The Grail," Lancelot said. "Yvain, do you recall when we were new knights — while Gawin was still a page learning to sing love songs for the queen's ladies? In those days I thought I would see the Grail if I were worthy."

"Gawin met a hermit who swears his uncle owns this cup."

Lancelot did not reply, only tapped Gawin's shoulder gently a time or two, like an older kinsman who foresees in the awkwardness of a younger good hope for improvement.

For all their friendly derision, Gawin did not give up his intention to speak with Lancelot until they reached the refectory of the monks. There, seated with brown-robed brothers at a long table under the low, oak-beamed ceiling, he learned that the chapter ate in religious silence. The only voice was that of a holy man who recited saints' lives, so elevating their minds above the gross, bodily act of feeding.

With a kind of aggravated despair he thought of Merlin hunched like a bag of old clothes over his blue, unearthly fire.

44

THE KING KEPT GAWIN waiting throughout the first month of the new year. This was partly, Gawin believed, because the political affairs of Britain were disturbed. Clamas, a certain chieftain who had been a king before Arthur's wars of unification, was gathering a rebel force, so confidential runners reported. Moreover, the people of The Isles pressed with growing restlessness and threats of revolt for the naming of Lancelot as governor.

Yet in Britain political affairs were always present to be dealt with. As Gawin considered Arthur's long delay it came over him that Kei was responsible for it. I was a fool not to see it at once, he thought. Kei includes me with Lancelot, he knows I will be dangerous to his ambition if I can reach my uncle. As the month dragged on he noticed too a narrowing of Arthur's cordiality. He was bidden less often to take his evening meat at the king's table, and a day came when state counsels were held and he was not asked to attend. He had not been excluded from the close group of Arthur's trusted knights since, at twenty-five, he first sat beside his uncle in the meeting chamber.

He felt a steadying anger that restored his ability to think. Without wasting his heat in a discussion with Yvain he took a day and night to weigh his strengths and weaknesses. His strengths lay mostly in the past, in his service and kinship to the king. His weaknesses were immediate. He had chased the wrong hare in delaying over Kei, he had lost time. While the seneschal fastened himself to the king and won the critical first engagements, Gawin had failed to force his case where it should be forced, with Arthur himself.

On a raw morning of sleety rain he walked to the monastery and asked to speak with a lay brother who sometimes wrote letters in exchange for charitable gifts. Gawin gave him a gold besant.

"This is to pay for a message to my uncle," he said, "and I make it a gold coin because I expect you to be silent about the matter I wish you to write."

"I will write whatever you ask, Messire Gawin," the scrivener said, "saving only blasphemy, a sin you aren't likely to commit. The gold will go into our common treasury, and as for my silence, it is given, it does not require a fee."

"Good. Here is the message. Begin with the proper custom, I do not know the usage. Then write, 'Messire —' "

Standing before the high, sloped desk in the scriptorium the scrivener worked rapidly with a narrow brush of stoat's hair, making beautiful, small letters in the Celtic style. " 'Messire —' What next?"

" 'In the name of my service to you, and my filial love —' "

" '— and my filial love —' "

" '— I ask you to receive me in private audience three days from this day, or give me leave —' "

"Wait a moment, Messire Gawin, I am behind you. 'Or give me leave —' I have it."

" 'Or give me leave to depart from your court on the mission we spoke of after Whitsuntide.' Are you still even with me, brother?"

"Almost. Now. Is there more?"

"A little more," Gawin said. "Write as I tell you. This is the part for which your silence was rewarded. Are you ready?"

"Yes, I am ready."

" 'In good conscience and with all my skill I searched for Lohot. No man had seen him or heard of him. I searched for his grave and did not find it. May God support you to hear what I believe, that the prince my cousin, in whose prowess I took much pride, has lost his life.' Have you put down what I tell you, word for word?"

The monk concluded a line. "Just as you said. I am grieved. Is it true that the prince is dead?"

"It is true that I believe he is dead, but as for you, you are only to write, not to wonder, not even to permit yourself to grieve. Remember what the besant paid for."

"I remember, only —"

"No 'only.' Remember without your 'only.' "

"Are you finished with your letter?"

"Nearly finished. Add, 'I am your loyal kinsman and servant as long as breath is in my body.' No, that is too much. Don't write that."

"I have written 'I am your —' Shall I remove those words?"

261

"Yes."

The monk scraped the vellum with a fine-edged tool, sprinkled white sand on the spot, blew it away. "Now we can resume."

"How is this? 'Sent to you by the hand of your loyal kinsman and servant, Gawin of Rhos.' "

"Dignified and fitting," the monk approved.

"Read what you have set down."

The monk rustled the pliable square of parchment, held it so Gawin could see and admire the neat script. " 'Messire: In the name of my service to you and my filial love, I ask you to receive me in private audience three days from this day, or give me leave to depart from your court on the mission we spoke of after Whitsuntide. In good conscience and with all my skill I searched for Lohot. No man had seen or heard of him. I searched for his grave and did not find it. May God support you to hear what I believe, that the prince my cousin, in whose prowess I took much pride, has lost his life. Sent to you by the hand of your loyal kinsman and servant, Gawin of Rhos.' "

"It is strange to hear one's thoughts fix themselves in a pattern like figured cloth," Gawin said. "Will you carry this sheepskin to the king, brother?"

"Willingly. Do you wish me to go now?"

"Yes," Gawin said, with the chill realization that he was committed. "At once. I will wait in the scriptorium for you."

The room was cold enough to show him his breath. Merlin's pot of charcoal had been removed. Gawin walked back and forth, stamped on the rushes spread over the stone floor, swung his arms for warmth. It was a long wait.

It was long, but not as long as the three days during which he watched with falling hope for an answer from the king. Arthur did not reply. On the third morning a runner, a page whose nose was white and pinched with cold, found Gawin in the common room.

"Messire," he piped, "I am sent from the royal residence with a message for you."

So, Gawin thought, Arthur shows me his mind by entrusting his decision to this half-frozen grasshopper of a page. "What are you sent to say, little messire?"

"Only this, that you do not need the king's leave for your mission, that you received the king's leave after Whitsuntide, that you are free to depart at once."

"This is all?"

"This is all, Messire Gawin. And may I stand on the hearth awhile to warm myself before I run back to the palace?"

Gawin dropped his hand gently on the child's head, surely the smallest, youngest, coldest page in Arthur's household. "Who was present with the king when he gave you the message for me?"

"Nobody at all, messire." The page edged toward the burning logs.

"The king was alone?"

"Yes indeed, he was alone. I think he must have been cold too, because his eyes were red and he wiped them with the backs of his hands. If he were not a man and the king, I would believe he was weeping, messire."

45

"AND SO," Gawin concluded the tale he was telling Yvain, "I knew my message to the king must either succeed or fail. And it failed."

The two friends had ridden to the ruins of a Roman bathhouse lying just inside the wall of the City of Legions. Needing privacy, they had pulled up among the tumbled masonry, wrapping their cloaks around them against wet fog.

"It was a risk to present Arthur with such downright alternatives, Gawin. I wish you had been more patient."

"With Lancelot's patience, you mean? But when I was shut out of the counsels of state I could not stand like a hall carl with my hat in my hand waiting in silence for Kei to sentence me to the kitchens."

"And now you are exiled." Yvain blew a long breath which was visible on the cold mist.

"No, not exiled, not by Arthur. Kei could not quite force that, he could only arrange matters so that I must exile myself."

"It is too fine a distinction. What will you do, brother?"

"The other morning when we were going with Lancelot to breakfast with the monks, do you remember speaking of the relic guarded by Peleur?"

"I remember you denied it and gave me a stare."

"I was surprised. I didn't know you knew I had spoken to the king. When I asked his leave to seek Peleur I gave him my word I would not mention the mission to any knight of his."

"I didn't know, what I said was only a wild throw."

"Wild throw or not, you are aware that the mission is set. And so I am still within my promise to the king if I ask you to come with me."

Yvain shook his head with such decision that his horse pranced as it felt him move. "I am the king's man, I go only where he sends me. Kei does not fear me as he fears you and Lancelot, not enough to be my enemy. But if he should scheme against me, that will be the moment to do what I must to defend myself."

"I do not ask you for the sake of taking you away from Kei or from any peril. I trust you to deal with peril. I ask you because of the relic itself."

"No, Gawin. Your quest is not for me."

"You do not believe in Christ's cup."

"I believe in it for you."

Gawin nudged his horse gently with the spur. The animal walked forward, picking its way among the rubble and frozen weeds. Yvain followed. The fog had closed off their view of the hills behind the capital, and they seemed to be moving in a narrow world whose limits advanced with them. "I do not wish to bid Lancelot farewell," Gawin said. "He holds me at arm's length. But tell him for me that I am his loyal man and will always be."

"I'll tell him."

"And now I must say farewell to you, brother." Gawin stopped his horse at the top of a brushy ditch. "It is hard to think we do not know when time will bring us back to the Round Table together."

Yvain drew close enough to grasp his hand. "You have an ear in the City of Legions as long as I am here, Gawin. Send me word. Tell me how I can send you a message if a message is needed."

Gawin thought of the bleak solitudes through which he had hunted Lohot. "It will be like finding a sleeping fox."

"Tell me at least how to reach Iglais."

"Joseus," Gawin said, "I will be with Joseus before I go to my combat for Iglais." And he described the Roman roads, the great bay of western Norgals, the villages, the strait, the estuary.

"When will you leave the City of Legions?"

"At daybreak tomorrow. I will lie in the monks' house tonight."

"I will come at dawn and ride with you to the milestone," Yvain said.

"No, brother, if Kei questions you it is better you tell him truthfully you did not see me depart. Let us say farewell here." He closed his fingers, then let Yvain's hand go. "I leave half my soul in the common room with you."

They turned their horses and rode back toward the hall. In the little time remaining Gawin thought of his days as a squire. So long ago, yet the years seemed short. Yvain had been a good-humored companion generous with his encouragement of a headlong lad, he had been a strong, kindly man showing the durable luster of a warm spirit. I cannot remember when we were not friends, I cannot remember when I did not fetch the tale of my victories and failures to Yvain. Life runs on too fast. And it may be that nothing, not even the sight of a vessel made holy by Christ's blood, can weigh against the loss of such a man, if it is our destiny not to meet again in this life.

They parted almost in silence, a brief, "God go with you, brother," their only words. Gawin left his horse at the domestic stables behind the sally port and walked straight on to the monastery. Through the hours of that day and night he followed the rule of the monks, rose with them at the canonical hours, shared their service. And when the prayers of the hour of prime had been said he departed from the house, and from the City of Legions, and from Arthur, the lonely man living with the sweat of fear, and from Yvain, and from ambitious Kei, the royal seneschal, and from the traitor Bryant of The Isles. From Lancelot too, the quiet, blue-eyed knight who believed in the impregnability of innocence. And from Merlin who had said, You can alter nothing time has prepared.

He rode through the north gate and into the Roman road, a knight delivered to the quest of the Holy Grail, whether moved like a chess piece by God, or hurried on by some dream of old enchantment, he could not have said.

46

I WILL RETURN to Pelles, he thought. I suppose the old man may rebuke me, since he gave me much instruction before he sent me away to do what I have not done. But how can I push forward on a quest whose size is unknown and whose country may be as large as all Norgals? Surely Pelles will tell me a direction in which to start.

Summoning his memory of landmarks, Gawin turned into the mountains. He held the thought of Pelles protectively against his loneliness and fear, feeling all the while oddly disencumbered yet in need of haste, like a man who dreams of running. He passed through the scrub and small trees and found himself in the old forest. Though in autumn these trees, now bare, had been in leaf, the gloom seemed grayer than then, and the silence absolute. Nothing was familiar, no iron-hard slope, no frozen stream. But I have only to keep moving on, Gawin thought, the green vale and hermitage of Pelles are less than half a day from the Roman road.

All the same, he was still toiling up steeps whose features he could not recognize when night fell. Morning did not enlighten him. Days passed, weeks passed, and he no longer hoped to reach Pelles and the hermitage, which now hung before him like a rich, legendary kingdom, but only to find a meaningful turning, to enter upon a road whose destination would prove to be his destination.

He did not live a soldierly existence of measured journeys, night fires, trapped food, rests in camp. Without any care for his body save to keep it alive he rode as far as he could, ate or did not eat as he was able to lay hands on a meal, slept when he could go forward no longer. From time to time he encountered men, danger, shelter — or dreams of them.

On a certain night he crept into the oozy ruin of a chapel, sat with his back against a stone, bent his arms and head onto his knees. In this posture he finally slept, and awoke to the wet fog of morning. I will say the prayers of prime, he thought, if I can find an altar stone still standing. It occurred to him with wonder that he had said no prayers for a long time, so full had he been of God.

He rose, stamped the stiffness out of his legs, clambered deeper into the ruin in search of its decayed hallows. He found the altar, and felt his heart swell with an evil sickness. The stumps of two thick, black candles stood in rotting sconces, and between them lay a tattered black glove that had once been rich with embroidery and pearls. Through its rents glared the knuckled bones of a man's hand. All about the altar, all about the floor of the chapel animal bones were flung, grinning, eyeless heads and the mildewed arches of ribs crazily decked with foul rags of hide. As he turned to flee, weeds matted over moldered planks gave way and cast him as deep as the shoulders into a narrow chamber of earth.

"Now, brother," he said aloud, "stand still lest this muck swallow you."

He had no room to move his arms save, pressing them against his chest, hands before his face, straight upward. But even as little movement as that drove his feet deeper into the slime. I am to die, he thought, in this defiled chapel, I am to die standing up like a man, and my eyes open.

He waited for his heart to settle and his breath to steady. Call out? Spread his arms into the weeds, swing his weight on his elbows, raise himself by the sheer power of willing? He closed his eyes and leaned his head into the dead thistles about the pit. He prayed aloud, for Arthur, for Yvain and Lancelot, for Britain, even for Kei. He prayed too for Iglais and Perceval, for the hermit Joseus who had deceived him once, for young Davith whose good land bore him vines and grain.

"For life," Gawin murmured, "against which sorrow and loss and the end of joy war, let me pray for life that leads in a circle from God to God."

As he leaned against the top of his prison it came over him that he had already died and that here was his grave. And it was as though he heard Pelles repeating, *Death is God's purest shape*. These were words which, like the Latin of the mass, had seemed serious and wise when Pelles spoke them. But now he understood them, an immeasurable, ineffable truth. In visionary silence he understood more, that Pelles had also said to him, "I saw one face of the Grail, the Vessel and Lance." This Grail of Pelles was the mother Vessel of Earth into which the Lance bled its paternal Seed.

270

Death that widows Earth is also the Divine Father Who restores Earth, Gawin thought, trembling because of the light that burst within him.

Later, he found himself stretched on a bed of oak leaves beside a spring around whose lip the grass was moist and green. Under his cloak next to his body lay his food sack. It had been filled with a loaf of bread and a skin bottle of mixed milk and water. His terror and exhaustion coursed out his arms and fingers, passing from him like a current through a conduit. He rose, and he was warm, refreshed, calm.

On a day of springlike sun, when the forest mosses were thickening and leaf-spikes, still tightly rolled, beginning to push through the deep floor of dead vegetation, he arrived at a walled house. It was too small to be useful as a castle, too large to be a cell for monks. He struck the fortified gate with the hilts of his sword.

It opened at once, and Gawin entered a little square of lawns. A procession seemed to be in progress, at least the household women were marching around a well in the center of the grass, casting sprays of dried grain into the water, and weeping in a fashion less suggestive of grief than of a ceremony of some sort. He watched until the rite was finished, then, advancing to ask for hospitality, found himself seized by the hands of the celebrants and dragged into the house. He was taken to a room, pushed within, and left alone.

Well! he thought. I should have resisted, only I supposed it was a springtime game of the kind villagers in remote corners of the land play on old, half-forgotten holy days. But these ladies are not playing a game. He examined the room. The door was a thick, oaken portal bolted on the outside by a heavy bar. The chamber was unfurnished except for a low bed. It was lit by two slip windows high in the wall. Even if he stood on the bed he would still be four feet below the embrasures. He was as much a prisoner as if he were in the dungeon of a baronial keep.

He could hit upon no rational explanation of a house of women capable of capturing a knight with nothing save their hands. He flung himself onto the bed to meditate the fact that he was, in fact, a prisoner. The bed was amorously soft, billowing about him in swamplike folds. He struggled to sit up, to escape it, but it drew him tight, held him fast. He could not lift a hand, not even a finger. He was overpoweringly sleepy too, and as he fought to keep his eyes open he thought, Somehow in the courtyard they drugged me with unholy herbs.

Later the oak door was opened and a woman entered and awoke him — or he dreamed the woman. She said, "Get up, Gawin, I have brought you supper." And two serving women set a low table and spread it with meats and fruits.

"You have given me a rude welcome," Gawin said.

"Rise and sit with me."

He did not wish to fight the spell of the bed before her, but when he moved he found that he could easily stand. He sat down at the table. "Do you imprison every knight who asks you for hospitality?"

"I am searching for a knight who will be my husband and become king of this land."

"Arthur is king of this land."

She studied him without emotion. "I will marry you, Gawin. You shall be my lord."

He shook his head. "This is not how marriages are made, my lady. Besides, I am sworn to fulfill a mission."

"Choose. If you do not take me to wife you must remain my captive." And she spoke threats unseemly in a woman, unseemly in any Christian. "Each winter my land is orphaned of its king. Each year when the season of spring returns it is laid upon me to seek a husband who will also become the king. If I am refused as you refuse me, it is laid upon me first to deprive you of your right to call yourself male, then to kill you."

This is a vile enchantment that endangers my quest, Gawin thought. He sat dumbly at the supper table. But when the woman left him he lay down on the floor, spreading his body in the shape of Christ's body hanging on His cross.

From this captivity too he emerged, unaware of the means of his delivery, as he had emerged from the grave pit in the destroyed chapel. From this, from others, from monstrous dream and the illusion of rescue, from faintness and starving, from the evil of things half seen, he stumbled again and again, until, on a day of broad sun and soft breezes from the sea, he floundered onto ground he knew. There, his strength gone, he fell into the neglected garden before the hermitage of Joseus, and felt himself being lifted in the arms of the holy man.

"I was expecting you," Joseus said.

47

WITHIN A FEW DAYS Gawin was restored.

"You give me no chance to show my skills as a physician," Joseus complained. "A little rest out of the weather has been all the medicine you need."

"I don't know where I have been or how I reached you," Gawin said, "and how could you have expected me?"

"You were lost?" Joseus asked him, with the habit his family seemed to have of not replying to questions.

"Yes indeed, I was lost. I have crossed Norgals ten times or more in the king's service, but on this journey I went where I have never gone before."

"And so you have learned that our world is familiar when we are at home in it, but strange when we are not."

They had walked to the shore and were sitting on the stony steps of a cliff. A few early flowers of yellow and white crept among the pebbles. Brown and gleaming at the foot of the cliff the wide strand lay in soft sunshine, and beyond it the sea itself, deep blue and ruffed in every direction with running foam. Birds rode the air currents up the face of the cliff, then tipped their round bodies and sailed, sailed on stiff, silvery wings.

Joseus pointed below. "If you were to walk into the surf, brother, and let the water sweep over your head even as little as a handbreadth, you would say, 'This sea is a foreign place.' Yet you behold it from the cliff and you say, 'I know this sea.'"

Gawin smiled. "Morals of your kind are easy to draw, Joseus."

"All the same, you understand it now, while we have the sea spread before us, though you did not understand it in the time you spent being, as you say, lost."

"I believe I have begun to understand," Gawin said. "Have you heard that I visited your father in his hermitage?"

"Yes, I have heard."

"And received his teaching?"

"That too," Joseus said.

"Pelles told me this: 'ask.' And now I believe I have walked a handbreadth deep under a foreign sea all these weeks in order to reach you, Joseus, and to ask you where your uncles Peleur and Mortelle are."

"Oh, oh!" The big hermit was laughing.

"Do you ridicule me?"

"Only a little." Joseus smote him a friendly blow between the shoulders. "You are such a trusting man, brother."

"Do I trust Pelles too far? Or yourself?"

"It is rather hard to explain," Joseus said. "What do you think the relic you seek is, Gawin?"

"I think it is Christ's cup. If it is not Christ's cup I do not know what it is."

"And why do you imagine Christ's cup has wandered so far and hidden itself in Britain?"

Gawin did not answer at once. Looking toward the restless blue deeps he saw close at hand Joseus's round head, his disordered curls, his strong neck. The holy man had changed somewhat. He was quieter, his great body was stretched and lean, his face was somehow less innocent. And he bore himself differently, wearing now a kind of submissive authority, like a king's officer in the first week of his tenure. He owned new powers but seemed not to know quite how to use them. "I have always heard," Gawin said, "that the Grail was an ordeal specially prepared for knights sworn to Arthur's service."

"Yet Christ accepted death for all men, not only for Arthur's knights. Listen, Gawin, the Grail is a *learning* and a *doing,* and it is older than Christ, it is as old as the men who first saw that life and death are the heartbeat of our earth. Pelles taught you this."

"Pelles taught me the nature of the animals and growing plants. It was from him I learned God's paternity."

"Yes, yes," Joseus said, impatient, "but there is more. The Grail is a secret — do you remember I told you last autumn it was a secret? I told you too its secret could be learned, but at a cost."

"I remember, I have thought of your words many times. Yourself, Joseus, are you willing at least to search for the secret?"

"No."

"I am satisfied to accept the cost," Gawin said.

276

Joseus sprang up and gathered a handful of small stones and threw them with an enormous sweep of arm and shoulder downward and across the strand. "The tide is just turning," he said. "I can hit salt water at high tide, and I hope some day to lengthen my throw and hit it at low tide."

"Give me a stone." Gawin rose, and threw, and passed Joseus's mark.

"Ah, if I could make a pebble fly like that!" Joseus said.

Gawin said, "No man can make it fly unless he has strengthened his arm practicing with the sword. I am a swordsman, you a hermit. You will never hit the water at low tide until you become a swordsman. And so sit down again and tell me what I need to know."

"You have a mighty argument," Joseus said, grinning.

"I do not wish to be put off any longer."

Joseus drew his robe under his knees and dropped down onto the rock. "God can take on natures that are not His, Gawin. He is not a spiritual body, as we are; not a beast, as the fox is; not a plant, as wheat is. But all these are members of His Being, and in them He shows Himself to us simply, so that we can understand. Do *you* understand?"

"Yes."

"Yet though He puts on many shapes, He is not a Shape. God has no habit, no extent, no features. He is the Source from which we issue and to which we return. He is not born, but we are. He does not die, but we must."

"He died once," Gawin said.

Joseus slowly nodded. "Yes, for love of us, He taught Himself our habit of death. He has taken our man-shape

277

many times and died many times, even before the sufferings He suffered in Christ's body. But still God does not die. And this is the secret of the Grail — that at the Source, Life and Death are One. And if you insist on seeing the Grail, Gawin, you must see the secret at the very moment it occurs, you must behold Life and Death embracing in divine ecstasy, becoming One."

Gawin had begun to tremble. Joseus said, "Are you afraid, brother?"

"Yes."

"My father could prepare you only so far. Since God has added a little strength to my holiness, I can prepare you a step beyond Pelles. But in the end you will be alone. And if you live to see the Grail, that will be the moment to ask a question."

Gawin leaned against his rock and closed his eyes. Almost he felt the foreign tide of a foreign sea take him, almost he felt his life lost in the smother and roll of breakers, lightless, salt, fatal.

GAWIN SLEPT on the pallet in the cell. But now he did not borrow the bed from Joseus, as he had done the summer before. Since those days, Joseus had adopted the pious habit of lying all night on the chapel floor.

The next morning Gawin awoke at daybreak. As he

listened to the subdued rumble of the devotions of his friend coming from the direction of the little church, he thought, I must get on, I am healed, Joseus has given me the teaching I require. Between now and the beginning of summer, when I return to Iglais, I shall ride north and learn at least the nature of the country of Peleur. And if I do not fulfill my mission before I go to Iglais, I shall come back afterwards and complete it.

He rose and put on his body linen and leather riding clothes, smiling as he wondered whether Joseus would take pleasure in squiring him into his mail. Through the days of his weakness and recovery he had worn the brown clothes of a hermit, and now as he dressed in the garments of his knighthood he regretted the coarse, long robe, the rope girdle, the soft boots.

He mended the cell fire, then, while he waited for Joseus to finish his prayers, went outdoors and walked about the weedy garden. The hermit's rich bass voice was vigorously lifted, as though, Gawin thought, he considered God to be slightly deaf. Yet to pray at the top of his voice, to chant the psalms like so many battle hymns, these are signs of joy. Joseus is a man who lives with joy.

Restlessly Gawin moved across the garden and entered the wood. He passed the stable where he had seen the hoofmarks of Perceval's mule, and pushed into the dead scrub over which tender spring bindweed was spreading. His old hope of finding Perceval rose in him again with almost unbearable desire. Before I leave this place, he thought, I will wring from Joseus the truth about Perceval, I will make him tell me who leads and protects him, who conceals him from me.

He emerged into a small, rude clearing between forest trees. It was not much larger than a human grave, and as Gawin stared down at the earth over which weeds and wild flowers were beginning to sprout it occurred to him that the spot was, in fact, a tiny burying ground. Tall trees shaded it all about, but, probably before the winter, the soil had been cleared of brush and heaped into a mound slightly longer than a man.

Gawin broke into a sweat. Perceval? Was this the narrow last bed of Iglais's son? He knelt, clawed at the earth with his hands.

"What will you do, brother?" Joseus asked him. "What turns you the color of clabber? The unhappy man here?" And he pointed to the grave.

"Why do you follow me?"

"To serve you — and because I have ended my office of prime."

Gawin got to his feet, feeling his legs shake. "Who is this man?"

"I believe he was a knight of the king," the hermit said. "I found his body in the forest horribly hacked and headless, and his armor hewn to pieces. Whoever killed him plainly wished to hide his name. I gathered up all, man and armor, and gave him Christian burial."

Gawin's mouth was dry, but he was recovering his nerve. "When was this, Joseus?"

"Last autumn, well before winter."

"After Whitsuntide?"

"Yes, after Whitsuntide. Why? Do you know a knight who lost his life after Whitsuntide?"

Gawin stood still, looking down on the unmarked grave. Young Lohot, eager, valiant, strong, his body should never have been found in Joseus's woods so far from the land of Logrins, not unless he had been decoyed here by treachery. He said, "Tell me what you can about him, Joseus. What size was he? Was he fair-skinned or dark? Was his cloak gilt-fringed, blue with a gilt fringe, I mean?"

"It was blue," Joseus said, "but the fringe was torn away. His body had been reduced to fragments, remember, but the leg bones were exceedingly long, as long as mine from ankle to knee. I noticed that, since I have few fellows in size. His skin was bloodied and torn, I do not know whether he was fair or dark, but one forearm showed a patch of sand-blond hair."

"Were there signs of the combat in which he lost his life?"

"No, nothing save his body, no horse gear, not even horse tracks. And I believe he was not killed where he fell, but carried there to be hidden. I believe too that whoever killed him beheaded and disfigured him, not with a sword but with an ax, after he was dead."

"Ah, ah." Gawin's eyes filled with fiery tears. "This is surely Lohot, this is my uncle's son. If he was murdered, Kei murdered him."

Joseus slowly nodded.

"Why do you nod, brother? Do you know for truth that Kei killed him?"

"I know it, though I did not know the dead man was the prince. Let us go back to the cell and break our night's fast, and I will tell you the story."

In silence they returned through the trees, past the stable, up the choked garden. Within, Joseus cut slabs of dark bread and poured milk and water into earthen bowls. He sat down before the fire and leaned his elbows on his knees, then raised a hand and crossed himself. "My sin was murder, Gawin."

"I remember. But you killed in the blindness of high feelings, not rationally, for advantage."

"Yet to the life that is lost, death is death. I hate Kei's deed, but I do not judge him."

"What was his deed?"

"He was my guest. He announced that he was a knight from Little Britain, but I had seen him in the world, and I remembered him."

"When?" Gawin asked.

"I have said — after Whitsuntide, I do not recall how long."

"Did you tell him you recognized him?"

The big hermit shook his head. "It is not my business to question men, only to listen to them and aid them if I can. Besides, Kei came to me with the larger part of his mind hidden, as they say ice hides itself under the waters of the northern sea. God has taught me to understand such wariness in the minds of men."

"Then why do you suspect him?" Gawin rose and stood over Joseus, who went on looking into the fire.

The hermit smiled into the embers. "How do I know you're an impatient man, Gawin? How do I know your will wavers this way and that when it should stiffen into purpose? I could see the fear and evil on Kei. Besides," he went on, with his surprising habit of practicality, "he got up in the night and stole into the woods. I followed him. I could not watch him, but I could hear him pulling brush together. In the morning after he left me I returned to the place, and I found what I have told you, the young knight's body hidden under a little earth and much rubble."

Gawin hit the stone facing of the hearth a blow with the flat of his hand. "You should have sent word to the City of Legions, you should have reported this murder the very day you learned of it."

"Why?"

"Because you are a subject of Arthur and a loyal Briton. Because it was a matter of simple justice."

"Justice — mortal justice — is not my calling. I wear God's clothes, not the kind you have chosen, Gawin. I am bound in God's name to receive every man who comes to me, I am bound to treat them all with love and charity, and to help them if I can."

"And so Kei has entrapped Arthur with the lie that it was he and not Lohot who killed Logrins. And so I spent four winter months searching for Lohot. I hunted him after he was already dead, I helped deceive Arthur with the ruinous belief that he was the good knight. If you had sent word —"

283

"If I had sent word, what? Your search led you to Pelles, didn't it?"

Gawin sank back onto the puncheon stool. *"I must send word, at least. Only, how am I to reach my uncle now? I am an exile, I have left the City of Legions because Kei conspires against Lancelot and the king and me."*

"What can be done at this day and hour, brother? Are you not delivered to your quest?"

"Yes," Gawin said, "I am delivered to it, but —"

After a considerable silence, Joseus sighed.

49

GAWIN TRIED TO MAKE the holy man understand. The murder not only stole from Lohot the renown of his conquering of Logrins, it was a crime of treason. And because of its success it was breeding other and more profound crimes of treason. Lancelot was in danger, and more than Lancelot, the king himself, and more than the king, Britain and its loyal men. Kei's act of murder was the first step in a plot of the seneschal to make himself tyrant of Arthur's broad land.

"No king but Arthur has ever brought peace to Britain," Gawin said. "Kei does not want to serve Arthur's peace, he wants to destroy it. Murdering Arthur's heir is only his opening move."

Joseus nodded intelligently. "I understand. You are next

of kin after Lohot, aren't you? And you've been removed too, though not by murder, not yet. What can you do to mend matters at the City of Legions?"

"First, send a runner to warn my uncle, then —"

"But you have told me your uncle chose between you and Kei, and put his lot with Kei."

"He has not chosen Kei," Gawin said angrily, "he has been captured by him. Once he learns the real fate of Lohot he will shake Kei off."

"You informed him of Lohot's real fate, didn't you?"

"I did not accuse Kei, but I told him what I believed. I could not prove then that the prince was dead by treachery."

"And now, can you prove it as you could not at mid-winter?"

"Yes. That is — you saw Kei —"

"I saw Kei, I heard him dragging brush in the night. I did not see a blow struck, I did not recognize the dead man in the morning, and you and I suppose it was Lohot only be-cause of a blue cape and blond hair on one arm. This might equally be the headless corpse of Logrins, mightn't it? Kei will swear it is. Believe me, Gawin, he has been prepared to swear it any time these eight months."

"No, no, Logrins was short and stocky, and his hair was blue-black, like the envoys from Rome."

"*We* know this is not the body of a man with blue-black hair, but we are too late to produce our evidence."

"Then I shall return to court and accuse Kei and appeal him for treason, body for body."

"Do you think Kei will allow you to reach the City of

Legions alive? Do you think he has not set a watch for you on every road? You have lived until now because he believes his murder safely hidden. But you are dead in ambush the minute you turn south."

"How do you know Kei will ambush me?"

"Because I am still capable of putting myself in his place. You have been a little simple through this affair, Gawin. You have done just what Kei designed for you to do. And whatever you do now, it too will be what Kei has planned and is ready for. And this," Joseus said, rising and shaking out his robe, "is one of the many things it means to be delivered to your quest. You cannot go back, you must go forward."

"I will not believe it," Gawin said. "If God is with my quest he will not advance me by means of Kei's treachery and murder."

"When God works with men he has only one material to work with," Joseus said, "the stuff of men, which is evil. You must be stouter, Gawin, you must gather your will for your mission. You cannot tarry, and ask God to use this dainty means and that sweet-smelling device for your sake. You do not have much time left, only until midsummer."

It was on Gawin's tongue to demand why Joseus set the term of the Grail mission at midsummer, but he did not. For one thing, the suggestion that the quest was allied to the pagan Mysteries of the seasons always chilled him with the fear of enchantment. For another, the certainty of Lohot's murder boiled his wrath and grief and confusion into a fire of indecision. He saw with crude force the helplessness of his position, the king beyond his appeal, and Kei entrenched past reach in the intimate council of knights who were Arthur's chosen men.

"But I can send a message to Yvain," he burst out. "He is a friend loyal to Arthur and to me too. He will know how to convince my uncle of Kei's treason."

Joseus did not reply.

Gawin said, "Will you find a runner for me?"

"If you must have runners flying between you and the capital, go to the royal fort." Jesus pointed northwest. "You will have your choice of experienced messengers — unless you think Kei has reached out after you as far as Norgals."

"It is a chance I am willing to take."

"And when you have dispatched the runner, what will you do, brother?"

"I don't know," Gawin said. "Wait for an answer. Wait here, or wait with Iglais"

"And your journey north to Peleur?"

"Soon, soon, in a little while."

Joseus spread his huge hands. "If this is your decision, I'll saddle your horse and say farewell and Godspeed."

"Wait, Joseus. Before we part, answer me one more question."

"If I have the answer."

"Where is Perceval? Let me see him."

"You will see him soon. He has gone west, perhaps to his mother's house. You may meet him when you return for your battle with the brother of the Knight of The Moors."

"Has he visited you since — since you hid him from me?"

"Often," Joseus said, without showing the confusion of a man caught in deception. "He has many things to do and not much time in which to do them, but when he can rest for a few days, or when he has been wounded and needs healing, he comes to me."

"Always I miss him."

The hermit smiled with the indulgence of a fond kinsman. "Poor Perceval, he has rather a streak of mischief in him, he's a little showy sometimes. He has teased you. But don't let this harmless playfulness mislead you, Gawin. He is a dedicated man."

"To what? Is his mission the same as mine?"

Joseus was slow in returning an answer. "Not quite, not quite."

"Sometimes," Gawin murmured, "he has seemed not a creature of this world to me, he has seemed a miracle."

Joseus's expressive face turned sad. "You, Gawin, God has given you forty years to feel the glory of being a creature of this world. Perhaps being a man, perhaps having lived forty years, are gifts you haven't fully weighed."

50

THE HERMIT saddled his horse for him, mounted him, and walked with him as far as the estuary, where he pointed out the crossing. "Now God go with you, Gawin, whichever way you ride."

Gawin said, "In these days when I bid a friend goodbye I have a feeling my life is running toward its end."

Joseus nodded. "I know, I know. Some portion of our hearts remains childlike, and when it is time to part we feel that all is over."

"Farewell, brother." Gawin moved onto the oily sand. He knew that Joseus watched him ride into the shallows, saw him flap his big hand in a sign of the cross for blessing, then turn back toward the hermitage. Of the members of the Grail family I understand him least, Gawin thought, but I love him best.

He pushed his horse at a fast pace, knowing the distance to the royal fort was short. Since Christmastide until this spring day, he had been riding through a Norgals both strange and hostile, and he had a superstitious notion that if he pressed on swiftly he could prevent the familiar west corner of the country from becoming mysteriously alien. Though he had no need of landmarks he watched for them with passionate care, and was relieved when a known milestone or a remembered sod wall appeared and was left behind.

And he thought of Perceval, of Iglais. Joseus had said Perceval was going home, as though it had been the youth's habit to return now and again to visit his mother. Though Gawin hoped this was true, he was also disappointed. I wished to bring him back, he thought. How long ago it seems that I promised her I would protect him. Now that he is no longer a mere runaway lad, now that he has achieved the sword and been helped by Merlin and his own kinsmen, now that he has become the good knight, what am I to say to his mother? What could I have said in any case? We cannot speak our meanings in words, she and I. I can only take her in my arms. And if she does not love me, nothing can be said between us at all.

God tosses me, he thought, between my love of Iglais, my duty to the king, my loyalty to Lancelot on one side, and on the other, this quest in which earthly love and duty seem to have so small a part. What am I? A man of flesh must love, he must defend the right with his arms and body, he must stand loyal to his friends to the death, if need be. Yet Pelles and Joseus teach me that within the man of flesh is a spirit whose business is foreign to the business of the flesh, they show me a spirit whose only work is to adore God perfectly and return to Him. Oh, God, Gawin prayed aloud, make me one thing or the other, make me flesh or make me spirit. I wish to love You perfectly, but how can I love You perfectly if I do less than my utmost as King Arthur's man? How can I adore You if I forget the treachery against Lancelot? How can I purify myself for union with You if I deny the desire I have for Iglais? For me, this is what love is — to love some *thing*, to love some *one*, to hope to do my best.

The prayer heartened him and relieved him of the vague fear of riding blindly into new enchantments. He began to feel like himself again, the Gawin who had served the king and lived with his fellows of the Round Table. He began to feel as though he were escaping some cloudy danger of which he was never quite sure but against which prudence urged him to take care. He began to feel younger, invulnerable. And so he was jerked back to the sense of peril when he saw before him, arriving from nowhere but simply filling the road, an enormous knight in black armor sitting on a black horse.

Gawin drew rein. Without a word the black knight cast his shield onto his arm and wedged his spear into the saddle feuter.

"Do you challenge me?" Gawin said. "Give me your name and rank if you mean to offer a fair fight."

"I hear that you have looked for me," the black knight said. Since his ventail was almost closed his voice emerged booming and hollow. "I am the knight Mortelle, and I do challenge you."

"What do you charge me with, Mortelle?"

"With having looked for me," the brother of Pelles said. "You must fight me or you must yield."

"Looking for you is no offense," Gawin said. "And I would rather challenge you to fight me than take up your challenge."

"I will not stand in my armor to talk. Defend yourself or yield recreant."

Gawin closed his own ventail and threw his shield forward onto his left arm. Mortelle was exceedingly broad and tall, and his horse stood a hand higher at the withers than Gawin's. I must tilt my spear up, Gawin thought, and hit him just under his shield's boss. And I must be galloping faster than he, since he has the advantage of weight and the downward blow.

The horses rushed into the charge, hurtling together so stiffly that both saddle bows were crushed, both stirrups loosened, both girths burst, both spears snapped short. Gawin dropped to earth with such a violent fall of steel that blood spurted from his nose. He was dazed and slow in getting to his feet, and expected every moment to feel the sword of Mortelle bite into his casque. Yet he did pull himself up, saw that Mortelle had taken a fall as disabling as his, and that blood was seeping through the gorget joint below his casque. Your nose is broken too, friend, Gawin mumbled, or else your teeth are knocked out.

Now they began to fight on foot. After two strokes Gawin realized that he had met a swordsman better than himself, not better in this or that lucky blow, but better in every thrust, every parry. Gagged with the blood in his throat, blinded by sweat, he cautiously gave ground. It will alter for me in a moment, he thought, I will set the pace, I will get my wind, I will see my advantage. He moved lightly, strategically, watching for the smallest shift of fortune. He knew that his chain had been opened, the flesh over his ribs cut, a shoulder gashed. He saw a cantle fly off his shield. He reached, reached, but he could neither overreach nor strike under the sword of Mortelle. He probed for the black knight's knees — and felt a hot blow sting his elbow. Moreover he could not turn Mortelle, but saw himself being turned, as he had turned many an enemy at will. This is not possible, he panted aloud, this cannot happen.

292

He expected to hear Mortelle shout the demand of the conqueror, "Yield yourself recreant or die —" as he himself had shouted it to knights struggling to avoid the final defeat of falling. To Gawin the angry return, "I will never yield" had always been unwelcome, since he had no love of fighting on to the uttermost. But I will never yield, he thought, Mortelle may kill me here on the threshold of Iglais's country, but I will never yield.

Yet Mortelle did not call for his surrender. Blows fell about his head and breast steadily, and Gawin had all he could do, more than he could do, to cover himself with what remained of his shield. He did not see the blow coming that overset him. He hardly felt it. He dropped straight down onto his face, his shattered shield still on his arm, and his right fist clenched around the hilt of his sword.

When he returned to his senses his casque had been removed and he was stretched in the grass on his back. Water was being poured gently over his head. He heaved himself onto an elbow and was immediately sick, vomiting the blood he had swallowed.

"Lie still, brother." The voice was the big bass voice of Joseus. "Do you know me?"

Gawin nodded.

"God be thanked. Can you move your legs?"

His legs seemed far away. But, thinking slowly, he moved one, then the other.

"Good. I do not believe you have caught a mortal hurt," Joseus said cheerfully. He rose from his knees and addressed someone whom Gawin could not see. "We have only to carry

293

him to my cell and wash him and search his wounds."

"Then let us get him there. Lay him across my saddle and I will lead the horse."

"Perceval!" Gawin tried to cry the name, but his voice would not strengthen itself into speech. "Is it you who protects me? I meant to protect you."

"He wishes to tell us something," Perceval said.

Joseus laughed. "Let us take him up, nephew. Our Gawin is not so wise but that his words can wait."

51

THOUGH NO BLOW had broken into the inner spaces of his body where his life was defended, he had many wounds and they cost him much blood. He fainted before Joseus and Perceval had done lifting him onto the horse, and he did not recover consciousness until the next day. Then weakness and attacks of fever made him a sick man for whom time was only an hallucination. When a morning came on which he knew himself and his circumstance, he saw no one but Joseus sitting near him in the cell.

"Where is Perceval?" he said.

"Are you better, brother?"

"I began to feel healed," Gawin said. "I am hungry for bread and news. Where is your nephew?"

Joseus rose and poured him drink and fetched it to the

pallet. "I have put a little wine in this milk, Gawin. At the fort when they heard of your wounds they sent you fowl and wine. I ate your fowl, since you could not, and since it is a sin to waste food. But I have saved the wine against the hour when you would ask for food."

"How long have I lain here, Joseus?"

"Four days, not long for such wounds as yours. You had health in your body to spare, by luck, and your flesh has not festered much. But you will need patience while these great rents close."

Gawin raised himself gingerly and sipped the milk and wine. He could feel it course into his blood hearteningly. He said, "I have learned that when I ask you a question and you do not answer it at once, you will never answer it. Yet I must ask you again. Wasn't Perceval here when I was wounded? And where is he now?"

The hermit hooked a huge hand over each knee. "Yes, yes, Perceval delivered you from the attack of our kinsman. I suppose he prevented Mortelle from killing you, Gawin. But I don't believe he wishes you to know it, and this is why I didn't answer you."

"I am proud to owe him my life. Why did he wish me not to know?"

Joseus gave it thought. "Listen, Gawin, among men Perceval is a man. But with you he still feels himself a youth. He loves you and feels he must earn your regard. If you can understand it, saving your life seemed to him rather presumptuous. Are you amused?"

Gawin's eyes filled with tears. "Where is he now?"

"He has ridden to the City of Legions to carry your message to Messire Yvain."

"Did I give him a message for Yvain?"

"You did not. Perceval asked me why you were here, and I told him the story of your exile, and Kei, and your belief that we have found Lohot's grave. In fairness to you I told everything, just as you related it to me. He chose to become your runner."

"I thought you were opposed to my sending a runner."

"I am opposed, but you were out of your senses, and I was speaking to Perceval in your stead."

"I am grateful, brother. I hope he goes and comes safely."

"He does not think of safety."

Gawin nodded. "This is what it is to be young. I thank God he was not wounded by Mortelle. Do you know, Joseus, this is the second time he has fought with his uncle?"

"I have heard of the battle on shipboard. But they did not fight here above the hermitage. Perceval surprised Mortelle just as you fell. He challenged him, but Mortelle evaded the challenge by claiming the right of a man who has just done battle to set a future date to meet. Perceval did what I wouldn't have done — let him go free." Joseus sighed with something near anger. "A pity, too. Though Mortelle is of my blood, I know well enough he has been asking for God's chastisement."

"Where are they to meet?"

"I am forbidden to tell you."

"You must tell me," Gawin said. "If you care for Perceval

you must overrule him. Tell me the day, and I will do for him what he did for me four days ago."

Joseus looked at him sadly, looked away. "I will not tell you. You have had your chance with Mortelle."

"I am too restless to lie here, Joseus. I must take a little exercise."

"I will help you. Let me lift you. Put your feet under you. Now. Raise yourself. Lean against the wall, let me look at your bandages. No fresh blood, good, no wound broke open when you stood."

"My legs shake, give me your arm." Gawin took two or three steps, hearing himself breathe as though he had been running. "Ah, a bed saps a man like a cup of poison!"

"A bed, and a fight, and ten sword cuts, and a hatful of blood spilled into the grass, these sap a man, brother. Can you walk the length of the cell and back to your pallet?"

"Yes, but not back to the pallet. Let me sit by the hearth awhile."

"If you hadn't got such a jungle of beard you would be as white as a girl."

Gawin sank down onto the puncheon stool, feeling the room turn, turn, then slowly settle. His mouth was dry and he was hungry and his hands were sweating. He said, "What did you mean when you answered that I had had my chance with Mortelle?"

"Did I say that?"

"Yes."

"I suppose I meant that men are lucky in this life if they

have a second chance to fight the same battle. It was only a manner of speaking."

"He took me by surprise. Next time I will be prepared."

Joseus made no reply.

Gawin stared into the empty hearth, aware of a sickness not related to his wound. He had a haunted sense that Mortelle had been sent against him by the enchantments always brooding over his quest, and that in failing this battle he had somehow failed whatever in men opposes evil, the struggling spirit of man torn so painfully between its earthly loves and the perfect love of God. He felt too that Joseus had realized he would fail, and pitied him as one pities a lame man or a child.

52

A FEW DAYS LATER Joseus trimmed his hair and shaved him. The slashes on his breast and arms were healing in long, horny, purple scars. A cut across the heavy muscle of his thigh made walking painful, but to spare himself a permanent limp he stumped about the woods, extending the distance each day until he could go to the shore and back.

One evening after a day spent alone he returned to the hermitage to find Joseus emerging from his prayers of vespers in the chapel. They went on to the cell together.

"I am a well man again," Gawin said. "and now I shall be your servant as you have been mine these weeks."

Joseus grinned and shook his head. "Being served would seem like labor to me. Besides, your wounds may be closed, but your patience has caught a fever. The more we wait for word from the City of Legions the more your peace of mind suffers."

Gawin admitted it. "At the end of eight days I began to look for Perceval, and now seventeen days have passed and we know no more than we did when he left us."

"What are you afraid of?"

"Kei. As long as his treachery goes unknown his hold on Arthur tightens," Gawin said. "I am afraid for Britain, I am afraid for Perceval too. I pray God he has not been sent to the same death as Lohot."

"Perceval is resourceful, and God defends him," Joseus said, undisturbed. "One of these mornings he will ride down from the Roman road with a message from your friend Yvain."

"But I am bound to fight the brother of the Knight of The Moors at the beginning of summer. And if I do not soon start toward my meeting with him I shall fail my pledge."

Joseus said, "You still plan to take this combat, Gawin? Why?"

"Because I am sworn in the king's name."

"Yet the king released you from his service so that you might seek Christ's cup. Besides, you have put yourself into exile from the king and court. What requires you to fight the brother of The Moors?"

"A sworn man does not come unsworn as easily as you

299

think, Joseus. Once he has pledged himself in the king's name —" Gawin broke off, trying to express a truth whose force he had never been required until now to define. "It changes him," he finished inadequately. "I mean he has no choice, no matter what words of release have been spoken."

Joseus made no reply. Though he smiled in his usual encouraging way, Gawin felt the constraint that had been growing between them. Since his encounter with Mortelle they could no longer pursue a discussion which led them into matters of duty and Gawin's quest, they could not talk away the hours on any subject as they had once been able to do. For this reason they had been spending time apart.

The days were burdensome to Gawin. He exercised on foot, practiced with his horse and spear, rode several times into the Roman road hoping to meet Perceval or Yvain or some traveler who could tell him news of Arthur's capital. But the hours passed blankly, one after another, and on the morning of his departure he still knew nothing of Perceval's errand or of Perceval himself.

He heard the prayers of prime in the chapel with Joseus, and afterwards shared a spare meal of dark bread and milk. The big hermit squired him into his mail and saddled his horse and led it out to the stump of a tree whose top he had leveled for a mounting stage.

"We say farewell a second time." Joseus reached up to grasp his hand. "God go with you, brother."

"I would be glad if I could reward you for your hospitality and your teachings, Joseus. No man ever befriended me more courteously."

300

Joseus sighed. "I envy you, though I pray it is envy without sin."

"Ah, Joseus!"

"I mean I lack your courage to seek the Grail. I am afraid of God's secrets, it is enough for me to try to understand what he shows openly to all men."

"If I live I shall come back."

"Send me word if I can serve you. Now I'll walk you as far as the estuary."

"No," Gawin said, "let us part here. God sustain you in health and holiness, brother."

Though he was moved with complex feelings of gratitude, love, and regret, he was anxious to get away from the big man who had radically altered the course of his life. And as he walked his horse down the overgrown garden he did not look back.

He passed the estuary, picked up the Roman road, fearing superstitiously that he would find his way blocked once more by Mortelle, and proceeded into the hill forest lying between him and the royal fort. He did not stop at the fort, but went on directly to the south reaches of the strait. Not even to secure a boat would he have ridden north to the inn of Luned's father. Now he felt himself removed by changes more profound than the mere passing of a year from all he had been on the day he bought the tear spoon. On the chance that fishermen would appear he made a beach camp, building a driftwood fire.

But no fishermen arrived. He slept in his cloak on the shingle. He was wakened at daybreak by screaming sea birds, and sat up to see several boats working close off-shore. He called to the crew of a broad-bottomed vessel of two sails and bargained for passage. The men, a father and son, agreed to ferry him and his horse.

The boatman's son said to him, "What brings you to this old countryside, messire?"

"I am on a mission of the king."

"Oh, I thought perhaps —" the young man considered his words, then fell silent.

"What did you think, friend?" Gawin asked him. "Is there trouble here?"

"No trouble at all," the father said. "He thinks nothing."

But the son did not wish to be muffled. "At this time of year we fishermen who work the strait always hope for the luck to see the green knight returning." He spread his hands apologetically. "My father fears you will think me a simpleton, but who knows what is true in this world? If there is a green knight, and if he does return, he must pass the strait, mustn't he?"

"Who is your green knight?" Gawin asked.

"They say he is the king of the harvest, messire."

The father ducked his head in embarrassment. "You must not think we believe these old lies, messire."

"Laugh if you like," the son said, "but whatever my father wishes, I am of a mind to ask you whether you yourself are the green knight."

Gawin could not help a snort of astonished laughter. "Not I, not I, I am Gawin of Rhos and knight of the Round

302

Table. I have never heard of your green knight. Does he have a name?"

"I do not think so. Everyone here knows who is meant when the green knight is mentioned."

"What does he do? I mean, where has he been and why does he return?"

"They only say he returns," the father interrupted, "they do not say where he has been. As for what he does, they say he makes the grain strong so it will set a fat harvest."

"He must be a pagan Demon," Gawin said.

"I don't know," the father went on, willing to talk once he was sure Gawin would not upbraid him for heresy. "I have looked for him many a summer, but I have never seen him. Perhaps he is pagan —" he paused, wrinkled his brow, "except —"

"Except what?"

"Except our priest allows us each year at Easter to burn a sheaf of last autumn's grain at the church door for the green knight's sake. Doesn't this make him a Christian, messire?" The boatman looked at Gawin with eager curiosity. "Like our Lord, the Son of God, Who also returns to His friends at the beginning of summer?"

53

BEYOND THE STRAIT the rich grain fields were ruffled by a west wind, and cloud shadows hastened dark and swift across their silvery stretches. The tossed grasses, the blue sky, the peaks and domes behind him to the east gave Gawin a sense of homecoming. So often he had thought of the rolling west shoulder of Norgals, so many times in dreams he had traversed its lonely roads that now its reality seemed to possess the intimate, special sanction of the long-known.

Once he was on Iglais's ground he wished to do all as he had done it before. Hence he turned right and followed the strait to its junction with the cliff road, thinking of Ewan and his twelve sheep, and of Luned who had loved him without love for a shilling. He ascended the hill beyond which lay the bay between its airy headlands. Just as it appeared a year ago, he muttered aloud, blue and peaceful, with the sun shining on the flying gulls. How can a winter of freezing gales pass over it and leave no change? Calamity changes nothing but ourselves.

He rode on northwestward, in time reaching the fishing village, the ruined church, the grove of blasted walnut trees. Finally he had pushed through the thin forests of Iglais's castle hold and emerged onto the field where he first saw Perceval. And now the idea of change became enormous, a racing Presence whose intentions were not knowable. Change had seized Perceval and marked him with God's unnamable sign. The youth with whom Gawin had made friends was become (in the life term of a single grain of wheat) the best knight, lost to him. Iglais too, was she lost?

The oat farms were not the same. The boundaries had been cleaned of weeds, and the cart lanes mended, and fat hanks of braided straw, stuck with hawk feathers, tied to poles so that as they fluttered in the wind they would scare away magpies and ravens and field mice. Gawin felt almost grateful for mundane changes which could be easily understood. This is what a year of quiet living has done, he thought, and enough men to work the land, and tools to make labor count. Does my lady ride out to look at her farms and remember who fought for her?

A rude, sudden desire for her stripped away the remote tenderness with which, in the year past, he had thought of her. A gentle, unworldly lady, victim of an oppressor, Perceval's mother, she had appealed to his chivalry. But she was a woman too, an attractive one. And as Gawin approached the barbican and drawbridge his heart shook in his breast because Iglais was a woman whom a man could love.

He saw that the barbican had undergone a certain degree of cleaning and patching, and that it was now manned. He gave his name to the sentry, who said, "Welcome, messire, I believed you would return to take up your pledge. And I am glad to see a knight as renowned as yourself."

The ancient drawbridge had been rejuvenated too, new planks replacing the rotted floor, and the machinery oiled and aligned. The sentry took his horse and sent a foot soldier with him across the moat. The guardroom was also manned, and the armory newly equipped with catapults and cross bows. A squad of foot soldiers in brown and green kilts shared the two rooms.

The soldier from the barbican said, "Here is Messire Gawin on the king's mission."

A kilted man stepped forward. "We still do not have a steward, Messire Gawin. Do you remember me?"

"Thomas! I remember you as though you were a brother."

Thomas's red face managed to glow a pleased shade brighter. "Things are different here in these days since our rights have been returned to us. We dress as soldiers, though I am bound to say we do not have much practice in war. But this time when you fight your combat, perhaps I can be your true squire."

"I shall be glad to have a true squire. Meanwhile, will you tell my lady I am here, Thomas?"

"Willingly."

It was on Gawin's tongue to ask whether Perceval had come home, but he did not. Here on Perceval's native ground he was overwhelmed by the size of the task of explaining the achievement of the sword, and the actuality of Perceval's uncles and the cup of Christ.

Thomas passed into the great hall, returned, and said, "My lady asks you to come in at once, Messire Gawin."

"I will lay off my mail first. Unarm me, Thomas, and give me water to wash my hands."

Thomas removed his chain shirt, his chausses and champons, which he replaced with soft boots. In his riding vestments and his own cloak Gawin entered the great central chamber where, a year ago, he had seen Iglais before her embroidery frames.

She stood by the hearth awaiting him, and his excited anticipation felt rebuffed. He had dreamed of her hastening to meet him, even running into his arms. Like a young lover he had imagined their sounds of joy, the half-spoken names, the quick endearments, the kisses. But she stood across the broad hall, wrapped in her own mood, strange.

"I have returned to keep my engagement with the brother of The Moors, my lady," he said.

"Welcome, Gawin." She seemed to cast about for more words, embarrassed. At length she repeated, "Welcome to this house, Gawin."

He moved toward her over the rattling floor rushes. She too had changed, though not in any large, visible way. She had not aged, she wore no open symtom of sorrow. Yet she was older and more sorrowful than she had been, as though the hues of her life had dimmed a little. But upon Gawin her beauty burst sudden and fresh, striking him like the light that streams past a curtain just drawn. He had forgotten the literal, small woman who stood before him, or he had remembered her only in musings and lonely dreams, which was the same as forgetting.

He said stupidly, "Iglais," and took her hand in his and kissed it.

"Have you come from the City of Legions, Gawin?"

"I have been afraid you would not receive me," he said.

"Oh, you should not have thought such a thing of me." She reclaimed her hand and somehow gave him a smile. "Let us sit down. What can I send for to make you comfortable? Will you take food or ale?"

"Have you believed I forgot my promise to bring Perceval home, Iglais?"

"No, but let us not speak of it. Tell me about yourself."

She sat down determinedly, and pointed to a chair nearby heaped with cushions.

"I can't tell you about myself without speaking of Perceval. This last year — it has all been changed because of him. And I have just come from your kinsman, the hermit Joseus, and while I was with him I saw Perceval."

"Yes," she said faintly. "You saw him? Was he well?"

"I had just been knocked off my horse and I was a little dazed," Gawin said, "and so I did not talk with him before he left. But I am sure he was well. He was — he is — he has become —"

She turned her head aside and closed her eyes. "I have seen him," she murmured. "I have seen the knight Perceval."

Gawin said, "Your son is the best knight, he has achieved the sword. Do you know this?"

"I know it." She drew breath, then opened her eyes. "I suppose we must speak of him, Gawin. I do not understand Perceval. I realize he loves me and I am glad of that, but he is not sweet and tender and cross and outrageous, like a son. He lives in a — I do not know — he is terrible, like an angry angel. I have seen him three times since he ran away from me, and each time he had moved a little farther toward — away from — beyond — I do not know the words. And now I have said all I can say."

She no longer blames me, Gawin thought, it has gone deeper than blame. She only feels the crush of his destiny. And for a moment Gawin thought of Perceval as a mindless energy, like a slide of mountain snow, impersonal, without malice, but smothering whatever opposed its awful force.

54

THE NEXT MORNING Gawin rose early, intending to take breakfast with the soldiers of the garrison. But he found Iglais and a boy about twelve years old waiting for him in the great hall. Near the hearth a low table was set with a white cloth, a silver cup, plate, and spoon, and a horn-handled knife.

"Good morning to you, Gawin," Iglais said.

"Good morning, my lady. I did not expect to find you awake."

Her eyes were on the page. She motioned the boy to come close, then smoothed back a lock that had slipped over his forehead. "We are trying to do things a little more politely than when you were here before. This is what you wished for us, isn't it?"

Gawin sat down on the mound of furs and cushions before the table. "Nothing was lacking before, Iglais. And my wish for you then was the same as now — peace and happiness."

"Run to the kitchen," she said to the youth, "and tell the cook Messire Gawin is ready to be served." When he had gone she went on, "I have taken the two sons of my chief farmer into my service as pages. They are not of gentle blood, but they are good, handsome boys, and perhaps they won't regret later on that they can't train for knighthood."

Gawin said, "Any lad will be improved by being in your service." He felt awkward, and heard himself speaking in tones that sounded false.

"Well!" she said. "At any rate, I have a household again." She still avoided his eyes. "I hope you didn't think me rude yesterday because I failed to mention our comforts, all the good things we lacked before you fought my husband's vassal, and perhaps today you will ride out to see how much is changed."

"I would be glad if you show me, and I hope you will ride with me."

"I keep a little horse for myself now, and that is one thing I didn't do when you were here before, partly because my boundaries were not very long in those days and I could walk them, but all the same I enjoy riding, I feel less alone when I am outdoors and my little palfrey is jogging along."

Her wistfulness upset him afresh, yet began to annoy him. She was insisting too much on the unwelcome alterations of her life, on her loss. Change and loss, were they not the common human bread, and must not all men learn to find nourishment in these harsh foods?

She brought her eyes to his and gave him a tremulous smile. "I mean to say it will be pleasant to ride with you."

But I am stupid and cruel to judge her, he thought, seeing her curved lip, her blue eyes slightly shaded with fatigue, as though she had been wakeful in the night, the smooth, fluid shine of her hair about her shoulders. The

3 1 0

blood swelled slowly into his head. *If she is not the woman for me, no woman is for me in this life.*

Preceded by the page, a kitchen carl bearing a huge board entered and set before Gawin a bowl of herb-scented mutton soup, thick porridge, cheese, cold roast fowl, and wafers of warm, unleavened bread. The servant was sweating and clumsy in his eagerness to do all as he had been instructed. When the food was placed he glanced at Iglais to learn whether his performance had been satisfactory.

This attempt at worldliness heightened Gawin's pity and embarrassment. He began to eat the enormous meal with the determination of a soldier faced with a duty, thankful that he could be silent. Iglais watched him anxiously, the page watched him, the cook stood off at a respectful distance and watched him. It was a long ordeal. As he neared the end the page suddenly collected himself and darted into the kitchen. He returned carrying a bowl, a ewer, and a white towel.

"This is for your hands, messire," he said, and poured water into the basin.

The table was cleared, and Iglais rose. "My people are still not used to guests," she said, "but practice will improve them, and I am sure they hope you were pleased, as I do, Gawin."

He dug himself out of the cushions. He was angry enough to stamp from the room, but he wished to draw her into his arms, to kiss her mouth, to speak all his tumbled memories of the year of his solitude and desire, to tear away her protective shams. He said, "I believe we will find the sun warm and breeze blowing. This will be a good morning for riding."

"I will send for the horses," she said. "Give me a little time, and let us meet at the postern."

Gawin went out by the barbican and walked back along the moat toward the stables. He discovered that a light, easily retractable footbridge had been thrown across the moat to connect the rear gate and the stables — part of Iglais's general renovations. Poor lady, he thought, she has ordered these patchings and renewals in order to convince herself that the life she must live is worth living. She was happier before, not only because she had Perceval, but because she is by nature a solitary soul best contented when life is simplest. She does not care a feather's weight about a garrison, bridges, pages, heaps of fine food. She has done these things to please — to please whom? The knight who fought for her? Gawin ridiculed the thought.

Iglais emerged through the postern and crossed the new footbridge. She wore an ankle-length riding dress, over it a leather jacket, and a silk-lined wool cape fastened with two enameled clasps. Her boots were cross-laced with wide, colored thongs from instep to ankle. She protected her head with a round cap brimmed with a rolled silk scarf. Under it a veil fell to her shoulders in the back, and passed below her chin and covered her throat. As she came along the bridge she looked charming, a girlish figure hurrying toward a pleasure.

There were few changes Gawin had not already observed on his ride from the strait. But he took them in again gladly as they walked their horses around the old boundaries. With a rising sense of shared delight they noted the green crops, the clean soil, harebells along hedges and pastures, and everywhere speckled white and yellow wildflowers. The field hands looked up and shaded their eyes to watch them pass, and the old priest came to the door of his cell to wave. Above them waterfowl swept in great curves, crying their plaintive cries.

Iglais led him to a bare, creased headland from which they could look down on the sea. The immense field of stone rounded up into a high, humped shoulder, then curved into a sheer wall. A calm sea lapped against the black-seamed cliff, running in on long, glassy, green swells that nuzzled and snuffed at the barnacled rock, then shattered in subdued bursts of white foam. The sound was low and lulling.

"Let us dismount," Gawin said.

"I sometimes sit here alone, though I am afraid it worries Thomas and Ewan," Iglais said. "Poor men, they are nervous, and I am not nervous."

Gawin fastened the horses by wrapping their reins around a stone. He and Iglais picked their way to the highest point and stood shoulder to shoulder, awed by the endless distance of blue, green, purple, and shadowed black. Below them on an island shaped like the paw of a huge animal they could distinguish a tiny house and, rising from the stark rock before it, a Christian cross.

"There is a hermit who truly wishes to be alone," Gawin said, pointing down.

"They say he can only go and come in a withy basket

he pulls back and forth by ropes," Iglais told him, "but it isn't true. At low tide I have seen him crossing on foot."

Gawin said, "Do you know why I returned, Iglais?"

"I suppose to keep your promise to the brother of The Moors."

"I mean, why I returned to you? If I had wished I could fight tomorrow without ever troubling you."

"I am glad you did not wish to fight without seeing me, Gawin. But I would rather not hear you say why you returned."

"Because you don't love me?"

"We are not young," she murmured.

"I was married when I was twenty," Gawin said, "and my wife died before I was twenty-one. Since then I have not seen any woman I could bear to love until I saw you. This is what I have come back to tell you."

She shook her head. "No, no, Gawin, I am sorry."

"Why?" he said.

"Let us sit down. A little farther on I know a ledge that is out of the wind."

She led him to a cramped seat sheltered on two sides by head-high walls. "I used to sit here with Perceval," she said. "Or rather I sat while he leaped about shouting at the birds."

"Is it for Perceval's sake that you can't love me?"

"No, no — or perhaps yes, Gawin. I don't know why. I am not a woman who thinks of love any longer. I live because God wishes me to live, and because I am Perceval's mother." She drew a loud, impatient breath. "I know he is

314

moving on some awful errand, I know he must yield himself to God's push. And I believe he will not live long. After he dies, if he must die —" she broke off to level a finger in the direction of the hermit's cell lying like an empty shell on the stony island — "I shall live like that holy man, praying, until I too reach the time to die."

"Oh, this is not good, Iglais, this is not right. You must not think such unnatural thoughts about your death and Perceval's."

She said with a kind of small, rueful mirth, "My family have been trying for I do not know how long, Gawin, I have heard it is as long as a thousand years — they have been trying to learn from God what secret He wraps up in death."

"Do you speak of the Grail?"

Suddenly she leaned against him and closed her eyes. "I am tired," she murmured. "Perhaps I could love you, except time is so big, and it lasts so long."

55

THEY DID NOT RETURN to the hall until the sixth hour, when the shadows were round and short and the sun stood almost overhead. There they found a squire armed with the bearings of The Moors. He had come with the formal duty of reminding Gawin of his pledge to fight the brother of the

Knight of The Moors on charge of treachery, and to state the time and place.

"You are expected, messire," the squire said, "an hour after prime, in the field before the keep where The Moors was struck down from ambush by an unlawful blow."

"I shall be there," Gawin responded, "in the king's name, to defend the king's justice."

With a curvet the squire turned his horse and rode away.

Iglais said, "I wish this fight did not have to be fought, Gawin. I do not need the land."

"But the king's law must be upheld."

"Yes, I remember. The battle is for the king, it only happens here."

He took her hand. "This is old ground, Iglais. Let us not allow my reason for fighting to divide us."

"You are right," she said with a sad little smile. "Me, I shall not think about it, I shall only pray for your safety."

They parted at the guardroom. Gawin went on to the armory to find Thomas and discuss with him the preparation for his combat.

"You must have had the services of a fine squire before you reached us, Messire Gawin," Thomas said. "Your arms and horse gear shine like silver."

"All that rubbing and oiling and sanding was done by a holy man," Gawin told him. "And I agree that I have never had such a squire as he."

"This is surely a good omen. Tomorrow you will fight with weapons that have been furbished by a blessing of God."

Gawin did not wish to see Iglais again before the combat. The end of a year ruled by an obsession with her and her son, a year in which he had met failure and mystery and isolation of spirit and the evil taint of enchantment, a year in which he had not been himself, seemed crushing to him. He felt damaged, not by any decisive wound but by many small ones, like a man who has pushed through a thicket of thorns. He did not wish to think of her, he did not wish to face his disappointment, he wished only to be alone, his mind on the duty he must perform in the morning. Hence he ate his evening meat with the garrison, and slept in the barbican with the post of guards.

With the first gray smoke of dawn he roused Thomas. Carrying his arms, they went in silence to the stable, and Thomas put him into his mail. They led their horses to the priest's cell, where Gawin had asked to hear his battle mass, received their communion, and emerged into the grove before the light was strong enough to show the color of the harebells.

Thomas, full of the dignity of his round shield and short sword, seemed to feel that a squire could not gossip and ask the simple questions a mere groom asked last year. And so they rode in silence. Gawin summoned his memory of the brother of The Moors, a man not so squat and sinewy as his kinsman, but perhaps quicker and better able to endure. He will not swarm onto me in a wild gallop, he told himself, but watch and think and try to take me in artful traps I am not expecting. I must fight with my head too. I hope the light is clear and long and falling onto the green from the side. I must not let him maneuver me so that the sun shines in my eyes, it is the kind of thing he will plan.

Am I ready? Yes, he thought, I suppose I am. Yet the fever of purpose, the coolness that lived with excitement and a heart knocking in the ears, these were missing. I fight because I know how to fight, I will prevail because it is my business to prevail. But he wondered whether a time came when such weapons lost their edge.

The sun poured down a sudden dazzle of gold. From a hidden chapel or wayside cross they heard a bell of prime. The horses jogged forward at a steady walk, and Gawin slumped in his saddle, lax, thinking. Perhaps it was intended that I should not fight this fight. Pelles asked me in a strange, half-clear way whether I was still the king's sworn man, and Joseus said I was not required to keep the king's pledge. Were these hints I did not listen to? It came over him that not only his search for Perceval, not only his meeting with the hermit father and son, not only his longing to achieve Christ's cup, but every motion of his life, every encounter of his days, all things large and small, were parts of the game of chess whose moves and pieces he could not see. God has me in His hand each moment, he thought, and the fact seemed new and enormous and terrifying.

"This is where we turn, Messire Gawin," Thomas said. "What instructions do you wish to give me?"

"If the tree still stands at the upper edge of the battle green, wait under it for me."

"I am not to help you if you need help?"

Gawin was touched. "If it were possible, there is no man

whose help I would rather have than yours, Thomas."

Thomas gulped down his disappointment. "Then God go with you, messire. We are near our ground."

They turned off the east-west road into a narrower trail running slightly northwest. Gawin spurred his horse into a trot, slung his shield forward at parade, and held his spear in his stirrup, standing it upright. His horse, feeling its own battle eagerness, arched its neck and pranced.

They entered a copse of ancient trees which lay beyond the battle green outside the wall of the castle of The Moors.

"Listen," Thomas said.

"I hear it," Gawin said, "and if it means treachery we have no time to listen." He kicked his spurs into his horse's belly. The loud clang of sword fighting shook through the trees, ringing blows like great, dull bells half-damped telling him two men of mighty strength were striving together. He knew this before he saw them. If someone anticipates me, he thought, if this combat in the king's name had been taken unlawfully from my hands a second time, is it to worsen the charge of treason against me, drag me before the king in my shirt, submit me to the ordeal?

He galloped into the clearing, then flung himself backward in the saddle, pulling his horse up so suddenly that it reared. On the long oblong of sunny sward two men were wielding double-bladed swords, crashing sparks from one anothers' helms and shoulders. One wore the bearings of The Moors, one silver-white arms blazoned with a glistering green cross.

Thomas panted to a stop beside Gawin, stared as though

he had been hit in the chest by an arrow, and crossed himself, muttering God's name. "The green knight," he said again and again, "the green knight."

Gawin leaned over, caught him by the shoulder, shook him. "Stop it, Thomas, stop it. What green knight?"

Thomas pointed. "There."

"That is no green knight, that is Perceval."

Open-mouthed, Thomas leaned over his saddle bow to stare. "How do you know it is Perceval? The green knight comes at the beginning of summer, this is his exact day, he —"

"I will not hear any more of this," Gawin said. "Go to your tree and keep your silly tongue to yourself."

"Wait, messire, tell me how you know it is Perceval."

"Because the green cross is his bearing. He has fought under it before. Go on, Thomas, move yourself off the field."

"You are sure?"

Gawin snatched Thomas's rein and led his horse beyond the battle lawns. "Either wait under the tree or ride home."

He rounded again to the field. In the moments during which his back was turned the man in the arms of The Moors had been struck to earth. Perceval ran forward and stood over him, sword raised in both hands. "Yield yourself recreant to King Arthur, or die!" The judgement-sentence of the good knight spoken in a deep singsong echoed and re-echoed about the field, bounding back from the castle walls and from the forest.

The fallen man said, "I will never yield, my brother died by treason and I will die by treason."

320

Gawin had pulled up to hear the reply. But when he saw Perceval kneel and methodically unlace the fallen man's casque, then begin to remove it, he rode to the combatants. "Wait, stop, let him get up."

Perceval heaved off the casque and threw it into the grass. Once more he stood and raised his sword.

Gawin swung his spear against the blade. "I forbid this killing in the king's name."

Perceval, with the advantage of leverage, swept the spear aside with his sword. Feet spread at the fallen man's shoulders he brought down his blade, a whistling, glittering arc of light in the morning sun. The head bounded away, mouth open, eyes staring, eyebrows raised as if in unbelief. The blow was clean, exact, and done the moment it began.

On the grass Perceval's shield lay, bearing up, in the bright light, its green cross blazing as though with green fire. The youth in white armor wiped his sword on the grass, sheathed it, and picked up the shield.

He said, "I took this fight for love of you, Gawin."

Behind him the veins in the neck of the beheaded man writhed as the blood hissed forth. His mailed fingers still feebly scratched at the grass.

"Now," Perceval went on, "I know what justice is. You were wrong when you said I must spare him in the king's name. I have set right the evil he and his family have done my mother." His face, austere, looked out of the raised ventail of his casque. The same dark eyes, the same fair, open brow, the same quick intelligence, they were all there.

321

But Perceval was no longer a boy, he had become a man, even, Gawin thought, stricken by wrath and disgust and awe and the end of seeking, even more than a man.

 56

AT GAWIN'S ORDER a horse litter was summoned from the castle garrison, and the body of the slain knight was carried to the priest's cell. Gawin followed on foot. He asked the holy man to bathe the corpse, see that it was moved into the chapel for appropriate prayers, then buried.

When he emerged Perceval was walking toward the chapel. He said, "Has all been done, Gawin?"

"Yes."

"Then let us remain together awhile. Thomas has unarmed me, and he is waiting to unarm you."

"Time enough to be unarmed when we return home." Gawin could not speak naturally with the man Perceval who had just dealt his justice with such unflinching conviction.

"There is a well at the lower edge of the battle green," Perceval said, "and a bench under an oak tree. Thomas is waiting at the tree. I have washed and drunk from the well. After Thomas serves you he will ride home with the news for my lady mother. I would be glad," he finished, "if you would delay with me an hour under the tree by the well."

322

"I do not need rest, I have not been dried by combat," Gawin said. "I am not fated to do battle on this field, however much a king's officer I am."

Perceval dropped a brotherly hand onto his shoulder. He was taller than Gawin, more youthfully lean in the hips. His color was glowing fresh, his hair thick and silky. Yet his style was not that of mere good looks. He was severe, preoccupied, a man who appeared young only in body. "I believe you, Gawin, you are not fated to do battle on this field. But all the same, battle has been done for justice, and your prowess is not in doubt. My family was injured, and it is my lawful right as well as my duty to defend the ancestral blood of my mother." He shook Gawin's shoulder in a friendly way, the gesture saying the affair was in the past. "Much was begun here, wasn't it? And now after a year, the much begun has become much achieved."

Gawin could not hit on any reply. In his physical body Perceval did not seem the mystery into which he had grown during the year of search. Enough of his vivid youth remained to inspire Gawin with the wish to reproach him for snatching into his own hands the matter of the kinsman of The Moors, to charge him with mischievous arrogance and secrecy, above all to make him feel the disappointments of his own confused wanderings. Moreover he needed to know whether Perceval had found Yvain in the City of Legions, and how the news of Lohot's death had been delivered. Yet though his sinews were still tense with what he had seen, the image of the severed head and bleeding trunk, some part of him stood away from his angry urgencies. For a year he had sought Perceval, and now they were met. He said, "Do you know I have looked for you?"

"My uncle and cousin told me, my mother too."

"Twice we might have met."

"More than twice." Perceval removed his hand and gestured in a way reminiscent of his old, childish restlessness, oddly unfitting now. "I needed time, Gawin. Besides, it was intended. From the moment I took the sword from the pillar I began to feel all was intended. Do you know what I mean?"

"I remember when I became a knight I had this same sense of destiny."

"And too," Perceval said, "I believed I had been right to kill the Knight of The Moors, and I did not wish to see you until I could show you that I had been right. Now you have seen my proof." And he pointed toward the battle green.

"And you can tell me what justice is?"

"Why do you dislike the idea that I know what justice is? Justice is your business too."

"My business is the *king's* justice. Sometimes a knight needs a while to see the difference."

After a long silence Perceval said, "It is hard to explain these things," as though to a younger brother. They were nearing the well. "Let Thomas help you out of your mail, Gawin. It is a shame to hold such a soft day as this at bay with a chain shirt." He sat down on the bench and leaned against the oak tree and closed his eyes. Without the light of his glance his face appeared colder and sterner. How can he speak of the soft day, Gawin thought, when he has just killed a man? And he remembered Iglais, who had called her son an angry angel.

Thomas removed his mail, led their horses away a distance and tethered them, then set out on his return journey home.

Perceval said, "Does it seem to you a long time that we have waited for this morning, Gawin?"

"Yes, longer than a single year."

Perceval ran his hands through his hair, lifting the helmet-flattened locks to the breeze. "I shall lie on the ground," he said. "I like to feel the sun on me." And he stretched himself on the thick grass beyond the shadow of the oak, hands under his head. "You know, Gawin, sometimes when I have bathed in a little, shallow, sun-cooked lake, I lie in the deep weeds near the water and let the wind dry me. There is the silence of the slopes, and the clouds going over, and nothing to speak louder than the roots of things growing."

Gawin was silent.

Perceval said, "Why do you not talk to me?"

"It is hard to begin. There is more to say than I can choose."

"What do you wish me to tell you, brother?"

Ask, Gawin thought. But surely not of the son of Iglais? He answered, "How did you achieve the sword?"

"I needed a sword, and it was at hand."

"Didn't you see the rune carved above it?"

Perceval shaded his eyes to follow the flight of a broad-winged bird high over the trees. "I saw it, but I don't know how to read many words. I was surprised when I learned the sword had caused so much excitement among the knights of the king."

"But," Gawin said, deflated, "wasn't it a special sword? Doesn't it have some unique power of its own?"

"Do you mean, is it magic? It is a perfect weapon, balanced to a hair, an edge that only crude abuse can dull, and so good in the hands that it seems to have its own leaping will to fight. If this is magic, it is a magic sword."

"Will you allow me to draw it?"

"Ah, Gawin, leave the sword! I use it for God's justice, and this is all that needs be said. Ourselves, we have other things to talk of."

"No man who has been a knight of Arthur's can pass over the sword as lightly as you, Perceval. From the days when we were pages we saw it standing in the pillar and we believed whoever achieved it would achieve it for a destiny beyond other men's. And as I followed you this past year I believed you did have a destiny laid on you by God."

"What destiny do you think mine is, Gawin?"

Gawin said slowly, "I have met your kinsmen and they speak of the Grail. Do you seek it, as I do?"

"I am of the family who guard the relic. And for this reason, if I seek it, I do not seek it in the same way as you."

"Will you tell me what the relic is?"

"Yes, indeed," Perceval said quietly. "It is a cup, first the cup of earth's bounty, then the cup of the shed blood of death, then the cup of the seed of resurrection. And at last it is the cup of the divine union of death and resurrection."

"And shall I hold it in my hands?"

Perceval laid his arm across his eyes. "My cousin Joseus believes you have given up your quest for the Grail, Gawin."

"I have not given it up, he has misunderstood."

"You are seeking it? Now? Today?"

"I have been pledged for a year to this combat for my lady your mother. But when I have sent the king word of your intervention and the outcome of your battle, and when the return of my lady's land is lawfully settled, I mean to go on trying to reach your uncle Peleur."

"The hermit, my uncle Pelles, says a man who elects the Grail cannot serve his quest at his own times, when this or that duty is done. Pelles says the Grail will have all of you."

"I know, I know, I will give it my whole self. But," Gawin said in despair, "I am the king's man."

"Pelles says 'the king' is the name of every barrier that stretches between a man and God."

Gawin rose. "You have never been sworn, Perceval, you are not the king's man, you cannot know what you are saying. As for Pelles, he deserted the world. And as for Joseus, he dissolved his oath in the penance done for a crime, the crime of murder."

"But I am a sworn man," Perceval said. "I am sworn to mete God's justice."

"God's justice is too vast for most men. God is there —" Gawin swept a pointing finger under the arc of sky, "and the king is here." He knocked his clenched hand against his breast. "When you achieved the sword you were still a lad,

327

a child, you were an innocent spirit untainted by the world, you knew nothing of the nature of men, you knew only God's goodness." Gawin wiped away the passionate tears with the backs of his hands. "But we men who learn the world's evil with our mother's milk, we are never innocent. How can a man who sees the wickedness he hates in others flourishing in his own heart, how can a man who lives his life with men day after day, love God perfectly? Only a soul born perfect, only a soul whose innocence has been protected and kept secret, only that soul can love God perfectly. The rest of us, we are imperfect, and we love imperfectly."

Perceval sat up, leaning on his hands. "God guided me, Gawin. Why do you not let Him guide you?"

"God does not appear, like a king's forester, when He is called."

"But He does," Perceval said earnestly. "He appeared to me the very day I achieved the sword. I met Him an hour later, just at dusk, on the road outside the City of Legions. He was wearing a black cloak."

"Merlin!"

"Merlin He was, if you like. But *I* know He was God."

GAWIN SAT DOWN. The silence within him felt like the silence of death.

Perceval said, "Will you hear what happened that night, brother?"

"Yes."

"I met the Being you call Merlin. He greeted me as best knight, and when I asked him what he meant, he pointed to the sword. And the sword glowed."

"He recognized the hilts," Gawin said, "and it was sunset, and the blade glistened in the last light."

Perceval bent upon him the young face that had been refined of the expression of youth. "Won't you hear me out?"

"I am sorry," Gawin said. "It is Merlin. He is practiced in trickery."

"Decide when the story is done."

Gawin nodded, repeated, "I am sorry."

"He seemed reverend and good to me, and I asked him what justice was. He said, 'Justice is the fruit of seeking.' I asked him where I must seek, and he said, 'That is a story which I think you had better hear.' He took me to the cottage of a royal hunter —" (Of course, the king's huntsman, Gawin thought, why didn't I remember him that night?) "— and we sat together while he told me who I am. I mean he told me the history of my family. Have you heard the name of Joseph of Arimathea?"

"Yes, I have heard it."

"He was the founder of the line of my mother. Joseph had listened to the teachings of Jesus of Nazareth, and he came to believe in the New Law. After the Son of God was crucified, Joseph pitied Him and begged His body from the soldiers, and washed the wounds and buried it. He preserved the cloth with which he cleansed away Christ's blood, and later, when he secured the cup Christ shared with His disciples at the last supper, he sealed the bloody cloth in lead and kept it in the cup."

Perceval thrust his hands into the deep grass beyond the oak tree and gently tugged at the roots. "Joseph was persecuted for his belief in the New Law. He was well acquainted with the island of Britain, he had worked for the Romans as a buyer of the British tin and lead they needed for their armies. On one of his journeys to the Vale of Avalon, where the metal was loaded into Roman ships, he had built a church of reeds and clay in honor of Christ's New Law. When he was forced to flee for his life he remembered Avalon and the wattle church. He found his way there, and he carried Christ's cup with him."

"Merlin told you this?" Gawin said.

"I was told it the evening I left the City of Legions with the sword. This and more. Will you hear it all?"

"I will hear what you wish to tell me," Gawin said, in torment as he thought of the king's counselor.

"Men who loved holiness were drawn to my kinsman Joseph," Perceval resumed, "and a company settled in Avalon. They professed the New Law of Christ, and because Joseph taught them and heartened their faith, the cup poured out nourishing meats in cruel winters when he could not feed them. But Joseph was unwilling to share the secret of the cup with men whose reliance on Christ's God faltered when it was tried. He told only one of his companions the real miracle of the food. In his old age he was troubled about the fate of the cup, knowing he could not trust any follower to hold it in reverence, without abusing its gifts. And when he knew he was near death, he hid it." Perceval sat up and held a wisp of grass under his nose, breathing in its cool, earthy smell.

"I thought the cup was passed on from man to man in your family," Gawin said.

Perceval slowly shook his head. His high color had faded a little and he had begun to grow pale. "Although my family were its natural guardians, they could only seek it, once it was hidden. In time God made it clear that He wished no man among my kinsmen save one worthy of the sacred relic to achieve it again and become its protector. But," he said, dropping back onto the sunny grass, "the same thing was true of the men of my lineage as is true of all men. Some were wicked, some were heedless, some were too foolish to understand. Yet when a seeker fit to behold the cup appeared, the relic would manifest itself to him, and he would learn in this way that he must take up the quest."

Suddenly Gawin pitied him. Had the relic manifested itself to him that evening outside the walls of the City of Legions? For a youth of sixteen this would be a heavy destiny. He must trade the taste of life, sweet or bitter, for a self-denial accepted for its own sake. He said, "Do you mean that only men of Joseph's lineage can achieve it?"

"God is good, Gawin," Perceval said. "God has promised His reward forever to the family who revered the body of His Son and buried it. But His goodness is given to all men.

331

And any true seeker who willingly yields himself to the terrible labor of the quest will see Christ live again within the holy vessel."

I cannot willingly yield myself, Gawin thought, I am the king's man. Yet I can. I will. I will endure the labors even if they are tortures, I will do all. I will forswear the king. But as he thought these words his blood clanged in his breast like the bell rung for the sentencing of a traitor. He said, "Have you achieved the cup, Perceval?"

"I saw it," the good knight said in a low voice. "From the hill above the City of Legions the Being you call Merlin sent me straight to the hall of my kinsman Peleur. I was only told how to reach him, not what I must do. And so I did the wrong thing, or rather I did not do the right thing, being still a child and heedless of secret things. The Grail appeared, all washed in light and sending out lovely scents. I thought it was a wonderful jewel. I watched it pass before me, and fade and disappear. And I did not ask the question."

"I too have been told to ask a question," Gawin said.

" 'Whom does the Grail serve?' This is the question I should have asked," Perceval said, agitated by the memory. He smote his open hand against the earth. "I should have asked, and I did not. And for this reason my kinsman Peleur has been forced to suffer the pains of his illness another year while I was growing wise enough through the ordeals of God's instruction to return and ask."

"I do not understand," Gawin said, "I do not understand."

332

"What don't you understand?"

"How any question asked or unasked could condemn your uncle to his illness."

"I am cold," Perceval said, and he jumped up with a violent spring and beat his arms across his chest. "I have been lazy too long. Let us walk, Gawin."

"No," Gawin said. "I wish to hear all the story you promised to tell me."

Perceval gave him a smile that seemed a little sly, reminding him of the glance he surprised now and then on the face of the hermit Pelles. Then he tipped his head boyishly and stared into the sky. Speaking rapidly he said, "Peleur is the old king. He is ill, he wishes to be done with his life, in his feebleness his land is hurt by many evils, drought and poor grain. But he cannot yield to the young king until the young king appears and asks the question and so releases the old king and achieves his own kingly quest."

"Yourself? Are you to become the young king and inherit your uncle's relic and restore his land to health?"

Perceval turned his back. "What you say is blasphemy, Gawin. No one knows the young king except God. I will tell you this much, that the Being you call Merlin has come to me again and again when I wished to follow my pleasures or was forgetful of my quest. He has come and reminded me that I must return to my kinsman. Before midsummer," he added.

With each word Gawin felt more widely removed from the youth he had hunted so long, from the hope, too, of succeeding in the quest he had undertaken without comprehending its awful confusion. Moreover he felt outraged by Merlin's equivocations, he felt he had been dealt with uncandidly by Pelles and Joseus, he felt he had been mocked for his ignorance and credulity. Or were the enchantments they hinted at fact? If they were fact, the whole quest was an abomination. God was not a magician, God dealt fairly with men, His miracles were clear, His goodness unsickened by trickery. Hence why were the old gods involved with the most holy of His hallows, the demon Spirits of Summer and Winter, the green knight of harvest, the fleshly divinities once served on the altar stone which the priest of Iglais had converted into a Christian cross? Why was Peleur, a king whose age and illness caused drought and starveling crops, the guardian of Christ's cup? Why must all be done by the heathen festival of midsummer?

I must know, Gawin thought, feeling his courage return. I will find out or I will die. He said, "Let me go with you, Perceval. Let me accompany you to the hold of King Peleur."

"It is not possible, brother. I would willingly take you if I could, but in this quest each man must go alone."

"Where is the hold?"

Perceval returned to the bench and sat beside Gawin and gave him a grave smile. "I will tell you the way, and God go with you." He began to lay out a route north, mentioning roadside crosses, hermitages, sentinel trees. "With good weather you will reach the place in three days. I have already described the road to Messire Yvain."

"Have you! Is Yvain to achieve the quest without even desiring it?"

"When I gave him your message about the death of Messire Arthur's son, he said he would come to you as soon as he had done what he could in the City of Legions."

"Has he told the king Joseus's story?"

"I don't know that, Gawin. I gave him the message just as it was entrusted to me, and I left without seeing anyone but him."

Gawin's mind leaped back to the south and his uncle and Kei and Lancelot. "What news was there, did you hear of —"

"Patience," Perceval said. "I have told you all I know. But Messire Yvain will follow you. I told him that he could find you at the hold of my uncle Peleur. I said that by the time he had ridden north you would be there."

"Why did you believe that?"

"I told him he could reach you before midsummer," the kinsman of Joseph of Arimathea said.

58

LATER, AS THEY RODE HOME together, Gawin said, "I will send Thomas to the City of Legions with news of what occurred this morning."

"No need," Perceval said. "I have one duty more, and when it is done I mean to return south to see the Being

335

you call Merlin. And I will carry our message to the king."

"Will you not remain awhile with my lady your mother? Your presence gives her much pleasure."

"My mother understands that I have work to do," Perceval said.

"Even if women understand such matters, their love is rewarded when we yield a little."

The young knight gave Gawin a perplexed look. "My mother's lineage should help her increase in holiness and outgrow the vanity of leaning on any love less firm than the love of God. I have explained this to her."

"Indeed! And what did she reply?"

"She replied that she hoped to please me. And I said I would be best pleased if she served God. And she said if serving God was my wish for her, she would do what I asked."

"What have you asked her to do?"

"Enter a convent of holy women."

"Oh, that will not make her happy," Gawin burst out. "Your mother is a young woman still, a beautiful woman. Her gifts are warmth and delight."

"I know. These are good gifts to offer God. It is true, she did not seem to feel the joy giving them should bring her. But I believe time will teach her the happiness of yielding to a great destiny."

This is what she meant yesterday on the cliff, Gawin thought. She has promised herself not to God but to Perceval, and she sets her promise before the love she has for me. She does love me, I am sure of it, I do not need words of avowal any more than she. And if she can be persuaded that giving herself to God is a different matter from the mere wish to please a son, she will gladly admit it. I shall have the chance to help her see this, he thought, since I must remain with her until the final transfer of her property is accomplished. And if Perceval leaves us to fulfill his other duty, she will not be influenced by his presence. Iglais and I shall have a few peaceful days together in which uncertainties of the future can be held off.

Yet he was conscious of the future, of his journey to the hall of ancient and suffering Peleur, and of his meeting with Yvain. Now it seemed a long time since he had heard of Lohot's death, longer still since he had exiled himself from Arthur. And his heavy sense of isolation was lightened somewhat as he considered that the story Joseus told would free the king from the deceits Kei nourished. Moreover (in spite of what Perceval might wish), he could return with Iglais to the City of Legions when he had finished his quest. And there treason would be met and defeated in its own stronghold.

At the barbican they dismounted. Perceval said, "I will come in with you, brother. I wish to see my mother and inform her of the deliverance I have worked for her sake from her enemies and the enemies of God. I will take meat with her."

"Will you not remain even overnight?"

The young knight only shook his head. "Let us say farewell here, Gawin. We were well met today."

"I owe you thanks for taking my combat." They looked

at one another shyly, constrained by the deep feelings of the year in which each had loomed so large to each. "I hope we shall meet again."

"I believe we shall meet again," Perceval said, "unless —"

"Unless what, brother?"

Perceval did not choose to finish the thought he had begun. He said, "Who can tell what the 'unless' is in this life?" And he took him by the shoulders and, like a king, kissed him on either cheek.

"I will not enter with you," Gawin said. "Your time is best spent with my lady. Farewell, and God go with you."

Perceval went on alone. Gawin was haunted by the meeting between mother and son, feeling as though by extension of Iglais's own senses her dazed pain as she faced the coldness and clarity of Perceval's mission on earth. Only a year ago he was a beloved child she had delighted to protect as she would protect a sportive puppy or a nestling bird. It was too much to ask her to understand that the boy she had nourished was become an elected spirit who did not question his partnership with God.

It is beyond my understanding too, Gawin muttered to himself. At one moment Perceval seems to me the good knight, at the next a soul already half of the stuff of heaven, at the next a stony judge of men whose weaknesses he does not share. And sometimes he seems still a youth, but a youth crazed by the teachings of kinsmen who have narrowed themselves to a fanatic belief in their own destiny. The achiever of the sword, the pupil of Merlin, the green knight,

338

the angry angel, the young king (of Summer, perhaps?), the guardian of Christ's cup, what is he? And Gawin remembered his own fear of madness a year ago when he had spoken to Yvain of the quest of the Grail. Perhaps, he thought, it is a dream from which I need to awaken.

To cure his restlessness he walked through the grove where the harebells were paling in the warm sun of afternoon, and entered the cell of the old priest.

"This is a good day," the holy man said, "since you return whole and Perceval has come home."

"Has Thomas told you the outcome of the combat, father?"

"Yes indeed. And he has told us too how Perceval appeared in green armor and fought the fight. Who would have thought he would grow into a knight as strong as Messire Lancelot in only a year's time? Much has changed," he concluded with a sigh.

Gawin sat down on the puncheon stool. "I asked you questions when we met before, and I have a question for you today."

"I will answer if I have the answer. Will you take bread with me, Messire Gawin?"

"Only a little milk and water. Before I ask, I must tell you about certain events that have befallen since last summer." And Gawin, overshadowed by the cross whose stones were carved with pagan runes, related his wanderings, and the reason for them. "Like Joseus and Pelles," he said at last, "you are a man of God. But I do not believe you share their blood, or that you have sought the Grail. Is this true?"

339

"I am the son of a freeman farmer, and I was born on this land, and I was taught by the monks who maintain a house west of the strait. I am not a man who can reach as high as the Grail."

"Then as one who can ponder it without the passion of birth, tell me why the quest seems one day a Christian search, and the next a secret of the Old Law of the pagans."

"Oh, oh, Gawin, you are a simple man!" The priest laughed without sound. "You want God to be like yourself, you want Him trimmed to fit the space you occupy and the time you occupy, seeing truth through your eyes. But God is not that. God is. God has been. God will be. And I believe He was present on every ancient midsummer morning when altar stones like mine —" without looking at it the priest moved a bony hand toward his cross — "were wet with the blood of the sacrifice our forefathers offered when they prayed to their gods of Winter and Summer to revive the dying year."

"But the Grail is Christ's own cup," Gawin said through stiff lips. "It is the very vessel of His death and resurrection."

"And do you think Christ denies us the bounty of His death because we act out at midsummer the death and re-birth of nature? You want too much, Gawin. You want all mysteries explained."

59

AFTER PERCEVAL'S DEPARTURE Iglais was depressed. And as the days passed Gawin used every device of easy companionship to coax her into better spirits. When the weather was sunny they rode together, often to The Moors, where he was questioning men who could best advise her in the matter of the farms. Fishermen were among the servants being returned to her, and the inspection of their fleet was Gawin's excuse for a day of pleasure. If storms kept them indoors they played chess before the hearth, or Iglais worked at her frames while he told her stories of his brothers of the Round Table.

"How good it is to hear you laugh," he said to her one evening when they had shared a supper by the fireside. "You are most beautiful when you open your mouth a little to laugh."

"It seems strange," she said, "to be sitting here all warm and comfortable and hearing you say pleasant things. You know, it has been a long, long time since I have felt like a woman or been treated like a woman or even thought about being one, and I believe if one happens to be a woman, the nicest thing is to feel like it."

"And how does a woman feel?"

"Safe," she said, "happy," she said, "at home, I suppose.

A woman feels like a woman when she does not have to think how she feels."

"Let me tell you something," he said, and lifted her hand and kissed the warm heartbeat in the wrist. "A man feels like a man when a woman looks at him with love."

"I know that, Gawin."

"I love you."

"I know that too," she said, remembering herself with a sigh. She pulled her hand gently, yet not enough to remove it when he tightened his hold. "Sometimes I am glad you love me, but often I wish you didn't, because I have promised the life I have left to God, and nothing can come of your loving me. Or," she went on after a long pause, "of my loving you either. I will not be foolish and pretend, like a girl, that I don't know my mind. I'm sure you know I do know it, and if I were to love any man again it would be you."

"Perceval has persuaded you that your life belongs to God, but if you asked only yourself how you wish to spend the years ahead, I do not believe you would answer, 'Among holy women.' "

"You must not unsettle me, Gawin."

"I wish to unsettle you, it is not wise to let another person, not even a son, decide what is to be done with all the passion and power of life. You must not run away, Iglais, you must —"

"Oh, stop, stop, I don't want to hear you. I am Perceval's mother, and I have got to — somehow I must — live up to him."

"And what about being safe, happy, at home? You have just said you are all these with me." He rose and drew her to her feet and held her close, kissed her, felt her respond, the two clinging, moving toward love. "Iglais, Iglais, let us not deny —"

She said, pressing her body to his, winding her arms behind his head, her mouth on his mouth, "You are my desire, Gawin, and this is a sin. Goodbye," she said, and kissed him profoundly, and pulled herself free.

She pulled herself free, she settled the long robe she wore, and the short jacket and little coif. And she turned away from him and walked across the great hall, the rushes whispering under her feet, and out the door that led to her private chambers. She did not look back.

Gawin did nothing until it was too late. Then he followed toward the door, of a mind to force it, or to raise an outcry that would bring her back to him. But when he reached it he stopped. His disappointment and affronted pride wished to blame her for rejecting him in the very moment she professed to love him. But a cold flirt was not the Iglais he knew. His dear Iglais had spoken the literal truth. For her, desiring him *was* a sin, for her, 'goodbye' *was* the only word she dared answer to the love of a woman for a man, for her, Perceval's will *was* God's will.

His heart still dunting in his dry throat, Gawin turned back from her door. He sat awhile before the fire, wishing what he knew was impossible, that she would come again across the shadowy hall. His hopes of the last days, a successful journey to the hold of Peleur, a return to Iglais and the City of Legions, and Kei's treachery defeated and shamed, seemed like dreams. He murmured aloud, "Is it dream? God's kingdom and ours too? Is it a world within us which does not resemble at all the world without?"

The bell of compline had long since rung when he made his way to his bed in the armory. In the morning, after he had eaten his meat at the soldiers' mess, Thomas joined him.

"I have a message for you," he said.

"What message, friend?"

"From our priest. He asks you to come to his cell."

"Now?"

"Now," Thomas said, "if you can go conveniently."

She will be with the priest, Gawin thought, she wishes to show me we are friends, but she is timid after last evening and seeks the protection of the holy man. Or perhaps in the night she realized that the life Perceval expects her to lead is not fitting, and she has consulted the priest, and he has advised her not to accept it without feeling her own conviction, and she asks him to tell me she is free. As he hastened down the grassy slope and into the grove, seeing the dew hanging everywhere like new-fallen rain, and hearing it drop, drop among the broad leaves, he fed his hope.

The priest was walking in the tiny garden before his cell. The moist scent of herbs, parsley, sage, savory, rosemary, blew on the clean air.

"Good morning to you, father," Gawin said.

"Good morning, Messire Gawin, and God give you a fine day."

"Thomas said you summoned me."

344

"If all men obeyed their priests as quickly as you have answered me," he said with a smile, "we could hope for a better world. Will you eat bread with me?"

"I took meat with the soldiers in the barbican." It occurred to Gawin that Iglais might be waiting in the cell, and he added, "but I shall be happy to sit before your hearth."

"If your hunger is satisfied, let us enjoy the sun. A morning without mist and clouds is too rare to shut away."

"You have a matter to discuss with me, father?"

The priest tucked his hands into his sleeves. "I have a message to deliver from my lady."

"Have you seen her this morning?"

"She came to my cell to say the prayers of prime with me."

"Had she slept? Was she well?"

"You, Messire Gawin, did you sleep?"

Gawin smiled. "Not as I sleep when I have a quiet mind."

"My lady lacked a quiet mind, as you did. And for this reason, it is better that you leave her house. You and she, your lives will run more peacefully apart."

"Is this the message she asked you to deliver?"

The priest stooped to pluck a tender spray of parsley, which he crushed and lifted to his nose. "She told me to thank you for your courtesy and kindness, and to say that she would always remember your courage, and that you were not to delay your departure. The rest of the message is mine. I believe she will be better served, and you too, Messire Gawin, if you do not try to change what can't be changed."

345

Gawin said harshly, "She does not wish to close herself away with holy women. She is being forced."

"I know, this may be true. But though we cannot see why God's work is done as it is, faith helps us understand that we are happiest when we accept His work without question."

Gawin turned away. This sort of pious adage outraged him, increased the pain of his loss. "Since you and God have settled my departure, I will leave at once."

"Will you send my lady a message?"

"Tell her," Gawin said, and stopped. What message would say more than she already knew? *I love her, I would have been her knight, this she understands.*

"Tell her farewell," he said.

60

BUT RETURNING THROUGH the grove Gawin thought, *I will not take the word of anyone save Iglais. If I am to be dismissed I will hear my dismissal from her own mouth.*

He did not find her in the hall. He went back to the guardroom and said to Thomas, "Tell my lady I have spoken with the priest, and ask her if she will receive me."

"I am sorry, messire, but my lady said I was to beg you to excuse her."

"When was this, Thomas?"

"When she came back from the prayers of prime. She

said if after your conversation with the holy man you requested a meeting I was to answer you as I have answered." Sullen, Thomas refused to lift his eyes.

"Is this all? Was my lady distressed?"

"I am a servant, I repeat what I am told."

"I believe my lady wept, Thomas," Gawin said. "I believe you hold me guilty of her tears."

"She did weep, and if you are not guilty, who is?"

"Has she ordered Iorworth to saddle my horse?"

"Yes, the order has been given."

"Then tell her this, that I leave because she wishes it, and that I am her knight as long as I bear the name of Gawin. For yourself, friend, take my thanks for your good service to me. I am sorry to part with you."

"Messire, messire, I was almost your squire at The Moors, and I wish I had not said you were guilty of my lady's tears."

Gawin went through the barbican and bade the soldiers of the watch goodbye. His horse had been led from the stable. Thomas armed him, conducted him to the mounting stage, and handed up his weapons. As he turned east, the breeze caught his cloak and spread it behind his shoulders. The men raised a cheer, crying after him, "Farewell, God go with you, Messire Gawin."

In all things it was an ordinary departure save in one, that it was made unnaturally vivid by the pain of finality. Everything he saw shone with a special luster, yet nothing was familiar any longer. From the meadows and low, rocky slopes and thin forests a haunting tune blown by the wind murmured, "Lost, lost, lost . . ." He had lost Iglais, and he had lost too this strange land of innocence and peace.

Since he had made a late start noon came and went before he reached the strait. At salt water he found a boat of six oars manned by a crew among whom he recognized men belonging to Iglais.

"Messire Gawin!" the skipper hailed him.

"Are you waiting for me?"

"Yes indeed, my lady sent us word at daybreak to be prepared for you and your horse. Will you board?"

Now, Gawin told himself, I must believe that she too wills the destiny Perceval has adjudged. Has she thought of me this morning as I have thought of her? No. She has already resolved not to think of me, she has given herself work to do so as to drive the memory of last night from her mind. And a year hence, or ten years hence, while I am still shaken by what might have been, will she have forgotten even my name?

On the other shore he rode through the village of Luned, looking with sore recollection at the monks' cookhouse. (Does any woman remember?) The day was nearly spent, but he did not wish to stop. Better to camp in his cloak than to deal again with Luned's father.

He slept that night in the ruins of a coastal tower from which a Roman sentry had once kept watch toward Ireland. The next day he reached a great, decayed, walled Roman city whose fort had guarded the frontier between conquered Britain and the savage North. Here, following Perceval's directions, he crossed a salt estuary and rode into the foothills of the wild, rising moors. That evening, the second of his journey to the hold of King Peleur, he camped in a wind-wrenched grove at the foot of a slope so immense it seemed to rise into the clouds. Yet it was not a high mountain, it was only wall-like, weighty, unfeatured by ravine or knob. This vast, inclined slab of earth was bare of trees, but grass whose green was made burning bright by the last rays of the sun wrapped it smotheringly to its top. Perceval had not distinguished this hill, he had only said, "Pass the slope." But, Gawin muttered, such a hill is memorable.

He slept badly, plagued with dreams of the cup and Kei. In his half-drowse he thought too of Perceval and Iglais and of Yvain, who awaited him in the stronghold of the Grail. Moreover he was always aware of the massive pitch of grass above him. In all that leaning space nothing could find cover, not a sheep, scarcely a hare. Yet again and again he roused with a sense that demons leaped along its cloud-wet crest or plunged headlong into the tough grass as swimmers plunge into water. Perhaps here the dangers of his quest took physical shape, he thought. Then he huddled closer to his fire burning inside stones he had dragged into a circle, hearing the wind moan and skirl in the gnarled trees or whistle evilly along the fleece of grass.

The morning was clear, but while the sunlight still lay in long golden fingers on the slope above him, clouds darkened the north. They were low and ragged, and they flapped over the ridge of the hill in boiling, damp masses, leaving, strangely, a narrow slit of ghastly gray-white brilliance between them and the crest. Each moment their purples grew more livid, each moment they swirled across larger spaces of sky. And before Gawin had led his horse a quarter of the way up the slope these furious wracks swept down on him and on all the grassy monolith of mountain, a cold, black, howling tide of rain.

He turned his horse, covered its head with his shield, and began to lead it back to the grove. But the torrent had already bred white veins of water that leapt down the slope, and at the foot roaring streams were widening into a lake. The trees stood in this lake like giant hunchbacks wading. If the storm continues long, he thought, we may drown on low ground. We must remain where we are. If we go up, rain will suffocate the horse. And so we must waste ourselves walking back and forth. At least we shall not die of cold.

He looked for a cave, an overhang, even a rocky shoulder under which they could shelter. There was nothing at all, nothing save the malignant, smooth, wet grass and the water crashing down. He led the horse what he judged to be half a mile east, turned it, led it back half a mile west. At each turn he tried to quarter upward a little, but so tight was the angle required to keep the rain out of the animal's nostrils that he could not measure progress. Moreover he had nothing to measure it against. The rain shut in his view to a prospect hardly larger than a man's grave.

Yet his spirits did not fail. A storm of this intensity could not endure, and soon the clouds would either pass off the sky or thin and settle down to a long, slow shower with intervals of intermission. His spirits did not fail the first hour. At the end of the second hour he was floundering along in an agony of cold and wet. During the third hour he tried to remove his chain shirt and could not, tried to get into the saddle and could not. After four hours the storm was still bellowing with its first furor. And Gawin's horse, coughing despite the protection of the shield, suddenly broke away and ran off into the brown mist. Within a second or so it was out of sight. After a minute he could not hear its feet.

The air grew black, he did not know whether because night had arrived or whether because the storm worsened. With his sword he tried to hack a little cave into the slope, but rain washed the soil into it as quickly as he removed it. He drove the blade into the ground and hung his sodden cape over the hilts and lay down with this flimsy shelter above his head and shoulders. He slept, or fainted, and revived when the wind capsized his cloak. Stiff, freezing, weak with hunger, he pushed himself to his feet. Now the rain seemed to be the element in which he was doomed to spend his life.

I will get to the top of this slope, he croaked aloud.

He climbed through the sightless dark. He abandoned his cloak. His shield and spear were gone, lost or carried off by his horse. But he clung to his sword, using it as a staff. He heard a voice and realized it was his own. Later he heard a man weeping and wondered what accursed soul was condemned to this evil green hillside that had no end. Green? Yes. Daylight had returned.

But the storm did not lighten at all.

351

hour. At the end of the second hour he was floundering along in an agony of cold and wet. During the third hour he tried to remove his chain and could not, tried to get into the saddle and could not. After a time knew the storm was still following him in its first position and that

61

HE DID NOT KNOW when he escaped the green steep, or even that he had escaped it. He only realized he was wandering among trees, and that wind whipped them with a sound of rending and rushing, and that whole branches were ripped away and flung along the air as along a stream. Sometimes the light was gray, sometimes there was no light at all. But, deadly cold and starving, he was afraid to stop, whether the time was night or day. Now and again he plucked at his chain shirt, but he could not remove the uniform of his knighthood. And he knew that in the moment when he tugged at it he wailed like a child.

One morning he saw ahead of him the edge of the storm. It was as clear as the wall of a room, and beyond it he believed sun was shining. He could no longer stand and had been creeping forward on hands and knees. He tried to get to his feet, to run, but he could not. He could make no haste at all. Yet in time he crawled through the limit of the rain as through a curtain. He rolled onto dry, bare earth, and at once fell into a stupor of sleep.

He was awakened and given water to drink, he was moved and carried, he was awakened again and told to drink mixed milk and wine. Now his senses began to return. He lay on a pallet of straw and old sheep hides in a dark, low-roofed room. Perceval, armed in white steel, sat on a puncheon beside him. Gleams of sunlight from the hutch-like door glinted on the speckless armor.

"I am not drowned, then," Gawin said.

"No indeed," Perceval told him. "How could you be drowned?"

"The storm. I think my horse was drowned."

"There is no storm, there has been no rain. Your horse and saddle are as dry as yourself, Gawin. You had a fall and a wound, and your horse stood over you. This drowning, it must be an effect of loss of blood."

"But the rain fell like breakers of the sea. It fell for days, for weeks, I do not know how long it fell. My horse ran away. I couldn't have fought anyone, I was always alone."

"Yes, yes," Perceval said in the tone of a watcher soothing a sick man. "You will mend. You lost blood through the cut on your breast, but it is shallow, it stops well short of your lungs."

Gawin raised himself on his elbow and stared at his breast. Torn strips of lint crossed his naked flesh, and on the lint were brown stains of blood. This is not possible, he thought. "Where is my hauberk?" he asked Perceval. "Show it to me."

Perceval rose and fetched him his rusted mail. Across the breast gaped a ragged tear. Dried blood stained the links on either side.

"I found you wounded and your horse standing over you," Perceval said. "The fall has shaken your memory."

"Is the horse safe?"

"Perfectly safe. It is tethered outside, only a dozen feet away."

"Where are we? What place is this?"

"We are in the forest beyond the hold of King Peleur. And this is the cottage of a forester of my uncle."

Gawin peered about the narrow, ill-smelling hut. "Much has gone to wrack with the country of Peleur," he murmured. "No forester of Arthur's lives in such a sty."

"It is not luxurious, but it is light and clean, a good home."

"It seems dark and foul to me."

"Try to sleep," Perceval said. "You are weak and you need sleep to restore your mind."

It was easy to sleep, yet in his dreams Gawin was disturbed by the fight he did not remember fighting, and by Perceval's denial that a storm had almost drowned him. As day succeeded day he was bewildered again and again by the difference between his and Perceval's reconstruction of past events, and even between the simple perception of their surroundings. To him the hut seemed each hour more miserable. But Perceval found their shelter pleasant and wholesome.

Gawin asked him whether King Arthur had been informed of the death of the brother of The Moors.

"Yes," Perceval answered, "though not by me, as I hoped. I did not go to the City of Legions."

"Will you tell me how it was done?"

Perceval sat down on a section of log which was upended to form a crude stool. Though he had not worn his mail during Gawin's illness he was always girded with the sword. Now he stretched his legs before him and let the sword lie between his knees. He said, "Do you remember that I had a mission to perform when I left the hall of my lady mother? I was going to meet my kinsman Mortelle and do battle with him."

"Oh," Gawin said, "that should have been my fight, Perceval. I have thought of it many times, I wished to do for you what you did for me."

The young knight said, "My uncle and I had agreed to meet in the same place, near the hermitage of our kinsman Joseus." He pulled the sword upright and leaned on the hilts. He was pale, looking beyond Gawin as though at the contest he had so recently waged. "We fought twelve hours, from prime to vespers. Mortelle died refusing to ask for mercy."

"Twelve hours! This was a fight for an old knight, for Lancelot himself! I have never known a young knight to live through such a combat. Since you are here, and whole, I must believe you were not wounded. Yet my mind refuses to believe it."

"God helped me, Gawin. Mortelle is God's great enemy, and his strong wickedness helped him. But God prevails. I was wounded a little, I lost blood. And while I lay in the hermitage feeling my strength return, the Being you call Merlin came to me as I had expected to go to him. I told him of my battle with The Moors for your sake, and asked him to inform the king of its outcome."

"The old man's arrival was a fortunate accident for you," Gawin said.

"It was not an accident. It was planned. God answers our prayers."

"I have not yet thanked you for my life, Perceval. I owe it to you."

"If there is a debt it is already repaid. You helped me fulfill God's will with Mortelle."

Soon Gawin was strong enough to exercise. Unarmed, he walked with Perceval in the woods. When he remarked that the trees appeared blasted by drought or bitter winters, Perceval replied, "Look about you, Gawin. Do you not see how rich all this forest is?" And when they ventured beyond the forest and reached meadows, Gawin had no heart to speak of what he beheld, only sparse grass choked with thistles, for Perceval said, "Here is good herbage that will make the cattle fat again."

On a certain morning Perceval rose very early and left the hut. Gawin, who had been wakeful, followed him. The youth had moved out of the trees and stood, hands on hips and head raised, looking at the eastern sky. Gilded clouds of pearly hues half concealed the sun.

"This will be a fine day," Gawin said.

"Yes. The third before midsummer. Three days more. It is a beautiful world, Gawin." A bright tear sprang into the corner of each eye. He flicked them away with his forefingers. "Why does a colored sky touch one so?"

"Because men are made to feel such things, I suppose."

"I must be on my way today, Gawin. I have an appointment on midsummer morning, one that I cannot fail."

"I am sorry we must part. Where will you ride?"

"To King Peleur's hold. The Being you call Merlin has a cell in the gate tower. I will meet him there — our last meeting."

"So this is his hiding place when he leaves court!"

Perceval shook his head. "When he finally enters that cell he will be done with his stay on earth."

"What business do you have with him?"

"I wish to tell him I have achieved my quest, and enter the cell in the gate tower with him."

Perceval had spoken quietly, yet it was as though he shouted. Gawin's ears sang, and the breath stuck in his throat. He said, "You saw Christ's cup?"

Perceval drew a long, ecstatic sigh. "I saw the holy vessel."

"The question," Gawin said, "did you ask the question?"

"My uncle was near death, but when I reached him he ordered his servants to carry him to the throne. I sat beside him. The Grail appeared before us, all gleaming with the light of suns and moons. I knelt and cried out, 'Whom does the Grail serve?' "

Gawin was trembling. "Were you answered?"

"My uncle raised his head," Perceval went on, transported. "He said, 'There be three things, *and these three things are one.*' His old face shone with the blaze of morning."

"And then? Did you hold the vessel in your hands?"

"I have told you as much as can be told," Perceval said. "The rest must be done alone."

Gawin could not say another word, so great was his longing to reach the hold of King Peleur. He could foresee his moment, kneeling, the gleaming cup of Christ before him, he could hear himself ask the question. I do not understand the question or its answer, he thought, but I shall ask, I shall hold the miraculous chalice in my hands.

"Now," Perceval said, "my uncle's suffering is done, and his country is healing, and justice will return to Britain." He laid his hand on Gawin's shoulder. It was tense and strong, like the talon of a falcon. He shook Gawin gently, saying, "What thanks can a man render God who is chosen to be God's arm in this world? I am God's elected Doer, it is through my unworthy humanity that He has poured His purifying fire. Britain *was* purified as I knelt before the Grail, Gawin, do you understand? Justice *has* returned. And King Arthur *will* put down the enemies of God and reign in peace, he will be a sinless monarch henceforth." He peered into Gawin's eyes as though to see his own belief there. "Do you understand?" he repeated. "Do you understand?"

The face, ageless and austere, staring at him so closely, alarmed Gawin with the physical alarm he would have felt had a hawk flown at him. Yet the young knight's fervor gave him a beauty at once severe and otherworldly, his great, dark eyes incandescent, and his mouth curved into an expression of amazed joy.

Perceval insisted, "Do you understand?"

358

"You have seen a miracle, and I believe the miracle."

For a moment Perceval continued to hold him tight, shaking him, willing the answer he wished to hear. Then he let him go. After they had walked a while in silence he said, "I must say farewell. I do not think we shall meet again, Gawin."

"I will arm you," Gawin said. "I will be your squire and mount you. Do you remember, Perceval? I was the first man who put you in a saddle."

"Gawin."

"What is it, brother?"

"It was you who sent me to the City of Legions to find the sword I needed for my quest."

"Perhaps. But destiny moves us sometimes, too."

"It was destiny, but it was also you," Perceval said. "And I believe this is why God has given you the chance to achieve His Grail."

Gawin looked at him, dumb with incredulity.

62

LATER, when they had returned, and Perceval was preparing his horse for the road, Gawin said, "Since I am going to the hold of King Peleur too, let us journey together."

"You must wait for Yvain," Perceval said.

"I do not believe Yvain is coming. He is long overdue."

"Your illness makes you feel more time has passed than

is the case. You were only three days' distance from my mother's hold when you were wounded, and I found you lying unconscious seven days ago — ten days. Yvain still has three days before midsummer."

Gawin did not argue. He no longer hoped to convince Perceval that the storm had persisted through many weeks.

"Remember," Perceval said, "from the forester's cottage it is only a short ride to the castle of Peleur. You can reach it, if you pass without trouble, in four hours."

"I remember. Now farewell, Perceval, and God go with you."

"He is with me, but He has left me one flaw still. I did not weep when I bade my mother goodbye, yet my heart fails me as I part from you for the last time."

"We have altered one another's lives, and this has made us brothers," Gawin said, feeling the hale man's inability to deal with a prophecy of death. "I shall not forget you."

"Nor I you, in the time I have left." He leaned from his horse to grasp Gawin's wrist, shook it lightly, let it go. Then he wheeled his horse in a wide sweep, made it curvet, and galloped away. This brave, boyish display brought into Gawin's throat a lump of remembrance. Does he truly foresee his death in the cell of Merlin? Whether he lives or dies he is lost to me as Iglais is. And I have lost more in these two than can be made up in this life.

He returned to the forester's hut to await Yvain. The hovel seemed smaller and dirtier than before, and even as he stood before it, reluctant to enter, a gust peeled off a clump of thatch sticky with mold. Within, the stench of decay was suffocating. He thought of Perceval's judgement, "clean and light," and felt again the unresting fear of enchantment. When truth wrapped itself in the secret illusions of the mind, how could it be truth?

For two days he lived in the evil hutch like a hermit, feeding himself on moor birds and a young hare he caught in snares. On the third morning Yvain rode out of the trees. His rugged body, his big shoulders and rough, dark head, above all his grin of greeting, seemed better to Gawin than anything he had seen since they parted at the milestone.

They seized one another in a rough embrace. "Oye, brother, but I am glad to see you!" Gawin said.

"I did not know whether you were alive or dead until your young friend from Norgals brought your message," Yvain said. "And hasn't he leaped into knighthood with a flourish! What deeds has he done with the pillar sword?"

"Perceval is more story than I can tell you now," Gawin said. "I am wild for news from court. I have heard nothing. Why didn't you send me a message by Perceval?"

"I am hungry," Yvain said, "thirsty too. Let us go into your great hall and unarm and make a meal."

"I'll unarm you within, but the meal will be better taken outdoors. This is the poorest roof I ever huddled under."

"Stinking too," Yvain agreed judiciously.

"Don't you think it light and clean?"

"Come on, brother, get me out of my chain."

They sat under a stunted wild apple tree sharing Gawin's hare and the bread and cheese Yvain carried. "Begin," Gawin said.

"Recall how affairs stood when you left: Kei and Bryant close to the king, and Lancelot walking on a sword blade, and the people of The Isles threatening to rise if Lancelot were not returned as governor, and the rebel Clamas and his clan rising in fact."

"I do not need reminding, I have thought of all this a thousand times," Gawin said.

"Well. Your departure convinced Kei that he had driven you off, and he began to show his power openly. But this had the opposite effect from what he hoped. It cooled the king's mind somewhat. Your uncle missed you, Gawin. He has depended on you too long to forget you overnight."

"Did he dismiss Kei?"

"No, no, just held him at arm's length awhile. And Kei was forced into a new plan. He persuaded Arthur to send Lancelot to The Isles as governor. Bryant's part in the scheme was to alert men in The Isles still loyal to him. These rogues were to hatch a plot that would make Lancelot appear to be using his new powers as a threat to the sovereignty of Britain."

"Surely this washed the scales from Arthur's eyes."

"You forget the lady," Yvain said. "You forget that Arthur is a husband as well as a king. He listened to the charge against Lancelot, he listened and believed it. And nineteen days ago he put Lancelot in prison."

Gawin leaped up from the shade of the tree. "Where? Where is Lancelot in prison? In The Isles?"

"If you will believe me, Gawin, Arthur ordered Lancelot

to return to the City of Legions, and Lancelot returned — *knowing he was to be imprisoned."*

"Why does he submit?" Gawin raged. "When he submits to Arthur he is only submitting to Kei. Can't he see Kei's treason?"

"He sees it." Yvain made a vehement gesture with a hand holding a piece of hard cheese. "But Lancelot is a man who loves his king. He believes Arthur to be a creature of destiny, a pure, godlike leader who happens to have the gifts Lancelot admires most, courage, strength, beauty, wisdom, knowledge of men. You know Lancelot, Gawin. Surely I needn't tell you this."

"In my judgement Lancelot's wits are at fault."

Yvain bit into the cheese and slowly chewed it. "Yes. I value his friendship more than any man's but yours, brother. I would rather fight shoulder to shoulder with him than any knight, even you. I would trust him with my life, my wealth too if I had wealth. But I have always thought him a little — uh — just a little — childlike in his view of the king."

Childlike? Applied to Lancelot the word was outrageous, Gawin thought. It was not the simple-mindedness of youth that made Lancelot vulnerable to Arthur's cruel fitfulness. A man could only fail to defend himself in Lancelot's situation if he had a guilty conscience. And it came over Gawin that Lancelot was, in all truth, guilty with Guenivere.

He hid his thought as though Yvain might see it through his skull. "Why don't his friends deliver him?"

"Because he sent Ector word that he would not leave the

363

prison if an attempt were made to free him against Arthur's wishes."

"Ah!" Angrily Gawin spat into the grass. "And so Kei has everything as he wishes. Wouldn't my uncle listen when you told him that Kei had murdered Lohot?"

"Wait for Lohot a moment, Gawin. As soon as Clamas learned that Lancelot was in prison he made common cause with the people of The Isles. And now there will soon be war — there is war, in fact."

"You should have sent me word of these events long ago," Gawin said.

"How could I send you word? I did dispatch a runner to the hermitage of Joseus."

"When?"

"Within a month of your departure."

"Joseus did not tell me. These kinsmen of the relic, they put aside matters that you and I would feel dishonest in suppressing. More than once I have wanted to choke the truth out of that holy man. Tell me about the war."

"Arthur has undertaken two actions, one toward the north against Clamas, one on the sea against The Isles. He has put Kei in charge against Clamas, and himself, he has sailed with a fleet of four ships to subdue The Isles."

"Oh, Yvain, a blind man could see that this strategy invites his destruction!"

"I know. When he summoned me to assign my duties in the war, I was foolish enough to protest. I told him," Yvain said, wincing at the memory, "that he must not depart from Britain, I told him he must not give Kei a military com-

364

mand. And this is why I am not helping fight the war."

"He exiled you?"

"Only confined me to the City of Legions. But when I heard from you, Gawin, when the story of Lohot's murder came to me, I thought the time had arrived to leave the City whether the king wished it or not."

"You did not tell him how Kei killed his son, then."

"No," said Yvain, "I can't reach him. He has put too much distance between himself and me."

"Then I will go back. I will appeal to him to receive me in the name of his sister my mother. I will tell him."

"I am glad you see it yourself, brother. He has had time to desire your return. I've come all this way mainly to urge you to go back to the City of Legions."

"I can raise troops in Rhos on my way. With a picked band I will come down on Clamas from the north. Will you fight with me, Yvain?"

"Yes. For the king."

"For Lancelot too. And against Kei. Let us swear to destroy Kei."

"I swore it when I left the City of Legions." Yvain swallowed the last of his cheese and brushed his hands together. "And so we have put things in motion, you and I. Tell me, Gawin, have you done with your quest?"

Gawin sucked air into his crammed lungs. Lie to Yvain? No. "This very midsummer day I am within four hours of the castle where the holy relic is guarded."

"What castle is it? I do not remember a castle four hours from here. This is my region, Gawin, I have ridden it a dozen times in Arthur's service. I have never heard of your relic in any castle."

"But I am sure," Gawin said. "It lies where three streams join. There are three bridges, three gates, three towers."

"Oh!" Yvain's face cleared. "I know the place. But it is in ruins, it was abandoned after an attack destroyed all but the shell."

"I do not believe it. It can't be the same place."

"Three streams come together, three bridges have fallen into the water, three towers are open to the sky. It was held by an old, ailing knight who had a younger brother. I knew their names once, but I have forgotten them. The older brother refused to surrender a family hoard of great value, I don't know its nature, only that it was precious."

The most precious of all hallows, Gawin thought, Christ's cup.

"The younger brother attacked him and killed him and stole the hoard."

And so Peleur is dead, and Mortelle prevailed. Gawin sank onto the thin grass where Yvain still sat. "What was the fate of the younger brother?"

Yvain shrugged. "They say he could feign death. They say if he realized he was about to be defeated he could appear stiff and blue, with the blood stopped in his wounds. But when he was left on the earth as dead, he would rise up again and run away. I do not know his real fate. But I have heard two or three times of his death."

Bitter questions seemed to smother Gawin. When did the battle occur between the brothers? How did Perceval achieve his quest in a ruined, deserted hold from which the Grail had been stolen? And was the good knight tricked by Mortelle's cowardly gift of false death and flight?

Oh, Time wound the past, the present, the future into tangles in the winter while I was bedeviled by mysteries, he thought, and again in the summer while I wandered on the terrible hill of grass. Or it has all been a dream, Iglais and Perceval too, and the kinsmen of the Grail, and the Grail itself?

But it was not a dream, he told himself, feeling for one blinding moment the incredible joy that would have been his had he won his quest.

He was cold, and hugged his arms across his breast to prevent himself from shivering. Under his hand he felt his traveling pouch, empty now of all its treasure save the tear spoon.

Courage wrung from the sorrow of men, he thought, this I understand. The spoon must be my hallows.

Stiffly he rose. "Let us arm, Yvain. It is our mission to defend the king and the king's justice." He remembered his torn and bloody hauberk.

Yvain clapped him on the back, let his arm lie on Gawin's shoulder. "Yes, we are still Arthur's, whatever Arthur thinks. And we can trust," he said, his gnarled face taking on a durable grin of hope, "we can trust that we may even enlarge the king's justice if we can make him see we are trying. Come on, brother, let us get into our mail."